759.2
43993

Graham Sutherland

A BIOGRAPHY

Graham Sutherland

A BIOGRAPHY

by
ROGER BERTHOUD

faber and faber

First published in 1982
by Faber and Faber Limited
3 Queen Square London WC1N 3AU
Printed in Great Britain by
BAS Printers Limited, Over Wallop, Hampshire
All rights reserved

British Library Cataloguing in Publication Data

Berthoud, Roger
Graham Sutherland.
1. Sutherland, Graham   2. Painters—Great
Britain—Biography
I. Title
759.2   ND497.S95

ISBN 0-571-11882-8

In the village the wind cowl on the
oast house has been removed.

Sight is a strange thing, for I still, from my window
see quite clearly the image of the cowl
exactly as it was; but it does not
veer with the wind!

GRAHAM SUTHERLAND, circa 1950

For Joy, Lucy and Lottie

Contents

7

CONTENTS

Illustrations

COLOUR PLATES

MONOCHROME PLATES

between pages 64 and 65

Acknowledgements

My first debts are to Graham Sutherland himself, for agreeing to co-operate on this biography; to his widow Kathleen, who courageously agreed to help once she had recovered from the shock of his sudden death in February 1980; and to the Trustees of the Graham and Kathleen Sutherland Foundation, at Picton Castle in Wales, for all their assistance in the production of this book. Kathleen Sutherland's help was indispensable. She bore patiently with my endless questions, lent me her invaluable engagement diaries covering most of her married life, and read both drafts of my typescript, offering some very helpful suggestions but never seeking to suppress the facts. I would also like to thank her for her permission to use a selection of photographs from her collection. Where it has been possible to trace the sources of other photographs, these have been acknowledged in the list of illustrations.

This is the 'authorized' biography in the sense that it had the Sutherlands' approval, a necessary condition for the co-operation of many of their friends and for permission to quote from Graham's writings; and in that I was granted access to some, though not all, of his correspondence. Other principal sources have been my own interviews with seventy or eighty of his friends and contemporaries, often taped; letters from several hundred others, mainly in response to questions; newspaper cuttings; and the main books on his work. For information about parallel developments in the art world I found Dennis Farr's *English Art 1870–1940* (Oxford University Press, 1978) particularly useful.

Among those whom I interviewed, often at great length and more than once, I would particularly like to thank Graham's brother Dr Humphrey Sutherland and his sister Mrs Vivien Ingman, his first cousin Aubrey Smith and the following: Lord Amulree, the late Roland Bond, Edgar

ACKNOWLEDGEMENTS

Larkin, Paul Drury, Milner Gray, Henry Moore, John Piper, Robert Medley, Prunella Clough, John Craxton, the late Sir Colin Anderson, Robert Wellington, Sir Roland Penrose, Lord Clark, Stella Mary Newton, Eunice Frost, William MacQuitty, Jill Craigie, Dean Walter Hussey, Canon Paul Miller, Provost H. C. N. Williams, Julian Andrews, Elsbeth Juda, Felix Man, Eardley Knollys, Alan Searle, Meary Tambimuttu, Lilian Somerville, Gilbert Lloyd, Harry Tatlock Miller, Sir Dennis and Lady Proctor, Sir Norman Reid, Sir William Coldstream, Ronald Alley, Denis Mahon, Dame Mary Soames, Anthony Blee, Lord Iliffe, Liam Hanley, Sandy Gall, Anthony Bell, Etti Plesch, Father James Ethrington, Alan Clark MP, Belinda Henderson, Wendy and the late Emery Reves, Pier Paolo and Marzia Ruggerini, Giorgio Soavi, John Ormond, Margaret White, Gordon and Catherine Bennett, André Devall, Hanning and Lady Marion Philipps, Jack and Betty Sulivan, Robin Chancellor, James Kirkman, Emile Marzé, Antoinette Ferrari, Lily King, Dr Frank Tait, Dame Sheila Sherlock, Alfred Hecht, Lord Airlie, Michael Standing, Dr John Hayes, Dame Adelaide Doughty and Monty Parkin.

Letters from the following were particularly helpful: Inez Bouverie Hoyton, Roderick Cameron, A. S. Frere, Father A. Whitehead C.R.L., J. H. Hockey, Maida Lunn, Jane Phillips, Baron Elie de Rothschild, Cecil King, the Marquis of Bath, Sir Sacheverell Sitwell, Lord Goodman, Lord Rayne, Mrs Signy Eaton, Louis Osman, Gianni Tinto and Humphrey Brooke.

My debt is heavy to all those who made available to me letters from Graham to themselves or their relatives, and especially Lord Clark, Dame Mary Soames, Maja Sacher, Stella Mary Newton, Elsbeth Juda, Aubrey Smith, the late Sir Colin Anderson, Pier Paolo and Marzia Ruggerini, Jack and Betty Sulivan and Milner Gray. I was also very grateful to the following for all the trouble they took in reading parts of my draft: Humphrey Sutherland, Milner Gray, Paul Drury, Eardley Knollys, Sir Dennis Proctor, Sir Norman Reid, Dame Mary Soames, B. D. Alexander, James Kirkman, Pier Paolo and Marzia Ruggerini, Hanning Philipps, Peter Cannon-Brookes, Anthony Blee, Lady Spence, Provost H. C. N. Williams, Dean Walter Hussey and Louis Osman.

I received much help from museums and public art galleries, especially from the Tate Gallery, the National Portrait Gallery, the Imperial War Museum, the National Museum of Wales, the Ashmolean Museum, Oxford, the Fitzwilliam Museum, Cambridge, Southampton Art Gallery, the British Museum and the Victoria and Albert Museum; and I would also like to thank for their help the following art dealers and galleries not already mentioned: Dr Heinz Roland; James Mayor of the Mayor Gallery, London; Valerie Beston and John Longstaff of Marlborough Fine Art; Gordon Cooke of the Robin Garton Gallery, London; William Weston; Erica Brausen; Reid and Lefevre, London; the Redfern Gallery, London; and Alexandre Rosenberg of the Paul Rosenberg Gallery, New York.

My thanks also go to: the British Council; the Beaverbrook Foundation, for access to its papers at the House of Lords Public Record Office; the Konrad-Adenauer-Stiftung near Bonn; friends at Buckingham Palace and Clarence House; Simon Rendall and Stanley Jones of the Curwen Press and the Curwen Studio; A. G. Quinsee, Librarian of Chelsea College; Raife Wellstead, Director of the National Postal Museum; Alan Scadding of Epsom College; John King, head of the *Daily Express*'s library, and Jack Lonsdale and the staff of *The Times*'s intelligence department; the borough librarians of Derby, Sutton and Merton Park for their invaluable researches; and those who preferred to remain anonymous.

For permission to quote from articles and transcripts I am most grateful to the *Daily Telegraph* and *Sunday Telegraph*, the *Illustrated London News*, the *Listener*, and London Weekend Television's 'South Bank Show'; and to the following, to quote from the source indicated: Lord Clark (letters from himself to Graham); Eardley Knollys (letters from E. Sackville-West); John Dreyfus (Oliver Simon's magazine *Signature*); A. P. Watt Ltd (letters from W. S. Maugham); Lund, Humphries (Douglas Cooper's monograph on Sutherland's work); Eileen Hose (letters from Cecil Beaton); the National Westminster Bank (letter from June Churchill); Dame Mary Soames (letters from Clementine Churchill); C. & T. Publications (letters from Sir Winston Churchill); Robin Chancellor (Andrew Revai's book *The Coventry Tapestry*); Noel Barber (his book *Conversations with Painters*); Anthony Blee and Lady Spence (letters from Sir Basil Spence); the Konrad-Adenauer-Stiftung (letters from Dr Adenauer).

Finally, I would like to thank William Rees-Mogg and Harold Evans, successive editors of *The Times*, for allowing me nine months' leave of absence to complete the research and to write this book; my wife and daughters for cheering me onwards; and my parents for their encouragement.

Introduction

I first met Graham Sutherland in 1961, when he was at the peak of his fame and I was a novice *Evening Standard* reporter doing my first big interview. Contact was maintained sporadically through the 1960s. In 1978, at about the time of his seventy-fifth birthday, I interviewed him again, this time for *The Times*, and commented on the apparent lack of a biography on him. Quite right, he said, in a tone of voice that suggested it was odd but true. Two publishers (Cape and Weidenfeld) had asked him to write his autobiography, he added—but he preferred to paint.

To plug the gap seemed a good idea when *The Times* went into limbo—for 11 months, it transpired—in late 1978. He agreed to co-operate within the confines of his overloaded and peripatetic schedule. We met a number of times in Wales, Kent and London for taped interviews, and exchanged some questions and answers by post. These covered the ground systematically up to his marriage and in patches thereafter. In February 1980, after a rapid decline, he died.

Other considerations aside, the best source had gone. But perhaps thereafter his friends spoke a trifle more freely, and certainly they were happier to lend letters. Kathleen's invaluable help I have acknowledged.

The aim has been to make this as 'open' a biography as possible. Imaginative supposition and invented or recreated dialogues have their place, but not here. Where possible, direct quotations have been used, even if sometimes at the expense of narrative flow, and sources given. Notes have sometimes been added to avoid cluttering the text with dates.

Where the source is not indicated or obvious, it is generally Kathleen's engagement diary which, apart from social engagements, frequently showed what Graham was working on; for instance, (first entry) 'G on Adenauer' and thereafter simply 'G on A' or 'G on CT' (Coventry tapestry). These diaries were particularly useful in tracing the evolution of portraits. As far as Graham's 'free' paintings are concerned, no such record exists. A weekly series of taped interviews with Kathleen was also a very valuable source of background information, which was checked where necessary.

Perhaps the most difficult task was to strike a happy mean between comprehensiveness and readability. Important events are not necessarily as interesting as less important ones. Another difficulty was to decide in what detail to write about Graham's work, especially the non-commissioned paintings (landscape, nature and so on). Since to a large extent his work was his life, and his free paintings were more important than the commissioned ones, I have tried at least to give an idea of how they evolved, without aspiring in any way to a 'critical' biography.

It is naturally less inhibiting to write a biography when the subject and his immediate family, friends and associates — not to mention tax advisers — are dead. On the other hand, they are also potentially the best sources in an age where letter writing is a dying art. Tact, discretion and the laws of libel may involve the occasional loss of frankness, but in exchange a good deal is gained. As Graham used to say (after André Gide) of the disciplines of his own craft, the kite only flies when attached to the string. I like to think of his spirit flying high up there, despite my attempts to haul him in.

I
Surrey and Derby
1903-21

MANY PEOPLE were perplexed by the apparent contrast between Graham Sutherland's manner and the nature of his painting. How could so courteous, charming, urbane, delightful a man produce work so spiky, sinister, baleful and even baffling? The brief answer must be that his personality was a great deal more complex than his manner suggested, and that his work reflects both that complexity and also, on closer acquaintance, a good deal of the charm.

Not infrequently, his behaviour was every bit as spiky as his work. Indeed, one of his oldest friends felt that to portray that side of him might detract from appreciation of his painting, so perhaps this book was better not written. My hope is that to show Graham in all his complexity will add to enjoyment of his paintings, which reflect it. 'Graham was born to complicate things,' another friend said. 'But it has been a miracle knowing him, and a lesson in living. He always gave us joy. We loved him for his personality even more than for his painting.'

Like his work, Graham was vibrant but imperfect. He gave much joy, but sometimes disappointed. One of his favourite concepts was of the 'precarious tension of opposites'. More, I think, than most people, he was the product of such a tension. He liked to speak, too, of the importance of shadows, likening them to a second tune in a piece of contrapuntal music, visible but impalpable. There were plenty of shadows in his life, but they were thrown by a strong light.

To deal with his charm first, since it was, overwhelmingly, the first impression of those who met him: that elusive compound was in his case a blend of wonderful manners, an extraordinarily attractive, light, very clear speaking voice, good looks—when young, rather those of the *jeune poète*, later of the 'distinguished' variety—a flattering capacity to focus on one entirely, and a considerable sense of fun and feeling for words. (Not for nothing was P. G. Wodehouse one of his favourite authors.)

The charm was real and deep, but it was adjustable. Graham sometimes used it to play on people's emotions. If you were out of favour, you knew it fairly rapidly. A day in Wales springs to memory. I had arrived at the Lord Nelson Hotel in Milford Haven (his invariable haunt there in later years), the compleat biographer, with tape recorder, camera, notebook poised, only to find the great man's mood strangely clouded. He had been swayed by one of his friends, whom I had interviewed, and was having doubts about the book. He was an impressionable man, influenced by the opinion of others — excessively, sometimes. As we waded through the mud of Sandy Haven estuary (or 'pill', as it is called there), he needed a lot of reassurance. Only in the evening did the full sun of his charm shine again. It had been cold in the shadows.

Part of his charm sprang from his gift of empathy — reflected in his portraits — and his real interest in people. This produced many fruits. One was a caring, Fabian socialism not necessarily at odds with a perfectionist taste for quality. He had a developed streak of compassion for those in difficulty; and he remembered the concerns and activities of others. For example, when he visited Michael Standing, a retired BBC executive, and his wife, Jean, in their village of Trottiscliffe in Kent, he always knew which of Standing's amateur landscapes were recent. 'I like that. You've done that piece of distance beautifully,' he would say.[1] Standing said: 'It was always a treat when he came.' Graham helped professional as well as amateur artists, especially in their relations with art dealers and patrons, from Francis Bacon and John Craxton in the 1940s to Bryan Organ and Monty Parkin in the 1960s and 1970s.

About his own work he was usually modest, sometimes seemingly convinced of its value, at others deeply in need of reassurance. That was why he was so vulnerable to the judgement of critics, second-rate though he knew many of them to be. He was full of contradictions. In some ways solitary by nature, he loved being with good friends and was easy of contact. He cherished the simplicity of the farm workers of Kent, Pembrokeshire and southern France, yet he was fascinated by power and, to some extent, by the *demi-monde*. He was deeply literate, yet, like many creative people, he could not spell. He loved Bach but could not appreciate Mozart and disliked opera. He had a streak of trusting naiveté, yet could be devious (not for nothing did he admire Cardinal Manning). He was quite shrewd with money, but foreign currencies baffled him — and he was absurdly generous with his work. He was unfailingly conscientious and so took on too many commitments (he hated to say no) and was often disappointingly behind schedule.

In all this he was complicated. But in a few respects he was relatively simple and consistent. He was, all his adult life, a ferocious worker, keeping more or less office hours. He lived to work. To be cut off from it by travel or, worse still, by staying with people was painful. He was highly intelligent (though not always clear-headed). And for fifty-three years he was a totally faithful husband.

Truth is never pure and rarely simple, said Oscar Wilde. In this impure and complex world, birth certificates stand out as beacons of straightforward reliability. According to Graham's, he was born at 8 Pendle Road, in the London suburb of Streatham—notable to non-residents for the dependability and duration of its traffic jams—on 24 August 1903, the son of George Humphreys Vivian Sutherland and Elsie Sutherland, *née* Foster.

No great event seems to have left its impress on that year. A few weeks later Evelyn Waugh was born. Orville and Wilbur Wright made the first flight in a petrol-driven aeroplane, lasting just fifty-nine seconds. Verdi's *Ernani* became the first opera to be recorded, a rather curious choice.

Britain's power was in decline, that of Germany and the USA in the ascendant. In the Western world, socialism and trade unionism were moving forward inexorably to counter the worst excesses of capitalism. Queen Victoria had died in January 1901, being succeeded by her son, Edward VII; and in 1902, when the Boer War ended, Arthur Balfour had taken over from Lord Salisbury as Britain's Prime Minister. Conservative domination was, however, threatened by the free trade issue, which was to sweep the Liberals to power in 1906. The first communications revolution was in full swing; the wireless, telephone and cinematograph were all fairly recent inventions, as were electricity and the motor car. There were still lots of horses around; deliveries of produce were by horse-drawn cart, and the sound of the blacksmith's anvil was everywhere in the air.

It was a vintage era for English literature. H. G. Wells, Henry James, Joseph Conrad, Rudyard Kipling, Arnold Bennett, Thomas Hardy and John Galsworthy were in full spate. In France the seeds of modernism had earlier been sown by Baudelaire, Flaubert, Rimbaud, Verlaine and Laforgue, among others; and in the fine arts, Britain followed in the wake of the Impressionists, largely unaware of the revolutionary work of Seurat, Van Gogh, Gauguin and Cézanne, soon to be so dramatically developed by Picasso, Braque, Matisse, Kandinsky and many others.

It was a Europe at once more ruthless than today's and more innocent, unaware that the incipient arms race would lead to the decimation of the First World War and, ultimately, to the concentration camps and genocide of the Second.

Graham came from the middle of the middle class. His father was a barrister who had been called to the Bar a year or two before his birth, having studied law and attended the Inner Temple after reading classics at New College, Oxford. He and Elsie Foster were married in the Chapel Royal, in the precinct of the Savoy, at the age of 29 and 25 respectively, on 7 October 1902, ten months before the arrival of their first-born. Unable to make a living at the Bar, and without private means, Graham's father—who was known by his third forename, Vivian—had become a civil servant. He was working at the time for the Land Registry Office, a government agency which 'gives finality and certainty by providing an up-to-date and official record of land ownership', to quote an explanatory leaflet. It still flourishes at Lincoln's Inn Fields, with branches up and down the country.

Not long afterwards, he transferred to the legal side of the Board of Education, precursor of today's Department of Education. At some stage after Oxford, he seems to have acted as tutor to one or more of the offspring of the Perronet Sells family. They had been wealthy coal merchants since the eighteenth century, and in 1859 the family firm had merged with Charrington's to form Charrington, Sells and Dale. They lived in Bishops-wood Road, Highgate, later moving to Beechwood, a large mansion on the Hampstead/Highgate border (bought in 1977 by King Khaled of Saudi Arabia for £1,900,000). Julia Perronet Sells became Graham's godmother; her husband had been one of the witnesses at his parents' marriage.

It was a less metropolitan union than it might have seemed. Graham's father, Vivian, was born and bred in Derby in the Midlands, where his grandfather, George Sutherland, had been headmaster of an establishment forthrightly called St Andrews Middle Class School. It seems to have been a minor day public school for the artisanal classes. He gave up the headship of the school in 1898 to become organizing secretary of the new Derby Municipal Technical College, where Graham was later to spend some unhappy hours. But he died the following year (and so well before Graham's birth) of apoplexy, aged only 54.[2] George Sutherland was also an active town councillor until two years before his death, became a Fellow of the Royal Geographical Society and was a familiar figure in Masonic circles. It was at the same Middle Class School that Graham's father was educated— and well enough to get to Oxford.

One result of the early death of Graham's paternal grandfather was a certain vagueness, tinged with romanticism, about the family's antecedents on that side. 'You see, my grandfather was Scottish', Graham would say.[3]

> I don't know what period he came down. The Countess of Sutherland married someone who became the Duke of Sutherland. . . . my grandfather claimed—and whether there is any truth in this I don't know: I have never pursued it, and am not snobbish enough to do so— that we were directly related to the Leveson-Gower side of the Sutherland family.

Graham rather relished the fact that one of the Dukes of Sutherland was 'one of the worst landlords Scotland has ever known' during the Highland Clearances. When asked whether he was related to the Duke of Sutherland, he would sometimes say: 'On the criminal side.'

The facts seem to be more prosaic. It is true that anyone called Sutherland is, unless he has changed his name by deed poll, in origin a native of Sutherland and a clansman.[4] But the Leveson-Gowers came from Yorkshire, not Scotland—and so, coincidentally, did Graham's great-grandfather. The best evidence is that he was a tailor from Sheffield who settled in Derby and was also called George Sutherland, but of him neither Graham nor his brother and sister had heard.

There was thought to be Welsh blood on that side of the family. Grandfather George had married a Miss Humphreys, whose father, though perhaps of Welsh origin, had come from Nottingham to Derby around 1840, marrying a servant called Martha Bird. Starting as a bricklayer, he set up as a builder in the year of revolutions, 1848, later building, *inter alia*, Derby market hall, St Pancras goods station and Bath station. Derby's covered market hall was opened in 1866 and still looks remarkably handsome.

Humphreys built Arboretum Square in Derby, once a pleasant cul-de-sac, in the local off-white brick, moving into number 6 himself. It was the only detached house and adjoined the Arboretum. Grandfather George subsequently lived there, and finally it passed to Graham's maiden aunt and uncle, Budge and Beatrice, who were to play a role in Graham's adolescent life. In Graham's young day, they were the sole link with Derby—though Graham's father's accent was a reminder. He would, for example, say 'castle' with a short 'a' rather than 'carstle'.[5]

What with the tailor's son turned headmaster and the daughter of the bricklayer who became a builder of considerable means, there was a good deal of 'upwards social mobility' in Graham's background on his father's side. The same is true of his mother's.

Elsie Foster was the eldest of three girls, Elsie, Bertha and Hester, and there were two boys, James, thought of as the black sheep of the family, and

Alastair, the engineer. James went to school at Tonbridge; Alastair went to King's College School, Wimbledon; and the three girls went to Wimbledon High School.

Elsie Sutherland's father, James Foster, was a remarkable self-made man who rose from office boy to company secretary at the publishing house of Macmillan. His mother, widowed young, went into domestic service at the Sussex home of Mr Alexander Macmillan, younger brother of the firm's founder and great-uncle of Britain's most literate post-war Prime Minister, Harold Macmillan.[6] No doubt a personable young boy—he was strikingly handsome in maturity—James Foster was accepted into the Macmillan family and taught by their governess. He later became an office boy at the firm, then confidential secretary to Alexander Macmillan and finally company secretary. 'My maternal grandfather knew and helped commission people like Kipling—the first *Jungle Book* came out under him,' Graham recalled. He was a man of some means.[7] He owned York House, near Amen Corner, in Tooting Broadway. 'It was the only house of splendour in the district, a big, partly Queen Anne, partly Georgian house,' his grandson remembered. 'It was really my first introduction to the fact that architecture was an important art. . . . Part of it was pulled down to make an engineering establishment for one of my uncles around 1925.'

There was a handsome library at York House, and Graham, his brother and sister all remembered Grandfather Foster with pleasure, his pleasant odour of cigars and port, and his generous way with half-crowns. 'We used to go out of the door literally holding out our hands, and he would put half a crown in each of them, which was a lot of money then for pocket money,' Graham's sister, Vivien, recalled.[8]

Graham believed that the Streatham house where he was born belonged to Grandfather Foster. Perhaps it represented a minor investment. Even in those days Pendle Road must have been a modest address. It is a street of small, two-storey terraced houses, where today scrawny roses and privet hedges straggle in tiny front gardens, and telephone wires lead from old-fashioned telegraph poles to the gables of pitched tile roofs. Graham would say he was born 'somewhere in Streatham—in what road I can't tell you'; yet the Spanish lady with the Pakistani husband who lived at number 8 when I called said they had had a letter from him in about 1978, saying that he would like to drop by one day to see his birthplace. 'Very famous, 8 Pendle Road,' she said, with a laugh.

By 1907, probably earlier, Graham's parents were living at a house called Allandene (now number 8) in Dorset Road, Merton Park, in vastly more spacious circumstances. In between, Graham thought, they might have lived in north London, perhaps to be near the bounteous Perronet Sells family.

Merton Park, now part of Wimbledon, then had its own identity as a village, made famous in 1801 when Lord Nelson bought Merton Place, living there with Sir William and Lady (Emma) Hamilton until his death at Trafalgar in 1805. Rather later, in 1881, William Morris established his dyeing, tapestry, stained-glass and carpet works at 10 and 11 Merton High Street, by the River Wandle. Graham remembered the family house there quite well.

> There, really, I think I had my first taste of landscape. We had a biggish garden with great elm trees in it. It was a semi-detached house, rather a nice one. There also I got my first conception of one space opening into another. Next door to us they had a quick hedge, between the two gardens, and I used to crawl through this hole. The difference between one garden and another was enormous, of course, and absolutely fascinated me as a kind of concept.

> I have always been interested in fire, and one of my pastimes was to have a piece of iron and hit it against a kerbstone, to see the sparks fly. Rather crazy, really.

The house backed on to a single-line railway track, which still joins Wimbledon and Croydon. He used to listen to the noise of the trains in bed. 'There was one night train. I used to hear it coming nearer and nearer. A terrifying sound. It was so persistent.' A snapshot survives, showing Graham, aged about 6, standing at the front gate in sweater and shorts, a rookery clearly visible in a large elm tree behind the gabled house with its mock-Tudor timbering. The elm trees' trunks were like great columns, he recollected.

Probably in 1910 or 1911 the family moved a few miles further south, to the first of three houses in Sutton, Surrey, but still within comfortable commuting distance of Whitehall, where Graham's father was progressing rather slowly up the hierarchy. The first two houses, both rented, were in Camborne Road, a long, curving, pleasant street where, in 1912, most of the fifty-odd houses had been built in the last ten years, according to borough library records.

The first house, called Adonholme, was a largish, detached residence on the junction with Stanley Road. Old street directories suggest that the family stayed there until 1914. Graham's memory was that the rent then went up, and they moved more or less across the road to a slightly smaller, semi-detached house (three floors, six bedrooms) called Storrington. The third house, built for them, was called Four Winds (now number 39) and was about a mile away, in Upland Road, a much posher street looking out over the valley of Carshalton Beeches to Croydon.

Graham's brother Humphrey was born in 1908. Graham had had his parents' undivided attention for five years, and no doubt he suffered the customary pangs attendant upon dethronement. Humphrey Sutherland later became a leading numismatist and Student (that is, Fellow) of Christ Church, Oxford. In 1913, after another five-year gap, their sister Vivien was born. She started learning ballet at the age of 3, and had a brief career as a dancer before giving it up for marriage.

Shortly after her birth, their parents built Green Bushes, a small country house (later enlarged) by the road down to the sea at Rustington, in Sussex. The same architect who built that house later built the house in Upland Road. Both were attractive and had pantile roofs, but both leaked. 'In Sussex we had to put bowls under the leaks in the roof,' Graham recalled. 'There was no pointing to the tiles to start with, and when the pointing was done, it was all right.' It was the same at the Sutton house. 'My father was too occupied or too lazy to get another architect. . . . he would certainly not have contracted the kind of arthritis he did if the house had been properly built. I remember his bedroom in the really bad weather streaming with water.'

Graham's father was of an intellectual bent. He had a deep love of classical literature and classical music, a wide-ranging mind and a good sense of humour. 'My father used to be very amusing,' said Graham. 'The older he got, the less amusing he became. But in his heyday he was really quite funny, and very affectionate, though a bit severe from the point of view of discipline.' He was rather a handsome man, with a bristly moustache, slightly crimpy, close-waved, auburn hair, and he wore a pince-nez for many years. Emotionally he was 'rather delicately balanced', Humphrey Sutherland thought. He had been very attached to his mother and had suffered from a form of nervous depression when she died. 'Father had himself under control for most of the time. But he was nervously charged. Mother was nervously charged in a different way, and the two, of course, produced sparks. It was not a happy household at all.'

Sutherland *père* was possibly a disappointed man. At the Board of Education he did not rise beyond the grade of principal (though that was then higher than now) perhaps, Graham thought, because 'he was much too useful training new people coming into the office. He was a very good teacher.' In those days civil servants were not well paid—Graham thought his father had never earned more than £1500—and Grandfather Sutherland had, according to family legend, frittered away a substantial inheritance from the Humphreys building profits on South American railroad stock. A legacy from Grandfather Foster was later spent on enlarging the Rustington house. Money was never in very ample supply, though middle-class standards of living were maintained.

Graham's father's consolation was music. He was a talented player of the violin, the viola and the piano. There used to be chamber-music evenings several times a week, either at the Sutherland home or with neighbours, and sometimes also readings of Shakespeare plays. Mabel Constanduros, later a well-known actress in radio soap operas, lived next door at one stage in Sutton and was doubtless sometimes of the party. She was a good friend of Graham's mother.

The stage was Elsie Sutherland's first love. But since the daughters of respectable families did not then become actresses, she had been sent to the Royal College of Music in Kensington, where she studied singing and pianoforte accompaniment from 1902 to 1904. She remained a competent pianist but was not basically musical. At heart a frustrated actress, she was a dissatisfied, rather restless woman, thoroughly undomesticated but a wonderful gardener.

The tower of strength of the family was Emily Collar, nicknamed 'Flea'. She had joined the family shortly before Humphrey was born, aged 15, as a helper around the house and ended up doing just about everything. She came from Sittingbourne in Kent and weighed some 15 stone. 'We were absolutely devoted to her,' said Vivien. 'She took us on as her family, and although she had one day off a week, she practically never took it, because she had nowhere to go. We were really her whole life. We absolutely adored her.' If a knee was pouring with blood, it was not to their mother they went, but to Emily. She stayed till the early 1930s. Graham never mentioned her to me. He said:

I was very fond of both of my parents, but there were difficulties, and my father, being a lawyer, was a very exacting type of person and liked the letter of the law. This irritated my mother very much indeed: 'You and your legal phraseology', that kind of thing.

My parents were always, almost invariably, quarrelling over something, alas. My brother wasn't affected as much as I was. I knew what was going on. I used to hear it when I got to bed. I heard it going on and on. It wasn't a violent quarrel. It was an attempt on each part to justify their particular actions. Over the years, the quarrelling was a constant. My mother, who dramatized herself in quite a big way sometimes, even attempted suicide. I don't think she could have killed herself by that particular method. She climbed out of a window and on to a sloping roof.

All she would have done was roll down and then drop about 6 feet. We had to pull her back, holding her ankles and saying: 'Oh, don't kill yourself.'

Graham's father was reflective, bookish and musical and loved walking. His mother was restless, never read a book, yet hated walks. By modern standards it was, brother Humphrey reflected, a curious upbringing: 'The children were in the family, but not really of it, in the intimate sense. I can't, for example, remember the children being truly invited to join the discussion of any subject of current interest.'

Graham's relations with his father were complicated by his parents' incompatibility. His father thought that Graham took after his wife's side of the family. 'My father quite clearly thought he had made a mistake in marrying my mother, and therefore all my mother's relatives, he thought, were awful . . . untrustworthy, and in fact one was. My father always thought at that time that I would turn out like this black sheep.' The black sheep was 'Uncle James or Jimmy', as he always signed himself on postcards. He had left Tonbridge under a cloud, according to family legend; started the First World War in the army and finished it in *The Bing Boys*, a musical which ran and ran at the Alhambra; abandoned a South American wife and two children; and generally went to the dogs.

It was against this rather unhappy background that Graham's schooling began. First, he went to a kindergarten called Clanrickard House, just beyond Sutton station. It was run, Graham recalled, 'by an old Fabian lady who wore very arty sort of clothes of the period. There was also "the black teacher", as we called her, who got very exasperated because I couldn't tie up my shoelaces. I didn't know how to tie a bow.'

There were end-of-term plays; in one of them Graham was dressed as a larkspur and Sholto Mackenzie, later Lord Amulree and already thin and tall, was a hollyhock. The Fabian lady was called Miss Close, and she had a pug dog called Rikki Tikki Tavi. The black teacher was called Miss Rice. Every morning began with the twenty-odd boys and girls singing 'All Things Bright and Beautiful'. Graham became friendly with Amulree in later life and inscribed a book on his work by their mutual friend Douglas Cooper with the words 'From' before a drawing of a lark and a spur and 'To' before a sprig of holly and a bottle of hock.[9]

Graham's father then decided that the education at Clanrickard House was inadequate and hired a governess, who came in to teach Graham and two or three other children from the immediate neighbourhood every morning. Her name was Dorothy Brown, and she was a nice-looking woman with brownish hair and beautiful handwriting. 'She was very good in her way,' Graham recalled. 'The repertoire of her teaching was very simple: she taught rudimentary French, English, arithmetic, history, and I suppose taught me to read perfectly and to spell—though she never really succeeded in that.'

Probably when he was about 9 or 10, Graham went to Homefield Preparatory School. It was within walking distance of their Sutton home, and it had recently been bought by two friends of his godmother, Julia Perronet Sells. They were Charles Walford and Rupert Gray, and both had taught at Highgate School. Homefield had been founded in 1868, but was set on its feet by Mr and Mrs Woodburn Bomford, who had acquired it in the 1880s.[10] By the time Graham got there it had a good reputation, which Walford enhanced. (Walford, eventually headmaster for forty years, Graham remembered as 'a Cambridge man, a very good teacher, very strict, and queer as a coot, I may say'—though Humphrey, who also went there, did not agree about this last point.) In a preface to a recent history of the school, Graham wrote:

Homefield Preparatory School—unique in the minds of many of us in having the marks of a miniature public school, and one of the better public schools at that, was intimate and friendly. Yet its structure and atmosphere were such as to prepare us for sterner things to come. Hardly aware of it at the time, I believe we were subtly filled with an eagerness to learn and compete, not only in school but on the playing fields. This provided a true foundation on which one could build and has proved invaluable to me in later life. . . . my days at Homefield give me a warm complex of emotions: that one was looked after, that one mattered, that one was encouraged and could make friends, could—a miracle!—learn and want to learn. For this I shall always be grateful.

It was basically a day school, with a few boarders. 'I had five or six very close friends. . . . we did all kinds of things boys do.' Graham recalled. 'We collected butterflies. . . .'

He seems to have been genuinely happy at Homefield. A photograph 1913 shows some eighty contented-looking boys in stiff white collars and suggests a pleasant, family atmosphere. Mrs Gray, sitting on Walford's right, has an infant on her lap, and Connie Bomford looks rather fetching on his left. Graham is one of the few boys not wearing a stiff collar and not looking at the camera. Even though Walford was a cricket fanatic (Colin Cowdrey was one of his products) and taught Graham's least favourite subject, mathematics, Graham seems to have liked him. He showed an aptitude only for English, he believed—'and I wasn't bad at Latin in those days, but of course my brother was infinitely superior as a scholar' (and indeed went, as a scholar, to Westminster).

He did not, in retrospect, believe that he gained anything from the art lessons of the Bomford daughter, Connie. But there was an admirable classics teacher, Miss Hallward, who was persuaded by Graham's mother to give him some art lessons at home. 'Of course, looking back, I realize she was a hopeless teacher with hopeless taste, and with no kind of conception of what she should be teaching,' he said. 'But, of course, I lapped it up at the time. I had to. We know better now.' Graham's father in particular thought he had some aptitude for drawing.

> I was not a prodigy by any means. I don't know quite how these things work out really. I suppose I must have drawn quite a bit at that time, at Storrington [the second Sutton house], and my mother made me draw when I was younger. Before we had the house at Rustington [in Sussex], we used to have digs at [nearby] Littlehampton. She used to make me draw on the village green. But it was really during the holidays at Rustington that I started to draw.
>
> There was a fairly strong strain of amateur painting in my father's family, and even a little in my mother's. But more in his. My aunt Beatrice, for instance, had a passionate interest in the work of Aubrey Beardsley, and wrote to Beardsley and was probably in love with him. She did minute, very beautiful drawings of illustrations to poems.

Rightly or wrongly, Graham did not feel all this made much difference.

> What did influence me was the fact that my grandfather at Macmillans oversaw the republication of classics like Thackeray, Jane Austen and George Eliot in a rather splendid edition which was illustrated by people like Hugh Thompson, E. M. Brock, and even Arthur Rackham, though he was slightly later.

Rackham became a family friend. In Humphrey Sutherland's memory he was a funny little gnome of a man, rather like one of his creatures, with a robust daughter called Barbara. He rented the Rustington house more than once when it was not required for holidays.

Well before his teens, Graham became 'mad' on these illustrations. 'I used to copy them, or try to. Then Macmillan published a big series called *Highways and Byways*, by E. V. Lucas. They had some jolly good illustrators, and I think that was another influence.' The young John Piper, an almost exact contemporary with a more topographical turn of mind, was also fired by *Highways and Byways*.[11]

Very few of Graham's juvenilia have survived. One of his maternal aunts, Hester, thought he had some talent and hung on to a couple of watercolours, now in the possession of her son Aubrey, Graham's first cousin and later director of a firm making industrial paints. One, believed to have been done by Graham aged about 6 or 7, shows a windmill looming up behind a long, low, white terrace of houses: quite a striking conception, but the execution shows no signs of precocity. It is signed 'GVS'—but then children love signing their works. A later one, probably done when he was about 12, shows a cottage with outlying buildings across the road from Green Bushes, the Rustington house. It is certainly competent, particularly in the relationship of the roofs, but does not make one cry 'Genius!'. Graham had no striking facility with the pencil in the manner of Picasso or Degas, but he was lucky to have been encouraged to do these watercolours out of doors, on the spot. How many childish talents have withered under the strain of being asked to paint or draw from the imagination? Drawing and sketching from nature was to be the foundation of Graham's art. He never started with something imagined.

Since there were five years between Graham, Humphrey and Vivien, they were all thrown on their own resources a good deal and tended to make their own separate lives. Graham went for long walks alone. He was later to recall:[12]

> The quality which I felt when I was about 10 of being in a wood, or at the side of a river, the warmth of the summer sun, was a thing which still stays with me, and I get enormously moved by this curious quality of enclosure . . . of being inside, as it were, a jewel in a way which a sunlit landscape seems to have. That is a thing which has been very constant.

There was a good deal of sibling rivalry between the two boys. Graham, who had the squarish forehead of some of the Fosters, was, if anything, his mother's preferred, while Humphrey and his father were physically akin and had a common interest in music and the classics. Their sister Vivien remembered a stage when they really did seem to feel like killing each other, and Graham recalled writing a note to Humphrey threatening to do just that, when he was about 12 years old. Later they became very close.

The house at Rustington, completed when Graham was about 10, cost only £400 or £500 to build and was used for all three school holidays, though Graham's father was not always there. 'The house was half a mile from the sea, next to Littlehampton,' Humphrey recalled. 'When my parents built it, there was only one house between them and the sea. It's very different now.' Next door was the composer Sir Hubert Parry, a dear old

31

teddy bear of a man, though his wife Maud, daughter of the Earl of Pembroke, was rather formidable. Quite a thicket divided the two houses. Sir Hubert used to go and stand on his lookout, a raised eminence in the corner of his property, and peer out to sea across the corn or stubble fields.

Graham had happy memories of tennis there. 'We were all tennis-mad, really. We had quite a nice grass court, and we used to organize tournaments with various friends.' Humphrey was the steadier player. 'I was occasionally quite brilliant, but I was a very erratic player. My father was very good, and my mother was even better. I don't know if the name of Mrs Lambert Chambers means anything to you? School of under-arm serves. The ball went like a corkscrew and was untakable. It didn't rise at all.'

Sometimes Graham's first cousin, Aubrey Smith, whose father was a colonial civil servant and was often abroad (after retirement he was killed by lightning on a golf course) would come for part of the holidays. 'Being three years older, Graham treated me and Humphrey as a couple of little rats and used to tease us,' he recalled. 'He was not a dull boy by any manner of means. He used to rather keep to himself, and didn't appear to have a lot of friends, but he had a good sense of humour and fun.' Later on there would be treasure hunts and dances at Rustington, from which Graham would frequently abstain, his sister Vivien remembered. 'He was different. He wasn't really very shy at all. He just didn't want to go to dances and dance with a lot of people he didn't like very much.'

While Humphrey learned the violin, as his father had, Graham was being taught the piano by a Miss Collier. She was the moving spirit of the resurrected musical evenings. 'I think Humphrey was more musical, not because he liked music better, but because he was more diligent in playing a musical instrument than I was,' Graham said. 'I played for a time, but I didn't apply myself. You see, I was really against my parents' interests at that time. I was very much the odd person out. I think their enthusiasm actually put me off.'

In the autumn of 1917 Graham went off to Epsom College, which was fifteen minutes away from Sutton by train. For no good reason, the standard potted biography of Graham in all books about his painting—no doubt based, in the first instance, on information from himself—gives his dates at Epsom as 1914 to 1918. But that is improbable. Boys from prep schools do not go to public school at the age of 11, but at between 13 and 14. The Epsom school registers of the period state unequivocally: 'The usual age for admission to the college is $13\frac{1}{2}$ to 14. No boy over 15 years of age is admitted.' The same rules state: 'A boy may remain in the school until the end of summer term of the year in which he reaches the age of 19, if his general conduct and his position in the school are satisfactory. Otherwise he must leave, if the headmaster so decides, after the term in which he completes his 16th year.'

School records are virtually error-proof. Epsom College's Yellow Book came out in the summer term, listing each form of the school with its members in form order. The 1918 edition, which first mentions G. V. Sutherland and would include boys arriving the autumn before, shows him second-bottom out of twenty-six pupils in Middle IVB, the lowest form of the middle school. The midsummer 1919 edition—the second and last mention of him—finds him promoted to Middle IVA and doing slightly better, at fifth-bottom out of twenty-five. The *School Register 1855–1954*, a sort of *Who's Who* of old boys, says: 'Sutherland, Graham Vivian . . . left 1919'.

Five years at public school being normal, it would not be surprising if Graham later thought that two would look a bit odd. But why should he choose to give the impression, to anyone who knew his date of birth, that he had left at the age of 14 or barely 15, a year younger than was in fact the case?

The transition from prep school to public school (indeed, from any primary to secondary school) is painful even in today's relatively enlightened circumstances. After being a biggish fish in a small pond, one becomes a minnow in an icy lake. In those days public schools were a great deal more spartan than they are now. In a sense, Graham was spared the worst by being a day boy. But day boys are second-rate citizens at boarding schools, often sneered at for their (sometimes) humbler backgrounds or local accents. There were only seventeen of them in the middle and upper schools in Graham's day, and school records suggest that they led a very shadowy existence.

One can imagine his heart sinking as he first made the walk from Epsom Downs station after a deceptively pleasant quarter-hour train journey. After a few minutes of skirting the Downs, the school buildings loom up, a tightly knit agglomeration of red-brick Victorian buildings with Tudor and Elizabethan overtones, seeming to glower from behind a high wall and topped by the inevitable crenellated clock-tower.

Epsom College was established as a public school in 1855, when it was known as the Royal Medical Benevolent College. It was intended to help to ensure that impoverished doctors and their families did not fall into the clutches of the workhouses of the time.[13] It had offered schooling for doctors' sons and accommodation for sixty doctors or dependants, each with an income of less than £15 a year. The pensioners left well before the First World War.

The school became known as Epsom College in 1902, and in 1914 it boasted 286 boys, a sound reputation and two former Prime Ministers, Lord Rosebery and A. J. Balfour, on its council. A high proportion of boys still came from medical backgrounds (at reduced fees), and the armed services were also well represented. Seven out of eighteen masters volunteered to serve in the First World War, no doubt to the detriment of academic standards.

The whole emphasis of the school was on the sciences. Graham said:

> It was a disaster from my point of view. A good school encourages you to learn. That's partly why you go there, and we weren't really encouraged to learn. I think this was partly due to the fact that all the best teachers were at the war. The public schools were drained of the cream. I should say probably the science teaching was pretty bad. Anything I know, sketchy though it may be, I have learned since.

The school stands on 80 windswept acres, 300 feet above sea level. There were wonderful playing fields immediately at hand, but even here tuition was inadequate.

> We were never really taught how to play games. I really rather liked rugby football. If I had known the rules, I might have been quite good at it. I was a three-quarter. In those days I could run very fast. I knew the rules of cricket, but I was always terrified I was going to drop a catch and was hopeless in the field. I was a fair bowler and an erratic batsman. What I really enjoyed was playing in the nets. One had no responsibility at all then.

Graham's memories show a certain fear of being laughed at, which remained with him. So did his dislike of physical intimidation. 'I was bullied at school, of course. There was a great deal of bullying. I think boys at school don't like timidity. I must have been very timid, really. They like to take it out on someone they think is weaker.' Graham compensated at home by taking it out on Humphrey and 'those awful boys my father thrust on me'—usually the hapless sons of his colleagues. 'They weren't really awful. I just disliked them because they were thrust on me.' Only an English master at Epsom inspired him at all, and in that subject he reckoned he did rather well.

It was on his teaching experiences in the junior or lower school at Epsom from 1908 to 1916 that Hugh Walpole based his novel *Mr Perrin and Mr Traill*. Like all public schools, it abounded with petty regulations. Each boy had to be provided with sixpence per week pocket money—but fines were deducted from that for being late in the morning. When the Derby was held at the nearby race course, the school was bolted and barred, the boys gazing out at the passing crowds like monkeys in a cage. School dress consisted of black, usually striped, long trousers and Eton jackets, known because of their brevity as 'bum-freezers'. Stiff collars were obligatory. Boys in the middle school were not allowed to put their hands in their pockets with the jacket behind their hands. That was 'swanking' and was reserved for boys in the upper school. Junior hands had to be inserted from behind.

Graham recalled that there was a good deal of homosexuality in evidence at Epsom in his day, but he did not really know what it was all about. Had he been a boarder, knowledge might have been thrust upon him. In matters sexual, Graham was to remain rather innocent and a touch prudish. He disliked crude jokes. Adolescence is normally an emotionally turbulent period. Graham was a good-looking boy. We do not know what, if any, lusts or passions tortured him. Probably he fought them down, along with his unhappiness, helping to lay (it may be surmised) the basis of that often decidedly erotic imagery that enriched the work of his maturity.

He was considered 'delicate' by his mother without, it seems, any good reason. But, probably at about the age of 15 or 16, he was allowed to acquire a motorbike. The love of speed was already there, though he did not keep the machine long. To his surprise, his father, who disapproved of motorbikes, sometimes asked for a lift.

By leaving Epsom at the end of the summer term of 1919, Graham just missed overlapping with John Piper, who arrived the following term and inherited Graham's *Shorter Latin Primer*, complete with his name and drawings of the Kaiser in it.[14] Piper's father was a successful Epsom solicitor. To mark the improbable feat of nurturing two such talents, the masters' common room at the College now displays a lithograph by each, presented in memory of an old boy.

Why did Graham leave before his sixteenth birthday? It was probably because the headmaster, the Rev. W. J. Barton, did not consider him university material, and neither did his father. The family debated what should be done with him. No sense of vocation was detectable, nor any great aptitude. Graham recalled:

> There were all kinds of suggestions: that I should be apprenticed to an architect; that I should even be a motor salesman. It was even suggested that I should become a farmer and go to agricultural school—all kinds of suggestions were made for someone considered to have no brains at all. Perhaps I didn't.

Although, unlike Piper, Graham did not frequent the art room at Epsom College, his own skills seem to have increased. A very adept watercolour survives, signed 'G.V. Sutherland 1918'. Perhaps a copy of a postcard, it shows two old men smoking very long, Korean-style pipes outside what looks like the door of an inn.[15] Despite what was evidently a growing talent and penchant for drawing and a general leaning towards the arts, he does not seem to have hankered at this stage after becoming a painter. Such an idea was probably outside his frame of reference. And so, eventually, it was decided to send him to Derby, where the paternal family roots lay, as an engineering apprentice at the Midland Railway Works. Perhaps it was argued that engineering required some flair for draughtsmanship. Uncle Budge and Aunt Beatrice lived up there, and Budge was a senior engineer at the works.

There was one serious flaw in the plan: Graham was no good at mathematics. It was as if someone tone-deaf were to be propelled—and Graham felt that he was being propelled into engineering—into a singing career. A remedy was tried: 'I was sent for a crash course in mathematics (a chap called Walker came in to teach me) and also to a polytechnic, Battersea Polytechnic, I think, where I learned physics, chemistry and mathematics too. This was thought to prepare me for engineering.' The transitional period of cramming lasted, he later thought, perhaps about eighteen months, though it seems likely to have been less in the light of subsequent timings. Although far from enthusiastic about going to Derby, Graham accepted the proposal. No doubt he was relieved to get away from school; and it is always pleasant to earn one's first wage, however meagre. 'It had its compensations,' he commented. 'Looking back, I don't think I would have missed it. I must confess it was a very formative thing in my life.'

Derby itself was, and remains, basically a pleasant, eighteenth-century Midlands county town with industrial accretions. In 1717 it had boasted the country's first silk mill. Indeed, the Industrial Revolution had its origins in the area: at Belper, 6 miles away, Jedadih Strutt owned the first factory in which stockings were manufactured by machines (later stormed by the Luddites); and at Cromford, Richard Arkwright, who revolutionized weaving with his invention of the spinning machine in 1769, established his first factory.

The coming of the railways in the 1830s set in motion the biggest increase in Derby's wealth and population. The Derby Locomotive Works, where Graham was to be apprenticed, was built for the North Midland Railway Company in 1840. In 1844 the North Midland amalgamated with the Midland Counties and Birmingham and Derby Junction companies to form the Midland Railway Company, a combined locomotive, carriage and wagon works covering nearly 50 acres by the railway station.

The carriage and wagon works were separated in 1873, spreading eventually over 128 acres, and remain the largest manufacturing and service centre of their kind in the world. Shortly after Graham's time, in 1923, the 120-odd railway companies in Britain were grouped into four big ones, of which the London Midland and Scottish was the biggest. The four were finally merged as British Railways with nationalization in 1948.

It was probably in the second quarter of 1920 that Graham went north. 'I don't think I'd ever been to Derby before,' he reflected. But he had met Uncle Budge and Aunt Beatrice on their visits south. Beatrice was his sister Vivien's godmother.

We must imagine Graham as 16, rising 17, a slim, good-looking youth with something of the self-contained quality of the oldest child, yet to some extent still his mother's darling, leaving home for the first time. Having always been a day boy at school, he had none of the dreadful resilience of those who have spent ten years as boarders. The move from relatively rural Sutton in Surrey to pre-Clean Air Act Derby was a sharp transition for a sensitive youth. 'It struck me very much, apart from the fact that they manufactured different things, as one of the Five Towns, as Arnold Bennett described them,' he recalled.

My uncle and aunt lived in one of the nicer parts, bang next to the Arboretum. The only industrial impingement was the Rolls Royce factory, which was very near them, and Crown Derby potteries. But I had the minimum of contact with my relations. My aunt and uncle didn't even offer to put me up. They valued their independence far too much for that. My uncle was sweet but dull: not a man of great attainment, but full of charm. My aunt, commandant of the St John's Ambulance Brigade, was intelligent and one of the most amusing women I have ever met—a real original. She had, as well as her own handwriting, a very curious, self-invented one which had to be seen to be believed![16]

So Graham had to find himself digs. At first he lived in a heavily Victorian, red-brick establishment called Melbourne House, on Osmaston Road and within walking distance of the railway works. It is now the seat of the Derbyshire Area Health Authority but was then a boarding house for young men at the railway works, Rolls Royce and so on.

I was not used to living in digs or sleeping in a bedroom—which was an ex-billiards room—with eight or nine other people. In fact, I prised myself away from this wretched boarding house. I was very depressed there, I must confess. I used to try to occupy myself mowing the lawn, rolling the grass. Then I met a chap who became a very good friend, a fellow apprentice. His mother was consumptive, though I didn't realize it at the time, in a very advanced stage, and she was very glad to have an extra lodger to help pay for his education.

At the works Graham had to clock on at 7.55 every morning.[17] Work continued until 12.30 p.m., when there was an hour's break for lunch, resuming at 1.30 until 5.30 p.m., with two mornings and three evenings of study at the municipal technical college, where Graham's grandfather, George, had briefly been organizing secretary.

The works then employed about 4000 staff, including about 500 trade apprentices training to be welders, platers, riveters, moulders and so on — the traditional craftsmen. Then there were about forty 'privileged' apprentices, of which Graham was one. Roughly half came direct from grammar and public schools between the ages of 16 and 18. The other half were promoted trade apprentices who had taken an internal examination set by the company. There were also about four engineering graduates, called 'pupils', fresh from university — the elite. The 'privilege' of Graham's group lay in being trained as all-round engineers and not as craftsmen, and also in being able to get up somewhat later two mornings a week, when attending lectures at the technical college.

The first sight of the railway works is not as daunting as one might expect, consisting as they do of a long line of low, red-brick buildings interspersed with railway tracks, turntables and capstans. But inside the enormously long bays of the various workshops, with their pitched glass roofs supported by steel struts and all the vast pressing, riveting and welding equipment, the turning, milling, planing, drilling and tapping machines and the overhead travelling cranes, are vastly impressive. Graham's record card has been destroyed, but he believed that he spent about a year at the works.

> I was mainly in the boiler-making department, working out the measurements of fire-boxes, etc., and later in the boiler repair shop, which meant entering the boiler through the dome cavity and marking up cracks with chalk, etc. I left before I could have entered the design department. The work was not tedious or especially difficult, but the hours were long.

According to Edgar Larkin, three years Graham's senior at Derby, as a privileged apprentice, Graham would have started off in the machine and fitting shop, which is still in the same building. There are five bays, each 450 feet long. The first has a huge walking crane powered by electricity, introduced in about 1870; and some vast, old planing machines were there in Graham's day. The glass roof, relatively clean today, would then have been grime-laden from outside pollution and from steam and dust inside.

The 'grease corner', where Graham probably started, is still a fairly mucky place. All sorts of small components—steel pins, bolts and nets, etc.—are made there. The thick, penetrating oil which gives the corner its name keeps both the tools and the components cool. Anyone using the vertical spindle-tapping machine, which puts the thread on huge nuts, was likely to find the oil soaking through his overalls on to his legs.

The dominant feature was a long line of machines, all then controlled by one 30–40 horsepower motor. 'With all those apprentices around, it was constantly breaking down,' said Larkin. 'When that happened, everyone was out of action. In the machine shop there were about 500 machines of all types, and at least 800 employees.' Roland Bond, an almost exact contemporary of Graham's at Derby, remembered how daunting it could be for the young apprentices.

The ordinary workmen were first-rate blokes, but they were inclined to pull your leg, and they certainly tried you out, as someone who was in a rather different position to themselves, with probably a totally different social background. You were given a rough idea of how to handle a lathe and expected to get on with it. Anyone coming completely fresh to the works would certainly find it pretty difficult. The men were on piece work. What one did contributed to their earnings. Their reactions were conditioned very much by the way in which one was prepared to work and get down to it.

It was the boiler-making and repair shops which left the deepest mark on Graham. The steel boilers were subject to corrosion and general deterioration, while the copper fire-boxes inside them suffered from the drastic changes of temperature. Patches had to be riveted on to cracked parts, and all the tubes had to be taken out and replaced. 'One of the fascinating jobs in those days was flangeing copper plates,' Bond recalled. 'One has a flat, red-hot plate, heated in the furnace. The plate is put on a flat iron table, and another lump of cast iron is put on top of it to hold it, and you bash the edge down with a wooden mallet to form the flange. That's the sort of work we all had a go at while we were in training.'

When riveting boilers, Graham would have used a 4 lb or 7 lb hammer. Larkin said:

It was a very heavy job, the heaviest in the works. The rivets were made red-hot in a portable fire beside the boiler, then pushed with a pair of tongs into a hole joining the two bits [of steel] together. There would be a head on one end of the rivet, and you had to form one on the other end by hammering it. You had to make a decent head, with a nice shape, so it didn't break away. Now it's all done with pneumatic or electric tools if it's done at all.

Electric-arc welding has largely superseded rivets.

Graham would undoubtedly have enjoyed many of the more craftsmanly of these tasks—especially those involving fire. One can imagine him giving a rivet head a 'nice shape'. The most disagreeable aspect of life in the works was the strain of being on one's feet virtually continuously from 7.55 a.m. to 5.30 p.m. 'If you were not standing, you were crouching in a pit under a locomotive—with an hour off for lunch, when we all went across to the Midland Railway Institute,' said Bond. The very heavy boots worn as a protective measure rubbed and blistered the feet until they got hardened.

Bond recalled Graham as 'clearly a fish out of water' at the works. 'I remember that he, almost alone among the pupils and apprentices, wore white overalls'—one of the privileges, but exercised by few. Most wore blue. Graham's white ones never seemed to get dirty. 'I remember him in the locomotive erecting shop. He never seemed to get down to any of the hard physical work involved in the erecting and repairing of locomotives. I don't suggest he idled his time away. I think it can only be said that he wasn't happy in that environment.'

Uncle Budge—more formally Major Frank Hubert Sutherland, but, coincidentally, known to everyone at the works as 'Uncle' owing to his gentle disposition—was a 'leading' draughtsman in the design department which Graham never reached. He was in charge of testing. This sometimes involved sitting in a shelter at the front of the locomotive or on the footplate, making diagrams as he went along. Both Bond and Larkin had a high opinion of his personality, as well as of his abilities, not least in mathematics. But his nephew did not share his facility with figures, and Graham did not take long to realize that his career had been misrouted. He told me:

> I *knew* I was on the wrong track immediately. But what was I to do but try? I drew in my lodgings after work, and rarely attended the courses at the technical college. . . . I was totally ill-equipped mathematically. Maths were crucial if it were intended that I should be a designer rather than a workman on the shop floor. Of course, a multitude of calculations would have to be thoroughly understood.

The old technical college which Graham spasmodically attended is a splendid bit of Victorian Gothic in Green Lane, near the main shopping area. It is all towers, turrets, buttresses and mullioned windows, its pinkish stone liberally spattered with pigeon droppings. Graham's studies there were the nearest he came to theoretical design. One of Larkin's old study books shows the sort of thing he had to to — like drawing a cam for operating a valve at varying speeds, very arid and precise. But from the pleasure Graham later derived from drawing and painting machines we may assume that something positive filtered through. The exams for which Graham's more serious colleagues were preparing were the equivalent of a university degree and involved a lot of homework as well as the course.

Graham had some social life.

I had a strong impression of the splendour of the Midland Hotel, with its bright red, thick carpets, its gilt, and splendid food in those days, incidentally; and of hunt balls, which were held in those days either in the Midland Hotel or in the Assembly Rooms [in the market place]. It was my only bit of social activity, really. I managed to get occasionally to a hunt ball.

The hunt was the Meynell, and a well-known bandleader of those days, Conri Tait, used to perform at the balls. Graham would go with his fellow apprentice friend with whom he lodged. 'I had really no timidity in this context. My mother taught us all to dance, and we went, of course, to dances when I was at school.' These occasional diversions were no real compensation for the rigours of daily work, however, and a traumatic episode at the works seems to have helped to focus Graham's determination to abandon engineering.

I got shut into the boiler of a shunting engine. There was one little man who was very slim and could slide down. You know the construction of the dome of a locomotive? It has a steam pipe which goes up one side [inside the dome, that is, taking the steam from the dome to the cylinders]. The maximum pressure is always at the top. He was able to slide between the steam pipe and the edge of the dome, in order to mark up faults. He had 'flu once, and I was next-slimmest. I had to do it, and I got shut in and couldn't get out. They had to take the dome off. I couldn't get out because you could get down with your arms together, but to get out, your arms became wide as you raised them by pulling on the edges of the dome. I think that's how claustrophobia started with me. There was a time when it was aggravated by agoraphobia. For instance, to cross a street was agony. I never had agoraphobia in the country, only when there were milling crowds crossing the road or something.

How long he was trapped he could not remember, but it seemed a very long time. The diameter of the dome through which he had to squeeze would have been between 18 and 20 inches, that of the boiler barrel just under 5 feet.

41

Probably in the first quarter of 1921 he decided that enough was enough. Cousin Aubrey Smith recalled Graham coming home from Derby one weekend and saying to his father, whom he called Didds: 'Didds, I can't stand this any more. I want to go in for art.' According to Aubrey, 'His father was appalled. In those days I think any parent would have been appalled.' Painting was essentially for those with private means, like the Bloomsbury set.

And so Graham went to see Sir Henry Fowler, chief mechanical engineer of the Midland Railway and head of the mechanical and electrical department in Derby. He was a tall, stout, imposing man with a wax moustache, who had played hockey for Derbyshire, introduced the famous *Royal Scot* locomotive and was ahead of his time in his ideas on the education and training of engineers. He was bald, wore pince-nez and had a kindly look, and he had been knighted for war work at the Ministry of Production.

Sir Henry was very tactful, Graham recalled. 'He said: "You have worked very hard, but you have no sense of mathematics. We know you want to pursue a career in art. I will speak to your father." He understood my feelings very well. He wrote to my father who, pressured by my mother, got me into the Goldsmiths' College, University of London.'

Looking back, Graham had no regrets about his stint at Derby.

I was at once amazed at the transformation of blocks and sheets of metal into the modern steam locomotive at its highest point, with all its intricate sophistication. The experience without doubt gave me a feeling for great machines which I have never lost. I had an admiration for the men and what they corporately achieved.

His experiences in Derby were to be reinforced by his years as a war artist, when he made studies of a number of steel works and armaments factories. Visiting the Derby works, one is struck by the 'Sutherlandish' look of some of the machines there, particularly some very old presses used for pressing the wheels of locomotives on or off the axles. Equally, his contacts with the Derby work force laid the basis for the compassionate socialism which in later years, ever contradictory, he combined with painting the portraits of, and dining at the tables of, the very rich.

2

Student and Etcher

1921-7

GRAHAM'S FIVE HAPPY YEARS at the Goldsmiths' School of Art laid the foundations for his adult life. He found his feet as an artist with remarkable speed; he met, and later married, the girl who was to be the mainstay of his life. But it was in no very confident mood that he arrived at the beginning of the spring/summer term of 1921, when he was rising 18.

'I went to Goldsmiths' on a slightly experimental basis,' he recalled.[1]

> I don't see how anyone at that age can have total confidence either in their ability or in the prospects which are possible. So I was always thinking: I am not sure. Then I got used to being unsure, and I didn't care so much. I was interested in what I was doing, and therefore didn't think of the future to any great degree.

Graham was too young to have been infected by the wave of interest in 'modern' painting which had swept London before the First World War. The reaction against the tyranny of the Royal Academy had begun in 1886, with the founding of the New English Art Club. Led by W. R. Sickert, the New English Art Club, broadly speaking, endeavoured to promote the cause of Impressionism. It was followed by the Camden Town Group in 1911, whose sympathies were with the post-Impressionists, and in 1914 by the Vorticists, who preached an idiosyncratic blend of Cubism, Futurism and Expressionism. Groups in which the more progressive spirits exhibited included, notably, the Allied Artists Association, which showed the first Kandinskys to be seen in England in 1909 and 1910, and the London Group, which the critic and painter Roger Fry joined in 1917, becoming the spearhead within it of the Bloomsbury painters.

Roger Fry had done more than anyone else to alert a wider public to the dramatic developments on the Continent. His two post-Impressionist shows at the Grafton Galleries in London came as a revelation. The first, in 1910, included twenty-one Cézannes, thirty-six Gauguins, twenty-two van Goghs, a sprinkling of Fauves, oils and bronzes by Matisse and two Picassos, one of them an early Cubist portrait. The second show, in 1912, ran to forty-one Matisses and sixteen Picassos, including Cubist works.

At the same time there were three exhibitions in London devoted to Futurism; the Diaghilev Ballet was fusing the fine and performing arts into a dazzling whole on stage; and Kandinsky, Mondrian, Paul Klee and the Russian Suprematists (largely unknown to the English) were adding a new, more abstract dimension to the vocabulary of painting. But the first flush of enthusiasm for the modern spirit did not survive the First World War, and amid the public at large the Royal Academy resumed much of its old sway.

Given Graham's immaturity as an artist and his uncertainty about his calling, it was lucky that he was not immediately exposed to such overpowering and intellectually stretching influences as Cézanne or Picasso, or to Fry's reassessment of primitive art. British art had long been torn between the dominance of Paris and a hankering after a national tradition. The end of the Great War set the clock back. It was not until the 1930s that the spirit of discovery and adventure returned. Graham was typical of his generation in being suspicious of Continental influences.

The Goldsmiths' school was not his first choice. First his father had tried the Slade School of Fine Art, where two years earlier Henry Tonks had taken over as Slade Professor (Principal). Graham often said later to his great friend at Goldsmiths', Paul Drury, that he wished he had gone to the Slade because of its emphasis on drawing. 'But in retrospect, I don't think Tonks would have helped him much,' Drury commented.[2] Graham was to learn the harder, more personal way. Perhaps his work would have been less intensely individual had he come under a teacher as strong as Tonks.

In the event, there were no vacancies at the Slade. The School of Art of the University of London's Goldsmiths' College, to give it its full title, was Graham's second choice, on the recommendation of a friend of his father, who was a senior Inspector of Schools. It had acquired a high reputation under its head, Frederick Marriott, and it was in south London and so more easily reached by train from Sutton, Surrey.

The college took its name from the Worshipful Company of Goldsmiths. The livery company had in 1891 purchased the 7-acre site and buildings at New Cross of the former Royal Naval School. The college first opened as the Goldsmiths' Company's Technical and Recreative Institute, a sort of polytechnic for south London, aimed at the working and artisan classes. Control was transferred to London University in 1903, but the Company continued to provide a subsidy, including £8000 for a new building designed by Sir Reginald Bloomfield. It was to the upper floors of this that the newly established art school moved in 1908. In the 1920s Goldsmiths' was also the largest teacher-training college in the country.[3]

When Graham arrived, the art school had some 200 students, of whom less than half were full-time. All the teachers were part-time except Marriott, who had been head since it opened in 1891. He was a tiny man with a handlebar moustache; he was knowledgeable about music and literature and a good friend of Arnold Bennett. Marriott had shown Graham and his father around the college during the previous winter term.

Drury's first impressions of Graham were of an outstandingly good-looking young man with a certain apprehensive reserve, yet with alert, intent eyes which took everything in. The handsome young man was also favourably noticed by one of the school's youngest pupils, Kathleen Barry, who was sitting in the architecture class trying to learn fashion drawing from Amor Fenn. She was only 16. Marriott had said she was too young but could not resist her. He told everyone that they had a lotus flower in their midst. 'The lotus flower got in and played merry hell,' she recalled fondly.

Graham always reckoned that it was at Goldsmiths' that his real education took place.

I learned a great deal more than art there. I learned to cultivate a taste for music and so on. All the proper reading I did, I did there. . . . A lot of my fellow students were great readers. Paul Drury really introduced me to the Russian novelists, to Jean-Jacques Rousseau, Balzac, and equally with music. I would go so far as to say that without him, I would never have developed a taste for music. A lot of people played rather well at the school; during the lunch break, we had two students who played excellently. One (Robert Barnes) was a specialist in Chopin. Paul didn't play frightfully well, but he played very fluently, and we went to concerts together in the Queen's Hall and so on.

The course which Graham followed at Goldsmiths' was a general one: the idea that Graham studied only etching there is mistaken. He recalled:

I did book illustration with Edmund J. Sullivan. He was one of the illustrators at the time of Sir Arthur Rackham and Hugh Thompson, one of the Macmillan boys. He was a very good teacher in his way, one of the very few there. . . . Then there was still life, antique class, life class. I never did the portrait class, but I attended the sketch club, which the head of the portrait section ran once a week. He was called Harold Speed, a society portrait painter. The sketch club was rather a misnomer. It was really more a means of learning composition—the composition of anything one had been interested in—and the composition was criticized.

Graham, Drury and their friends were much impressed by Sullivan's illustrations for Carlyle's *Sartor Resartus* and by the free simplifications and bold, nervous penwork of his illustrations for Tennyson's 'Maud'. Sullivan wore a floppy bow tie and had white hair, save for a streak of yellow, where he stroked it back with nicotine-stained fingers. 'He would drink with us students in the Rosemary Branch, a pub a few yards from the school,' Drury recalled, 'and introduced us to Henry James and talked about Wilde'—in a soft, diffident voice, laced with 'ers' and 'dontcherknows'.

Such was the prevailing enthusiasm for etching at Goldsmiths' that even 'old Sully' himself started doing some there around 1923, and Graham, by then more experienced than his distinguished teacher in that medium, helped him with the 'biting' of some plates.[4] Freddie Marriott was himself a painter and topographical etcher in a somewhat conventional style. Although the great boom in etchings did not really get under way until 1924 or so, it was a popular medium, and Marriott thought that etching was a good line to pursue. It was Marriott, Drury believed, who first showed Graham the basic techniques. Etching is not to be confused with engraving, though the term 'engraving' is sometimes used in a generic sense to cover a variety of incised techniques. Engraving itself involves making a shallow incision directly on to a polished copper or steel plate with a sharp burin. Ink is worked into the engraved part and the surplus wiped off, and the plate is passed through a mangle-like press which transfers the ink to the paper from the recesses of the plate. Drypoint is akin to engraving, but the steel or diamond-tipped needle raises a slight burr or furrow on the metal, which retains the ink and gives the end product its slightly furry line.

Etching is a much freer medium. The plate is coated with a wax-like ground, which is impervious to acid. The artist lays the metal bare with a pen-like needle where lines are required. The plate is then placed in a bath of diluted nitric acid until those parts which are to be lightest are judged to be sufficiently 'bitten' or eaten out. They are then covered—the plate having been dried—with acid-resisting varnish. The plate goes back into the acid, the process continuing till the darkest parts have been deeply enough 'bitten'. Etched lines are softer because of the uneven action of the acid on the metal. Just how long to leave the plate in the acid calls for fine judgement, one of the many factors tending towards a heavy preoccupation with technique among practitioners and collectors. Endless rejigging is possible: hence the different 'states' which so fascinate connoisseurs.

Graham's first etching teacher was Alfred Bentley, in whose own later work a poetic tranquillity and echoes of Corot have been discerned. But Bentley, who had been gassed in the war, contracted bronchial pneumonia and died in 1923. He was succeeded by his great friend Malcolm Osborne. Graham thought:

> They were both very nice men, but I don't think either would, by today's or any other standards, be considered particularly interesting as artists, and they were not even technically experimental. The whole thing was really on the basis of a preconceived plan: foregrounds had to be done in a certain way, that kind of thing.

Osborne went off to the Royal College of Art in 1925 and was replaced by Stanley Anderson. He was anxious to help, diffident when it came to general criticism but precise in technical matters. Like most people, he admired his own qualities in other people: 'sterling', 'probity' and 'guts' were words of praise. Graham considered him to be almost as hidebound in his imaginative approach as Bentley and Osborne, but Anderson appreciated Graham's ability, and in 1926 recommended Graham to fill his post as teacher of engraving at Chelsea School of Art.

The teacher whom Graham came to respect most at Goldsmiths'— though mainly in retrospect—was Clive Gardiner, whose wife had been a pupil of Sickert and who had drunk deeply at the fount of the Impressionists and post-Impressionists in Paris and London. Gardiner, whose father edited the liberal *Daily News*, taught the still-life class at Goldsmiths' (and was later Principal from 1929 to 1958). Graham was to recall him as a 'young, shy, faintly mocking and sarcastic figure', who would peer over their shoulders from time to time, 'tolerantly amused at the results of our ignorance, and viewing—not quite so tolerantly, I suspect—the mediocre and threadbare academic tradition affecting both staff and students alike'.[5] Gardiner gave them a glimpse of a new world.

> One heard for the first time such names as Cézanne and Matisse, and we were shown reproductions of their work. . . . one began to feel there was more to drawing than copying more or less what we thought we saw. . . . I for one certainly at that time thought the work he showed us superficial (a word then much in currency) and inept.

Yet forty years later Gardiner's words would rise constantly in Graham's mind, and he was no longer blind to their significance.

Of more immediate influence were Harold Speed's sketch-club classes. He was no protagonist of the modern French school, but he spoke good sense with real warmth. 'The most important thing in a picture is to decide the mood, and to see that you sustain that mood, unless for any particular reason you wish to shock,' he would say.[6] Then again: 'Of course, these horizontal lines give you a feeling of peace. The vertical lines which go across the horizontal lines give you great stability, exemplified to a treat, if I may so, in Hobbema's *Avenue*.'

Drury remembered Graham showing Speed a watercolour of a fish as an illustration of a poem by Rupert Brooke. It was in opalescent shades and revealed some Japanese influence. 'This is most poetical,' Speed commented. Drury also recalled Graham later doing a Descent from the Cross in oils for Speed, an interesting prefiguration of his later religious work. It was a tightly knit composition with a good deal of *Angst* in it. Conceivably, Graham showed Speed a self-portrait that he did as a student — 'a very finished sort of work, which I destroyed, over-finished', Graham remarked.[7]

Graham's 'close little band' of friends at Goldsmiths', as he was to call them,[8] consisted of Drury, William Larkins and Edward Bouverie Hoyton. Drury was a young man of wide-ranging culture and son of the distinguished sculptor Alfred Drury who was responsible, *inter alia*, for the statue of Joshua Reynolds in the forecourt of the Royal Academy building, off Piccadilly. Bouverie was splendidly scruffy and good-natured, a natural butt for humour (Graham and Larkins once etched a spider on the bottom of a boy on one of his etching plates). Both Bouverie and Larkins had arrived at Goldsmiths' a couple of years before Graham, and he doubtless benefited from their experience.

Larkins was a ferocious worker. If Graham arrived at Goldsmiths' at 7 a.m., he would find Larkins had been there since 6.30. He was the son of a steeplejack who cleaned Nelson's Column. 'The family lived at Whitechapel, and were as Irish as can be,' Graham recalled.[9] 'In spite of his mocking, slightly acidulated manner, he was a real friend. I admired much of his work.' When the 1929 crash came, Larkins turned first to films, then to commercial art, designing the famous Black Magic chocolate box and the Lux packet with elongated lettering.

Together they would go on expeditions to the Tate and the National Gallery, sometimes adjourning to Snow's Chophouse in Piccadilly. Drury recalled:

> We used to have something like gravy soup, made from meat; chips, braised onions, baked beans and coffee, and it used to come to around 10 pence or a shilling. Sometimes we had meat. There were three waiters, all Dickensian characters, and wooden stalls. The waiters had white aprons

and always a dirty white napkin. There was a tall, thin one called 'Arry, who looked a bit like Eric Fraser [a fellow student], who did all those designs for the *Radio Times* later.

This little band of like-minded etchers worked together, not infrequently, in the so-called 'Bijou' room at Goldsmiths', sometimes in the anatomy room, which was usually empty. Only the actual etching was done in the admirably equipped etching room, with its tools, stopping-out varnish and so on. To a large extent they were left to their own devices.

Four of Graham's first five surviving works were drypoints, done in 1922 and 1923 and printed at the school.[10] It was a medium favoured by Bentley. The first, called *Les Sylphides*, showed six female ballet dancers with arms raised, reflecting Graham's enthusiasm for the ballet at that time. Next came a slightly more ambitious study of a wharf at Arundel, not far from Rustington, with part of a ship in the foreground. The third was a rather attractive study of two greyhounds, coursing neck and neck over well grazed turf. It was based on a bronze sculpture by Frémiet, a French *statuaire* of the 1870s and 1880s, which belonged to Paul Drury's father. These three, and a heavily worked study of houses done from the 'Bijou' room's window, date from 1922, Graham's first full year at Goldsmiths'.

His first real success came with *Barn Interior* the following year. To the great excitement of his family, it was hung 'on the line' (that is, at a favourable height) at the Royal Academy's Summer Exhibition that year. By chance, his cousin Aubrey Smith stumbled on Graham when he was doing the preparatory drawing:

In those days Carshalton Beeches, near their home in Sutton, was very countrified. At the bottom of the valley was a very rickety old barn. I was on my own once, having a walk around. I was 16, so Graham was 19. I went into this barn, and there was Graham drawing. He was absolutely shattered and told me that on no account was I to disclose this to anyone. I think he felt they might all laugh at him. It was the interior of a barn—lots of old sacks and rubbish.

It is an astonishingly assured, if slightly 'busy' work, full of intricate detail, the scene lit by a dramatic light and bisected left of centre by a strongly drawn ladder, a useful compositional device. Graham went on in 1923 to do his first etching to show a real feeling for rural landscape: a striking distant view of a pub near Arundel called *The Black Rabbit*. The pub nestles at the foot of a hill. The River Arun winds its way along the valley. In the foreground are large elms and, just visible, the rim of the quarry from which the scene was sketched. It was shown at the Royal Academy in 1924. Graham was to show one or two etchings there every summer until 1930.

He was later to attach some significance, as a landmark, to a pen-and-wash drawing he did in 1923 called *Mill Interior*, probably inspired by the inside of the same windmill which he had drawn in Sussex as a child. He was fascinated by the intricacy of the complicated machinery inside and recorded it in a factual, descriptive style.[11] '*Mill Interior*, I think, really marks the beginning of my ability to control a line,' he told me. There seems to be little doubt that Graham's experiences at Derby had predisposed him to taking an interest in the shape of machines.

By the second half of 1923 he felt bold enough to enter for the Rome Scholarship's engraving section. Six drawings and six prints had to be submitted by the end of January 1924. Four finalists then spent four weeks working on two plates or blocks, one on a compulsory theme—in Graham's year, the Expulsion from Eden—under strictly controlled conditions in special studio accommodation.

The scholarships were tenable for three years at the British School at Rome, founded in 1901 as an archaeology school. In 1923 there were twelve candidates in the engraving section. Graham and his friend Edward Bouverie Hoyton were finalists, but the winner was one Edward Morgan, from the Slade. Bouverie, as he was called, went on to win in 1926 at his third attempt. A disappointed Graham did not try again. In the sculpture section that year Barbara Hepworth was runner-up to John Skeaping, an engaging character but a vastly lesser artist, whom she later married.

Artists whose work influenced Graham and his friends at this stage included Rembrandt, Dürer, Whistler, Charles Méryon and Jean-François Millet.[12] There was more than a touch of Dürer in the crumbling farm buildings which feature in several of the etchings of rural scenes that Graham did in 1924. Another, *The Sluice Gate*, is heavily indebted to Rembrandt. Two others, called *Cudham, Kent* and *Barrow Hedges Farm*, were among the few which Graham did straight on to the etching plate in front of the subject. Generally, he made sketches first, in pencil or water-colour, working on the plate later.

In October that year, 1924 (not 1925, as all the reference books say), Graham had his first exhibition, at the Twenty-One Gallery in Durham-House Street, Adelphi, not far from the Strand. He recalled:

I hawked my work all around London. I took portfolios to every dealer. Eventually I went to this Molly Bernhard-Smith, who was a remarkable woman, and she *was* the Twenty-One Gallery. She was very much in advance of her time, and had Epstein, Gaudier-Brzeska, the best of William Nicholson: a lot of people who were not really considered academic.

The Bernhard-Smiths were a very, very eccentric family. Her sister was the wife of the composer Clifford Bax. Her husband had been one of Lister's house surgeons. He was a great stunt man. He stood on the cliffs at Ramsgate, I think it was, and swore he would dive into the boiling sea, which in fact he did.

Graham's debut was a success. 'A new draughtsman', proclaimed a headline in the *Morning Post* on 10 October. The article dwelt on Graham's youth (he was 21), his 'odd yet curiously familiar way of looking at and representing inanimate things', his sense of the picturesque and of line. Rembrandt and his later mentor F. L. Griggs (whose *Highways and Byways* illustrations Graham had much admired) were seen as apparent influences. *The Times* was equally enthusiastic. Mr Sutherland was very clearly to be added, the reviewer said on 11 October, to the growing body of young artists who aimed at an artistic effect by co-ordinating detail rather than leaving it out (a swipe at those Continentals, perhaps). The show was a most encouraging successor to Graham's Royal Academy exhibits and established the beginnings of a market for his works.

As a healthy corrective to the rather rarefied, finicky work of etching, Graham, Drury and Larkins gathered some experience of great practical and aesthetic value, as Graham later called it, when they and others helped Clive Gardiner to carry out some large decorative panels, in a style reminiscent of the Douanier Rousseau and Gauguin, for a pavilion at the British Empire Exhibition of 1924 at Wembley. 'They were brilliant designs by Gardiner, rather like huge posters, which we squared up and enlarged from drawings: he couldn't do it all himself,' said Drury. The superimposition of a squared grid on a drawing was a technique widely adopted by Sickert and others—which Graham was to use regularly in later life for transferring a sketch to a canvas without losing his grip on the original inspiration.

One day that autumn Larkins brought to the college an etching by Samuel Palmer called *The Herdsman's Cottage*. Graham was amazed at its completeness, both emotional and technical.

It was unheard of at the school to cover the plate almost completely with work, and quite new to us that the complex variety of the multiplicity of lines could form a tone of such luminosity . . . as we became familiar with Palmer's later etchings, we 'bit' our plates deeper. We had always been warned against 'over-biting'. But we did 'over-bite', and we burnished our way through innumerable states, quite unrepentant at the way we punished and maltreated the copper.[13]

It was not only Palmer's etchings which excited Graham, but also the drawings of his famous Shoreham period, named after the idyllic Kent village where Palmer lived at the time. 'The best of the Shoreham drawings, the very best, were unsentimental,' he said.[14] 'The landscapes were daring, and were drawn from unexpected viewpoints: *The Girl in the Ploughed Field* astonished me with its total disregard for conventional composition. The drawing is almost what we today called naif . . . .'

One of the things that fascinated Graham about Palmer's work was the way in which a strong emotion could change and transform the appearance of things. It was an idea which never left him.[15] William Blake had, perhaps, started it all with his visionary watercolours and especially his wood engravings for Dr Thornton's Virgil. Samuel Palmer and his circle, including Edward Calvert and George Richmond, had become Blake's disciples. Wearing cloaks—as Graham and his friends were sometimes to do, in imitation (Graham borrowed his mother's Royal College of Music cloak)—and calling themselves the Ancients, Palmer and friends transmuted the gently folding landscape around Shoreham in Kent into visions of ripe innocence in which shepherds tended their flocks under vast moons, and everywhere was peace, abundance and honest toil. After 50 years of neglect, these works were being rediscovered by a handful of museum officials, like Martin Hardie of the Victoria and Albert Museum, who in December 1926 organized with James Laver a memorable exhibition of work by Samuel Palmer 'and other disciples of William Blake.'

'You must not think that this period was *all* hard work and seriousness,' Graham said.[16] 'We had great jokes which we thought hilariously funny. We read all the Russian novelists in the Garnett translation, and assumed the characters . . . and I was walking out with K.'

Kathleen Barry—later frequently also called Katharine—was half-Irish. Her father had been in the Consular Service in Hong Kong (where she spent the first eight months of her life), then returned to England, where he worked first as a schoolmaster, then at Woolwich Arsenal, living at Eltham. She and Graham at first just gazed at each other. Then, during that first July holiday, he wrote inviting her to the Diaghilev Ballet. When they met at Charing Cross station, it was the first time they had spoken to each other. 'I remember I was very surprised at the timbre of his voice, being so high and light, like the Duke of Windsor's,' she recalled. 'It was all very agreeable. We had Fuller's cake, and he had to borrow half a crown to get his train home.'

Graham had his rivals. At one stage Kathleen dropped him in favour of one of them. Then she decided that she had backed the wrong horse and asked Paul Drury to give Graham a note saying she would meet him again. Drury said: 'Well, I'll give your note, but, you know, Sutherland has his pride.'

Holidays were, naturally, also for drawing. Graham's sister Vivien remembered an incident at Rustington when she was 11, in about 1924, in the summer. Graham asked her: 'You wouldn't let me draw you, would you?' She was longing to get out into the sun to play tennis or to swim, but sat for about five minutes, keeping absolutely still. Then she said: 'I'm fed up with this,' and went. Graham was absolutely furious, she recalled.

No doubt finding both the commuting to Goldsmiths' and the troubled atmosphere at home tiresome, Graham decided that same year to move into digs with a friend at Blackheath, not far from New Cross. The friend was a shyly ambitious young man called Milner Gray. Four years older than Graham, he had left Goldsmiths' in 1921 but still turned up on some evenings. He had set up a design consultancy called the Bassett Gray Studio and was to become one of the leading designers in the country. 'When Graham found me, I had a bedroom and a ground-floor sitting-room in a nice little Queen Anne house in Grote's Place,' he recalled.[17] He secured another bedroom for Graham, and they shared the sitting-room, where Graham soon installed his own small printing press.

In January 1925 Graham was elected an associate member of the Royal Society of Painter-Etchers and Engravers. This body had been founded in 1880 by Whistler's brother-in-law, Sir Seymour Haden, a fierce evangelist of original graphic work, and was then being presided over by the not much less autocratic Sir Frank Short. Until 1931 Graham was to exhibit between one and three works there every year. More important, being an ARE (an illogical abbreviation) was recognized as a qualification for teaching at art schools and elsewhere. Graham's father was among those who expressed his relief at this development.

Graham's work was maturing rapidly. A large etching called *The Village*, finished in the first half of 1925, was another landmark, more reminiscent of Millet than of Palmer but richly pastoral, with its furrowed fields in the folds of a valley. In the foreground sits a girl, her basket full of eggs (or possibly potatoes). In the background are oasthouses, and just off-centre is a shed. A broad shaft of sunlight enters right. It was based mainly on scenery around Cudham, in Kent, but included elements from Warning Camp, in Sussex. Graham was already using his imagination not to invent but to regroup and distil. It was really only in the period between his work on *Pecken Wood*, which he did later that year, and *The Meadow Chapel* of 1928 that Graham's etchings were heavily under the influence of Palmer—a mere half-dozen of them. They are heavily 'medieval' in overtone. Evening stars and setting suns illumine a hushed world of thatched cottages and toiling peasants.

An element of this was due not so much to Palmer as to F. L. Griggs, to whom Graham was introduced by Paul Drury's father at the Royal Academy vernissage of the summer 1925. Griggs was profoundly moved by *The Village*, Drury recalled, and a correspondence began between Graham and both Griggs and his friend, the writer and painter Russell Alexander.

Griggs had become a Roman Catholic convert in 1912, had settled in the beautiful Cotswold village of Chipping Campden and had become a doughty champion of rural preservation. Graham greatly admired his drawings (he enriched thirteen volumes of the *Highways and Byways* series with pen-and-ink and pencil drawings). Graham said:

> His etchings, of course, were technically miraculous. But for me they were a bit too much imaginings—and I think partly false imaginings—of Olde England: rustic, and highly Catholic in the religious sense. His medievalism was part of his Catholicism: he dreamed of old cities and towns furnished with pure and perfect Gothic churches, and of the monastic life. He thought real England had been damned, as one of his titles, *Ex Anglia Perdita*, suggests.
>
> But he taught me a great deal about printing. Everything I know about printing I know I owe to him: how thick the ink should be, how to use the hand in wiping it off [Griggs, he said elsewhere,[18] had 'a palm as delicate as gossamer'], how many rags one had to use, and at what kind of stages: not I think the actual 'biting' of the lines, because I knew that before. Certainly, we never came across a printer who had that particular acumen.[19]

In late 1926 Griggs invited Graham and Paul Drury down to Chipping Campden. They spent some three bitterly cold days there in November. Graham recalled:

> We took some plates down. He printed them and stamped them with his special stamp. Then he made the mistake, which I think I never made myself, of trying to re-teach or direct me. . . . I was a bit independent, and I didn't take to this advice, and I'm very glad I didn't. The friendship didn't finish, but certainly I didn't see very much of him after that, and then [in 1938] he died.

Equally certainly, Graham was for a time somewhat infected by the Griggs outlook on life. A letter of 15 May 1925 to Russell Alexander finds Graham talking of 'this country seemingly fast sacrificing itself to progress (so called) at the expense of calm nobility'. A certain ceremoniousness of style matched the nostalgia. 'I do indeed feel the greatest sympathy and harmony in the way you mention,' he wrote to Alexander after the visit.

> Yet for a man of my years to give outward assent to such thoughts seems to me very near presumption. I do, however, know that the thoughts and loves (to quote yourself) which prompt the art of such as Mr Griggs and yourself and those masters of the past who made their art (or, as you say, craft) the servant of the thought, are nearest to my heart.

The Catholic faith was another bond with Griggs. Religion was in the air. Graham and his friends seem to have been little interested in politics. There was not much youthful idealism around. Peace had brought two years of boom, followed by slump and disillusion, hunger marches and strikes. T. S. Eliot caught the mood in *The Waste Land* and *The Hollow Men*. Ramsay MacDonald had formed the first Labour Government in 1924, but before the end of the year Stanley Baldwin was back with a huge majority. His Chancellor of the Exchequer, Winston Churchill—later to bulk large in Graham's career—deepened the depression by returning sterling to the gold standard. Bright Young Things, Noel Coward plays and P. G. Wodehouse novels were a welcome diversion. Popularizers of Freudian psychology like Havelock Ellis, and writers like D. H. Lawrence, Aldous Huxley, E. M. Forster, James Joyce and Lytton Strachey led an onslaught on Victorian values. Continental artists celebrated the liberation of the subconscious with the Surrealist Movement, launched with André Breton's manifesto in 1924. In Britain uncertainty prevailed. Paul Nash was marking time, Ben Nicholson still groping, Henry Moore not quite launched. The General Strike of May 1926 was the nadir of a miserable decade. Graham's only involvement was to be obliged to use his bicycle more intensively— though emotionally he was always, he said, 'on the side of the workers, especially at that time'.

In this atmosphere the certitudes of Roman Catholicism must have been welcome. He said that his interest in it evolved basically through Kathleen

> but we were all interested in religions of all kinds at that time, in much the same way as people at Cambridge were later interested in communism. . . . Chesterton and Belloc were an influence in a way. Then, of course, there was the Oxford Movement: Cardinal Manning, Newman—all, of course, starting as Church of England.[20]

Kathleen's parents were strict Roman Catholics.

TO19436

She hated going to church three times a day on Sunday, for instance. . . .
But fundamentally she thought religion was an important thing. Before I
was received into the Church, I had to go once a week to be instructed. I
was what is called a catechumen, someone who is favourably disposed
towards Catholicism but has not yet been received into the Church. One
of the priests was a jolly old thing, of whom I was very fond indeed, and I
wept buckets when he died. The second one was much more scholarly,
higher in the hierarchy and a much better teacher.

Kathleen recalled Graham sitting at the end of Christ Church, in Eltham
High Street, when she went to confession. It had been since 1906 in the care
of the Canons Regular of Lateran, part of the Benedictine order which had
been confined to Italy until 1881. The 'jolly' priest was Abbot White, a
generous, impulsive and uncomplicated character, according to those who
knew him.[21] He died in 1932. The 'more scholarly' one was Father Isidore
O'Leary, CRL, DD, a sound theologian and keen-witted scholar, very well
read and an admirer of Ruskin and of Italian culture. A natural hesitancy
added weight to his opinions.

Graham would have gone for instruction once a week for some six
months, each session lasting between half an hour and an hour. He was
received into the Roman Catholic Church on 21 December 1926. He
recalled:

> I kept on for a long time being highly observant of the ordinances of the
> Church. Then, when I started to get claustrophobia, I found I couldn't
> go to church without considerable distress—I felt I was hemmed in and
> couldn't get out. I have never abandoned it . . . but one is bound to
> speculate on certain things which have a relationship to science, which, of
> course, the Church has until recently not acknowledged.

Shortly before he died, Graham wrote:[22]

> although I am by no means *devout*, as many people write of me, it is
> almost certainly an infinitely valuable support to all my actions and
> thoughts. Some might call my vision pantheist. I am certainly held by the
> inner rhythms and order of nature; by the completeness of a master plan.

Roman Catholic churches were not easily accessible when Graham and
Kathleen were living in Kent after their marriage; and in later life Graham
would go to church invariably on Good Friday and, when possible, on
Christmas Eve, but otherwise rarely, according to Kathleen.

In late 1925 or early 1926 he began a two- or three-year stint of teaching
on Friday evenings at Kingston School of Art (one of the places to which he
had to bicycle during the General Strike of 1926). The school's head was a

large, bumbling and rather tactless Manxman called A. J. Collister, who used to say: 'If you don't feel like a wet rag when you have taken a class, you haven't been teaching.'[23] Graham remembered the atmosphere of the place all too well: 'I would be trying to follow the best traditions of life drawing in reaching the students, talking about Michelangelo and so on. The headmaster would come up to me and say: "We have no use for Michelangelo here, have we, Mr Sutherland?"'

Graham left Goldsmiths' at the end of the spring/summer term of 1926. The etching boom was well under way, and the market was particularly strong in America. By this stage, he reckoned, he was making around £700 a year from etchings and drawings, and his best customers were in the United States:

I don't know what that's worth nowadays, but it was certainly enough to carry one. It was only when the American recession came along that I *had* to teach. I generally did a maximum of four plates a year. The etchings were four guineas each — we worked in guineas in those days. There was an edition of seventy-five almost invariably for the major works. Then I sold a few drawings in addition.

Each edition sold out, though not necessarily in the year in which it was printed. Graham's father was also delighted by his success: 'At last he began to take an interest,' Graham recalled with a touch of bitterness. Paul Drury and William Larkins were enjoying similar success at this stage.

Gratifying though his growing reputation as an etcher was — Campbell Dodgson, the formidable Keeper of the Prints and Drawings Department at the British Museum was among his admirers and buyers — Graham wisely decided to consolidate his position by accepting the offer of Stanley Anderson's job at Chelsea School of Art. The annual report of the school for the academic year 1926–7 states: 'Mr Stanley Anderson, the teacher of etching, resigned in December [1926] and Mr Graham Sutherland was appointed in his place.' The Principal at the time was a somewhat shadowy figure, P. H. Jowett. He was succeeded in 1930 by a very able painter, H. S. Williamson, who had a remarkable eye for talent. He recruited Henry Moore (in 1931), the painter and stage designer Robert Medley (in 1932) and Ceri Richards (in 1938). But Jowett recruited Graham.

With marriage to Kathleen no doubt in his mind, Graham brought a pleasingly pastoral touch to his wooing as well as to such Palmer-like etchings as *St Mary's Hatch* and *Lammas*. When down at Rustington, he used to go to Dover Woods, near Hammerpot, and pick bunches of primroses for her. Then, his sister Vivien recalled, he would collect some unwanted shoe boxes from shoe shops, pack them with damp moss, and send bunches and bunches of primroses to Kathleen.

Kathleen herself had left Goldsmiths' a year earlier and had gone to work in a fashion studio called Henschel, off Fleet Street, in London. She was paid £1 a week, and when she asked for an increase, it was refused. 'So another girl and I took our paint brushes and drawing boards and rented a room across the street. A very nice old man knew we were struggling girls, and said we didn't need to pay the rent straight away. One girl used to go out and get the orders, another did lettering jobs and I did the fashion.' By mid-1927 she was earning about £10 a week, which was good money then. 'My mother wouldn't speak to me when I said I was giving it up to marry Graham.'

They were engaged in October 1927. 'Sincerest and loving congratulations,' Graham's father wrote on the 28th from Whitehall, before having met Kathleen.

> I am unfeignedly glad to hear it, my dear lad, and I can say this because I am so confident that you will have made a right choice. . . . I feel very sure that, with your high ideals, and your experience of life, you would not have taken this step (the most important, apart from matters of faith, in life) unless you had been quite certain that your ideals, your dreams would be realized. . . . Of course we shall be eager to be introduced. . . . I am *greatly* looking forward to it.

It is indicative of the poor rapport between Graham and his parents that he should not yet have introduced to them the girl he had been courting for six years. Equally—though perhaps more from fear of hurting them—he seems to have kept quiet about his conversion to Roman Catholicism a year before. The parental meeting with Kathleen took place on 3 November, and for Graham's father it confirmed that his son's 'momentous choice' was, indeed, a 'blest and happy one', as he wrote next day. 'I am particularly glad to be able to tell you that she has made a complete conquest of Dear [Graham's mother], and the more so because this fact should ease your further disclosure, when you consider that the time has come to make it.'

Any easing was marginal. 'My conversion to Catholicism shocked my mother unbearably,' Graham said.[24] 'She at first refused to come to the wedding. Her background was strongly anti-Papist.' Although without Kathleen he would almost certainly not have been converted, she did not attract odium on that score. 'Kathleen's family tolerated me: but my family were entranced by K. and loved her immediately. She was one of a handful of people who could really get on with my mother.' Not the least entranced was Graham's brother Humphrey, who had risen to be head boy of

Westminster School and was now a classical scholar at Christ Church, Oxford. 'She was a classic beauty: flawless skin, wonderful features, wonderful hair,' he recalled.

Graham and Kathleen were married on 29 December 1927, at St Etheldreda's church in Ely Place, by Hatton Garden, the centre of London's diamond merchants. The church had been the first pre-Reformation shrine to be restored to Roman Catholic hands in England or Wales, and its history went back to the thirteenth century. The same Father O'Leary who had received Graham into the Roman Catholic Church officiated. It was a quiet little wedding. Kathleen would have liked the full works. 'But Graham thought it destroyed romance to make things public which should be kept private,' she said.

It was a bitterly cold day. Humphrey was best man. He and Graham drove up from Sutton in the family bull-nosed Morris Cowley, and Humphrey remembered the panache with which Graham negotiated the south London tram lines. There were only a few members of the family and friends at the marriage, and there was not enough money for a honeymoon. After the service the newly-weds took a taxi, in which Graham changed, down to their new home in Kent. In their excitement they left their suitcase on the pavement outside the church, and a Goldsmiths' friend, James Hockey, brought it down for them that afternoon by train.

Home for Graham and Kathleen was now a top-floor flat in a handsome, three-storey Georgian house, built in 1743, called the White House, in the main street of Farningham, a pretty village barely 25 miles from London, full of white clapboard houses. Palmer's beloved Shoreham was only a few miles away, and Graham had probably discovered the village, if not the flat, on a sketching expedition. During their first night there the pipes froze, and next morning Graham had to find a plumber to unfreeze them. It was not a very propitious start, but the marriage was to endure for more than half a century.

3

Teaching and Design

1928-33

A NEW, more responsible life was beginning. On 4 January 1928 Graham
wrote to Milner Gray, his former digs companion in Blackheath:

> My dear Milner, I called this afternoon to turn out my 'things' upstairs
> and most reluctantly (from some points of view!) to fetch my Palmers and
> the brass rubbing. I hope in a week or two to be able to let you have the
> duplicate of the one we took at Fordwich. Also the three proofs of my own
> I promised you (if you could put up with them!). I put Bouverie's
> *Hedging and Ditching* up again, but the cord requires lengthening. My
> acids and dishes, as well as the drawing boards etc., I will call for next week.
> I do hope you will get your plate done — do not hesitate to use my press or
> any acids, etc. that you require.
> I rather think we forgot to wish you well for the New Year, when you
> were over on Sunday. *We do so now indeed*. Excuse scrawl. In great haste.
> Graham.

What a fresh, innocent, happy, pastoral, craftsman's world that letter seems
to summon up. Life must have seemed very good. His etchings were selling
well. He was teaching two days a week at Chelsea, which brought in some
£250 a year. He was extremely happily married to a girl of beauty and wit.
They were comfortably installed in a beautiful setting. Another exhibition
was impending at the Twenty One-Gallery.

If the barometer seemed set fair, it deceived. Graham's nerve and courage
were to be severely tested in the next five years, during which he considerably
broadened the range of his activities and began to develop a much more
personal style. They were important and formative years, a time of questing
and experimenting. In 1928 Graham was still relatively little known. Mainly
by venturing into the field of design, he was to achieve the makings of a
public reputation by the middle of the decade and to prepare himself
technically for the big leap forward of 1934, when the scenery of

Pembrokeshire unlocked his inspiration.

Towards the end of 1927 he was beginning to realize that the quasi-religious, quasi-romantic, Palmerish preoccupation with idealized villages was, as he put it, a 'total cul de sac'.[1]

> It was fascinating in its way, and one tried to do it as beautifully as one could; but one knew that other things were happening in the world at the time, and that one really must alter one's direction to a certain extent. This was just about the time, I suppose, when we were all becoming conscious of modern French painting.

For the time being Graham continued with his etching. But one only has to compare his *The Meadow Chapel* of 1928 with *May Green* of the previous year to see how he was gradually shedding the mystic, Olde England overtones of the Palmer influence. In *Hanger Hill*, which he completed in 1929, a touch of menace is detectable in the trees which overhang the scything woman, with a suggestion of twisted roots protruding at their base.

Looking forwards now rather than backwards, he turned to the field of design and, as he had at Goldsmiths', demonstrated remarkable adaptability. Milner Gray was to play no small role in helping him to spread his wings. His design consultancy, the Bassett Gray group, had initially concentrated on copywriting and the design of publicity material, including advertisements. Later it did pioneering work in product and packaging design and in 1935, with Misha Black by then a partner, became well-known as the Industrial Design Partnership.

Anxious to keep his design work distinct from his etching and drawing, Graham occasionally used the pseudonym 'Humphries'. It was, for example, as 'Humphries' that he signed an early design for Bassett Gray, a pen-and-ink drawing of a sports car rounding a bend in a country road.[2] Another specimen of Graham's handiwork from this period shows two heraldic-looking horses with helmeted men, under which attractive lettering proclaims: 'Bassett Gray: A Group of Artists'. It is rather in the style of the Bayeux Tapestry.

There was a social side to this work. A good deal of somewhat heavy-handed jollity marked the annual dinners of the Bassett Gray Studio, which Graham attended in his capacity as an associate. 'We knew that Freemasons wore aprons, so we decided we would wear bibs,' Milner Gray recalled. 'We used to initiate, or 'bib', what we called patrons, who were people we admired.'[3] A photograph in the *Advertising World* of October 1927 shows Paul Drury, Edward Bouverie Hoyton, Graham, Milner Gray and others at such a dinner, at which the patrons who were being 'bibbed' were Paul

Drury's father, Alfred, the sculptor; Freddie Marriott, the head of Goldsmiths'; and the illustrator Edmund Sullivan. The initiation ceremony involved an exchange of dog Latin; for example, 'Byshop [Mr Hoyton]: Watsier nomen? Responsum: Fredi Marriottus. Byshop: Ubi natus est? Responsum: Id forgeto. ... Byshop: Legem tuam pulere licet? Responsum: Asu licet. ...'

Innocent days. Graham's brother Humphrey recalled with nostalgia the holidays in Dorset on which he sometimes accompanied Graham and Kathleen from 1928 onwards, when he had just finished his first year at Oxford. 'I remember we sort of jaunted along at whatever high speed one could then jaunt along at—wheel wobble generally set in at about 50 m.p.h.' (This was in the family bull-nosed Morris, registration number XW 4528.) 'Once a whole portfolio of Graham's drawings blew out of the car. . . .' They would stay in the village of Corfe Castle—dominated by the castle of that name—at a hotel called The Greyhound. 'They were trips of sheer enjoyment, looking at a countryside that was as beautiful and pastoral as now and infinitely more private. There seemed to be all the room in the world for the few people who had a car. It was a golden sort of time.'

By the time of Graham's second one-man show at the Twenty-One Gallery, in September 1928, his reputation as an etcher was beginning to look established. The tiny catalogue listed several museums which had bought his work, including the Victoria and Albert, the Boston Museum of Fine Arts and some smaller ones. Most of Graham's earlier etchings were shown, twenty-five in all, and some watercolours and other drawings not in the catalogue. Graham kept *The Times*'s review. The critic saw him as more homely than Palmer in his reaction to landscape and praised a pastel drawing of sloping fields with rooks. None of the drawings of this period has been traced, though a photograph of one, of some deserted-looking cottages shrouded by trees, is reproduced in Dr John Hayes's study of Graham's work.[4] As Hayes says, it harks back to Dürer rather than Palmer.

By the autumn of 1928 Kathleen was pregnant. It was not an easy pregnancy; she suffered from a great deal of morning sickness. A boy was born—at home, with the aid only of some chloroform—on 16 April 1929 and was christened John Vivian. A living-in nurse had been hired. She upset Graham by telling him that Kathleen was so pretty she could have married a duke; and when she helped Kathleen do up her stays, she would say: 'You realize you will never be a Venus again.' The absence of lobster at the dining-table was the subject of unfavourable comment.

The baby cried constantly, as if in distress. The unpleasant nurse said that she was sure he was a 'blue' baby with a heart problem. It was soon evident that something was indeed seriously wrong. Those were desperate days. The local doctor was ignorant and made reassuring noises. The baby kept on screaming. Graham used to sit watching him being bathed, and wept a lot himself. Then Graham's mother, rising to the occasion, as she had over Graham's desire to go to art school, came to take over for a fortnight.

She found Kathleen and Graham near to collapse and sent them down to recover at Rustington, to which Graham's family, abandoning Sutton for good, had moved that year. The baby had bouts of semi-recovery. Graham's mother had a photograph taken, which shows a beautiful child. 'I am sending you this because a miracle has happened,' she wrote, enclosing the picture. They rushed back. Graham wrote to Russell Alexander on 14 June: 'We have had a very trying and anxious time during the past month as our son had been very desperately ill, and was at one time not expected to live. He has *mercifully* recovered, I know you will be glad to know; but our time has been so very occupied that I have had literally no time to write. . . .'[5]

The recovery was short-lived. Graham took the baby to a young heart specialist at St Thomas's Hospital, London. Whether the baby had a hole in the heart or, as Kathleen believed, an enlarged heart we do not know. The specialist warned that he could die at any time or might survive some twelve years without being able to take strenuous exercise. On 14 July, barely three months old, John Sutherland died. It was only when they were on their way to a short holiday in Dorset that Kathleen's pent-up tears began to flow, silently.

Perhaps, she later wondered, the baby's death had been a disguised blessing. She was not particularly maternal. Graham, being very conscientious, might have been tempted to make compromises in order to bring up the boy in a fitting way. They resolved not to run the risk of trying for a child again, a decision which must have taken its toll on their emotional lives. Graham told me in 1979 that he did not believe the child's death had made any real difference. That assessment is hard to accept.

It must have affected his relationship with Kathleen, laying the basis for that often fierce mutual protectiveness which later characterized it. Childless married couples frequently have a more intense relationship than do those with children. Her hands relatively free, Kathleen was able to devote her considerable energies to protecting and promoting Graham as an artist. He, sensing his debt and the sacrifices this often entailed, sometimes seemed to raise her on to a pedestal of love, rather like a medieval poet.

The child's death must also have affected their social life, reducing contact with contemporaries who had children. Later many of their friends were homosexuals; gifted, creative, amusing, more available, they also eliminated the difficulty that Graham and Kathleen frequently experienced of liking only one half of a couple.

As a painter, Graham was spared the distractions and divided loyalties which come from trying to reconcile intensive work at home with family life. Henceforward a good deal of his emotional energy (Kathleen had no complaints on the sexual side) was to be canalized into his work, which was not without its erotic element. It may be naive to suppose that happiness is the enemy of creativity. Nonetheless, this domestic tragedy probably helped to fuel the deep springs of his inspiration.

History too was conspiring to widen his range as an artist. On 23 October 1929 the New York stock exchange began to collapse. By 13 November some $30,000 million had been knocked off the capital value of shares there. Etchings had been treated like stocks and shares during the boom. The largely American-based market for them, too, was virtually wiped out.

It seems odd that anything so cheap should be hit by the Slump. Paul Drury recalled:

> It wasn't because people couldn't afford two or three pounds. At the height of the boom, in 1929, people were buying editions they hadn't even seen, and putting them into folios and strong rooms as investments. Everyone was doing it, and people who weren't artists at all were turning out specious things. It was a case of entirely fabricated values. I was sorry to see it going that way.

Many artists were financially broken, including F. L. Griggs, who in 1930 had to borrow money to survive and was obliged to sell his own collection of engravings.

Graham had probably earned a good £900–£1000 from etchings in 1928. His main source of income had now been removed. He still had his Chelsea salary, and he tried to sell more watercolours and drawings. In 1929 he showed these in mixed exhibitions at the Cotswold Gallery in Frith Street, Soho, at the Twenty-One Gallery and, in November, for the first time, at the annual show of the New English Art Club. The brilliant Futurist C. R. W. Nevinson and the New Zealander Frances Hodgkins were co-exhibitors.

These sporadic showings cannot have brought in much, and Graham and Kathleen faced a period of acute financial difficulty. Kathleen even sold her sapphire engagement ring from Hatton Garden, tried to sell the etching press (unsuccessfully) and, as Graham later put it, 'nobly and with great self-sacrifice augmented my teaching salary by taking up her work again, thus enabling us to survive'. There was still a market for fashion drawings.

(*Top left*) Graham with his mother, aged 3
years 4 months
(*Top right*) Graham with his father, aged about
4 years
(*Above*) Graham's father, Vivian Sutherland
(*Right*) Grandfather James Foster

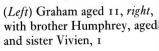

(*Left*) Graham aged 11, *right*, with brother Humphrey, aged and sister Vivien, 1

(*Below*) Graham's mother Elsie Sutherland, in her 70s
(*Bottom left*) Graham aged 13 or 14
(*Bottom right*) Graham aged 2

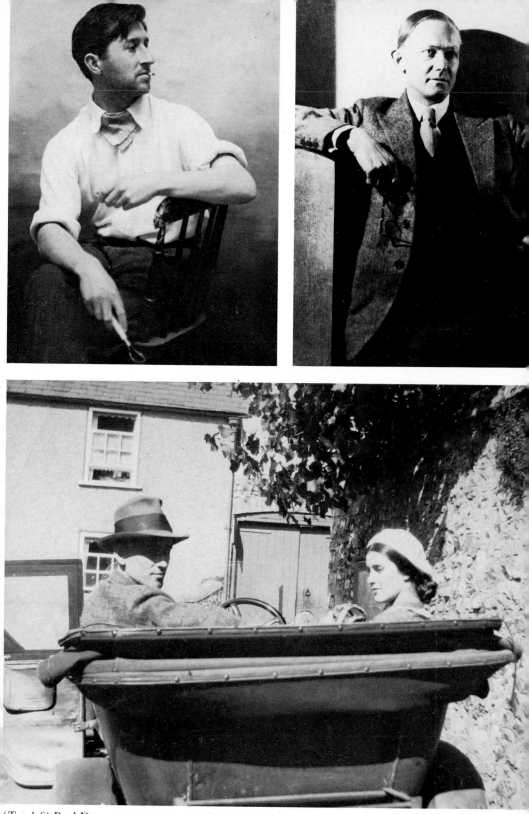

(*Top left*) Paul Drury as a young man (*Top right*) Milner Gray aged 30
(*Above*) Graham and Kathleen not long after their marriage, in the family's open Morris

Kathleen and
Graham and
Henry Moore on a
Chelsea School of
Art outing, in late
1930s

Graham and
Frederick Ashton
looking at Margot
Fonteyn's costume
for *The Wanderer*,
the ballet he
designed in late
1940

Colin Anderson, Kenneth Clark and Kathleen en route to the Moore/Sutherland/Piper exhibition in Leeds, July 1941

(*Top*) Graham sketching during the filming of *Out of Chaos*, probably at the ICI limestone quarry near Buxton, Derbyshire, in late 1943 (*Above left and right*) Graham's letter to Kenneth Clark about his experiences down the Cornish tin mine in 1942

Graham at work on *Origins of the Land* in a studio at the Tate Gallery, in early 1951

Basil Spence, who arranged for the Coventry tapestry to be commissioned from Graham in 1952, in front of part of the tapestry in about 1961

The White House, Trottiscliffe, Kent; first rented in 1937 and bought in 1945 with Kenneth Clark's help

Top) The Village. Etching, 1925. $6\frac{7}{8} \times 8\frac{7}{8}$ in (17.5 × 22.5 cm)
Above) St Mary Hatch. Etching, 1926. $4\frac{7}{8} \times 7\frac{1}{4}$ in (12.4 × 18.7 cm)

(*Top*) *Pastoral*. Etching and engraving, 1930. $5\frac{1}{8} \times 7\frac{5}{8}$ in (13 × 19.3 cm)
(*Above*) *The Great Globe, Swanage*. Poster designed for Shell-Mex Ltd, 1932. 30 × 40 in
(76.2 × 101.6 cm)

(*above left*) One of Graham's three designs for a George V stamp, abandoned when the monarch died, 1935

(*above right*) Two examples of china decorated by Graham for E. Brain & Co of Stoke-on-Trent, shown at Harrods in 1935

Crystal glass decorated to Graham's design for Stuart & Sons, Stourbridge, 1935

Black Landscape
Oil on canvas,
1937. 32 × 52 in
(81.3 × 132.1 cm

*Roads and Hills
Setting Sun.* Oil
on canvas, 1938
24 × 20 in
(60.9 × 50.8 cm)

ntrance to Lane. Oil on canvas, 1939. 24 × 20 in (60.9 × 50.8 cm)

Tin Mine: Emerging Miner.
Pen and ink and gouache, 1942.
$45\frac{1}{2} \times 28\frac{3}{4}$ in (115.5 × 73 cm)

Devastation: East End Street.
Pen and ink and gouache, 1941.
$25\frac{1}{2} \times 44\frac{3}{4}$ in (64.7 × 113.6 cm)

Study of a Tin Miner. Pencil, 1942.
$9 \times 5\frac{3}{8}$ in (22.8 × 13.6 cm)

Study of Kathleen Sutherland. Pen and ink and pencil, about 1938. $4\frac{1}{2} \times 4\frac{3}{8}$ in (11.4 × 10.8 cm)

The Lamp. Oil on hardboard, 1944. $30\frac{1}{8} \times 24\frac{7}{8}$ in (76.5 × 63.2 cm)

Kathleen would go up to London with Graham on his teaching days and hawk her drawings— hints on how to alter a dress to make it look up to date and so on —around the fashion magazines. Sometimes they brought in £10 a week.

Although Graham was teaching only on Tuesdays and Thursdays at Chelsea, it was a draining activity. Part of each Monday and Wednesday was often devoted to preparing for his classes, examining students' work and so on, and by Friday he was often worn out. But he liked the place. 'The atmosphere was excellent,' he recalled.[6] 'All the staff knew each other very well . . . but the majority of the students were very "debby". One and a half per cent were worth the trouble: the odd eccentric, and retired naval people (even admirals) were the ones, apart from the exceedingly rare genius.'

Graham made a strong impact as a teacher. One of his students, Diana Murray Hill, remembered her first impression of him as a

> neat, slightly built, dark-haired and good-looking young man who emerged from a room with a sink, bearing a copper plate. I was told he was in charge of etching, lithography and wood-engraving classes. He was an unusually good-tempered, enthusiastic and patient teacher but, in spite of his apparent gentleness and diffidence, had an extremely strong influence on the work of his pupils. . . . I for one—I am extremely inefficient and cack-handed—found myself turning out a very different product from the one I had expected to turn out. It was like entering a new and exciting world where shapes and designs took over. 'Your vision should develop at the same time as your technique,' he told us.[7]

Nina Orloff (later Sagovsky), who studied etching with him from 1929 to 1931, remembered him as a 'very beautiful young man' and a very thorough teacher, who took a lot of trouble with interested students, including herself.[8] But he could be touchy. 'I was once thoroughly squashed by Sutherland,' she recalled. At the end-of-year exhibition she had won three first prizes and one second prize, for etching. 'Not realizing that Sutherland stood behind me, I said to a friend: "What a pity—I should have had a first in etching too"—and before I had time to add: "It spoils the continuity," Sutherland said: *"Not at all,"* and looked furious. It didn't seem worth explaining what my meaning was.'

Teaching no doubt helped Graham to focus his ideas. In *Wood Interior*, an etching dated 1929–30, he abandoned all signs of human habitation to plunge in among the tree trunks, which are sunlit but have a hint of disquiet in their sinuous forms. Then in *Pastoral* (1930) he produced his first genuinely individual work. No trace of Samuel Palmer remains. The gnarled and hollow bole of the tree trunk in the right foreground has a faintly human shape. To the left, pressed against the wall, two thinner trees lean over sharply, while in the centre some bushier ones throw long shadows in the evening light. The mood is dramatic yet enigmatic, poised between calm and menace. It is a great deal more sharply focused than his earlier work. Already he was singling out the more expressive features of nature to convey their subtle relationship with man.

Both Milner Gray and Paul Drury remember Graham doing a good number of watercolours while living at Farningham. 'They were beautiful little watercolours,' said Drury. Some were done in the lanes, some in the walled garden of the White House. Drury's father encouraged Graham's interest in colour, for example by showing him his collection of butterflies. Alfred Drury was also a rose enthusiast. Roses were to be one of Graham's favourite themes in later years; but the first one that he etched in 1931 led to a breach with the Royal Society of Painter-Etchers.

The new work was called *The Garden*. It shows a disproportionately large rosebush in front of a wall, behind which there is a house or barn. The rose seems to be caught in a nimbus of light which emphasizes its overall shape and gives it a curious mystical quality. For the first time there are overtones of Paul Nash, who was fourteen years Graham's senior and was soon to become a friend. Nash's early visionary landscapes, influenced more by Blake than by Palmer, had been followed by some haunting evocations of the battlefields of the First World War.

The Garden was not to the taste of the Society, and the committee decided that it should not hang in the annual exhibition. F. L. Griggs, too, was shocked. 'What is Sutherland up to? I wish he would leave Nash alone,' he wrote to Paul Drury. Graham resented the Society's rejection and it led to a complete break. Graham and his protagonists always said he was *expelled* from the Society: 'I was expelled because I refused to pay my subscription if my work was not shown,' he told me.[9] In fact, although he exhibited nothing at the Society in 1931 and 1932, he did show a trial proof of *Pastoral* there in 1933. On 2 March 1934 it was recorded in the minutes that he and others were in arrears of their subscription of nine guineas a year. They were warned by the secretary that their names would be removed from the list of members if the arrears were not forthcoming. That is what happened. It was more a lapsing than an expulsion.[10] Resignation might have been more effective.

Graham's last recorded etching in anything resembling his old manner was a straightforward Kentish scene, *Oast House* (1932). It is more modern in feel than earlier work, though less highly wrought than *Pastoral*. It was to form the basis of his first poster design.

It was the age of the poster, and the two big patrons of the new art form were Shell-Mex and BP, and London Transport. Commercial art was flourishing as never since, and artists hoped that the hoardings would become a people's art gallery, a happy union of art and commerce.[11] The man who raised Shell's advertising to its near-legendary status was Jack Beddington, a suave, worldly but imaginative man. From 1928 onwards he employed such brilliant artists as E. McKnight Kauffer, pioneer of lettering as an integral part of design, Paul Nash and indeed Clive Gardiner, from Goldsmiths'. Milner Gray had shown Beddington some of Graham's work—hence, no doubt, this first commission, the first Sutherland to hit the public eye.

Graham was defensive about his 1930s excursions into commercial art. 'You should remember the climate of the time,' he said.[12] 'It was a very fortunate one in that field, so what was done by me and a few others could hardly be considered commercial art. It was more a question of gouaches literally copied, often by hand.'

In the case of Shell, the resulting lithographic prints were, strictly speaking, lorry bills rather than posters. The delivery lorries had flat sides, to which the posters were stuck. It was a cheap and mobile form of advertising, and one intended to restrain the march of hoardings through the countryside. They were a standard size—30 inches high by 45 inches wide—and were soon recognized as collector's items.

Graham's first poster, one of the series called 'Everywhere you go, you can be sure of Shell', was quietly appealing rather than striking. It showed two oast houses in a setting more sylvan than the one in the related etching, and was unrevealingly captioned 'Near Leeds, Kent' on the left, with Graham's name prominently displayed opposite. The original gouache (a medium somewhere between watercolour and oils, sometimes called poster paint) hangs in the managing director's office at Shell-Mex House in the Strand.

During his periodic trips to Dorset, Graham was beginning to find subject matter—hills, fallen trees, megalithic stones—stimulatingly different from the Kentish landscapes which he had come to associate with his more Palmer-ish etchings. At Swanage, on the Dorset coast, he also found the subject of his second, much bolder poster, issued later in 1932. The Great Globe at Swanage is a chiselled relief map of the world, 10 feet in diameter and weighing 40 tons, erected in 1887 by George Burt, a local entrepreneur. In Graham's hands it became a mysterious monument, standing pearly grey on its curious little plinth, with green fields and sky filled with scudding clouds beyond.

As with the rosebush etching, there were overtones of Nash, who was also attracted by the Globe as a theme. Graham had been greatly struck that year by Nash's illustrations to a strange seventeenth-century disquisition, Sir Thomas Browne's *Urne Buriall and the Garden of Cyrus*, published by Cassell in a limited edition of 215 copies hand-stencilled at the Curwen Press. Graham was later to describe them as 'a poetic and imaginative achievement without equal today in this country'.[13] Nash had seen the work of the Surrealists in Paris and had written on Chirico and Magritte in the *Listener* in 1931. Graham never considered his own work remotely Surrealist, but Nash's knack of focusing on the latent mysteriousness of part of a landscape encouraged his own similar experiments.

Milner Gray, the intermediary in these and other commissions, had recently joined Graham and Kathleen as a lodger. In 1931 the rent of the flat at Farningham had gone up, and Graham and Kathleen, perhaps anxious also to get away from painful memories, decided to move to Eynsford nearby; the two villages are joined by Sparepenny Lane, which winds attractively above the River Darenth. There they rented a charming old clapboard and brick house called Willow Cottage, which at the back looked out over a meadow lined with willows; a pub called the Malt Shovel was almost opposite in front. The rent was just too much, and Milner Gray, whose parents lived nearby, joined them to ease the burden. Although Palmer's style had lost something of its pull, Eynsford happened to be even nearer to Shoreham, and Graham still foregathered for walks in that wonderful valley with Willie Larkins and Paul Drury, both considerable talkers.

By 1932 Graham was groping his way in the largely unfamiliar medium (student work apart) of oil paint, adjusting to much larger surfaces, a wide range of colours and the complex problem of their relationship to light which had so preoccupied the Impressionists. He began by painting painstakingly and objectively from nature, copying what he saw and trying to match, tone by tone, the colours on the canvas with those in nature.[14] There was no attempt at originality. The aim was to learn and to gain confidence. Virtually everything he did at this time in oils he destroyed. But one such study has been reproduced: called *Farm in Dorset*, and dated 1932, it is sub-Impressionist in manner, conventional and competent.[15]

In watercolours, by contrast, his artistic personality continued to evolve, and several studies of hill and tree forms inspired by visits to Dorset in 1932–3 give more than a hint of things to come.

Graham chose to live in Kent because he loved the countryside there and disliked living in cities. One consequence was that he kept a certain distance between himself and the various little London-based groups into which the avant-garde of British art was then splitting. It is true that in 1930 he had become a founder member of the National Society of Painters, Sculptors, Engravers and Potters, whose other members included Henry Moore, William Nicholson (father of Ben) and the potter Bernard Leach. But that was mainly an exhibiting society, offering common ground for those with academic or modernist sympathies. Exhibitions were held at the Royal Institute Galleries in Piccadilly.

Graham shunned more ideological groupings, like the Seven and Five Society, which by the early 1930s had swung from lyrical post-Impressionism to abstraction and was largely under the influence of Ben Nicholson, seven years Graham's senior. Its last exhibition, in 1935, was purely abstract, the first such show in England.

Equally, Graham had no part in Unit One, launched in June 1933 by Paul Nash with a flourish of rhetorical trumpets in, of all places, the letters column of *The Times*. Nash saw a revival of the 'nature cult' looming. Unit One members were at variance with the Great Unconscious School of painting and lacked reverence for nature as such, he said. They were interested in design, considered as a structural pursuit, and in imagination, explored apart from literature or metaphysics. Members included Moore, Hepworth, Nicholson, Nash, Edward Wadsworth, Hodgkins, Edward Burra and the architect Wells Coates. The secretary was a wealthy young man called Douglas Cooper, destined to bulk large in Graham's life, and the focus of the group was Freddie Mayor's gallery in Cork Street, London W1, of which Cooper was the chief financial backer.

Moore, Nicholson, Hepworth, Nash and Herbert Read lived in Hampstead: 'a nest of gentle artists', their guru Read was to call it.[16] Later they were joined there by some brilliant refugees, including Walter Gropius, Laszlo Moholy-Nagy, Naum Gabo and Piet Mondrian, whose arrival between 1934 and 1938 greatly strengthened the 'Constructivist' element within the group.

A looser grouping, the Artists International Association, was political in emphasis. Graham had still not set foot abroad and did not feel strongly enough about Fascism to join that group either, though Milner Gray was a member and Gray's partner, Misha Black, a founder.

Graham was not a great joiner. But, in common with most other 'progressive' artists of the time, he did show with the London Group, along with Moore, David Bomberg, William Coldstream, Rodrigo Moynihan, Victor Pasmore and others (between 1932 and 1949, six times in all, usually only one work in each show).

Henry Moore, Graham's colleague at Chelsea since 1931, had been far more open to new developments from his early days as a student in Leeds and at the Royal College of Art under Sir William Rothenstein. He paid his first visit to Paris in 1922 (Graham's was in 1944—his first trip abroad), and was dazzled by what he saw of Cézanne's work there. Moore's chief memory of Graham at Chelsea was of the coffee breaks at 11 a.m. in the staff room, when they all chatted. 'Sometimes we had lunch in the Polytechnic, which was cheaper, or in the pub—the Eight Bells—that's how one became friendly.'[17]

For Graham, teaching etching was becoming increasingly anomalous, and in the academic year 1933–4 he switched to book illustration and composition.[18] At the same time Kathleen was taken on, at Graham's suggestion, to teach fashion drawing two afternoons a week. 'The class was full of extraordinary people, including men', she recalled. 'I used to put some clothes on the model and ask them to draw them.' Partly on Graham's recommendation, Milner Gray too was appointed in 1934 to teach design.

Robert Medley, who had joined the staff in 1932 and was teaching life drawing and a bit of painting, recalled Graham as

> plainly extremely intelligent and an extremely good artist. There was no doubt about that. He hadn't, of course, got quite the steam behind him that Henry [Moore] had. Henry likes to make out that he had no public — but he was always supported by Herbert Read, and he had some pretty solid patrons behind him. Graham was totally hypochondriac. He used to arrive muffled up in scarves and with pills and things Kathy had given him, because he was always supposed to be ailing and having some sort of nervous complaint, which I'm sure he had, out of sheer frustration of having a lot of talent and not getting it placed. . . . But he was very clear-headed, very shrewd. He used to grumble a lot in those days, but we all grumbled.[19]

One of Graham's most remarkable and talented pupils at Chelsea was Gerald Wilde, who was to establish a name as a painter and lithographer. Wilde seemed to be bent on self-destruction. He had been a student from 1927 to 1930. 'Then in about 1932 Graham gave me a place in his teaching room and was always ready to help me at all times,' he recalled.[20] 'He showed real interest in my work and method of working and use of materials.' Graham took endless trouble with Wilde, bought several of his lithographs, and helped procure him commissions for others. Wilde in fact outlived him.

Graham's sympathies were no doubt the more readily aroused, in that he was himself still groping around for a way forward and was very far from being well-off. In 1933 he was 30. He had sold watercolours, but not a single oil painting, as far as is known. For the rest of the decade he was obliged to continue with design work to supplement his income from teaching. In 1933 he did his first poster for Frank Pick, who had been commissioning posters for the London Underground since 1915 and had become chief executive of the London Passenger Transport Board in 1933.

Pick had helped forge a design policy which covered every facet of the recently amalgamated Underground companies, from rolling stock and stations to litter bins. The theme of Graham's first two posters was 'London Transport opens a window on London's country'—part of a campaign to attract off-peak passengers. One showed a brown-framed window looking out on to a garden and a white gate leading to a orchard; it was based, Milner Gray believed, on the view from the Farningham flat. The second was called *Cottage Interior*. Again, it was a quiet beginning.

As with Beddington, Graham was probably introduced to Pick by Milner Gray, who was certainly responsible for Graham's next major venture in the design field. Gray had been very much concerned with the founding of the Society of Industrial Artists and Designers, on the Council of which Graham also served. In 1933 they had started a branch in north Staffordshire. Gray had got to know T. A. Fennemore, an advertising man who a year earlier had become marketing director at E. Brain and Co., makers of Foley China at Stoke-on-Trent. Fennemore, Milner Gray and Graham thought it would be a good idea, Gray recalled, to launch an experiment to improve the standards of certain commercial products; bone china and earthenware would be the first targets. They drew up a list of fairly 'modern' artists who should be asked to execute designs, including Paul Nash, Nicholson, Hepworth, Albert Rutherston, Vanessa Bell and Duncan Grant.

In addition to E. Brain and Co., the Burslem firm of A. J. Wilkinson, makers of earthenware, were to take part. As a result of pressure from their managers, the list was enlarged to include several artists, like Laura Knight and Frank Brangwyn, who could not be considered remotely modern. A third firm, Stuart Crystal of Stourbridge, Gloucesterhire, was also brought in.

Milner Gray had hoped that the artists would be able to design their own shapes, but this was deemed too risky and too expensive. So all they did was the decorations, and these were transferred by other hands to standard shapes. No documentary records of Graham's decorations appear to have survived,[21] though numerous specimens have. He seems to have done at least four sets of decorations for tea and coffee services. Some examples are in the Victoria and Albert Museum. One has a white rose on a bright green background; another, green splodges over a spidery pattern. All look fresh

71

and original. His designs for Stuart of Stourbridge were equally successful: spiralling grooves cut into clear crystal, with an Art Nouveau look to them and judiciously varied to suite the shape of the half-dozen vases and dishes into which they were incised.

Altogether twenty-seven artists took part in this considerable exercise, and a large exhibition of the resulting products was opened at Harrods in October 1934 by Sir William Rothenstein, Principal of the Royal College of Art. 'It was a flop,' Milner Gray recalled sadly. 'The store buyers were just not interested. As usual, they just looked back on what were good orders last year and ordered again for next year. Anything new was not acceptable.'

But the show got a good press, and Graham's work was often singled out. Improbably, it seems to have been there that the brilliant young critic Raymond Mortimer first saw his work. In the *New Statesman* of 27 October he praised Graham's 'extraordinary intuition of the demands made by the material alike in porcelain, earthenware and glass' and said that his work was all remarkable. In the *Spectator* of 26 October Anthony Blunt—on a year's sabbatical from Cambridge and not yet recruited to the Soviet cause by Guy Burgess—also singled out Graham's work, along with that of Duncan Grant and Vanessa and Angelica Bell.

Throughout his career Graham kept his hand in on the design side. At this stage he needed to do it for the money; later it kept him in touch with reality, and it was fun. But all along it was, strictly speaking, a diversion from the real issue of painting.

Finances continued to be a source of difficulty. In 1933 an increase in rent once again obliged Graham and Kathleen to move. Milner Gray was to marry in June 1934, and probably towards the end of 1933 they took on a converted stables near the front gate of an estate called Sutton Place, on the edge of the village of Sutton-at-Hone, situated a couple of miles on the Dartford side of Farningham. Coincidentally, the rather better-known Sutton Place, near Guildford in Surrey (later the home of Paul Getty), then belonged to the Duke of Sutherland, and Graham was startled one day to be telephoned and told that his boat was ready.

One of the attractions of Sutton-at-Hone was Sir Stephen Tallents, who lived up the road in a house called St John's Jerusalem, a former Commandery of the Knights of St John and Jerusalem, rebuilt in Georgian style. He was a very cultured, unorthodox civil servant who, in 1933, had become public relations officer at the General Post Office. Like his friend Frank Pick, he commissioned many excellent posters, including one or two from Graham, who may well have met him through Pick. Sir Stephen invited Graham and Kathleen to stay for a couple of nights while the moved into Sutton Place Cottage. He and his wife Bridget and their daughters Miranda and Persis were all rather taken with Kathleen, which brought on one of Graham's bouts of jealousy.

He was to the end a man of inner uncertainties and a prey to insecurity, yet was driven on by ambition and a fierce desire to do good work. So far, since the Slump not much had happened to promote a feeling of security, but he was on his way to making a name for himself, and all his hard work in equipping himself as a painter was about to pay off.

4

Self-discovery in Wales

1934-9

THE MID-1930s were a deeply disquieting time for Europe. In Germany,
Hitler had become Chancellor in 1933, and the following year succeeded
Hindenburg as *Reichsführer*. The Stalinist purges were under way in the
Soviet Union. The British response to the advance of Fascism on the
Continent was predominantly supine. In February 1933, the Oxford Union
had reflected the mood by passing its famous motion 'that this House will in
no circumstances fight for King and Country'.

For Graham Sutherland, now rising 31 and still without any standing as a
painter, it was to be a period of rapid evolution. In 1934, a visit to
Pembrokeshire helped him to find himself, and at much the same time he
met three of his most stimulating and generous patrons: Kenneth Clark,
Colin Anderson and—of a rather different sort—Oliver Simon. By mid-
1940 he had graduated from group exhibitions to two very successful one-
man shows containing some of the finest works of his career, and had come
to be seen by an influential group of admirers as the most talented painter of
his generation. It was a remarkable transformation, brought about by an
unleashing of creative energies hitherto either canalized into the finicky
concentration of etching, or in search of the necessary catalyst.

To an extent unusual among contemporary artists, patrons were to play a
big part in his life. Lacking confidence as he did, they were important even
more for their moral than for their financial support.

Kenneth Clark was supremely well placed to give both. Although only a
few weeks older than Graham, he had taken over as Director of the National
Gallery in Trafalgar Square on 1 January 1934, after three years as Keeper
of Western Art at the Ashmolean Museum in Oxford, following a couple of
years with the art historian Bernard Berenson at I Tatti, near Florence. He
was not only knowledgeable about Italian painting of the Renaissance but

also enthusiastic about post-Impressionism and some contemporary painting and sculpture, and his houses at Lympne, on the Kent coast, and in Portland Place, London W1, were hung with fine examples of Cézanne, Renoir, Seurat, Matisse and Bonnard.

Clark's great-great-grandfather had invented the cotton spool, and enough of the family fortune had survived his father's Edwardian idleness to leave him very well off.[1] He and his wife Jane, a history graduate whom he had married in 1927, were heavily in demand at the dinner tables of social figures like Sybil Colefax, Lady Cunard and Philip Sassoon and entertained a wide range of the privileged and the talented themselves. It was what Kenneth Clark later called the 'Great Clark Boom', and Graham and Kathleen were to benefit from it.

The truth habitually comes in alternative versions. Clark believes that he first met Graham through Jack Beddington at an exhibition of Shell posters which he opened at the New Burlington Galleries in June 1934 and at which he greatly admired Graham's poster of the Great Globe at Swanage.[2] Graham's brother Humphrey, who as an assistant keeper of coins had known Clark at the Ashmolean, believed that he introduced them for the first time at the Harrods exhibition of artist-designed china, earthenware and glass of October 1934, mentioned above. Whichever it was, Graham struck Clark as a self-possessed, highly intelligent man of the world, 'with bright eyes which suggested, but in no way revealed, exceptional depths', while Kathleen was 'as pretty as a geisha'.[3]

Clark may have somewhat telescoped events in his autobiography when he said that a few days after they had met Graham came to see him with some recent watercolours and an oil painting, all of which he bought immediately, with great—and, no doubt, mutual—excitement. Kathleen's memory was that Oliver Simon of the Curwen Press drove them both to Portland Place with some gouaches, of which Clark bought one for about £20, had it magnificently framed and later asked them to come and have a look at it. What matters, however, is that in Graham's work Clark was to find visionary intensity and colouristic freedom in the lyrical tradition of Blake, Palmer and Turner. It showed him, he said, a way out of the 'virtuous fog of Bloomsbury art'.

Colin Anderson, whom Clark introduced to Graham before long, was a year younger than Graham. He radiated good looks and charm and came from the wealthy Scottish shipping dynasty which owned the Orient line. He used his position as a director to pioneer the application of good modern design to shipping, notably with the SS *Orion*, whose interior the architect Bryan O'Rorke designed in 1934–5.

'Graham was still very obviously struggling,' Anderson recalled.[4] 'He did posters for me, and for one of our ships he did a painted ceiling which was not accepted—to my horror—by the architect Bryan O'Rorke. . . . we used Ted [McKnight] Kauffer, who did a big mural; Ceri Richards did some murals; Piper, Bawden, all sorts of people.' Anderson reckoned he met Piper and Henry Moore, as well as Graham, through Clark. He had opened Ceri Richards's first one-man show at the Glynn Vivian Gallery in Swansea in 1931.[5]

The role these two wealthy, discriminating, charming men played in supporting and encouraging the most promising artists of their own age can hardly be exaggerated (though they were not alone). It was, however, neither of them but Robert Wellington, seven years Graham's junior, who recommended the Pembrokeshire landscape. The son of Hubert Wellington, the painter, art critic and former Registrar of the Royal College of Art, Wellington was running the Zwemmer Gallery in Charing Cross Road. He had met Graham in 1932, and on the strength of a watercolour seen shortly afterwards at the National Society in Piccadilly, had asked Graham to consider an exhibition of paintings at Zwemmer's. Graham replied that he had none, Wellington recalled.[6]

He had visited Pembrokeshire in 1933 for the first time with his parents. Advising Graham to visit Solva, on the coast, he also spoke highly of St David's—giving him the address of his lodgings there—and thought he might be particularly interested in the view from Whitesand Bay looking north to where the Preseli Hills come down into the sea. 'I thought it had the same sort of feeling which he had enjoyed so much in the chalk pits which came down to the Thames near Gravesend'—the subject of a painting which Graham had proudly shown him in 1933.

So, in the summer of 1934, Graham and Kathleen headed for the most westerly peninsula of Wales in the second-hand MG which had replaced the Morris. Nothing in their previous travels to Devonshire and Dorset had prepared them for Pembrokeshire's medley of tightly packed hills, valleys, cliffs, estuaries, and moorland, the land visibly shaped by the powerful rock movements and inundations of the sea over millions of years. Its impact was also a matter of timing. Graham had (belatedly) become increasingly conscious of the work of Picasso, Matisse, Miró and other Paris-based artists, through the magazines *Cahiers d'Art* and *Minotaure*. He was looking for a way of using what he had learnt without abandoning his individuality. In the contours and details of that landscape, he found it.

'It was in this country that I began to learn painting,' he wrote in a famous letter to Colin Anderson.[7]

It seemed impossible here for me here to sit down and make finished paintings 'from nature'. Indeed there were no 'ready-made' subjects to paint. The spaces and concentrations of this clearly constructed land were stuff for storing in the mind. Their essence was intellectual and emotional, if I may say so. I found that I could express what I felt only by paraphrasing what I saw. . . . it was in this area that I learned that landscape is not necessarily scenic, but that its parts have an individual figurative detachment.

That lesson, coupled with the feeling there of being 'on the brink of some drama', influenced him profoundly, he said.

I wish I could give you an idea of the exultant strangeness of this place — for strange it certainly is, many people whom I know hate it, and I cannot but admit that it possesses an element of disquiet. . . . the whole setting is one of exuberance — of darkness and light — of decay and life. Rarely have I been so conscious of these elements in so small a compass.

They had, that first time, approached St David's Head across a wide plain, its emptiness relieved by strips of field and bounding walls of turf-covered rocks. Then came the classically perfect forms of Carn Lidi and Carn Lleithyr, two hills shaped like small mountains, and finally a 'vast congregation of rocks, fallen cromlechs and goats' caves' plunging down the terraces of St David's Head into the sea. Heading south through bud-like valleys and along roads forming strange arabesques, they came to the estuary of such 'exultant strangeness': Sandy Haven, where the black-green ribs of half-buried wrecks, the bleached skull of a horse or cattle horns all seemed to emphasize the extraordinary completeness of the scene. And then there was the light, henceforward so important for Graham and here 'magical and transforming'.

At first he tried to make pictures on the spot. Then he gave this up and took to walking through, and soaking himself in, the country. 'At times I would make small sketches of ideas on the backs of envelopes and in a small sketch book, or I would make drawings from nature of forms which interested me and which I might otherwise forget.' Sometimes, lying on the warm shore, he would notice that some sea-eroded rocks precisely reproduced, in miniature, the form of the inland hills. The fragment could be as revealing as the panorama, sometimes even more so. Graham returned to Sutton Place Cottage not just with notebooks filled with drawings in pencil and watercolour from this and later trips to Pembrokeshire but also with a stored imagery of shells, roots and stones. These he would later transplant into landscapes which distilled the mood of what he had seen and noted.

Graham dated his use of sketchbooks—usually Rowney's $5\frac{1}{2}$- by 4-inch ones 'containing eighty leaves of good white paper'—from 1934.[8] He used them partly for on-the-spot drawings of a subject which he had encountered. Some such drawings turned out to be useless. Others he had to redraw several times in order to simplify and clarify them. Sometimes he had to return to the spot because he had failed to grasp the structure of the subject. He also used them to plan several versions of ideas for a painting. The same notebook might thus contain fragmentary notations and ideas more fully worked out, and it would not always be easy to tell which had been executed on the spot and which in the studio:

> I make notes following the first *frisson* of an encounter.[9] Gradually an idea emerges: there is the knowledge that, almost in spite of myself, something significant has arrived. . . . the preliminary stage, the direct contact, leads then to something else, controlled and ordered by the mind.

The difficulty was to preserve the feelings of the first encounter while paraphrasing it in the studio into something new yet the same.

St David's, where Graham and Kathleen stayed that first summer, is the smallest city in Britain, notable for the wonderfully romantic ruins of the fourteenth-century Bishop's Palace next to a remarkable, earlier cathedral. A few lush, green fields away is the old settlement site and outcropping of rock known as Clegyr Boia, which in 1936 was to inspire Graham's first etching-and-aquatint in his new manner.

During the next few years they stayed variously in the pretty harbour town of Solva, at the Cumbrian Hotel or in the hilltop cottage of Miss Nellie Pierce, who ran it; in cottages at Dale and Sandy Haven; and at the Mariner's Arms in Haverfordwest. Once, Kathleen recalled, they took a caravan. The sheep used to rub against it at night, and after a thunderstorm Graham had to put a piece of hardboard, on which he had started a painting, under a rear wheel of the car to get it out of the mud. It is nice to think of an early Sutherland lodging in some lonely grassland.

The Pierce cottage at Solva looked out to the Gribin, a ridged headland where Graham loved to walk and draw. Not far away is Porthclais, where two roads, intersecting above a stream-filled valley, form a sensuous Y-shape which Graham painted many times in both his early and his late Welsh periods. To the exploding light and dramatic pink rocks of Sandy Haven Graham added in 1936 the marshier mysteries of the foreshore of the Eastern Cleddau near Picton Castle, where a remarkably friable type of shale rock provides many strange shapes, and the exposed roots of oak trees reveal the struggle of organic things which so fascinated him. Most haunting of all, perhaps, was the beauty of Monk Haven, a tiny bay within a bay, first glimpsed through the open gateway of a 20-foot-high, castellated wall, covered with ancient ivy sinews. The tops of the ivy-festooned oaks and ash enclosed by the wall seem to form a roof, and a stream splashes over the pebbles of the beach beyond into the breakers of the Atlantic.

This immensely rich subject matter Graham transmuted at first mainly into small, simplified but highly charged watercolours and gouaches, in which blacks and reds often predominated: roads through hills, an outcropping of rock against the sky, a roadside boulder looming against a sulphurous sky were typical themes, and colour was used to create mood rather than to describe. From 1936 onwards he moved from this relatively panoramic manner towards a greater concentration on his discovery that landscape is 'not necessarily scenic, but that its parts have an individual figurative detachment'.

He arrived back from Wales in 1934 feeling that he had begun to find himself as a painter.[10] Oliver Simon, who was among the first to appreciate his new work, was introduced to Graham and Kathleen in June 1935 by Robert Wellington at the Museum Tavern in Bloomsbury.[11] Simon had become obsessively interested in typography while studying in Germany, near Weimar, and had been taken on by Harold Curwen. Curwen had transformed the family firm at Plaistow, in the East End of London, from a visual wilderness into an oasis for artists and designers, and Simon's life was soon dedicated to proving that books set by machines could be beautiful. He had shared an office in Bloomsbury with the famous typographer Stanley Morison, and the clarity, the restrained use of ornament and the judicious choice of founts which marked his books became a legend.[12]

Both he and his wife Ruth liked Graham and Kathleen immediately. They frequently visited them at Sutton-at-Hone, and felt that Graham's work, with its fresh vision and lyrical quality, provided another good reason for launching Simon's new journal of typography and the graphic arts, *Signature*. But no artist who came to Simon's office and saw examples of Graham's work there actually liked it—except Paul Nash.

In the first issue of *Signature*, in November 1935, Nash hailed Graham and Edward Bawden as artists of great accomplishment and promise. Nash contrasted the feeling of nervous, scarcely controlled energy which pervaded Graham's drawing with the precise, orderly, perhaps slightly cautious approach of Bawden, whom he saw as an applied rather than a 'free' draughtsman.

Graham reciprocated the compliment in the July 1936 issue, in an article entitled 'A Trend in English Draughtsmanship', in which he listed Nash and Henry Moore, as well as Blake, Palmer and late Turner, as being in the same (his own) genealogical tree. The trouble with Blake, he said, was that he rarely refreshed his imagination by making studies from natural phenomena. But in Blake's late works he saw a mysterious grandeur and flaring ecstasy. Moore, Graham said, discovered one thing with the help of another and by their resemblance made the unknown known. It was a phrase which he was often to use about his own aims and to illustrate the function of metaphor.

Even at its peak *Signature* never sold more than 1100 copies, but it was read by many fellow artists. 'It was a difficult time for fairly intellectual artists and composers,' John Piper recalled.[13] 'It was a time seething with experiment and adventure, but no one was particularly interested. *Signature* was something you could show around a bit. None of us had anything to advertise ourselves with.' Graham himself spoke of Oliver Simon as 'of immeasurable help to me in every possible way, encouraging me to write and reproduce my work in *Signature*. . . . he was not only a great typographer, but also one among very few patrons of great intelligence.'[14]

Kenneth Clark came out in open support of Graham in the November 1936 issue with a pat on the back for the 'rich and coherent design' and the extraordinarily personal style of a drawing he had done to illustrate a passage from Emily Brontë's *Wuthering Heights,* a rather slight pretext for such an encomium. In the issue of July 1937 Graham had not only a charming five-colour lithograph of two fishes, called *Under Water,* but also an article (rather ponderous) entitled 'Graven Images: Line Engraving and the Illustrated Book'. It was basically a plea to book publishers to take advantage of a·technique revived by Harold Curwen for the lithographic reproduction of engraved plates. Graham used the opportunity to show and to praise the work of one of his more talented pupils, Jock Kinneir, then only 20, who in the 1960s devised Britain's new road-signing system.

Graham's first, pre-Simon contacts with the Curwen Press had been of an extremely modest nature, starting in February 1935 with the design of a cover for a house journal, the *British Industries House Weekly*. That April he earned twenty guineas each for six Southern Railways posters, on bathing, rambles, racing, cricket, football and docks. If printed, these have become elusive. There cannot have been much excitement in designing the china and glass list for the Christmas gifts catalogue of Barrows, the Birmingham store, for which he earned three guineas that September. In 1935, at Simon's invitation, he joined the Double Crown Club, which Simon had founded in 1924 for those interested in good printing. The menus were traditionally designed by members to reflect the subject of the after-dinner

addresses. Graham designed one in October 1936. Paul Nash was to speak
on 'Surrealism and the Printed Book', and Graham's playful design showed
a ham with a human head speared by two forks, one supported by a cigar.

Towards the end of 1935 he was one of four artists to submit designs to
the Post Office for a new seven-penny stamp. The stamp had to bear a
standardized head of the monarch, George V, the value and the words
'Postage and Revenue'. There was little more than the lettering, borders and
colours to play with. Graham's three designs used different combinations of
yellow, dark pink and grey, and he worked hard at the borders. Barnett
Freedman's had vastly greater boldness and clarity. But it was all wasted
effort: in January 1936 the king's death paved the way for Edward VIII and
the abdication crisis.[15]

At about this stage, Graham's father, who had retired from the
Department of Education on reaching the age of 60, went to live in Jersey
with a lady friend. The wholly unexpected news came in a letter from him to
each of the children, passed on by the faithful factotum Emily Collar.

In the preceding years Graham's mother's restlessness had become much
more pronounced; she and Graham's father had lived at four different flats
in Soho, Marylebone and Holland Park before settling at the Embassy Hotel
in the Bayswater Road, from which he decamped. The three children
foregathered in London and went to explain what had happened to their
mother. 'We found her sitting in a shelter in Hyde Park, and we had to say he
had gone off to Jersey,' Graham recalled.[16] As the oldest, the burden fell on
him. 'I didn't dare say he'd gone off with somebody. The ironical thing was
that my mother knew this woman, and she knew that my father saw her.
They belonged to the same musical circle. She would say to my father:
"You would agree with *her*." She never knew, right to the end, that he had
gone off with somebody.'

Both Humphrey and Vivien thought their father's liaison, which had
probably been going on for a decade, was wholly platonic. 'They were both
desperately keen on music and walking in the country, neither of which
appealed to my mother,' Humphrey said. But Graham was not convinced.
His father had once said to him, 'You see, my dear boy, I am a very ardent
character.' Graham's view was that this was said 'meaningfully': 'She was a
good deal younger, and very serious.'

With Kathleen and Humphrey's wife, Monica, they saw Elsie Sutherland
through that dreadful day. 'Then the crunch came,' Graham said.

We decided she could not be left alone at this point. Kathy was absolutely
marvellous. We took her to Wales. We had hired a cottage [at Solva].

There were some jolly steep cliffs near. Kathy had to be always near her. . . . I was drawing some of the day. It was a terrible responsibility for Kathy, and I blame myself for putting this on her. But it did save the situation. My mother gradually recovered. . . .

A rare venture northwards had brought Graham, in the autumn of 1935, to Brimham Rock, in Nidderdale, north-west of Harrogate in Yorkshire. Jack Beddington had suggested it for a series of advertisements with the slogan 'To visit Britain's landmarks, you can be sure of Shell'. In a description which prefigured the later letter to Colin Anderson about Pembrokeshire, Graham described what they found there:

> a vast congregation of rocks. . . . they obscure the earth and sky with their forms . . . many of them rise, like unmentionable bathers, from pools of water. Supporting on their backs small rocks like slothful heads, they bend forward casting their huge shadows into the depths which half obscure their bulk.

One mass of stone was 'shaped like a growth which one sometimes sees attached to the nose of a peasant', yet it was divested, 'owing to the fact that it exists in stone, of the horror which such an affliction inspires. . . .'[17]

Graham was not a man to waste a good idea, either literary or pictorial. In the Welsh letter to Colin Anderson he was to write: 'One soon notices an irregularity of contour on the horizon'; in the Yorkshire one, 'the attention becomes drawn to an irregularity on the horizon.' In Wales the farms and cottages 'give scale and quicken by their implications our apprehension of the scene'; in Yorkshire a house 'not only gives scale, but quickens by its implications and associations our apprehension of the strangeness of the scene'. It is a highly anthropomorphic or animistic vision, which his prose style strove painfully hard at times to express.

Set like a sentinel on an upland hill, Brimham Rock made a perfect Sutherland subject, anticipating in its way those strange standing forms of the post-war years. In the resulting poster, issued in 1937, it mingled elements of mushroom, owl and human being in an ambiguous configuration outlined against a blue sky full of white, sickle-shaped clouds.

Perhaps Graham's finest poster—one not dependent on the exoticism of its subject matter—had been issued in 1936 by London Transport, under the slogan 'From field to field'. With two larks ascendant against two rounded hills, fields and a blue sky, and with some strategically placed shrubbery, it is a serenely sensual work resembling, at a closer look, a disguised female nude. A second Sutherland poster issued by London Transport that year mystified some poster gazers, who rang the *Daily*

Express. Graham had shown a haymaker's fork, a butterfly and a puzzling object. Tom Driberg, a journalist and later a Labour MP and life peer (he became Lord Bradwell), explained helpfully: 'Peculiar object illustrated herewith is not an instrument of discipline at a particularly posh school. It's what's called a corn baby.'

Surprisingly, considering his lack of experience as a painter, Graham showed his influences less at this stage than in the later 1940s and early 1950s. One might detect traces of Blake, or Masson, in some of the swirling forms of his Welsh landscapes; and something of later Turner and of Palmer, or indeed of Matisse or Nolde, in his expressive use of colour. Yet it is all highly individual. The later influences of Picasso, Matisse, Max Ernst, Grünewald and Bacon were more easily detectable.

He survived even association with the Surrealists without being obviously marked by the encounter, though it proved to be emboldening. The International Surrealist Exhibition opened in London at the ever-hospitable New Burlington Galleries in July 1936, the prime movers being Roland Penrose and David Gascoyne. Penrose, a painter and collector from a prosperous Quaker family, had recently returned from thirteen years in Paris, during which he had become a friend of Picasso, Ernst, Miró, Man Ray and the poet Paul Eluard, among others. He had met Gascoyne there in 1935. 'This is extraordinary', Gascoyne had said to him.[18] 'Why do people in London know nothing about the marvellous things going on here?' Penrose said he had to go back to London, adding: 'Let's go together and see what we can do.'

'When the first cases came from Paris for the exhibition, people were absolutely astonished,' he recalled. It was a vast show, with some 400 exhibits. The foreword to the pink catalogue was by André Breton, high priest of the movement, but no one was very fussy about Surrealist credentials. In addition to numerous works by recognizable Surrealists like Chirico, Ernst, Magritte, Picabia, Man Ray, Tanguy and Dali, there were also eleven Picassos, fifteen Klees, eight Giacomettis, seven Moores — and two paintings by Graham: *Thunder Sounding* and *Mobile Mask*.

Proceedings were enlivened by a girl wearing a fencing mask covered with red roses at the private view. She later fed the pigeons in Trafalgar Square. One corner of the gallery smelt strongly of fish: a kipper had been attached to a painting of a kipper. Among objects on view was the famous tea-set lined with fur. Incongruous juxtapositions, images of the unconscious, Freudian associations: on these and other Continental exotica the British could feast for the first time.

Neither of Graham's two oils was particularly Surrealist, though there was perhaps an element of unconscious sexual imagery in *Mobile Mask*: it resembles a behind more than a face.[19] A subtly modified version in red and grey crayon and pen-and-wash has appeared as a cover on the June 1936 issue of the Curwen Press newsletter, when, Oliver Simon noted in his autobiography, it evoked some hostility.

Graham disliked suggestions that his work was Surrealist. He had, it was true, shown at the 1936 exhibition, he said.[20]

> It is true too that the Surrealists sometimes came upon those *accidental* juxtapositions which produced in me that *frisson* which I find so satisfying. But I should hate my painting to be called Surrealist. I am quite unmoved by that sort of painting where one finds a head growing out of the thorax instead of out of the neck. For the most part I think Surrealism far too smooth and very badly done.

But, he conceded, the Surrealists did help him to widen his range by propagating the idea that worthy subject matter existed in objects at which the painter would never have looked before.

> My *Red Tree* of 1936 [which Kenneth Clark was to buy] was inspired by a piece of flotsam I saw washed up somewhere. Surrealism helped me to realize that forms which interested me existed already in nature and were waiting for me to find them. In nature lies the key. You see, I'm lost without nature; that's the fact. I can't do a thing without it. I can't invent unless I've got something to invent from. But I *can* carry it further.

There were, naturally, exceptions, and one of them was his first venture into lithography. It was for a scheme called Contemporary Lithographs, started in 1936 by Robert Wellington and John Piper. Among Wellington's customers for the reproductions (printed in Germany) of Impressionists and Post-Impressionists which he was obliged to sell at Zwemmer's was Henry Morris, the pioneering Director of Education for Cambridgeshire. Morris was implementing his plan to provide thinly populated rural areas with educational focal points, and he wanted the prints for the first of his village colleges, at Sawston.

Wellington thought it a pity he could not involve living painters in his schools. A mural by Robert Medley and a fountain by Henry Moore were mooted, but rejected as too expensive. Knowing what the French had done with limited-edition lithographs, Wellington decided to commission some. Piper, he knew, had the ability to adapt his own work and encourage others to explore a new medium. 'It meant having people like Paul Nash, Ivon Hitchens, Frances Hodgkins and Graham go to the Curwen and Baynard Presses, and make drawings on the stones or plates,' Piper recalled.[21] Most were wholly inexperienced. 'It was an awful sweat'.

Graham was asked to do something specifically for infants' schools, in place of all the gnomes on toadstools and fairies coming out of bluebells by Margaret Tarrant, then prevalent. He came up with *The Sick Duck*, a charming and humorous study of doctor and mother duck flapping around the woebegone sick duck with a thermometer in its bill. The white ducks were set against orange, pink and green. It was shown with other lithographs by Bawden, Medley, Clive Gardiner and H. S. Williamson, the Chelsea Principal, in January 1937 at Oliver Simon's Bloomsbury offices, and the critics were much taken by the ducks. Medley recalled a trip to Bristol in Graham's MG to sell lithographs to the headmasters of Clifton College and Bristol Grammar School. Both he and Graham loved speed. 'We used to take turns at the wheel, and he always managed a couple of miles an hour better than I did over a set distance. But it was his car!'

Graham's work was gradually being more widely shown. Freddie Mayor's gallery in Cork Street, where he first met Douglas Cooper in 1936–7,[22] usually had a selection of his watercolours and gouaches in stock, and sold about a dozen between 1936 and 1938 for eight to twelve guineas each. Some were shown, with works by Miró, Klee, Rouault and others, at an Exhibition of Inexpensive Pictures there over Christmas 1936. The mouth waters retrospectively.

There was a minor breakthrough in January 1937, when he sold an oil (*Welsh Landscape with Roads*, later bought by Oliver Simon) in a mixed exhibition at a smart new gallery in Bruton Street, London W1, called Rosenberg and Helft. Its main partner, Paul Rosenberg, handled Picasso, Braque, Matisse, Léger and Masson in Paris, where he was based. He had opened his London tributary in 1936, and felt an obligation to 'participate in and support some worthy achievements of the local school', his son Alexandre recalled.[23]

Kenneth Clark, inevitably, knew him. 'Dear Mr Clark', Graham wrote shortly before the show—it was still a rather formal relationship: 'As you were so kind in mentioning my name to them, would you help me by saying if you think I am wise in sending the Welsh Landscape to this exhibition . . .? I want to send something representative, and I was rather puzzled. Yours sincerely, Graham Sutherland.'

For a French dealer to show British painting was considered a flattering gesture by the *Scotsman*'s critic. In cricketing terms, the *Sunday Times*'s Frank Rutter (27 January) thought Steer, Sickert and Augustus John were the obvious three to lead an England painting eleven, while Rosenberg's other choices—Grant, Gertler, Matthew Smith, Stanley and Gilbert

Spencer, Wadsworth and Paul Nash—were fairly safe, with Sutherland perhaps as spare man, and Vanessa Bell as an odd woman. But Graham batted higher up in a younger and more progressive eleven exhibiting that same month at Thomas Agnew and Sons, of all places, whose sombre Bond Street premises had been lent for the purpose. The other ten artists were Ivon Hitchens, John Piper, Ceri Richards, Julian Trevelyan, Victor Pasmore, Robert Medley, James Cant, Arthur Jackson, Roy de Maistre and his close friend Francis Bacon. The show was, the catalogue announced, 'in connection with a scheme to provide a permanent gallery for the constant display of works by Contemporary Painters and Sculptors'.

This was another brainchild of Robert Wellington, conceived in the summer of 1934. It was based, he recalled,[24] partly on the Bloomsbury-orientated London Artists' Association formed by Maynard Keynes and Samuel Courtauld in 1925, which guaranteed member artists a minimum income, and partly on the practices of big Paris dealers like Kahnweiler and Vollard.

Roy de Maistre, who had good connections, helped Wellington draw up a memorandum outlining the idea. Henry Moore said that he could give up teaching and concentrate on his work if guaranteed £400 a year. Wellington then tried to raise the necessary capital to start a gallery and set a scheme in motion. He remembered having lunch with de Maistre, Keynes, R. A. Butler and his wife Sydney, who was Sam Courtauld's daughter, at the Butlers' home in Westminster. Kenneth Clark and Lord Balniel (later Lord Crawford and Balcarres) were also canvassed. But nobody would put up the capital, which would have given them first choice of the paintings shown. Then Wellington split with de Maistre, and the Agnew's exhibition was the only outcome. Of the thirty-six pictures shown (Graham and Bacon had four each), none cost more than forty guineas.

This was certainly the first time Graham and Bacon had shown together, but they may well have met earlier through de Maistre, who was a Catholic too. The high noon of their friendship was to be in the mid and later 1940s. Bacon, born in Dublin in 1909, was six years younger. His father was an (English) trainer of horses, and the young Francis left home aged 16, after a minimal education, to live in London, Paris and Berlin on a tiny allowance, with occasional commissions for interior decoration in the Bauhaus style. He started drawing at 17 or 18 and never went to art school. Later he settled in London, designing some furniture and rugs and doing odd jobs unconnected with art.

He had shown individual paintings at the Mayor Gallery in 1933 and had put on a show of his own work in a Curzon Street basement in 1934. The result was discouraging. Herbert Read, however, had perspicaciously included Bacon's *Crucifixion 1933* in his seminal book *Art Now*, published that same year, and—even more perspicaciously—Sir Michael Sadler had bought it from Mayor. In Graham's battered, paint-spattered copy of Read's book (which did not mention him) the illustration of the *Crucifixion* was the most heavily thumbed page. He rapidly became one of Bacon's most enthusiastic admirers.

In early 1937 Graham and Kathleen were faced with another accommodation crisis. Sutton Place, the big house by whose gate their modest cottage stood, was sold. 'The new landlord seemed friendly,' Graham recalled,[25] 'and told us we would not be disturbed, whereupon we did the house up—gleaming white paint!—and were promptly given notice on the grounds that they wanted the place for their gardener!'

This time luck was on their side, and a good deed was rewarded. Graham had spent a whole day driving an American bandleader friend around Kent in search of a house to rent, and they had discovered an enchanting former oast house in the main street of the village of Trottiscliffe. Shortly after being given notice, Graham and Kathleen found themselves in front of this friend at the theatre. 'Did you know the White House in Trottiscliffe is to let?' he asked Graham. Its tenants, the actors Franklin Dyall and Mary Merrall, had decided to move.

Graham and Kathleen hurried down to see it. Trottiscliffe (pronounced 'Trosley' by the locals) lies some 15 miles further south than their previous three homes, just below the rim of the North Downs, from which there is a wonderful view of the Weald of Kent and along which a pilgrim path to Canterbury still runs.

The White House (their second of that name) faces a little segmented green on the edge of the village, by the George pub. It is a very attractive, white clapboard house with warm-red roof tiles, dating from the seventeenth century or earlier, which was, long ago, first a bakery and then a butcher's shop, as large hooks in the sitting-room testify. The front door is left of centre. On the left of the entrance hall a narrow dining-room overlooks the back garden. On the right a large sitting-room—two rooms knocked into one by the Dyalls—runs the length of the rest of the house. Between it and the kitchen at the back there is a small breakfast room, usable as a cosy second sitting-room.

Up narrow, twisty stairs, the first floor has three bedrooms, two bathrooms (the second was added much later) and a boxroom; on the top floor a long, attic-style room with lots of windows makes an admirable studio, and there is a smaller room for storage. All the rooms on the first two floors are low-ceilinged and beamy. The rear garden runs to a little over an acre, with fruit trees, an old wall down one side and kitchen garden beyond.

Graham and Kathleen fell for it, and it was a measure of their growing confidence that they felt able to rent so substantial a home. It was to serve as their base in England for the rest of Graham's life.

It was no doubt a wrench to leave the 'Palmer country' of the Darenth valley, where they had spent the first nine years of their married life. But among the gains was the proximity to Trottiscliffe of some fine woods on the edge of the Downs, full of old yew trees from whose overhanging branches great tresses of old man's beard dangled and whose exposed roots and knotted trunks were to provide Graham with many an 'encounter'. Not far away, he later discovered, lay Mereworth Woods, full of Spanish chestnut plantations, cut back periodically to provide chestnut paling for fencing. The pollarded limbs of these chestnuts were much to Graham's later taste.

Twice-weekly sorties to London for teaching at Chelsea continued, and from 1936 or 1937 (no records survive) Graham taught on an occasional basis at the Ruskin School of Drawing and Fine Art in Oxford, whose head (from 1929 to 1949) was Albert Rutherston. Rutherston, who had changed his name from Rothenstein and was Sir William's brother, was a charmingly decorative designer and illustrator and a stalwart of the Curwen Press team. The Ruskin assignment lasted until the war; to simplify the difficult journey, Graham sometimes spent the night either with his brother Humphrey in Oxford or with the Clarks in London.

As the confidence of his own work grew, so did his impact as a teacher. One to receive its full force at Chelsea was Paul Miller, later Canon of Derby Cathedral. Fresh from Haileybury, he had seen Graham's *Red Cliff* and *Two Flowers* at the 1937 London Group exhibition before meeting him at Chelsea. Used to the gentler tonalities of the Euston Road School painters like Pasmore, Coldstream and Claude Rogers, Miller was amazed by Graham's cruder, more passionate work. 'It fired me with a joy, a happiness and a fulfilment of a kind I had never known before,' he recalled.[26] It was, he believed, his first and most important step towards finding God through imagery. 'More particularly, it was the discovery of the "givenness" of God's world, of its relentlessness, of its secrecy, of its masculinity.'

Miller was soon discussing with Graham such topics as the conflict between man's natural fulfilment (artists 'expressing themselves') and the need for the Christian to deny himself and to take up his cross daily. Kathleen he found equally striking: women then usually wore pastel colours, not the magenta, mustard and emerald green she teamed with her black dresses. 'She was extraordinarily beautiful, and the pair of them reigned as twin deities in my imagination, appearing frequently in my dreams five years later when I was a prisoner-of-war of the Japanese.'

Dirk Bogarde, the actor, was also at Chelsea and has recalled how Graham coped with his attempted design for a cover of H. E. Bates's *The Poacher*.[27] He had put in fields, woods, rabbits, guns, traps, fishing rods, the lot. Graham explained that what was needed was an uncomplicated symbol which might tempt someone to read the book, not a map of England with all its blood sports. Swiftly, economically, he drew a face, a cloth cap, some rabbit's legs, a long, wavy line which was clearly a field of corn — 'and the entire subject was before me'.

Graham had a wonderful gift for making every student feel that he or she was important, Maida Lunn recalled.[28] Few under him failed to extend such ability as they had to its fullest — but he did not suffer gladly the idle or fidgety. (He once offered ninepence to anyone who preferred to go down the road to the Classic cinema to see the Marx Brothers' *Duck Soup*, which, he said, would give them a legitimate cause for mirth.) 'He made me see and share that joy and love for Blake and Samuel Palmer which has become part of my life.' Graham and Kathleen would put in an appearance at the common-room hops and attended the annual picnics.

By 1937 he was getting into his stride. *Red Tree*, of which he had done two very different versions the previous year, had been striking if not wholly convincing. *Welsh Mountains* and *Black Landscape* of 1937 were magnificent in their sombre, brooding quality and skilful use of black, providing what Edward Sackville-West was to call a bass octave of 'fuliginous obscurity'.[29] Graham often used it to heighten the impact of his flame-reds, oranges and a wonderful range of yellows.

Red Monolith (1938) provided an impressive first example of a new penchant for focusing on detached elements of nature, not dissimilar to that which had produced the 'controversial' rose bush etching of 1931. The studies show a vase-like tree form as the point of departure. Into this he inserted a quasi-human, shadowy figure, setting it against a flat horizon line. It makes a cryptic, ambiguous, somewhat phallic double image, full of portents of his more mysterious creations of the later 1940s and early 1950s.

In 1938 came the moment of truth: Graham's first one-man exhibition as a painter. 'I have managed to arrange with M. Rosenberg that you have a show at his [London] galleries in October,' Kenneth Clark announced casually in a letter from Paris of 25 February. 'I made it that month as it allowed you a summer holiday to prepare in. ... The Surrealist show in Paris is really degrading — like a squalid entertainment park.'

Graham's relations with Clark had warmed considerably in the last eighteen months. It was now 'Dear K.', as he wrote on the 28th, 'What really staggering news! and a complete surprise to me, since the idea seemed so far beyond the bounds of possibility. Thank you à thousand times. I'm immensely stimulated; but break into a cold sweat at the thought of the work letting you down, or my not getting enough done!'

In fact, he completed eight oils that year before the exhibition and a number of drawings. Early September found him and Kathleen in lodgings in Dale, Pembrokeshire, wrestling with Rosenberg and Helft over the opening date of the exhibition and the private-view invitations. The gallery wanted to advance the opening to a time when 'no-one would have been in town', Graham told Clark.[30] Another room was to contain a group of contemporary British painters, and to Graham's annoyance, the gallery insisted on a *joint* private-view card.

To Paul Nash, whom he had come to know better through Oliver Simon, Graham wrote on 16 September from the same address: 'We are in Pembrokeshire, alternating between enjoyment of this superb country and desolation as we scan the European horizon. My show opens (I trust) on Tuesday, and I hope we may see you there. . . .'[31]

Kenneth Clark contributed, anonymously, a typically succinct foreword to the minimal, unillustrated catalogue, stressing the poetic nature of Graham's work and his magical vision of nature, which 'gradually convinces the spectator, who ends by discovering Graham Sutherland in nature'. 'Nearly all the pictures in this exhibition have been painted from small, careful drawings done on the spot, squared for enlargement and followed most accurately,' he explained for the benefit of doubting spirits. 'As a result Sutherland's work is the reverse of abstract.' Those prepared to trust their eyes would recognize a rare and precious talent, which could furnish the mind with memorable images.

There were fourteen oils and eleven watercolours and gouaches. The oils included Clark's *Red Tree* (on loan) and the two Surrealist show works. Some of the gouaches seem subsequently to have disappeared. What happened, for example, to *Woman with a Face Ache*, inspired by Kathleen wearing a kerchief? Or a study of the Bishop's Palace at St David's in Pembrokeshire? Both represented unusual subjects at that stage. In the gallery's front room there were eleven works by six youngish painters, including Coldstream, Pasmore, Graham Bell and Geoffrey Tibble.

Press reaction was enthusiastic. *The Times*'s critic[32] found in Graham's work 'an extreme distillation of landscape moods', the taste for black and dark red suggesting Gauguin, the approach Braque—painters also cited by Raymond Mortimer in the *New Statesman*,[33] who hailed Graham's 'scrumptious' details of handling and sumptuous oranges and pinks in an article gratifyingly headed 'An Arrival'. He placed Graham firmly among 'the most arresting painters of his time'.

Seven works were sold—'and everyone thinks this v. good for crisis time,' Graham wrote to Clark, offering him a medium-sized gouache called *Estuary* by way of thanks for all he had done.[34] According to Graham's own marked catalogue, the buyers were Lord Sandwich (a particularly luscious landscape, *Road and Hills in Setting Sun*); Peter Gregory and Peter Watson, both major patrons of contemporary work; Colin Anderson and Oliver Simon; the Redfern Gallery; and—most important—the Tate Gallery. Through the Contemporary Art Society and the good offices of Sir Jasper Ridley, who later became chairman of its Board of Trustees, the Tate was eventually (in 1946) to acquire one of the larger oils, *Welsh Landscape with Roads*, then priced at £35. The gouaches in the show cost around £15 each. *Red Monolith* did not sell (it was later acquired by the American mega-collector Joseph H. Hirshhorn).

The buyers may not have been numerous, but they were discriminating. The reviews had been very good: Graham had indeed arrived, at least in the small circle of those interested in modern art. Rosenberg and Helft were pleased, and the following May they suggested another show in 1940, with Henry Moore and, perhaps, Victor Pasmore. But that was not to be: Paul Rosenberg was Jewish and soon had to flee from Paris to New York.

Buoyed up by these affirmations of confidence, so important to boost his faltering faith in himself, Graham went on in 1939 and early 1940 to paint three of the accepted masterpieces of his career: *Entrance to Lane* and *Green Tree Form: Interior of Woods*, both now in the Tate Gallery, and *Gorse on Sea Wall*, now in the Ulster Museum, Belfast. All three were inspired by Pembrokeshire, to which Graham and Kathleen had returned at least once every year since 1934—though he could have found similar subject matter elsewhere. They reflect his shift away from the scenic and towards a more psychological approach.

> After I had been to Wales I began to notice in landscape that almost everything, if one keeps one's eyes open, is potential material for painting; and, more than that, certain elements of nature seem to me to have a kind of presence . . . shadows had a presence; certain conformation of rock seemed to go beyond just being a rock, they were emanations of some kind of personality.[35]

In 1939, this tendency to endow natural forms with human overtones produced *Gorse on Sea Wall*, in which he superimposed on the formal shape of *Red Monolith* the clawing fingers of a spiralling gorse bush. Aptly, a critic later called it 'a grave and noble portrait'.[36] 'It is not a question so much of a "tree like a figure", or a "root like a figure", it is a question of bringing out the anonymous personality of these things,' Graham said.[37] 'At the same time, they must bear the mould of their ancestry. There is a duality: they can be themselves, and something else at the same time. They are formal metaphors.' In those few lines he summed up the essence of much of his work.

Detached forms had another advantage. 'I have never liked the idea, in looking at a landscape for pictorial purposes, that something is going on outside the canvas — that a hill, for instance, continues right and left.'[38] He preferred something which could be self-contained.

In *Entrance to Lane* he contrived, by the skilful disposition of black, white, singing green and yellow lozenge-shapes of paint, to suggest a tubular lane with sun at the end without in any way literally portraying one. *Green Tree Form: Interior of Woods* (the studies date from 1939, the main oil from 1940) represents his darker side: tree trunk as quasi-human form, poised eerily in a melancholy green void.

Some of the depth and intensity of these works may have sprung from seeing Picasso's *Guernica*, shown with its sixty-seven preparatory studies in London in October 1938, first at the New Burlington Galleries (3000 visitors in a month) and then at the Whitechapel Gallery in the East End (12,000 visitors in two weeks). Graham came to regard Picasso's evocation of the horror of the bombing of the Basque town in the Spanish Civil War as 'the great picture of the twentieth-century'.[39] 'Picasso's *Guernica* drawings seemed to open up a philosophy and to point a way whereby — by a kind of paraphrase of appearances — things could be made to look more vital and real.' Everything he saw at that time — probably including a major show of contemporary German painting that July — seemed to exhort him to a greater freedom, he said. 'Only Picasso, however, seemed to have the true idea of metamorphosis, whereby things found a new form through feeling.'[40]

That was to be another central concept: not a new one, since it ran in one sense from Grünewald through Goya to Munch and the Expressionists. Graham chose a painter with a similar approach as the starting point for his first known mature religious work: an interpretation of El Greco's *Agony in the Garden*. It was shown in 1939 with other 'paraphrases' of Old Masters at the Storran Gallery, which was off Piccadilly in Albany courtyard and owned by Eardley Knollys. He was to introduce Graham to the South of France, and Erica Brausen, a German immigrant who was then his secretary, was also to play a role in their lives.

In these last two years of peace, Graham designed a fifth and last poster for London Transport, and one for Colin Anderson's Orient Line; and shared an exhibition of his china and earthenware (mainly it seems of earlier design) with Marion Dorn, the American-born carpet and textile designer, at her gallery off New Bond Street. Beside her extreme professionalism, his efforts were adjudged a trifle amateurish.[41]

Finally, he made his debut in the USA, chosen by Kenneth Clark, along with Pasmore, Coldstream, Moore and others, to represent Britain at the World Fair in New York in the summer of 1939, complementing older artists like Sickert, Steer and Clausen. The 'vibrant emotional quality' of Graham's 'amorphous and pleasingly coloured designs' struck one American critic as undoubtedly original, but not easily understood.[42]

At home, Graham's reputation was spreading to a wider public. 'Fashion in collecting?' asked an article entitled 'People who Collect' that August in *Queen* magazine. 'The coming "tip" for English contemporary painting, say many, is Graham Sutherland. . . .'[43]

With war looming, it was an oddly-timed exercise in cultural crystal-ball gazing, but showed how far he had come in the last five years. In the event, Hitler's war was to enrich Graham's work by diverting it, and to speed the spread of his renown.

5

War Artist

1940-5

Hitler attacked poland on 1 September 1939, and Britain declared war on 3 September. The ostrich days were over. Like most people, Graham was deeply troubled that autumn. 'Although we have been expecting this war for so long, it finds me in a state of great mental bewilderment,' he wrote to Jane Clark on 14 September. 'The idea of killing a man seems awful, and for me wrong. It would be equally awful to stand back while others go. Yet this war seems as just and inevitable as any war could be, though I cannot believe that war today can bring anything but further evil in its wake.'

At first sight it looked as though Graham's career was going to be blighted just when it was blossoming. It seemed certain that he would lose his main source of income, teaching. What should he do? How could he and Kathleen scrape a living? Should he go on the land? Should they go to live with his mother in Rustington or in a caravan that they had been offered by some neighbours in Trottiscliffe? In a series of anxious letters, they turned to the Clarks for advice.

Kenneth Clark was crisply reassuring. For Graham to go on painting was the highest form of national service he could perform, he wrote. The idea of going on the land was rubbish. 'Why does he think he is serving his country better by digging potatoes than by painting the few pictures now being produced in Britain which have any chance of survival?' he asked Kathleen. As for living with Graham's mother, he advised against that too: 'Family life is really fatal to any creative work.' Graham should go on painting at the White House; and then they should come and spend the winter at the house that he and Jane had rented and were getting ready at Upton, near Tetbury, in Gloucestershire: 'I believe that voluntary communism should precede the real thing,' he wrote. Meanwhile they should not worry about money. He would do what he could to make up for Chelsea—and enclosed an 'interim dividend', a cheque for £50.[1]

As Director of the National Gallery, Clark had been busy overseeing the evacuation of its paintings to country houses and castles. Later they were transferred to a cave in a disused slate quarry in north Wales. He thought that his own house at Lympne, Kent, overlooking Romney Marsh, was also at risk: any German invasion force was likely to be deployed there. When captured later, the German invasion plans confirmed his suspicion. Gloucestershire, well to the west, was reckoned safer.

Clark knew that he had the answer to Graham's problems. A few weeks after the outbreak of war, he had set in motion a plan for artists to be commissioned to make a record of it, along the lines of a First World War scheme pioneered by the Canadians.[2] Graham had thought he might be suitably employed in camouflage work. The war artists scheme would make much better use of his talents and would prevent him and others from being killed. So, at least, Clark hoped.

Pending the fruition of the scheme, Graham tried to fulfil Clark's injunction to carry on painting in Kent. He had been invited to have a show the following February at the Leicester Galleries, in Leicester Square, London W1 (it was postponed eventually to May). Two evacuees who had been billeted on the Sutherlands were a diversion. They were school-teachers and were in a state of perpetual warfare with local special constables over blackout lapses. Graham's own teaching, at Chelsea, was after all to continue, but on a week-to-week basis.

Overwhelmed with feelings of gratitude to the Clarks, Graham and Kathleen made arrangements to sublet the White House and to join their benefactors at Upton House. They seem to have settled there finally in December 1939 but soon took off for a spell over Christmas in a new part of Wales: Abergavenny, Brecon and the Brecon Beacons, a range of hills more obviously dramatic than anything in Pembrokeshire. 'I have been working every day, and have found some electrifying motifs,' Graham wrote to the Clarks from Brecon on 27 December.

> It is not easy country, and perhaps needs a closer familiarity than most. I believe that I may have secured enough material for eight new pictures — perhaps! Yesterday we were spell-bound at sunset by the effect of the sun coming through holes in the clouds and making orange red patches on the blue-black mountains.

The following day they went off to the Gower Peninsula.

Upton House, to which they returned, was a handsome Georgian residence large enough for the Clarks, their three children (Alan and the twins, Colin and Colette), Sir Kenneth's mother and, before long, Edward Sackville-West. There was a large sitting-room, and Graham and Kathleen had a bedroom and studio. The studio was not large and contained a large Sandy Calder mobile and a collection of Italian paintings, stacked against the wall, belonging to Henry 'Bogey' Harris, a typical Clark friend who had known everyone from Oscar Wilde to Pope Pius X.

Eddy Sackville-West combined great talents and considerable achievements with acute hypochondria. A precociously gifted pianist at Eton, he became the *New Statesman*'s music critic, did much to promote young composers like Britten, Tippett and Walton, had a famous collection of gramophone records—which he often played at Upton—and was, with his friend Desmond Shawe-Taylor, to write the *Record Guide* in 1951. He was also a novelist, wartime BBC producer and connoisseur of paintings; he wrote the first considered account of Graham's work in 1943. He balanced his hypochondria and melancholia with bursts of gaiety and lived to be 63. He always seemed to be huddled up in a velvet cloak at Upton, writing in a chair, Colin Anderson remembered from his visits there. Kathleen recalled him playing the piano with great *brio* and rushing from the room with a nosebleed.

The Clarks, often in London during the week, entertained at weekends rather too much for Graham's taste—'actors, duchesses, etc., Gaby Pascal (an eccentric film producer), Willy Walton, Oxford grandees such as Maurice Bowra, Air Force chiefs,' Graham recalled.[3] 'Apart from the intellectuals, I found this, in spite of the Clarks' great consideration and kindness, a very wearing period. But I did a good deal of work, mostly culled from studies made in Wales.'

One friendly refuge from Upton was the house, at Woodchester nearby, of Hiram Winterbotham, of the cloth-manufacturing family, who was in charge of 20,000 personnel in some twenty aircraft factories. Winterbotham knew the local area intimately, and Graham and Kathleen explored it with him. He also had his own pump and used to make petrol available to Graham in days of rationing. Cars seemed to represent freedom to Graham, he recalled. 'One day he complained that his beloved MG was not going as it should. I took him to see my garage mechanic, who said the carburettor needed "taking abroad" [Gloucestershire for 'to pieces']. "Surely", said Graham, "there is something that can be done to it in this country in time of war".'[4] Graham gave Winterbotham a watercolour, *Dark Hill with Hedges and Fields*, and inscribed it: 'For services during the war 1939– .'

Winterbotham's friend and assistant was a good-looking ex-Rhodes scholar called Alan Jarvis, who became a personal assistant to Sir Stafford

se on Sea Wall. Oil on canvas, 1939. $24\frac{1}{2} \times 19$ in (62.2 $\times$ 48.3 cm)

Pembrokeshire Landscape. Pen and ink and gouache, 1936. $14 \times 21\frac{1}{2}$ in (35.6×54.6 cm)

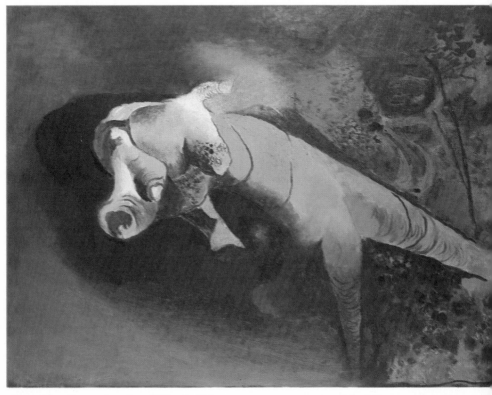

Green Tree Form: Interior of Woods. Oil on canvas, 1940. $31 \times 42\frac{1}{2}$ in (78.7×107.9 cm)

Cripps and, after the war and probably on Kenneth Clark's recommendation, Director of the National Gallery of Canada. Kathleen remembered Winterbotham wearing a white boiler suit—he believed in dressing the part—to dinner at the Clarks and playing table skittles with him in a local pub.

From the declaration of war to April 1940 was, as far as Britain was concerned, the period of the so-called 'phoney war', an uneasy calm while Hitler prepared the swift occupation of Denmark and Norway, then Belgium and Holland. Graham and Henry Moore (who was old enough to have served in the First World War) began to feel restive about their failure to make any contribution to the war effort. Moore recalled:[5]

> We knew that Chelsea [School of Art] was going to be evacuated. We talked together and thought we ought to do something to help. So we applied to learn munition gauge making, which was being taught at Chelsea Polytechnic, which the art school was part of. They said we should wait—they would call us. One month, two months, three months went by, and we heard nothing. They had too many volunteers.

Graham's first effort as a war artist was of a non-commissioned nature. No doubt at Clark's suggestion, in the early part of 1940 he went off to an airfield in the vicinity of Tetbury to draw some bombers based there. The result was three gouaches, one of which, *Camouflaged Bombers at Dawn*, was shown in a mixed exhibition called 'England in Wartime' at the Leicester Galleries in early June. It was a tentative start, with no feeling of involvement.

His main preoccupation at this stage was his own exhibition at the Leicester Galleries, at whose modest premises many of the post-Impressionists had first been shown in London. It opened in early May, preceded by a lunch party given by the Clarks at the flat in Gray's Inn to which they had moved from Portland Place.

Graham's second one-man show as a painter was as successful with the critics as the first. He had managed to muster thirty works, mainly gouaches, and sold twenty-two of them. Among the buyers were the Clarks themselves, Colin Anderson, Cecil Beaton, the novelist Hugh Walpole (who had taught at Epsom), Raymond Mortimer, Lady Hinchingbrooke, Sidney Bernstein (then working with Clark at the film division of the Ministry of Information), the Contemporary Art Society and the Tate Gallery, and Peter Watson.

Watson had already bought *Gorse on Sea Wall*, which he lent for the show. Now he bought *Entrance to Lane* (then called *Approach to Woods*), demonstrating his uncanny eye for quality. It was Watson, second son of a rich baronet, who in September 1939 had decided to back *Horizon*—with money derived from the family firm, Maypole Dairy Co., a chain of grocery stores that had pioneered the sale of margarine and been bought by Unilever in the 1920s. While Cyril Connolly (and, more briefly, Stephen Spender) edited this brilliant magazine devoted to literature and art and got most of the credit for it, Watson paid the bills and was its art editor. He was a dandy and a dilettante who was to do a great deal to sustain Graham and other artists, notably John Craxton, Lucian Freud, Robert Colquhoun and Robert MacBryde, through the war. (He liked to change his pictures around and sold *Entrance to Lane* to the Tate in 1953.)

Prices in general ranged from ten to forty guineas, though the Tate paid fifty guineas for *Green Tree Form*, its first Sutherland; Colin Anderson bought the large gouache study for this for a mere fifteen guineas. So frequently has the latter since been exhibited that its reverse side is scarcely visible through the stickers of exhibitions all over the world.

John Piper was among the reviewers. Colour was the connecting link betwen Graham's visions, he said in the *Spectator*.[6] It was so rich and concentrated that each picture seemed like an urgent revelation. Raymond Mortimer was lyrical in the *New Statesman*:[7] 'A cumulative effect of certainty and power that I have never had from an English contemporary,' he wrote, though he found *Green Tree Form* 'too breasted' and *Association of Oaks* too much a caricature of a human couple. In the *Sunday Times* Eric Newton found a suggestion of primeval chaos in some of the paintings, and in each an 'almost frightening intensity'.[8] By any standards the exhibition was a *succès d'estime*, even if both buyers and critics represented a small group of relatively intellectual enthusiasts, a good number of whom had come to Graham's work via Kenneth Clark.

It was noteworthy that this show sold three times as well as the previous one. That was no doubt due in part to Graham's growing reputation, and to his greater confidence as a painter. Perhaps, also, collectors were happier to spend money now that war had been declared than when it hovered as an intangible shadow.

The exhibition out of the way, Graham had his first contact, in June, with the War Artists Advisory Committee, which had been drawing up lists of artists to be employed and deciding how they could best be used. The aim, broadly, was to produce a record of all aspects of Britain's involvement in the war and to help bolster morale by showing the resulting pictures at exhibitions up and down the country. Clark chaired the Committee, on which sat representatives of the armed services, government departments and the art world. Its secretary, the linchpin of the operation, was E. M. O'R. Dickey, a former Ministry of Education Inspector for Art and member of the London Group.

There were three main ways in which war artists were employed by the Committee. They could submit work speculatively, in the hope that it would be bought—as Graham soon did with one of his studies of bombers, which was eventually bought by the Committee for fifteen guineas. They might be employed for an agreed sum to do a specific task. Finally, they might be paid a salary for a fixed period, usually six months, all their war-related work theoretically becoming the government's property.

Without having reached any agreement yet on the manner of his employment, Graham went off in early August for a brief holiday in Pembrokeshire with Kathleen, during which they discovered lodgings at a farmhouse which was to be their base in Wales for the next few years. Called Lleithyr Farm, it was less than a mile from Whitesand Bay and hard by the hills of Carn Lidi and Carn Lleithyr which Graham was to describe so well to Colin Anderson. 'At last', Graham wrote in the visitors' book on leaving, 'we have found a perfect place in which to stay in Pembs, and real friends in Mr and Mrs James [the owners]. . . .'

He reacted cautiously when, later that month, the War Artists Committee came up with the suggestion that he should undertake 'pictures of damage which may be caused by enemy action', the amount of work being a matter for mutual agreement. He had undertaken to be trained as a munition gauge maker, he explained, and wondered how many pictures would be expected and how soon. Dickey suggested that he could take up his munition training later. As for quantity, it was all very civilized:

> Our plan has been to leave it more or less to the artists to produce what they think is fair for the fee in cases of this kind, and to get the work done at the pace which suits them best. I need hardly say that we have had to take strong measures from time to time in order to prevent artists from being too generous![9]

By August, Hitler's Luftwaffe was beginning to provide an all too adequate supply of damage to record: the bombing which had begun sporadically in June was now growing in intensity and hitting civilian as well as military and industrial targets. Cardiff had been bombed off and on since 25 June, and Graham arrived there—with Kathleen, as ever—on 31 August, poised to grapple with his first major assignment and armed with a special petrol allowance to facilitate his movements. But damage there had in fact been slight, and he was advised to try Llantwit Major, on the coast. He was in an anxious state. 'There was I, who, up to then, had been concerned with the more hidden aspects of nature,' he was to recall.[10]

I had been attempting to paraphrase what I saw, and to make paintings which were parallel to, rather than a copy of, nature. But now, suddenly, I was a paid official — a sort of reporter — and naturally not only did I feel that I had to give value for money, but to contrive somehow to reflect in an immediate way the subjects set me.

The bombing continued. In another village, Barry, also on the coast, they stayed in a room above an oil merchant and general stores. The bed backed on to a window, which Graham covered at night with his drawing board against the danger of flying glass.

Swansea, with its florid, Victorian architecture, gave Graham his first sense of the possibilities of destruction as a subject, though some studies of a damaged farmhouse were among the more effective works he did on this first venture. His experience of drawing in front of natural forms was to stand him in very good stead. But confronted by a bombed building, he had to work in a much more hectic atmosphere, with people peering at what he was doing — the 'too curious crowds', he called them[11] — sometimes with firemen in action, and the subjects were at first alien.

Before returning to Upton House, he retired in early October to the peace of Lleithyr farm to work up his on-the-spot notes and drawings, usually requiring a secondary stage before producing the finished work. His first subjects included a Masonic hall and hospital as well as various houses. 'Some of the final drawings, as you see, I have completed within reach of the "motif", as the complexity of the subject necessitated constant reference,' he wrote to Dickey on 1 October. 'Doing the scenes of devastation I have found most absorbing, though with the accompaniment of nightly raids, at all events during the early part of the work, not without its nerve-wracking element.' Not long afterwards he delivered no less than thirty-six drawings and was told the Committee was delighted with them.

He was less happy himself about his next assignment, a gun-testing site at Melton Mowbray, not far away. He could not make much of guns, gun barrels and breech blocks as subject matter, though everybody on the range was very helpful, and the commandant, a Colonel Skentlebury, played Bach to him in the evenings in the local church.

His assiduity was soon rewarded, however, with a six-month contract carrying a salary of £325, payable in three instalments, that was contingent on the delivery of works which the Committee considered to warrant payment. All original drawings and paintings (including preliminary sketches) done during the period concerned, and all rights of reproduction, were to be vested in the Crown. This contract came into effect on 1 January 1941, and it was only then, therefore, that Graham became a fully employed war artist. With the relative security which the contract provided, Graham decided to move back to the White House that December (1940). He felt nostalgic for Kent, and the need to 'mind his Ps and Qs', as he put it,[12] at Upton House was very wearing. He even felt that he might be heading for a nervous breakdown. After a day spent trying to portray the reality, the feel of a bombed home, to have to change for dinner with, say, Maurice Bowra, the Warden of Wadham College, Oxford, must indeed have been tiresome. Yet it was impossible to enjoy the benefits of Clark's patronage without some of the snags.

Another Clark contact was about to bear fruit, in the shape of Graham's first, and only, design for a ballet. Graham had been a modest balletomane at Goldsmiths'. While at Chelsea in the 1930s, he had taken considerable interest in the plays of W. H. Auden and Christopher Isherwood that were being performed by Group Theatre. Graham's Chelsea colleague, Robert Medley, was the main stage designer. Henry Moore had designed a mask for Auden's first play, *The Dance of Death*. John Piper designed *Trial of a Judge* for Stepher Spender, his first experience of the stage. But Graham had not become professionally involved.

The Clarks were ballet enthusiasts. Among their friends in that world were Frederick Ashton and Margot Fonteyn, respectively principal choreographer and prima ballerina of the Sadler's Wells company, which had been founded in 1931, and Constant Lambert, the composer, conductor and pianist. Periodically, Margot Fonteyn stayed near Upton with the designer and painter Theyre Lee-Elliott, a friend of Clark's from schooldays at Winchester. Clark had taken Graham over to meet her in May 1940, on her twenty-first birthday, shortly after the company had narrowly escaped from Holland during Hitler's *Blitzkrieg*.[13]

One upshot of these contacts was that Graham was invited by Ashton to do the sets for his next ballet, originally intended to be based on Tchaikovsky's incidental music to *The Tempest*.[14] In the event Ashton decided instead on a choreographic fantasy on Schubert's piano Fantasia in C, named *The Wanderer* after the song which supplied the theme for one of the movements.

In December Graham went down to Dartington Hall in Devon, where the company was resting and rehearsing, to see a run-through of the ballet, and thought it an 'awful mess',[15] as he told Jane Clark. As backcloths he produced nothing novel: simply two medium-sized (8 inches by 10 inches) gouaches of Pembrokeshire landscapes, one of them closely related to an earlier work. These were then squared up and enormously enlarged by other hands. The costumes, for which Graham was also responsible and which were being made by Matilda Etches, were a novel assignment and proved to be decidedly difficult.

The first performance was on 26 January 1941, at the New Theatre (now the Albery) in the West End: matinées only, to avoid the Blitz, which had begun in earnest the previous September. Constant Lambert and Hilda Gaunt provided music from two pianos. The critical reception was mixed, but Margot Fonteyn's performance was widely praised, as were those of Michael Somes and Pamela May as the young lovers.

If Graham's decor drew one or two favourable comments, the costumes, on which Kathleen had given her advice, were poorly received. At one stage Robert Helpmann, the Wanderer himself, was flanked by two pairs of young men in shorts—'one of the most unfortunate costumes in modern ballet, with its suggestion of the Boy Scout movement, or even the Hitler Youth', David Vaughan later called them, perhaps over-severely, in his book on Ashton.[16] After the London season, *The Wanderer* went on a provincial tour with other items but achieved no lasting place in the repertoire. Nonetheless Graham had enjoyed the exercise and ended up as an admirer of Ashton's choreography.

The ballet had eaten into his official time, but he had taken to walking through the bombed City at twilight and had done a number of sketchbook notes. He now decided to get down in earnest to recording the destruction of London, which had increasingly become a substitute rather than a preparation for the long-feared German invasion. The most intensive bombing of the capital had taken place during the previous autumn, when Graham had been mainly in Wales and Gloucestershire. Cardiff and Swansea, by contrast, suffered most heavily when Graham was in London. But when one is being bombed, it is the bomb nearest that counts, not the overall tonnage of high explosive and incendiaries dropped.

It was January 1941. On a typical day, Graham said,[17] he would arrive from Kent with very spare paraphernalia: a sketch book, two or three coloured chalks, a pencil and an apparently watertight pass—though, in fact, he was arrested several times, especially in the East End (when penetrating cordoned-off areas). He would look around. 'I will never forget those extraordinary first encounters: the silence, the absolute dead silence, except every now and again a thin tinkling of falling glass—a noise which reminded me of some of the music of Debussy.' He started off in a flattened 5-acre area just north of St Paul's Cathedral. There was a terrible stench about, perhaps of burnt dirt, and just a few policemen to be seen. Occasionally, there was the crash of a collapsing building.

I would start to make perfunctory drawings here and there; gradually it was borne in on me amid all this destruction how singularly one shape would impinge on another. A lift shaft, for instance, the only thing left from what had obviously been a very tall building . . . with a very strong lateral fall, suggested a wounded tiger in a painting by Delacroix.

At first he was a bit shy. Then he grew bolder and went into some of the ruins. One was a factory for making women's coats. 'All the floors had gone, but the staircase remained, as very often happened. And there were machines, their entrails hanging through the floors, but looking extraordinarily beautiful at the same time.' Here too, amid the destruction, Graham was spotting correspondences between different worlds: the wounded lift shaft, the entrails of machines. Both were among his most memorable images in this series.

In the East End, where homes rather than offices had been destroyed, the atmosphere was more tragic. Even a mattress blown into the middle of the street looked more like a body than a mattress, and Graham at first thought that meat spewed on to the street from a bombed butcher's was human flesh. He became tremendously interested in the perspectives of destruction offered by bombed terraces of houses in Silvertown, which seemed to recede into infinity, the windowless blocks like sightless eyes. The resulting studies, one of which is in the Tate Gallery, capture the feeling of desolation to perfection. They were done with the aid of photographs which Graham had taken, applying to Dickey for a photographic pass in mid-May. It was, he explained, difficult to draw in some places 'without arousing a sense of resentment in the people', who may have felt he was capitalizing on their misfortunes. It was perhaps Graham's first use of photographs as an aid to drawing, which not infrequently—as in the case of Silvertown—extended to squaring them up with a sharp edge for more accurate reference. Photographs being frequently deceptive, they are by no means an infallible guide, and he remained an amateurish photographer.

It was at much the same period that Henry Moore was doing his sketches of Londoners sheltering in the Underground system. At first, he had been reluctant to do work as a war artist. 'But when I saw the shelters, and got caught in them one night, and saw all the people undressing their children and putting them to bed with the trains going by, it was quite something,' he recalled.[18] Where Moore generally used chalk, pen and watercolour, Graham often used pencil and gouache in addition. Technique aside, Moore's work is much more serene and classical in mood, and he has the sculptor's preoccupation with the movement of the human figure.

That summer of 1941 Moore, John Piper and Graham shared an

exhibition which opened at Temple Newsam, the large, rambling museum on the outskirts of Leeds, on 21 July. Each was to have a mini-retrospective, and Graham was decidedly bothered by the difficulties of borrowing works from private purchasers. 'Provincial loan shows aren't worth it by a long chalk,' he complained to Dickey, who had referred to a war drawing to be shown as 'abstract'. 'I'm glad you used inverted commas,' Graham wrote, 'as it is really a very close and exact study of what these bombs do—apart perhaps from the colour.'

The Leeds City Galleries were then run by Philip Hendy, who was to succeed Clark after the war as Director of the National Gallery and now asked him, as a known sponsor of the three artists (Clark was sometimes nicknamed the Earl of Moore and Sutherland) to open the exhibition. They all travelled up together by train with their wives and Colin and Morna Anderson. Jane Clark had bought braces for the men decorated with seductive mermaids, and provided a dozen half-bottles of Orvieto Secco, which they hung in their raffia jackets over each seat.[19] It was a warm summer afternoon, and there was a general feeling of escape from the worries of war. Hendy greeted the jolly group soberly and nervously, anxious about how the great Clark would react to his efforts. In fact, the exhibition was a considerable success. Graham showed thirty works, dating back to 1936 and including a recent oil landscape. Clark lent five, Anderson three. 'Hendy did a really splendid job,' Kathleen wrote to the critic Eric Newton,[20] with whose *European Painting and Sculpture* Graham was then much taken.

A work which Graham perhaps did too late for Leeds, and which has since secured a niche in Sutherland literature, was shown that July at the Leicester Galleries in London and found a friendly owner. 'Terribly late, I went today to see the show at the Leicester Galleries, was instantly smitten by the same lightning which struck your "Blasted Oak"—and bought it, blast it!—which I ought not to have done,' Eddy Sackville-West wrote to Graham on 31 July. This largish (15 inches by 12 inches) pen-and-wash drawing, in which the stricken tree resembles a cross between Hokusai's *The Wave* and a snarling sea lion, was a virtuoso piece of draughtsmanship and suggested that Graham's sense of drama had been quickened by his war experiences.

Armed with another six-month contract and refreshed by a short holiday in the Gower Peninsula in Wales, Graham went off, in the autumn of 1941, to tackle steel and munition works in Cardiff and Swansea. Among the factories he visited was a Guest, Keen and Baldwin works in Cardiff. Still fascinated by fire, he was much struck by 'the very primitive method of making steel from stones thrown in with iron, mixed, of course, with chemicals', he recalled, and the danger to the workers from those great vats of molten iron.[21] 'I am never surprised when steel workers ask for a rise. It was a Dantesque kind of atmosphere.'

Here his beloved reds and oranges could glow through a rich gloom of black. He caught the long scoops plunging into the furnace openings, the metal containers like great, encrusted mouths pouring molten iron into ladles, moulds glowing with their molten cargo and the almost suppliant look of the strange towers of the blast furnaces. Here groups of men appeared for the first time in Graham's work, stripped to the waist, only dimly seen through the smoke and gloom, probing a furnace with giant rods, tapping and examining others. Here and there flashes of green and violet add to the sombrely infernal atmosphere.

Graham had to fight to keep his petrol allowance. A Women's Voluntary Service driver had been suggested. He explained to Dickey:

the whole difficulty lies in being present at certain variable times, and at different factories, in order to watch operations at the exact time they occur. When I go to the works in the morning, for instance, they may say that a 'tap' will take place at 1.30. Meanwhile I have to go back for a quick lunch (no time to get in touch with WVS driver unless she is prepared to wait all day) and rush back to the works at 1.30. This is a typicle [sic] sort of happening. . . .

He got his petrol.

He found time too for some literary excursions. One was a BBC radio-broadcast discussion in November 1941 with Moore, Clark and V. S. Pritchett, on Art and Life.[22] Those were more formal days. It was 'Yes, of course, Sutherland', and 'You seem to be assuming, Clark', or 'What you mean, I take it, Pritchett. . . .' The main theme was the role of emotion in the artist's work. It was the force of the emotion in the presence of, say, bomb damage that determined and shaped the pictorial form one chose, Graham said. If sordidness and anguish were implied, one invented forms which were their pictorial essence—symbols of reality.

Then came the famous letter to Colin Anderson, printed in the April 1942 issue of *Horizon*. Anderson had told Graham that he wanted to visit some of the places Graham had painted. Graham said he would never find them, since he had altered so much: the letter was a sort of guide. The two men were close at that time. Strangely, however, the fair copy of the letter, found among Graham's papers, opens not with 'Dear Colin' but with 'Dear Peter'. That could only have been Peter Watson, *Horizon*'s backer. It would have been in character for him to say, as the original addressee, 'would it not look better if it were addressed to someone *outside* the magazine?'

As a war artist, Graham was not immune to enrolment in the Home Guard, the citizens' army formed, originally, to save middle-aged volunteers for military service from being cold-shouldered. He had volunteered for it in 1940 but was away too much. Now he was based at Trottiscliffe again and joined in May 1942, periodically doing guard duty, sleeping at the local waterworks—and parading in his uniform, to the detectable benefit, Kathleen recalled, of his rather round-shouldered posture. He turned down a suggestion that he should become an officer, preferring to muck in with the (ageing) lads.

In June he headed for Cornwall and the assignment which was to produce perhaps his finest work as a war artist: the tin mine at Pendeen, on the north side of the narrow peninsula. It was not strictly a 'war subject', any more than steel production, but it was all part of the war effort, and British tin was urgently needed to compensate for lost imports. Graham did not argue: he was delighted to explore 'a world of such beauty that I shall never forget it'.

'The mines are stupendous and thrilling to a degree which I wouldn't have believed possible,' he wrote to the Clarks in a letter showing him as a diminutive black figure 1200 feet below the surface—which was in parts under the sea—and with writing running up the lift-shaft.

> Life below is awe-inspiring. . . . the records I make should either be easily the best I've done or a failure. . . . the miners are grand, handsome da Vinci types who move easily. I like them very much and have ideas for one or two portraits (perhaps two combined in one design) in addition to any other work.[23]

There were hair-raising moments. Graham was afraid that to go down in the lift would bring on claustrophobia, so he was taken down in a sort of bucket. 'Put your feet on either side of the bucket and we'll hold on to the rope,' he was told, and he dropped down the 1200 feet like a bullet. The last stage was by ladder. Pitch dark and 100 feet of ladder: I know I'm going to faint, he thought. In fact, there were staging posts, and he could not have fallen the whole way.

Some of the tunnels were a mile long, and at first he had to mark his way on the walls in chalk to avoid getting lost. 'Far from the main shaft, the sense of remoteness was tangible and the distances seemed endless. Faintly, far away, was the sound of work on other levels.' The diagonally descending shafts which followed the veins of metal from one tunnel to a lower one revealed precipitous perspectives of extraordinary beauty.

> Often one would come across a miner sitting in a niche in a wall, like a statue, immobile. . . . one would flatten oneself against the wall when

trucks passed. . . . All was humid. The walls dripped water, and the only light was from the acetylene lamps fixed to each man's helmet.

Graham would draw underground from 9.30 a.m. to one o'clock and work up his sketches in the afternoon, when the mine was closed for blasting fumes to clear. During these very satisfying weeks he stayed with his Goldsmiths' friend, Edward Bouverie Hoyton, who had been Principal of the Penzance School of Art for a year, and his wife Inez, who lent him her studio. Through them Graham met Ben Nicholson and Barbara Hepworth; Naum Gabo, the Russian-born sculptor who had arrived in London in 1935; and Adrian Stokes, the writer, all of whom lived not far off, at St Ives. It was, surprisingly, the first time he had met Nicholson, whom he found 'very agreeable and pleasant', he told Clark.

Clark urged Graham to take his time working out the implications of what he had found in those extraordinary depths: the Committee would not expect to see any results for months. Graham spent an initial three weeks there, then went back again after a short break and spent much of the rest of the year working on his drawings.

As befitted the subterranean and darkly mineralogical nature of the setting, his colours were more subdued than they had been in the glow of the steel works—mainly reds, browns, blacks and yellows—and his textured effects with ink, pencil, chalk, wash and gouache were equally subtly orchestrated. For the first time, human figures were not just a part of the composition but, in many instances, the main subject. With enormous tenderness, Graham portrayed his da Vinci miners wielding their drills or resting in one of those wall cavities. Several he showed in close-up, pipe jutting from a finely aquiline profile. Without being sentimentalized, the miners exude a passive acceptance of their hard life. Looking back on these portraits in later life, Graham realized that from them to his formal portraits was not such a big step after all.[24] In other drawings the miners were more generalized, and there were evocative inscriptions, such as:

> Suggest miner in distance coming round curve of slope (very strong feeling of shut-in-ness and weight of stone). Miner emerges from entrance of slope. Very mysterious. Approach associated with noise of boots and falling stones and with approaching light of lamp. Remember light flesh colour derived from light reflected from close walls.

Despite his contractual obligation to hand over all his production, Graham hung on to many sketches—and so, Kenneth Clark believed, did most of the war artists. 'They probably sent in more than half the ones they did. But they would not have been human not to have kept back some of the best,' he reckoned.[25] Graham no doubt disliked the idea that the harder he worked, the more he handed over. But he gave value for money, delivering ten fully worked studies in December 1942. 'The Committee are more than satisfied with the artist's output, both in quality and number,' its acting secretary (Dickey having returned to Education) observed in an inter-office memo of 10 December.

By now Graham was pursuing another semi-literary sideline: illustrating a volume of recent poems by one of the animators of the 1936 Surrealist exhibition, David Gascoyne. These were published eventually in December 1943 by Tambimuttu's *Poetry London*. Meary Tambimuttu, always known as Tambi, was an erratically brilliant Tamil from Ceylon (as it then was), whose flair T. S. Eliot, for one, much admired. Herbert Read suggested Graham as illustrator, Tambi recalled.[26] 'David Gascoyne liked the idea. Peter Watson was also interested in the project, so I did it.' Graham did eighteen drawings loosely related to Gascoyne's often violent verse. Seven were used—evocative landscapes full of mysterious rocks, moons, tongues of flame and some strange human figures. It was being designed, Graham wrote to the painter Keith Vaughan, 'as something to be read and carried about in the pocket . . . slightly reminiscent of the "knockabout" quality of the original editions of Blake's *Songs of Innocence*.'[27]

At first Graham found Tambi 'immensely stimulating and intelligent . . . a poet publisher who, to say the least, anticipates one's ideas', he told Colin Anderson. Later he came to feel that Tambi's somewhat Bohemian life-style was intruding on his professional activities.[28] During the enthusiastic phase Graham did three lithographs for the May 1943 issue of *Poetry London* (No.9), illustrating some lines from *Hieroglypics of the Life of Man*, by the seventeenth-century English poet Francis Quarles. David Gascoyne had introduced him to Quarles's work, which he found enchanting, and to that of the Jesuit Emblemists. Graham liked to quote Quarles's lines:

> Ev'n so this little world of living clay,
> The pride of nature glorified by art. . . .
> Triumphs awhile, then droops, ethen decays.[29]

For the same issue Graham did a cover design of the magazine's symbol, a lyre bird; thirty-six years later, when the magazine was revived, he was to draw another, more phoenix than lyre bird.

Clark called Graham's illustration to Gascoyne's poems 'the most complete realization I have yet seen of your landscapes of the spirit'. He wrote solicitously:[30] 'the externalization of this intense and subjective inner landscape must impose a very great strain, and my only fear is that you will suffer from nervous exhaustion.' That was the easiest part, Graham replied.

> I could have gone on making innumerable drawings of such a kind, since it is one of the ways I naturally think. But to decide the precise position of a line—or the direction of one mass in relation to another—that's the difficulty and the sweat, and it's so immensely important—the verification *by the eye* of what has been done.

No doubt for some more technically facile painters the opposite would have been true: sorting out the images would have been harder than rendering them. On the danger of losing inspiration, to which Clark had alluded, Graham wrote:

> I don't think one's muse deserts one unless one is physically exhausted, or unhappy, or very far from some sort of state of grace. Mine deserted me very much when I taught too much. I think it deserts one if one does too much of the same kind of thing in too much the same way.

Graham's reputation, spread by the regular exhibitions of war artists' work at the National Gallery and up and down the country, and by booklets with forewords by such disparate writers as Stephen Spender and J. B. Morton ('Beachcomber'), was bringing in a variety of design commissions: a lithograph for the Council for the Encouragement of Music and the Arts, forerunner of the Arts Council; some more china for Fennemore; a fabric design, possibly for Courtauld's. He wrote of these to Clark. He felt he needed the money, Graham told him, but feared that 'too much adulteration may be a bad financial and spiritual policy—in the long run'.[31] Clark recommended a severely limited number of designs every year. 'You know I am not much in sympathy with the modern notion that the artist must be in closer touch with the common man,' he wrote. 'I believe that magic and mystery are of the essence of art.' But there was the opposite danger of in-breeding. Design could act as a link with the world and could actually benefit his painting.[32]

Searching for a new subject for his war work in the spring of 1943, Graham spent six weeks exploring Imperial Chemical Industries concerns, including the Dye Stuffs group at Manchester, where M & B and anti-malaria specifics were made, but mainly some limestone quarries at Hindlow, near the Derbyshire spa of Buxton. The restrictions made, not in the interests of defence but out of fear of trade competition, were extremely irksome. 'Buxton was full of the aged and infirm, loudly complaining (in a

perfectly excellent hotel) that *Salmon* was *boiled* and not grilled and so on,'
he told Colin Anderson in May.[33] Looking back on the experience, he
wrote to Eric Newton:

> In the quarries the chaos of form was bewildering. I had to find for my
> pictures an *ordered* chaos, which still retained characteristics of chaos. . . .
> it was the idea of a quarry and what it stands for *transcending* nature, and
> formed by the mind and emotions, which interested me.[34]

One or two images added something: a study of a worker loosening stones
from the stepped face of the quarry seemed to prefigure some of Graham's
later mineral 'conglomerates'. But in general it failed to stimulate him as
London's destruction, the steel works and tin mines had done.

Graham's exhibitions of 1938 and 1941, and the voyagings of his war
drawings (including overseas—two were sunk with 109 others in a boat
heading for South America), had made him an inspiration to younger
British artists of a 'romantic' bent, such as Michael Ayrton, John Minton,
Robert MacBryde, Robert Colquhoun, Keith Vaughan and John Craxton.
Ayrton, Vaughan and Craxton were friends. That summer of 1943 Craxton
and Peter Watson joined Graham and Kathleen for a holiday at Lleithyr
Farm in Pembrokeshire. Craxton had met Graham over lunch at the Ivy
restaurant in London in 1942 and again at Peter Watson's flat in Palace
Gate. He recalled:[35]

> Graham was my hero. It was Graham who had suggested that Lucian
> Freud and I should go to Goldsmiths' College under Clive Gardiner. I
> was well aware of the danger of being influenced by Graham, and I
> certainly had been influenced by his work earlier, around 1941. What was
> wonderful about him was that he did not want to make one do Graham
> Sutherlands.

Graham helped Craxton—who was 19 years younger—to extract the
elements from a landscape and to invent it afresh. They went drawing
together in Wales, and Graham demonstrated how he took a detail of
landscape and enlarged it. He showed Craxton where he had drawn
Entrance to Lane: at the estuary end of the path from the road to Sandy
Haven. 'I asked him where he got the leaves, as there weren't any, and he
said: "I brought them in from somewhere else." ' During the war, he said,
Graham was always complaining that he would have to go back to teaching.
'Peter Watson and I would say he was the best painter in the country—
which he was at the time—and how could he?' With youthful
pretentiousness, he once asked Graham: 'Would you say paintings were
made of two facets, flesh and bones?' 'No, flesh and spirit,' Graham replied.
Exit Craxton. Graham would say: 'I want you to meet this fantastic painter,

Francis Bacon. He's like a cross between Vuillard and Picasso.' Craxton and Lucian Freud seem to have first met Bacon at the White House in 1943. Graham had made contact with Freud after admiring some drawings of his in the May 1943 issue of *Horizon*. Bacon, then alternating between a cottage in Petersfield, Hants, and a studio in Glebe Place, Chelsea, had resuscitated his acquaintance with Graham in February, with a letter suggesting that they get together for dinner in London.

In retrospect we can see that the period 1943-47 was when Graham was most closely integrated with the small world of contemporary painting of a linear, English tendency and was regarded by a number of younger artists as its natural leader. From 1938 until the time of his first Mediterranean work, in 1947, was also the period when he was generally held in highest esteem by his fellow artists and by art critics. Broadly speaking, his reputation with these two groups declined as his public fame grew. From the end of the war onwards, there would always be those who 'so much preferred his early Welsh drawings'—and not only among painters and critics.

And now, for the growing band of culture-hungry, war-weary *aficionados*, came the first book on Graham's work. It was by Eddy Sackville-West and part of a pioneering new series, Penguin Modern Painters. Other titles were devoted to Henry Moore, Duncan Grant, Paul Nash, Matthew Smith and John Piper, shortly followed by Edward Bawden, Stanley Spencer, Ben Nicholson and Frances Hodgkins. The series had been suggested, almost inevitably, by the ubiquitous Kenneth Clark, whose friend William Emrys Williams was then editor-in-chief of Penguin Books, as well as a prime mover in the Council for the Encouragement of Music and the Arts. The ball landed in the court of Eunice Frost, then a youthful director of Penguin. 'K. Clark drew up a list of the artists he thought should be used,' she recalled.[36]

He said: 'If you think this is a good idea, you can cost it and we can see how many colour plates there should be, and so on.' In those days we worked fast and instinctively, and without too much agonizing. They were the first thing of their sort, which tried to show what artists of this calibre were doing. The standard of production was quite a big achievement under wartime conditions.

Graham was conscientious but appreciative. 'Being a technician, I think he knew the difficulties the printers were under.' There were thirty-two plates, of which sixteen were in very good colour.

Eunice Frost was transfixed by her first sight of Sackville-West. 'He looked such a suffering, delicate and emaciated little man. I felt he might blow away like a leaf.' But his text showed foresight as well as insight: he saw Graham as at heart a portrait painter, whose subjects had so far been mainly tree trunks, grass blades, old stones rather than human faces: and there were some nice phrases amid the rather lush vegetation of his prose. But why did Graham allow him to say he had been at boarding school? Since he had been a day boy, it was misleading, if technically true.

Kenneth Clark also played a part in the making of the first film about the work of Britain's war artists. Called *Out of Chaos*, it was directed by Jill Craigie (later Mrs Michael Foot) and concentrated on Graham, Henry Moore, Stanley Spencer and Paul Nash. Jill Craigie had been writing documentaries for the British Council and had never made a film. 'I was very keen on art,' she recalled.[37] 'I went to Kenneth Clark, and he agreed to be in it, and because of that, the others fell into line.' Films were regarded as rather frivolous in those days. Jill Craigie was suspiciously pretty and wholly inexperienced.

> I discovered later I was suspect to Graham for another reason. I was then living in Malcolm MacDonald's house. He was High Commissioner in Canada but still an MP, and there was much criticism of him, because his constituents were in effect disfranchised. Just because I occupied his house, Graham thought I was some sort of MacDonaldite.[38] I wasn't. I was on the far left.

Although they did not discuss politics, Graham made it clear that he was a socialist.

The film was made for a company called Two Cities, which had been set up by an Italian lawyer, Filippo del Giudice. He had negotiated his way out of internment on the Isle of Man and was backed by the Rank Organization. Sidney Box was the producer, his associate the son of a Belfast newspaper proprietor, William MacQuitty. Graham was fascinated by MacQuitty's tales of his days in the Punjab Light Horse and as a banker in China, less fascinated by Jill Craigie.

He wanted to be filmed in the Cornish tin mines, which, he wrote to MacQuitty in August 1943, 'had for me a much closer relation to the "feel" and "tempo" of my real work than any subjects I have tackled, except perhaps the "Blitz" subjects'. They reconnoitred in Cornwall, and Jill Craigie was much impressed by the speed and skill with which, from memory, Graham did some pencil portraits of the miners after they had resurfaced one day. The tin mines turned out to be too difficult to film and light, however. MacQuitty suggested Welsh steel works, but Graham thought these would look hackneyed and would be hard to relate to his work, in which colour was particularly important (the film was to be in black and white). So they compromised, unsatisfactorily, selecting the Derbyshire limestone quarries, where he was shown sketching. At the end of the exercise, his studio was partially recreated at some film studios in Merton Park—his first return to the scene of his early childhood.

Graham was a more self-conscious participant than the others. He was keen, Jill Craigie recalled, to be filmed in his safety helmet, to show he was not doing a cissy job while others risked their lives. Moore, filmed observing sleeping shelterers at Holborn Underground station, had shown rapid understanding of the complex lighting system. Scruffy little Stanley Spencer—shown talking to workers on Clydeside—had enjoyed shocking them. 'Of course, all my painting is masturbation,' he would loudly explain in a crowded railway compartment.

The film finally ran to twenty-eight minutes. It was privately shown to film critics in December 1944 and released soon afterwards as a supporting 'extra'. The critics found it a well intentioned and novel attempt to interpret modern English painting to a largely unsympathetic public, but the difficulties of showing paintings on film had not, it was reckoned, been overcome, and Graham in particular was held to have suffered from the lack of colour.

By the autumn of 1943, when Graham's salary as a war artist was increased from £650 to £750 a year, he seemed to have 'peaked'; it would evidently take a wholly new experience to inspire him to produce his best again. Meanwhile, he jogged along. Open-cast coalmines near Wakefield, Yorkshire, yielded some fine panoramic studies of the scarred land, with more detailed images of excavators depositing waste earth on little conical hillocks. Probably in the first half of 1944 there were also some studies of Woolwich Arsenal. Other commissions were not lacking. Graham did the fabric design—on a lobsterish theme—of which he had written to Clark, and a visit to Northampton in February 1944 produced much to think about.

Kenneth Clark had been invited to 'unveil' the *Madonna and Child* which Henry Moore had done for St Matthew's church, some 2 miles from the town centre, at the invitation of its vicar, the Rev. Walter Hussey, a lover of modern art and music. Hussey had been struck by Moore's work at a National Gallery show of war drawings. H. S. Williamson, head of the Chelsea School of Art—evacuated to Northampton in 1940—brought them together over dinner. Eventually, when the *Madonna* was nearly finished, he asked Moore which painter he thought might do something for the opposite transept, mentioning as possibilities Stanley Spencer, Graham Sutherland,

John Piper, Matthew Smith, Ben Nicholson, and Barbara Hepworth. Moore replied: 'Of those, the only one who might do something of the quality you require is Graham Sutherland.'

That February, Hussey put the proposition to Graham and showed him the site. 'What do you have in mind?' Graham asked. Hussey replied: 'I thought, knowing your work and knowing El Greco, with whom you have perhaps certain affinities, perhaps an *Agony in the Garden*.' Graham said he had just been copying an El Greco (perhaps a reference to the 1939 paraphrase). 'Two or three minutes later he added—and I remember his exact words—"One's ambition would be to do a *Crucifixion* of a significant size. Would that be all right?"' Hussey recalled,[39] and he answered: 'Absolutely fine.'

There it was, a landmark-in-waiting. There was no deadline, and Graham did not tackle it until his war work was over. Meanwhile, he reflected on it. There was no reason why such a theme, and the great myths, should not be tackled if one could feel strongly enough about them, he told Keith Vaughan two months later. It was important to understand the subject and not just to illustrate it—and to believe in its reality. But he seems to have had doubts about the Crucifixion theme: 'It is an embarrassing situation, to say the least of it,' he told Vaughan, 'to contemplate a man nailed to a piece of wood in the presence of his friends.'[40]

A three-man show at the Lefevre Gallery in New Bond Street—later postponed—was being mooted for the autumn of 1944. That August Graham went off with Kathleen to Pembrokeshire for further material, staying first at the Mariner's Arms in Haverfordwest with John Craxton and Lucian Freud, then retreating from their high spirits to a cottage at Sandy Haven. Craxton took them over to Picton Castle, not far away, to introduce them to Sir John Philipps. In his last decade Graham was to have many dealings with the Philipps family, which was large, complex and rich; but not with Sir John, a gently eccentric, cultured bachelor who died in a hot bath after taking a sleeping pill at his flat in Albany, Piccadilly, in 1948. (Curiously, Peter Watson was to die a very similar, equally premature death in 1956.) 'The castle was being used by the army,' Craxton recalled. 'Johnny had a wing. It was very romantic: rough grass with sheep grazing around.'

Once back in Wales, it was 'G. Pembrokeshire Sutherland' (as he once called himself) again, and 'the ideas started welling up and crowding each other for daylight', as he told Kenneth Clark.[41] A whole series of paintings and drawings sprang from this trip: *Horned Forms*, a largish oil now in the Tate Gallery, and many studies for it, all inspired by a dried-out tree stump set in a glowing, invented landscape; and numerous *Triple Tiered*

Landscapes, and *Landscapes with Pointed Hills*. Here too he conceived two ravishing oils called *The Lamp*, based on a paraffin lamp in the Sandy Haven cottage.

By now—as *The Lamp* almost proclaims—peace was in prospect at last. In June Normandy was invaded, and on 25 August Paris was liberated. After Wales Graham fancied an unpaid month or two. 'I'm far from unmindful of my good fortune during the war,' he told Clark. 'War art has not been irksome until recently. On the contrary, I have learned a great deal. . . .'

His last fling as war artist was to be in liberated France. The initial idea was that he should have a look at the V2 rocket constructions along the French coast, but these proved to be too inaccessible. So instead, after a month of strenuous endeavour by the Air Ministry, he was sent off in war correspondent's uniform, on 9 December, to Paris, in quest of flying-bomb ('doodle-bug') sites in the region. 'It was the first time I'd been abroad in my life,' he recalled.[42] 'Before the war I hadn't been able to afford it, and before that I was leading a really insular English life. When we were children, it was thought too much of an upheaval to travel abroad.'

Nobody in Paris was very helpful. There was a lot of hanging about, he wrote to Kathleen on 13 December (it was their first extended separation). 'The whole thing so far has been one long muddle.' The journalists, mainly American, at the Scribe Hotel were distinctly unfriendly, the noise was awful—and he missed her madly. 'It's jolly tiring walking about a city; as you know, I always hate doing so in London. I've got a map, and unashamedly flaunt it.' However, a bored RAF group captain suggested some marshalling yards near Paris, badly bombed by the RAF and with railway engines piled on top of each other. These yards, at Trappes, provided the former Derby apprentice with some fine studies of wrecked locomotives: thrown on one side, dismembered, noses buried in bomb craters.

With great difficulty, he located the flying-bomb sites at St Leu d'Esserent, some 30 miles north-west of Paris, and was astonished by what he found there. The Germans had taken over caves in which the French had grown mushrooms and had fortified them to store the flying bombs. The RAF bombs had made holes in the tops of the hills, and blue sky could be seen from the caves.

I've never seen such a panoramic piece of devastation in my life—for miles the bridges and remnants of houses on either side of the river were like black spokes. A lot of Germans had been killed inside the caves, and there was a terrible sweet smell of death in them. . . . There were bits and pieces of people knocking about, and I did draw some, but they were not allowed to be shown; and I think probably rightly.[43]

Other relics were more poignant, like an abandoned volume of Goethe.

Graham returned to Kent and Kathleen on Christmas Eve, after just a fortnight in France. He spent the next few months working up his French sketches and preparing for the Lefevre show, re-scheduled for April. An attack of mumps in February was a set back. His relations with the War Artists Advisory Committee petered out in wrangling over his expenses for France: the Information Ministry's finance division drew the line at the new pyjamas and braces which Graham had bought for the trip but allowed an extra five shillings a day for meals. That spring of 1945 President Roosevelt died, and the remains of the civilized world reeled at the horrors of the concentration camps. Photographs of what was found there and in the extermination camps were to affect profoundly Graham's treatment of the Crucifixion. The war ended with the Japanese surrender on 15 August 1945.

The War Artists Advisory Committee collected some 6000 pictures in all from 300 artists.[44] In 1946 these were distributed among national, provincial and Commonwealth museums and public galleries. Of the fully worked up paintings and drawings which Graham surrendered to the Committee, twenty-three went to the Imperial War Museum, where more than a dozen languished until 1970 in a box categorized as 'odds and sods', and a further eighty-seven went to twenty-eight different public galleries.

According to Joseph Darracott of the Imperial War Museum, it was agreed after the war that artists could keep their sketches.[45] With Graham, the distinction between finished works and preparatory sketches was always a fine one. In the event, he retained more than 250, some of which were indeed very small and very sketchy.

Slightly to his own regret, one senses, he had a rather protected war, thanks to Kenneth Clark, who did not want to lose him. Three gifted artists, Thomas Hennell, Eric Ravilious and Albert Richards, died on official duty. Some of Graham's contemporaries travelled far and dangerously: Anthony Gross was in Egypt and the Far East, where he crawled to within 20 yards of the Japanese lines; Edward Bawden ranged through the Middle East; Feliks Topolski was virtually everywhere, including Moscow when the Germans were only 55 miles away; Edward Ardizzone took part in the Dunkirk retreat and was later in North Africa and Italy.

Looking back, Graham felt that on the whole his imagination would not have been aroused by mechanized warfare on a grand scale. House-to-house fighting might have been another matter: sudden uprisings, revolutions and riots had 'mysterious, timeless qualities of drama which grip the imagination', he found. At the root of his work, he concluded, lay memory and emotion, which modified and transformed facts. But the facts were a necessary starting point. 'In the particular context of modern warfare it is more than likely that I would have found these facts difficult or impossible to gather.'

At first the task of being a war artist had seemed alien and journalistic. Then Graham came to see that it required not so much a change of approach as an adaptation of his usual sketching techniques and a broadening of subject matter. For the last four years his 'encounters' had been mainly with his fellow men, with their factories, their machines, their toil, their sufferings. It had been a deeply educational experience, in both human and artistic terms. Because most of the war drawings were soon spread thinly around or lost to sight, it surprised many people that Graham, the painter of Welsh landscapes, should turn his hand to religious themes, to portraiture and to the strange affinities between man, nature and machines. Yet there was always an underlying unity in Graham's variety and in his development: even the beautiful textures which he achieved in his war drawings owed something to his years as an etcher. The suffering he recorded implicitly in his Blitz studies helped to prepare him to portray the symbolic sufferings of Christ. His drawings of tin miners and his heightened interest in human psychology were a further step towards portraiture. His renewed contact with the great temples of heavy industry rekindled his love of machinery, first sparked by his year in Derby.

Previously Graham had approached man via nature. The war enabled him to tackle man on his own ground. Man was now part of the oneness of nature.

6

Via a Crucifixion to Maugham

1945-50

GRAHAM'S CAREER as a war artist was over by the spring of 1945. But the Germans did not surrender until 7 May, and the Japanese fought on till mid-August, when the rest of the world was as stunned psychologically as the inhabitants of Hiroshima and Nagasaki were physically by the impact of two atomic bombs. In Europe suffering continued at a high level; the east–west division of Europe created millions of refugees and prefigured the Cold War. The horrors of the time made their mark on Graham. A painter, he believed, is a kind of blotting paper, absorbing impressions and very much part of the world: 'He cannot therefore avoid soaking up the implications of the outer chaos of twentieth-century civilization.'[1]

But for him, as for most Britons, hope prevailed for a time over *Angst*. Though Britain had been, by Continental standards, but lightly scarred by the war, the huge victory of the Labour Party at the general election of July 1945 showed a strong desire for a fresh start.

British painting had been isolated by the war, despite the voyagings of some war artists. Consciously or otherwise, abstract art had been seen to be unsuitably devoid of content and out of tune with the times. The spirit of poetic realism still prevailed, and it was to be a couple of years before the old 1930s thirst for experiment returned, symbolized by Victor Pasmore's dramatic switch to abstraction.

Graham however soon showed that after the *petit-point* of the war drawings he was anxious to broaden his range and open his style to the influence of the great modern masters. The next five years were to find him moving away from Wales and towards France, both spiritually and in actual fact. Not all his admirers welcomed the change. But Pembrokeshire could no longer satisfy fully his inner needs and ambitions.

A mixed show at the Lefevre Gallery in April 1945, in which he had seven oils and four gouaches, gave him a chance to demonstrate how he was evolving. If *The Lamp*, which now made its debut, owed something to Matisse and Braque, it also bore Picasso's imprint, as did *Smiling Woman* and *Woman in a Garden*, which was bought for £68 by Graham's solicitor Wilfrid Evill, who also collected Stanley Spencer's work and porcelain. The woman in question was a Trottiscliffe villager called Mrs Justice, and in different pictures Graham showed her smiling enigmatically beside a hedge, eating an apple and, in an oil not shown on this occasion, picking vegetables. An *Intruding Bull*, thrusting its powerful horned head over a hedge, was no less novel or Picasso-esque. This was bought by Colin Anderson for £85. Others were in Graham's familiar Welsh vein and included a fresh version of the entrance-to-lane theme called *Lane Opening*, which the film producer Michael Balcon bought for £105. When shown at the same gallery in 1975, this picture was priced at a sum well into five figures.

Graham's work—all of which was sold at the private view—must have looked benign indeed by comparison with Francis Bacon's triptych, *Three Studies of Figures at the Base of a Crucifixion*, already replete with the horrors of war. It caused consternation. Reviewing the show in the *New Statesman* of 14 April, Raymond Mortimer found it 'gloomily phallic', a symbol of outrage rather than a work of art. As for Graham, the seemingly extravagant terms in which he had written about the painter six years earlier were commonplace today, Mortimer said: 'If he continues to fulfil himself, he will be one of the great painters of our time.'

Trying to pin down the essence of the change in his work in a letter to Colin Anderson, Graham wrote: 'Whereas hitherto I've tried to invent forms which give a feeling of reality, I now want to try and invent forms which not only give the feeling but something of the appearance as well.' The *Intruding Bull* was the first result, and he thought it aesthetically the best of his recent pictures.[2] In what looked like a discreet thrust at Kenneth Clark, whose munificence must sometimes have been hard to bear, Graham added:

> *I do thank you* for being literally the only one of my earliest supporters who follows what I am trying to do as I try to do it, naturally, and without the slightest prompting on my part. You never seem shocked, never worried as to whether my work is erotic or not or different or not . . . nor do you think my work is always like Samuel Palmer or maddeningly like Picasso, or too hard now or too soft before.

Was Picasso indeed the Dracula of modern painting, sucking the lifeblood of young talent and blocking all roads to progress? Eddy Sackville-West

started a lively controversy in the *New Statesman* at this time by accusing
Michael Ayrton of having said so in a radio broadcast and of having singled
out Graham Sutherland to lead the martyrs from the wood. Yet Sutherland himself admitted that Picasso was the principal influence on the
development of his art.[3] Ayrton defended himself. Graham waded in on 28
April. Painters could borrow forms for good or bad motives, he wrote. They
could be influenced through idolatry, for better or worse, or by a way of
thinking which an older artist had opened up. 'Mr Ayrton says he thinks I
am more influenced by Blake, Palmer and Turner than Picasso. I have been
influenced by these painters, but I cannot and do not intend to weigh
precisely the degree of their impact on my thought as compared with the
impact of Picasso.'

Delighted with the success of the Lefevre show, Graham and Kathleen
went off to Pembrokeshire in mid-April 1945. This time they also met Sir
John Philipps's sister, Sheila (who became Lady Dunsay two years later), on
a visit to Picton Castle. She recalled walking along the foreshore of Picton
estuary that spring. Graham stopped at one stage to sketch the exposed roots
of an oak. He did a very meticulous drawing and asked her: 'What do you
think of that?' 'It's absolutely delightful,' she replied. Graham countered:
'You wait till you see what I do with it.' When he showed it to her later, she
told him: 'I liked the other one better.' 'You see,' he said, 'I've eliminated all
that isn't necessary.'[4] Had Graham *not* eliminated what he considered
unnecessary, his work would doubtless have had wider appeal, but at a
shallower level.

The weather was particularly fine. Graham was pondering his *Crucifixion*
commission, and in particular the crown of thorns. But he had made no
drawings. 'For the first time I started to notice thorn bushes and the
structure of thorn bushes as they pierce the air,' he recalled.[5]

> I made some drawings, and as I made them, a curious change developed.
> As the thorns rearranged themselves, they became, while still retaining
> their own pricking, space-encompassing life, something else—a kind of
> 'stand-in' for a Crucifixion and a crucified head. . . .

The thorns themselves were, of course, quite small. Graham enlarged them.
He saw them as a sort of open sculpture, defining points in space, which he
could use like dividers. He searched for their inner rhythm and pruned away
the inessentials, as with the Picton oak roots. For the next two years he was
to paint these thorns with passion and intensity, reverting to them
sporadically for many years thereafter. From them he developed his 'thorn
heads', which were more sculpturesque and self-contained, but still, he

maintained, close to the reality of what he saw when peering into a thorn hedge or bush. (They were also slightly reminiscent of some of Picasso's sharply distorted heads of the 1930s.) And the blue skies of that April in Pembrokeshire left their mark on these thorn studies. He said:

> The thorns sprang from the idea of potential cruelty—to me they were the cruelty. I attempted to give the idea a double twist, as it were, by setting them in benign circumstances: a blue sky, green grass, Crucifixions under warmth—and blue skies are, in a sense, more powerfully horrifying. . . .

Looking back later, Graham was surprised by how the Mediterranean blues of these thorn skies anticipated the lighter palette which he adopted in the South of France itself.[6]

Kenneth Clark's taste was keeping abreast of Graham's new work at this stage, and he bought a particularly fine *Thorn Tree* that autumn. 'I like it better every day, and get more pleasure from it than from any of your works,' he wrote to Graham in November.

> I said five years ago that waiting to see what you and Henry [Moore] are going to do was one of the few things that kept me going in these times, and I haven't altered in my feelings. Having overcome your detractors, you are now in the process of overcoming your admirers, which is far more difficult (failure to do so by Whistler and Steer was fatal). . . .

That was very heartening, but not much money was coming in. Graham's father's pension had been frozen in occupied Jersey, and he was helping to pay off the resulting accumulated debts. The Lefevre show netted just under £500, but as the cost of materials and framing was rising, that was not pure gain. Graham's war artist's salary was ending, and the future was uncertain. A year before, he and Kathleen had even contemplated going to the USA or 'sliding out of the struggle for places in the sun', and living on honey and rabbits in a cottage on Johnny Philipps's estate in Wales, as Kathleen had written to their friend Cecil Beaton.[7] Above all, Graham was anxious not to be dependent on teaching again.

Against this background, darkened by worries about the tenure of their house in Kent, he concluded various agreements to design textiles. Earlier in 1945 he had done an attractive rose design for Courtauld's through Milner Gray and had signed a contract with the Czech emigré Bernard Ascher, who had commissioned a number of well-known artists (including Graham) to design headscarves for him. Now he contracted with a new Sutherland enthusiast, Hans Juda, to do twenty fabric designs over twelve months for £250.[8]

Juda had settled in Britain in 1933, after being beaten up by a storm trooper when working as a financial journalist in Berlin.[9] In London he started up an export promotion magazine called *Ambassador*, which was at first strongly oriented towards textiles and for which his wife Elsbeth took excellent photographs. He was one of those ebullient, larger-than-life characters, generous yet egocentric, and saw himself not just as publisher and patron but also as an active promoter of good design, in this instance through British textile firms. Graham and John Piper became his favourite artists. He celebrated VE Day in May 1945 by buying a version of *Entrance to Lane*, and among the two dozen Sutherlands which he eventually collected, *Gorse on Sea Wall*, bought from Peter Watson, took pride of place. Graham was to paint his portrait in 1955.

Courtauld's, John Heathcoat and Hill, Brown were among the textile firms which took Graham's designs, the fabrics being used for furnishing and making up clothes. (Kathleen at one stage sported a rose-pattern by Graham to considerable effect.) The contract with Juda was renewed in 1947, and the fee rose to £300.

The most serious financial problem was created by the decision of the owners of the White House, a Mr and Mrs d'Elboux, to sell it on the expiry of the lease, three months after the end of the war. Graham did not have the necessary capital to buy the house. To raise it by conventional methods would involve regular payments, to which his irregular income was ill-suited. First he asked Peter Watson whether he could help, but he did not feel able to.[10] There seemed no choice but to turn again to the ever-supportive Kenneth Clark. 'I don't know whether I dreamed it or not, but did you say that you might be interested in the matter of our house?' Graham wrote to him on 30 October. 'The position is this: W. A. Evill has been acting for us in "beating down" our landlady. She originally asked £5000; dropped to £3000 and now after a good deal of astute bargaining on Evill's part has dropped to £2500.' He explained that owing to the difficulties created by his father's debts in Jersey, he wanted to raise £3000. 'If you feel such a proposition is too much, we shall entirely understand, and think no more about it. . . .'

Clark advanced the capital and guaranteed Graham's overdraft. Graham paid interest at 4½ per cent and eventually repaid the capital. Meanwhile the deeds of the house went to Clark. Graham, a proud man, cannot have enjoyed being so indebted. It is easier to be patron than patronized, and Clark had already done so much to help. Those misgivings apart, it was no doubt a relief to have clinched the deal.

Perhaps more out of loyalty than financial need, Graham agreed with

Clive Gardiner, whom he so admired, to teach once a week at Goldsmiths' from that autumn term of 1945. The arrangement brought Graham up to London on a Tuesday each week, but after two terms it proved impracticable and lapsed.

The big excitement of the winter of 1945 was an exhibition of twenty-four works by Picasso and twenty-five by Matisse at the Victoria and Albert Museum. Those who loathed modern art came to mock; for admirers who had been starved of the work of the two giants of contemporary French painting—Graham's twin deities—the exhibition was confirmation of their continued vitality. If Picasso had taught Graham about the expressive use of form, he learned much from Matisse about space and colour. For Graham, Matisse used colour as a composer uses certain instruments in an orchestra and always with passion and justice.[11]

Picasso was expected in person at a dinner at the French Embassy the evening before the exhibition opened. Graham, Henry Moore, Roland Penrose, Duncan Grant and Herbert Read were among the guests of the ambassador, René Massigli, a collector himself (he bought one of Graham's *Thorns*) and friend of the Clarks. At the last minute, the great man sent a message from Paris that he could not make it. The sort of resentment which Graham's relatively privileged position could arouse was illustrated by an encounter, at this same exhibition, with his old Chelsea colleague Robert Medley. 'I had been in the army in the Middle East, and I had been completely out of it,' Medley recalled.[12]

> Graham, of course, had been in, patronized by K. Clark along with Henry Moore. . . . we encountered each other bang on the steps of the V & A, and Graham cut me dead. I don't know why he did it—whether he wanted only to be associated with success, or what. I found that absolutely unforgivable. But, of course, I forgave him, and we saw each other from time to time. . . .

No one, Medley included, would have denied that Graham had earned his position through ability, intelligence and hard work. The issue was the way in which he handled it, and here his moodiness no doubt played a part, as perhaps did the thinness of Medley's skin.

Certainly, there were friends in plenty. Among the closest at this stage (apart from the Clarks and Colin and Morna Anderson) were Francis Bacon, Eardley Knollys, Raymond Mortimer, Rory Cameron (who had bought *The Lamp*) and Cecil Beaton.

Graham and Kathleen had seen a good deal of Beaton during the war. For a time he had been in love with Peter Watson but his feelings were not reciprocated. Watson often preferred to walk around the garden with Graham, talking about Picasso and Matisse. Kathleen remembered Beaton seething with jealousy indoors and positively stabbing his *petit-point*. Graham and Kathleen had spent the Whitsun weekend of 1945 at Beaton's country home, Ashcombe, a smallish, theatrically decorated house near the Wiltshire village of Tollard Royal. Lord and Lady Weymouth were there: he became Lord Bath the next year, and eventually Graham did his portrait. So were Sir Henry 'Chips' Channon, the American who had become a Conservative MP and married a Guinness, and his friend, the playwright Terence Rattigan. Beaton received them in Austrian garb, Channon recorded in his diary, and 'also there, an uninteresting couple, the Graham Sutherlands. He is a painter.'[13] No meeting of minds *there*.

By the autumn of 1945 Graham's main anxiety was his first show in New York, now due to open on 26 February 1946 at Curt Valentin's Buchholz Gallery, at 32 East 57th Street. Valentin had emigrated from Hamburg in 1937 and had given Henry Moore his first New York show in 1943. He was well acquainted with the British art scene and also handled John Piper.

New York, which played no part in European art before 1939, had then become the focal point for exiled artists. Among those who spent much of the war there were Yves Tanguy, Max Ernst, Marc Chagall, Fernand Léger, Piet Mondrian, André Masson and Matta Echaurren. Their presence had acted like yeast on gifted Americans—some of them also immigrants—like Arshile Gorky, Hans Hofmann, Robert Motherwell, Mark Tobey, Jackson Pollock and Willem de Kooning, who by 1946 were producing work of a quality which later finally destroyed Paris's supremacy. So it was no place to score an easy success. American painters had drawn their own lessons from the French masters in their midst and had moved on to do something bold, new and predominantly abstract.

This exhibition of Graham's came too soon. He had not yet accumulated enough work which embodied and digested fully what he had learned. It must have looked eclectic, with eight oils and twenty-eight gouaches and drawings, ranging from rocky landscapes and a *Horned Form* to a *Lamp*, thorns and thistles and the Picasso-like women. It was the first major showing of the thorns and also of a new theme, here called *Staring Tree Form*. So far just a chalk and gouache drawing, it faintly resembled a rocking-horse with a thatched but semi-human head and a single Cyclopean eye shape. Later Graham worked it up into a balefully staring hybrid called *Chimère I* and *II*, with overtones of Max Ernst and Bacon.

In those days one did not just hop on a plane to New York. Graham did not in fact get there till 1964. It was consoling for him to hear from Valentin in March that the show was 'going very well' and that they had sold nine pictures.[14] Among the buyers were the Museum of Modern Art, which bought a version of *Horned Form* (the catalogue showed a photograph of Graham with the stump which inspired it) only marginally different from the Tate's; and the Albright Art Gallery of Buffalo, New York, which bought a large *Thorn Trees* that Kenneth Clark had, in vain, recommended to the Tate Gallery.[15] But if the reaction of the critic of the *New York Times*, Edward Alden Jewell, was in any way typical, the show got at best a mixed press. He found Graham's work gravely disappointing: 'mannered, obscure in its motivations, frequently not too felicitous in its colour. . . . he reaches his best statement in the handsomely designed *Thorn Trees*, his nadir in the lamentable *Smiling Woman*,' Jewell wrote on 3 March.

Given Graham's heavily Eurocentric view of the world and the contemporary British ignorance about developments in American painting, he was probably not unduly worried about his failure to take New York by storm. To the end, Paris bulked larger in his mind. He had scarcely had time to scratch its beautiful surface on his end-of-war mission in 1944, and on 3 April 1946 he and Kathleen set off on a 6 a.m. plane to Le Bourget airport to make good some of the omissions.

The trip was largely the idea of Eardley Knollys, who was now looking after National Trust properties in the south-west of England and was sharing Long Crichel House, at Wimborne in Dorset, with Eddy Sackville-West and Desmond Shawe-Taylor. Knollys was a keen collector (Matisse, Bonnard, Braque and others), and his years as a dealer in the 1930s had left him with a detailed knowledge of the Paris art world. He spoke good French, Graham and Kathleen virtually none; he made the next eleven days an agreeable crash course in Parisian culture.

They stayed at his favourite hotel, the Royal Condé in the rue de Condé. They lunched with his friend, the novelist Maurice Druon, who had escaped with Joseph Kessell and had joined the Free French in London during the war. They went to one of the famous Thursday parties of Marie-Louise Bousquet, when almost everyone worth knowing in the art world was packed into her small, rather shabby flat. They visited and lunched with some leading dealers, Madame Guillaume, Bing, Leiris, Charpentier, and dined with Camille Pissarro's son, Rodo. They went to see the picture collection of the dress designer Captain Edward Molyneux, a former client and friend of Eardley's, and they saw collections at Jacques Fath and Lelong (Graham came to share Kathleen's interest in beautifully made clothes). They dined at the Catalan, a Spanish restaurant in the rue des Grands-Augustins, near Picasso's studio, where Graham recognized his mentor's mistress, Dora Maar, from the well known portrait. They visited Notre Dame, Versailles, Fontainebleau—and the Folies Bergère, returning home a well spent £100 poorer.

Before settling down to work on the Northampton *Crucifixion* commission, Graham rather incongruously tackled two carpet designs for the Dorchester Hotel in Park Lane, which the McAlpine family had built in 1930–1. They had hired an architect, Frankland Dark, to mastermind an ambitious refurbishing scheme. He admired Graham's work and collected it. The commission brought in £71, and later Graham did another two designs. Only one was used, in the restaurant, where it survived the well heeled for some ten years. Kathleen used other sample pieces to lend an original touch—with their subtle use of olive green, yellow and black—to the sitting- and breakfast-rooms at the White House from the later 1940s until Graham's death.

Although by now he had roughed out some ideas for the *Crucifixion*, only after Easter 1946 did he tackle his biggest and most difficult commission to date. The thorns had helped to bring the project alive; so too had an examination of the photographs in a gruesome American document on the concentration camps, as they were found by the liberating troops. Called simply *K-Z* (the illogical German abbreviation for *Konzentrationslager*), it had been issued in about June 1945, in German, by the Office of War Information, with the aim of bringing home to the Germans just what the Nazis had done. Graham was sent a copy. He was intensely moved by the photographs of Belsen, Buchenwald and other camps. 'Many of the tortured bodies looked like figures deposed from crosses,' he said.[16]

> The whole idea of the depiction of Christ crucified became more real to me after having seen this book, and it seemed to me possible to do the subject again. In any case, the continuing beastliness and cruelty of mankind, amounting at times to madness, seems eternal and classic.

Some of the hideously emaciated bodies reminded him of the Christ figure in Crucifixions by Dürer's contemporary, Grünewald, patron saint of the Expressionists. The most famous of these forms part of the Isenheim altarpiece, now in the museum in Colmar, Alsace. Grünewald had used the technical advances of the Renaissance painters to heighten the emotional impact of his late Gothic religious imagery. In Graham's mind the writhing fingers of the Isenheim Christ fused with the twisted limbs of the Nazis' victims.

The auspices for the commission were not otherwise promising. The Church, whether Roman Catholic or Anglican, had long since lost touch with what contemporary art there was in Britain, and churchgoers had become used to bloodless or sentimental renderings of Christ. It was not only Graham's first religious commission but also his first large figure study. The church setting was 'only moderately sympathetic', in Graham's phrase; and the structure and decoration ruled out a promising idea to portray the Cross, like the thorns, against a warm blue sky.[17] On the other hand, he was not concerned, as a Roman Catholic, about working for an Anglican patron. Even faith itself was not important. 'I think there is a juice in certain people that makes them, whether believers or not, capable of producing a profoundly religious work,' he said.[18]

The patron himself was wholly sympathetic, however. Walter Hussey had taken over St Matthew's, a large, late-Victorian affair designed by Matthew Holding, in 1937. He built on his father's musical enthusiasms, commissioning Benjamin Britten and Michael Tippett to compose works for the fiftieth anniversary celebrations in 1943. Later Kirsten Flagstad sang there twice. The unveiling of Moore's *Madonna and Child* in 1944 had enraged enemies of modern art. Hussey's church council gamely stood by him over his plan for a Sutherland *Crucifixion*. For a man as gentle as Hussey, it must have taken courage to press ahead.

Graham had himself decided that his work for the church must be 'immediately intelligible and within the tradition', tempted though he was to do something more detached and less naturalistic.[19] He started off with drawings of a very elongated and emaciated Christ. But the space required something wider, and he brought the arms down from an almost vertical to an almost horizontal position in several much larger oil sketches. Two of these measured nearly 3 feet by 4 feet; a third was more than twice as big. In July he showed a fourth large sketch first to Kenneth Clark, then to Walter Hussey and Eric Newton, who came down to Kent together. Clark thought it 'a truly great work, entirely you, without concessions either to the Rev. Hussey or P. Watson'.[20] Hussey was less rhapsodic. 'I wasn't awfully happy with the sketch, and I think Graham saw the slight reserve in my enthusiasm,' he recalled.[21] Graham told Clark:[22]

The Rev. Hussey is worried about the Hemlock Plants (!). I name those forms thus, but anything as botanical or exact is far from my intention, as you know. . . . I still have great difficulty over materials. Church decoration, so I learn, is not high on the priority lists. . . .

Only through great effort did he obtain the four panels of hardboard he required for the size on which he had decided (8 feet by 7 feet 6 inches), a 'significant size' indeed, too big for his studio, so he rented a nearby garage in Trottiscliffe. In the final version he eliminated the foliage about which Hussey had reservations and a skull and crossbones which had appeared at the foot of the cross in the 'final' sketch.

On 5 November Graham took this and the last sketch up to Northampton in his car with Felix Man (a pioneer of photojournalism who had joined Stefan Lorant in setting up *Picture Post* in London in 1938) after the first of many sessions in which Man recorded Graham's work in progress. On the way they almost crashed with a lorry, Man remembered.[23] Graham then showed the nearly completed work to the church council, some of whose members were startled by what they saw. Graham soon won them over by describing how he wanted to try to sum up the agony and suffering of the war in the agony and suffering of Christ. Hussey recalled one rough diamond on the council asking Graham why he had eliminated the skull and crossbones in the final version. 'What do *you* think?' Graham asked. 'Is it better with or without?' The rough diamond pondered, then said: 'Well, without, I think.' 'Well, so do I. That's why I took it out.' The rough diamond was very flattered. 'He wanted to know my opinion,' he said, half-incredulously.

The final version was very different from the last sketch, Hussey said: 'Everything I felt unhappy about had gone.' Graham returned to the church on 11 November. The huge painting had been fixed in place, and he spent six days there, making adjustments required by the light and the sandstone background, staying with Hussey at the vicarage next door and laying the basis of an enduring friendship. Graham struck him as a deeply religious person, unsure of his faith, yet anxious to keep it.

Clark had again been asked to do the unveiling, but he thought that if he did, it would look as if Graham and Henry Moore worked for a clique, instead of being admired by 'all serious lovers of art'.[24] Instead the ceremony was performed, on 16 November, by Sir Eric Maclagan, the former Director of the Victoria and Albert Museum, after a celebratory luncheon attended by, among others the Clarks, Moores, Andersons, Pipers and Peter Gregory, of Lund, Humphries.

What they saw when Sir Eric pulled the cord was 'by its vividness calculated to make the average onlooker gasp', in the awed words of the *Northampton Independent*.[25] Yet it did not arouse the same incomprehension as the Moore *Madonna and Child* because the distortions were explicable in terms of the subject matter. The *Independent* put it well: 'Whereas in the popular mind there are rigid limits to an artist's licence in dealing with womanhood and motherhood, there can be none when his subject is as imponderable as agonized death.' Commentators in general felt

rucifixion. Oil on hardboard, 1946. 96 × 90 in (243.8 × 228.6 cm)

Standing Form against Hedge. Oil on canvas, 1950. $52\frac{1}{8} \times 45\frac{5}{8}$ in (132.4 × 115.9 cm)

that the work, while flawed—for example, in the treatment of the legs—and not without its searchings and immaturities, represented a sincere and a brave effort to unwrap much of the cotton wool which had covered the subject for generations, as Hussey later said.[26] It is generally considered—in so far as anything is 'generally considered'—the most deeply felt and successful of all Graham's religious works. (The fee, raised from contributions to a special collecting box and the receipts of recitals given free by Britten and Peter Pears, was around £350, Hussey thought.)

Like many artists, Graham liked to work a theme through. While grappling with the *Crucifixion*, he also did a rather garish *Deposition*, later given to his solicitor, Wilfrid Evill, in lieu of fees (Graham had envisaged something smaller, but Evill took an unexpected fancy to it),[27] and a *Weeping Magdalen*. Both are heavily influenced by Picasso. A sunny *Laughing Woman* of the same period was inspired by a newspaper photograph. 'I never knew who she was,' Graham said, 'but the expression caught my attention, and I used the idea to build a picture.'[28] After the unveiling he also did some more work, while 'letting the engine run down slowly',[29] on the preliminary *Crucifixion* sketches. With Graham, some sketches were more preliminary than others, and these ones were to be shown at the Lefevre Gallery.

Francis Bacon, who (as a non-believer) had done several *Crucifixions* of a very different sort himself, was fretting to see photographs of Graham's *magnum opus*. Since renewing their links in 1943, he and Graham had become close friends. In 1943 or 1944 Bacon had moved to Millais' former studio in Cromwell Place, South Kensington, with his old family nanny, to whom he was devoted. By 1945 Graham and Kathleen were dining there roughly once a week. It was a large, chaotic place, where the salad bowl was likely to have paint on it and the painting to have salad dressing on it, but the wine and food were good, and the conversation, Kathleen recalled, marvellous. Bacon also used the studio for gambling sessions (then illegal), and nanny would be the hat-check girl.

Graham greatly admired the power of Bacon's work and was fascinated by his personality and way of life. Apart from their intelligence, charm and obsession with painting, the two men were very different. Graham had had a thoroughly conventional upbringing, liked to work office hours and within a supportive context of loving wife, patrons, friends and sympathetic dealers. While Graham was full of inhibitions, Bacon had few—that was perhaps part of his fascination. When Graham had been in Sutton and at Gold-smiths', Bacon was in Berlin and Paris. His life was essentially spasmic: first a painting spasm, then a drinking or social spasm. He liked the hazards of Soho by night and was by nature a gambler. He had little time for bourgeois morality—but good restaurants were another matter. Patrons of the kind who supported Graham he would have found oppressive. Bacon's painting was brutal, yet tinged with compassion. He believed that idea and technique must be inseparably fused. With Graham everything was more interior, except the starting point, which was in nature, where Bacon rarely found inspiration. Graham started as an etcher. For him the line remained paramount.

Bacon found Graham charming, easy to talk to and highly intelligent, but he did not greatly admire his work. Some of the war drawings were all right, perhaps, but he disliked the spikiness which intruded later.[30] Graham, by contrast, was at this stage one of Bacon's leading evangelists. Both Kenneth Clark and Colin Anderson recalled that it was he who first brought Bacon's work to their attention,[31] probably around 1943–4. Anderson came to like it and bought *Study for a Crucifixion* (1933) from the Redfern Gallery in 1946, and *Owls* (1956–7) from the Hanover Gallery in 1957; at Graham's suggestion, Clark actually visited Bacon's studio, probably in about 1944–5. Bacon remembered that Clark walked in and out again. Kathleen's memory, generally good on such matters, was that Clark came in with his tightly rolled umbrella, very much the Director of the National Gallery, gave Bacon's work a swift appraisal, and said, 'Interesting, yes. What extraordinary times we live in,' and walked out again. Bacon turned to Graham —who had been telling him that one could not work in a vacuum—and said, 'You see, you're surrounded by cretins.' But when Graham and Kathleen dined with Clark that evening, he said to Graham: 'You and I may be in a minority of two, but we may still be right in thinking that Francis Bacon has genius.' Buying a Bacon was another matter, however. Clark did not fancy such strong meat on his walls.

In June 1946 Bacon went off to sample life in the South of France, basing himself in the Hotel de Ré, Monte Carlo. From there he wrote Graham a series of letters about life on the coast, his hopes and fears, their work and various exhibitions which he had seen. In what seems to have been the first (not all are dated), he described how he loved the light, went to the casino in the evening and felt pleasantly isolated: nobody was at all interested in art. Thanking Graham for all he had done for him, he said he knew he would not have been able to sell anything if Graham had not mentioned his work to other people.

At Bacon's request, Graham had sprayed a fixative over some passages in magenta pastel in Bacon's *Painting 1946*, which showed a gruesome-looking man under an umbrella against a huge, hanging beef carcase, set against raspberry-coloured blinds. (Erica Brausen, then of the Redfern Gallery, had bought it for £100 and two years later sold it to the Museum of Modern Art in New York for £150, through Alfred Barr.) Writing to thank him for doing this on 20 August, Bacon said that he hoped Graham would decide to show at the UNESCO exhibition at the Musée d'Art Moderne in Paris in November. He was sure that Douglas Cooper, who had been a friend of Bacon's and was becoming well-known, would launch an attack on Graham, but since Cooper was becoming a champion of decorators, that was all to the good. Bacon wrote that he did not feel he wanted to go back to England for a long time: he might try finding a studio in Paris that they could use alternately.

Then came news in October that Bacon was working on three studies of the Velasquez portrait of Pope Innocent X. He had practically finished one but was not yet sure if they were going to succeed or not. Come 30 December, he was glad the *Crucifixion* had been well received, though he knew Graham shared his feelings about the boredom of being liked by well-meaning fools.

By now Bacon had been to the UNESCO show in Paris, at which Graham had shown *Chimère I* and a thorn tree, and Bacon the painting which Graham had sprayed. Bacon wrote that he had found the show awful—including the Braque and the Picassos in the French section. As for their own things there, he had been shocked by their boring lack of reality and immediacy, of which they had so often talked. He thought that was why so many Picassos were beginning to look jaded: decoration was contaminating everyone. He felt sick to death of everything he had himself done, but continued to think—childishly or foolishly—that he was on the point of doing something good.

Bacon told Graham that he had seen Balthus' show in Paris at Wildenstein's, but had thought his things were no good. Balthus was trying to get the tenderness they would all love to achieve. But he thought it couldn't be done until someone made a new technical synthesis which would carry over from the sensation to the nervous system. He longed to see them, he concluded—and details of the *Crucifixion*.

By 22 January 1947 he had managed to see a copy of *Picture Post* (containing Felix Man's photographs) and thought the *Crucifixion* looked 'most awfully good', and the colour sounded very exciting, he wrote in his last surviving letter. He urged Graham to bring more details if he came to France—but, in fact, Bacon went to London for ten days in February. They all had lunch together at the White Tower restaurant on the 13th, progressed to an exhibition of Spanish painting at the National Gallery and went back to Bacon's Cromwell Place studio for tea and drinks.

Bacon's had not been the only siren voice luring them to the South of France, with his descriptions of the gorgeous, pearly haze which Renoir had tried to catch. There was also Roderick Cameron, whom they had met in London during the war through the Clarks and whose mother, Lady Kenmare, owned La Fiorentina, a villa on the peninsula jutting out from Cap Ferrat. Graham later inscribed a book: 'For Rory, whose description of this region—so true, so felicitous—first fired me with the idea to work here. . . .'[32] Eardley Knollys had happy memories of a visit there before the war. Kenneth Clark, by contrast, was anxious about the effect of the Mediterranean on Graham's work.

Graham, ambitious as he was and avid for new experiences to nourish his painting, decided to risk it. Once again, Eardley Knollys came along as cicerone and interpreter (though Graham had been trying to improve his French). Graham had recently acquired a Standard tourer, and off they went in it on 10 April 1947, via Dover, Paris, Avallon, Tournus and Aix, where Knollys introduced them to Matthew Smith, who was revisiting old haunts in search of work he had left behind before the war.

Even in today's image-soaked world, the first experience of the south and of the Mediterranean is intoxicating. The sound of the cicadas, the subtle light of the avenues and squares of peeling plane trees, the red of the soil, the dark, slim verticals of the cypresses, the singing greens of the bushy-topped pines against the often flawless blue of the sky, the first sight of the Mont Ste-Victoire: coming from the north, the thrill is infinitely renewable, and for Graham it was a different world—and one which made him think quite differently about certain painters: 'To see Provence for the first time is to know Cézanne properly, and the painting of van Gogh had suddenly for me a new excitement,' he said later.[33]

Once on the coast, the immediate problem was where to stay. Eardley Knollys had spent the winter of 1928–9 at the Welcome Hotel in Villefranche. 'Let's see if it still exists,' he said.[34] It did, and they settled there. The Welcome, then a simple, five-storey hotel, had been reopened in 1946 by a couple called Galbois. It is in the old port, almost on the water's edge, in the middle of the bay formed by Cap Ferrat and the Cap de Nice. The steep, narrow streets behind have a Neapolitan flavour: canaries singing, washing hanging out, neighbours chatting from the windows across the street. Walking down towards the hotel, there are dazzling views across to Cap Ferrat.

Francis Bacon was back in Monte Carlo, now staying in a flat with his friend Eric Hall. That first evening Graham, Kathleen and Eardley Knollys visited him, and they all went to the casino, where they lost 500 old francs. It was Graham's introduction to roulette, to which he and Kathleen became mildly addicted in the next five years. Like painting, it involved risks—and revealed one's own character, Graham believed. 'When one should be bold, for instance, one is timid; when one should be timid one is bold,' he said once.[35] Over the next five weeks Graham, Kathleen, Bacon and Hall (Knollys left after ten days or so) met roughly twice a week for meals, visits to the casino and trips to the interior.

The Riviera, Graham soon grasped, is a place of extreme contrasts, the sybaritic luxuries of the coast (less sybaritic in 1947) being superimposed on an ancient land of olive groves, vineyards and smallholdings belonging to peasants of very limited means (less limited latterly for those who have sold land for development). He was to find more inspiration inland than by the coast: in vine pergolas, palisades of palm branches, dried gourds, hanging maize cobs, bursting pine cones, bamboo groves, tall grasses and strange rock formations. One expedition with Bacon was to Tourette-sur-Loup, not far from Vence, where the rocks and grasses of a dried river bed were to be a fruitful source of ideas. Objects seemed more alive in the hallucinating sunlight there, Graham found, and everything seemed to have a back to it, like sculpture.[36]

For ten days Graham and Kathleen moved from the Welcome Hotel to the luxury and beauty of La Fiorentina, which Rory Cameron lent them when leaving for a trip. It was a kind of eighteenth-century dower house— red-tiled floors, white marble stairs and pinkish-ochre walls—set in a spectacular garden, with shallow grass steps lined with cypresses leading down to the sea.[37] Somerset Maugham's Villa Mauresque was nearby. Graham had an introduction to the novelist—then still on a high plateau of fame—almost certainly from their mutual friend Kenneth Clark. They were invited to lunch there on 20 April: impeccable table, marvellous food, conversation acute and sometimes acid, Graham recalled.[38] Maugham showed them around: 'This is the writing room, where the books are done,' he would say, and they nicknamed him the Caretaker, Knollys recalled. Two days later they met Maugham again at lunch at La Fiorentina. Lord and Lady Bearsted were also there. They had a villa called La Serena, very near Maugham's, and it was at a cocktail party there that Graham and Kathleen met him for the third time in four days.

How did Graham's first portrait commission come about? In the Japanese film *Rashomon* the director reconstructed several wholly different eye-witness accounts of how a murder had taken place. The '*Rashomon* effect' may be seen here too. Graham's usual version was that on the way back from lunch at the Mauresque, he said to a friend (presumably

Knollys): 'If I was a portrait painter, I think that's the kind of face I could do.' The friend reported this to Monroe Wheeler, of the Museum of Modern Art in New York, who spoke to Willie Maugham. Maugham wrote to Graham suggesting the portrait. According to Graham, Maugham's version was quite different. Maugham said that he did not ask Graham to paint his portrait; Graham begged and begged him to let him do it. Graham told him on television: 'Well, Willie, this is not the true story, and you know it,' to which Maugham said, 'Well, you stick to your story, and I'll stick to mine, and we'll have a truce on this.'[39]

Knollys had yet another version. After they had returned from the Mauresque to the Welcome, Kathleen drew a sketch of Maugham with a pencil on a napkin, showing him in profile, his hands clasped in front of his face. Graham said, 'No, he wasn't a bit like that,' and drew something quite different. Knollys said, 'You ought to paint a portrait of him, Graham' — 'Then I came back to England, and said to Monroe [Wheeler], who was going to stay with Maugham: "You must egg him on to get Graham to paint his portrait." ' But Alan Searle, Maugham's private secretary and ever-present companion, thought that the crucial meal had been the second lunch *chez* Cameron at La Fiorentina, and not the first one at the Mauresque.[40] Rory Cameron thought that Graham's remark about Maugham's paintability had been made to *him* and that he had played it back to Maugham.

Such is the raw material of history before time and the historians tidy it up. Maugham's letter asking Graham to do the portrait — and it seems likely he wrote one — has not survived. Graham recalled:[41]

> First of all I said, 'No, I'm not a portrait painter, and I don't feel I can really undertake this.' So he wrote back then and said, 'I'm very sorry to hear this, won't you reconsider?' I said: 'Well, look, if you treat it purely as an experiment with no strings on either side' — absolute freedom, he to reject, me to withhold — then I would have a go.

The idea of trying to pin down that memorable face, so reminiscent of one of Graham's gnarled old roots, appealed to his gambling instinct, though he cannot have suspected that the stakes would be as high as they were two years later.

They left Villefranche on 20 May, spending two nights in Paris on the way and lunching there with a future friend and ally, Frank McEwen, the very able and energetic respresentative of the British Council, the arm of the government that promotes British culture and, above all, the English language overseas.

In the tranquillity of his Kent studio, Graham tried to digest the experiences of his first visit to the cradle of European culture. It was a fresh world in several ways. He had met the famous in England at the home of the Clarks, but in elegant Mediterranean villas, with their swimming-pools and beautiful gardens, fame takes on a more glamorous aspect, wealth a pearlier sheen. Then there was the new subject matter, sketchbooks full of it, and the hazards attending a drastic change of scene. It cannot have been easy to sort it all out, as he settled down to a series of studies of spiky palm branches, cactuses, gourds, palisades and cicadas. Although some new soft pinks, blues and yellows now emerged from his palette, both the brighter colours and the spikiness had been heralded by the thorn trees against blue skies. It was, Douglas Cooper later observed, as if the visit to the south had been the logical fulfilment of an earlier spiritual need.[42]

By late summer Graham was impatient to be back there, and on 23 September they set off again, this time with Lucian Freud replacing Eardley Knollys in the Standard tourer. Freud, Sigmund's grandson, was then 26 years old to Graham's 43, his great gifts only partially concealed by a wild Bohemianism. Graham was laid up with a temperature for three days in Paris, where Freud bought some cage birds, releasing them periodically from hotel bedrooms on the way south.

At the Welcome Graham agreed with the proprietor, Guy Galbois, that he should do an oil in lieu of five weeks' bed and breakfast for them both. The result was a handsome pergola study, *Tunnel de Vignes*, painted in a former chapel a few yards from the hotel, which Cocteau, an old Welcome *habitué*, later decorated. (The painting hung for many years in the hotel's foyer; then Guy Galbois died in 1971, and his widow, a tough lady of Greek origin, removed it for safety to her flat.) Bacon was still in Monte Carlo, and there were further meals and roulette sessions with him, but more work was done on this visit, including many days' sketching near Vence and Peille, a hilltop town behind La Turbie.

Picasso and Matisse lived tantalizingly near. Graham had been much impressed that spring by a visit to the Picasso museum at the Château Grimaldi, on the water's edge at Antibes, where Picasso had recently decorated huge panels with centaurs, fauns and still lifes in a burst of creativity exceptional even for him. (Pottery and further paintings were added later.) It was, improbably, through an old acquaintance, Tom Driberg, the journalist and Labour MP, that he was to meet both Picasso and Matisse.

Driberg, who had founded the *Daily Express*'s 'William Hickey' column in the 1930s, was now a columnist for *Reynolds News*, a moderately left-wing Sunday newspaper (since defunct). (Chapman Pincher has convincingly

claimed that Driberg was an MI5 agent and also sometimes spied for the
Russians.[43] He himself later exhaustively chronicled his taste for
homosexual encounters in public lavatories.)[44] Driberg carried out his
varied assignments with uniform charm. Journalism was perhaps
uppermost when he arrived at the Welcome on 14 November 1947,
admiring Graham's vine pergola painting on the way in. He had come to do
a series of articles about famous writers and painters and asked Graham
whether he could introduce him to Picasso. 'I said: Well, I didn't really think
I could—I didn't want to disturb someone I respected so much,' Graham
recalled.[45] Driberg persisted: 'I thought I could introduce him to Matisse. I
eventually did introduce him to Picasso. I discovered he was working at the
pottery factory in Vallauris, so I had less compunction in disturbing him.'

Four days after Driberg's arrival, they set off with Kathleen to see
Matisse, who since 1943 had been living in Vence, in a villa called Le Rêve.
He was now 77 and had never fully recovered from two major operations in
1941. They rang Le Rêve's bell. 'Personne,' said the maid. After some
delay—intended, Kathleen surmised, to enable Matisse to put on a camel-
hair coat and to tidy himself up—they were allowed in. Graham
remembered that he was painting a dummy model which looked just like the
girl in many of his paintings. It was a dull day, Driberg told the readers of his
column on 7 December. All the sunlight was concentrated on the canvases
on Matisse's studio walls, 'a compacted blaze of crimsons and yellows'. He
found Matisse to be a 'venerable, slightly formal figure now, chubby, white-
bearded, his clothes as spick and span as his paint brushes'.

Picasso, by contrast, struck him as a 'trim, spry, unassuming, cheerful
little chap with very close-cropped grey hair'. They called on him on 20
November at Vallauris, an ancient potting village where that summer
Picasso had begun to do some work at the Madoura pottery, first learning
the skills of the craft, then producing some two thousand pieces in a year:
horned heads, nymphs and centaurs, owls and bulls, and girls with hips like
rounded vases. Suddenly, Graham recalled, 'there were those large brown
eyes staring at us from a doorway.' Picasso welcomed them unaffectedly,
Driberg wrote in the same column, and showed them his work with almost
child-like pleasure: several hundred plates and pots in vivid and amusing
adaptations of traditional designs, laid out on the floor of a barn-like attic—
'"something useful and practical," he said, "something that everyone can
take pleasure in"'. Driberg's article on the two masters made no more than 6
column inches, but for Graham the encounter had broken the ice with
Picasso, whom he came to know quite well later.

Driberg stayed ten days, while Graham and Kathleen this time spent ten weeks in France, returning to Kent in mid-December in time for a quiet Christmas at home.

The next year, 1948, was to be a year of exhibitions: two group shows in Paris and Brussels; two one-man shows in London and New York. The group shows abroad were organized by the British Council. Less favoured artists sometimes claim that colleagues like Graham, Ceri Richards, Alan Davie, Victor Pasmore and even Henry Moore owed much of their reputation to the patronage of the British Council and the Arts Council. This is both true and untrue. Certainly, the British Council did much to put contemporary British painting and sculpture on the map in those post-war years. It was a misfortune for an artist not to be admired by Mrs Lilian Somerville, director of the British Council's art department for more than twenty years, or by Philip James, her almost equally durable Arts Council equivalent, and their respective selection committees. On the other hand, an artist had to be found good by foreigners to survive the exposure. Powerful taste-maker though the British Council was, its prophecies were not wholly self-fulfilling: Matthew Smith, for example, went down like a lead balloon at the 1950 Venice Biennale.

Graham shared the Paris show, which ran for four weeks from 23 January 1948 at the Galerie René Drouin in the Place Vendôme, with his friends Craxton, Freud and Vaughan, and with Ben Nicholson, Ivon Hitchens, Edward Burra, Robert MacBryde, John Minton and William Scott. It was an impressive group, though slanted towards the linear, romantic tradition. Three of Graham's thorn paintings were shown, together with *Chimère II* (not a very imaginative selection). In an introductory essay René Guilly hailed Graham as one of two Englishmen (the other being Moore) who had rediscovered the universality of Constable and Turner.

The Brussels exhibition, held at the Palais des Beaux Arts in October–November, offered a wider range; Matthew Smith, Louis le Brocquy, L. S. Lowry, Stanley Spencer and John Tunnard were represented, in addition to the Paris team sans Burra and Freud. Graham had ten works in this exhibition, mainly recent but including *Gorse on Sea Wall*, lent by Peter Watson, and a war drawing of a tin miner. Taken together with the UNESCO show of autumn 1946, these were Graham's first steps towards a Continental reputation which was to vary sharply from country to country.

In June 1948 he faced his first post-war one-man show in London, which was also to be the opening exhibition of the new Hanover Gallery, just off Hanover Square. The gallery was being set up by Erica Brausen, who had had a row with the Redfern's founder, Rex Nan Kivell, and an anglicized

American, Arthur Jeffress. Erica Brausen was a crisply intelligent German, born in Düsseldorf, who had lived in Paris and then worked for the Republicans in the Spanish Civil War, escaping to London where, as noted, she had worked for Eardley Knollys's Storran Gallery.[46] Arthur Jeffress was 42, had spent most of his life in England and was rich—the money was thought to come from Virginian tobacco. Behind his sometimes cruelly witty façade, close friends detected an inner melancholy and a variety of inferiority complexes. Like many insecure people, he was a bit of a snob. He was also, to a degree then hazardous and in his case fatal, an active homosexual.

Graham worked very hard for the show. Some nine oils and a dozen drawings remained from 1947's output; to them he added eighteen more oils, though many were smaller than usual. He was still revelling in the exotic subject matter of the South of France, and many of the pictures showed insects like the praying mantis or the grasshopper, or banana leaves, gourds and hanging maize cobs against backgrounds often of a single colour: he was running the risk of being contaminated by that 'terrible decoration' which he and Bacon had so often discussed. Later he rather disapproved of this phase: 'I find it a little bit gimmicky to be influenced simply by things which are exotic and new, to the exclusion therefore of real interest in a more generalized idea of structure,' he said.[47] But the exhibition made a considerable impact and decisively marked the emergence of the new, Mediterranean Sutherland. Prices were slightly up, larger oils (roughly 4 feet by 3 feet) going for £210, the smallest for £52. Ten works sold for a total of £1246 gross, or £774 net of the gallery's one-third commission and other costs.

His second New York show, in November and again at the Buchholz Gallery, included roughly a dozen unsold oils from the Hanover show and eight or so others and eighteen gouaches. 'There have been misgivings about Sutherland before,' Sam Hunter wrote in the *New York Times* of 21 November. 'Reputable American critics have found him provincial and a fundamentally weak abstractionist.' But he noted a progression towards a more sanguine outlook: the pergolas were observed not entirely with rancour; the orchard had become more fruitful.

The indications are that the show was not a tremendous success, though most of the works on offer ended up, sooner or later, in American collections, including those of Mrs Benjamin Watson of New York City and Wright Ludington of Santa Barbara, California, both of whom became Sutherland admirers. From the point of view of Graham's development, the most interesting items were two recent gouaches, *Turning Form I* and

Articulated Form, in which he seemed at last to have succeeded in investing Mediterranean themes with the same kind of mystery as the boulders, tree roots and hills of Wales.

In May 1948 Graham took a fateful step by accepting an offer to become one of the Tate Gallery's trustees, of whom four were customarily artists. (Henry Moore had just completed a seven-year term.) The other trustees then were Sir Jasper Ridley (chairman), Lord Jowitt, Henry Lamb, John Piper, Hugo Pitman, Lord Harlech, Lord Justice Somervell and Philip Hendy. The trustees were theoretically responsible for all decisions about acquisitions, whether by purchase, gift, bequest or transfer, though works for purchase were usually brought forward by the Director, then John Rothenstein. Graham had strong views about the Tate's failure to acquire good examples of the work of great living French masters. He was articulate, knowledgeable, anxious to help. The duties did not seem arduous: there were meetings on the third Thursday of each month, August excepted. It seemed a good appointment.

Was it, however, compatible with a growing taste for the South of France? Graham may possibly have pondered on that—though he was not always good at thinking things through, being too often prey to sudden enthusiasms, which faded away—as he and Kathleen spent much of the second half of 1948 in the Villefranche area. This time they rented a house, most of whose furniture had been destroyed by the Germans, for less than £2 a week.

Again they returned to Kent for Christmas and a brief burst of tapestry design, Graham's first venture in this field. He did four gouaches for the Edinburgh Tapestry Company. The best of these emerged as *Three Wading Birds*, an attractive, slightly stylized work.

Then, in March 1949, they at last went off to stay with Willie Maugham at the Villa Mauresque to tackle the strictly experimental portrait of the novelist, then aged 75. Eardley Knollys travelled with them as far as Paris, and they went together to see Braque in his studio. Graham had met him over dinner at the St John's Wood home of Lilian Somerville. Braque was tall, handsome and impressive. His studio was exceedingly neat, Knollys recalled:

> There were three big easels with paintings, and perhaps thirty small ones on tiny stands on the floor, like a flight of swallows. He had a big stand-up desk, where he did drawings and graphics, with all the tools laid out in rows and lined up. I remember Graham leaning over the desk with him and examining brushes and things and having a very technical discussion, while I mooned around looking at the paintings.

Graham and Kathleen arrived at the Villa Mauresque on 14 March. Monroe Wheeler of the Museum of Modern Art in New York was staying there, and next day Alexander Frere and his wife arrived. He was chairman of William Heinemann, Maugham's publishers, and became a friend of Graham, who later painted his portrait. The Mauresque itself was a slightly gloomy place, with its gilt buddhas, blackamoors and dark Spanish furniture, but the setting was beautiful—terraces of tangerine and lemon trees, a view over the pines to sea, the air heavy with the scent of arum lilies and verbena—and the food delicious.

Maugham could be very waspish, and he sometimes tried to intimidate his guests, but to Graham and Kathleen he was always kind and considerate. His own collection of paintings showed discrimination, consisting of sunny works by Renoir, Monet, Gauguin, Matisse, Pissarro, Boudin and others. Only Toulouse-Lautrec's rather kinky male nude of a man polishing a floor, *Le Polisseur*, and Picasso's early *Death of Harlequin* struck a sombre note. Surprisingly for a basically shy man, he had had himself painted several times: by Edouard MacAvoy, for example, a Frenchman of Scottish ancestry, and by Marie Laurençin. Neither portrait set Graham a very daunting precedent. There were, Graham believed, two main ways of painting a portrait.

> One, which I admire enormously, is the real paraphrase such as Picasso does, which to me is marvellous, because the likeness is always preserved. The other is to make a straight attempt at what you see, and that is my course. It is much the same practice, on the whole, which I used in my war drawings . . . to make as clear a presentation as one's gifts allow for what one sees in front of one's face. I think that if one does that, sometimes the thing comes full circle, because if the thing is intense enough, in itself it becomes a kind of paraphrase.[48]

In his drawings of natural forms Graham felt that he was drawing attention to something unfamiliar by isolating it from its environment. Faces, by contrast, were familiar. The task was different, even though in Maugham's case it was the resemblance of his face to a weatherbeaten *objet trouvé* which had perhaps first made Graham feel he might be paintable. From the start, Graham felt he had to be 'as absorbent as blotting paper and as patient and watchful as a cat'.[49] His aim was not the 'so-called speaking likeness of attempted imitation, but the likeness which is the result of an attempt to fuse all the characteristic directions, movements and tensions of the head and body into terms of paint'.[50] As when sketching an oak root or rock formation, he filled a whole sketchbook with small pencil studies of his sitter's head, arms, legs and notes about his clothes and so on, later making two larger preparatory drawings on tracing paper in his studio. One emphasized the right side of Maugham's face, the other the left. Deciding the former was the better likeness, he traced it on to the tall, narrow canvas which he had chosen for the final portrait.[51] (Later he copied both working studies;[52] these were bought first by Hans Juda for £50, then in 1967 by the Fitzwilliam Museum in Cambridge for £3300.) With later portraits he used his usual method of transferring sketches to canvas by squaring them both up. All final portraits, rather than sketches, were done in his studio, away from the sitter.

After a week at the Mauresque, Graham decided that it would be easier to work in more relaxed surroundings, where a splash of paint on the floor would not damage a valuable rug, and moved to La Mignonelle, a pleasant villa which Kathleen had found not far off, with its own little beach down a flight of steps. The ten sittings which he and Maugham had had proved to be insufficient. While he was working on the canvas there, Maugham came for more detailed drawings of ears, mouth and so on, and when the author retreated to the mountains of Valberg for a rest, Graham had to follow for an extra sitting. Adopting what became his standard practice—based perhaps on lack of confidence in his skills—he did not allow Maugham to see the work in progress.

Graham had difficulty painting the clothes, and especially—for the first of many times—the legs. 'The trousers gave me just hell,' he wrote to Craxton that July. They had to borrow Maugham's velvet jacket and grey flannels, and Kathleen had to pose in them. The round-backed chair on which Maugham had sat was wrong for the vertical composition; they had to search for a suitable stool in nearby cafés. When it was found, Graham furtively sketched it.

On 24 May, just nine weeks after it had been begun, the portrait was ready. Maugham and Searle were invited to La Mignonelle to see it. Searle recalled that it was hidden under rather a dirty sheet. 'I can't bring myself to unveil it till we have had a glass of champagne,' Graham said. So first they braced themselves with a drink.

'The first time I saw it I was shocked,' Maugham said later.[53] 'I was really stunned. Could this face really be mine? And then I began to realize that here was far more of me than I ever saw myself.' He saw himself portrayed as the sardonic, aloof and quietly amused observer of human frailty, perched on the café stool with arms and legs crossed, mouth down-turned, face lined and generous bags under his eyes, against a plain background unusually thickly painted (for Graham) in shades ranging from apricot to yellow-green, with a few palm fronds suggesting a hint of the Orient at the top. Perhaps it was these which led Sir Gerald Kelly—then President of the Royal Academy, who painted Maugham eighteen times in all between 1907 and 1963, without once exciting the same interest—to remark: 'To think that I have known Willie since 1902 and have only just recognized that, disguised as an old madame, he kept a brothel in Shanghai!'[54]

The tall, narrow canvas (54 × 25 inches) heightened the monolithic effect. It was a telling likeness yet far from flattering, bold, if a trifle coarse, in treatment and with a trace of caricature. The somewhat skeletal right hand and the legs were perhaps not completely convincing. But the power was terrific and the originality undeniable.

Once Maugham had recovered from the shock, he asked the price. Eardley Knollys had urged Graham to settle this in advance, but he had failed to grasp the nettle. He suggested £500. The following day Alan Searle came around with £300 and said that as it was in cash, it really represented £500, and anyway Mr Maugham couldn't afford more.[55] Graham was not pleased with this arrangement, and some minor altercation with Searle ensued.

Maugham rapidly acquired a taste for the portrait. He called it 'magnificent' when interviewed soon after taking delivery by the local *Time* magazine correspondent. 'There is no doubt that Graham has painted me with an expression I sometimes have, even without being aware of it.'[56] *Time* printed the first photograph of it; other publications hastened to follow suit. Graham was on his way to being a celebrity, thanks to a single portrait.

Up the road at Cap d'Ail, Maugham's friend Lord Beaverbrook saw the photograph at his Villa Capponcina, built near the water's edge by Captain Edward Molyneux, the fashion designer. Soon the diarists of Fleet Street were announcing that Sutherland might be going to paint the Beaver's not much less remarkable physiognomy. Suddenly Graham was news. 'I am very glad that you have accepted a commission to paint Lord Beaverbrook,' Maugham wrote on 25 August—not wholly sincerely, since he would have preferred to remain Graham's only sitter, Kathleen recalled. 'I think you will find him a subject very much to your taste, and I hope you are stinging him a lot of money. Don't forget the income tax will claim half of all you get.'

Maugham, for all his cynicism, was impressionable. His enjoyment of Graham's portrait increased as the praise flowed in. 'I am sure you will be glad to hear that K. [Clark] is enthusiastic about your portrait,' he wrote to Graham on 18 March 1950.

When he first looked at it he smiled and said 'Pretty good', then he chuckled and said 'Jolly good', and after that he clapped his hands and said 'It's remarkable.' Since then he has been telling everyone that came to the house that it is undoubtedly the greatest portrait of the twentieth-century. So that's that.

Only once, in early 1958, were Graham's very harmonious relations with Maugham disrupted. In a television interview that January, he had said that during their sittings, Maugham had talked extremely well about his early life, and about how much money he had earned—'and it seemed to me rather a lot', Graham had commented. Maugham wrote to him on 25 January: 'I very much resent your having said during your BBC talk that when I sat for you I talked to you about my money. I have been accused of many things during my long life, but so far as I know never of vulgarity. It was hardly a friendly act on your part to do so.' The row was short-lived.

Graham's work was evolving rapidly. In 1949 he produced not only his first portrait but also the first of his bizarre standing forms. His interest in *objets trouvés* was strong at the time. He kept finding interesting shapes on the little beach at La Mignonelle, where there was a garden with old walls and hedges covered with creepers. He had the idea of portraying the objects against this background: 'they seemed to me the sort of things that I wanted to place in an environment, things which were part figure, part a natural organic object . . . in the same way that my earlier trees were organic, and . . . appeared to be figurative in a sense. . . .' The standing forms were a sort of half-way house, he said, between a thing in a setting and a figure, a bit like a statue seen in an old Italian or English garden.[57] Sometimes Graham saw their origins more simply: 'The standing forms stemmed from seeing figures in gardens—half-hidden in shade. At the time I wanted to try and do forms in such a setting which were not figures but parallel to figures—figures once removed.'[58] He wanted to catch 'the mysterious immediacy of a figure standing in a room or against a hedge in its shadow, its awareness, its regard, as if one had never seen it before, by a substitution'. The standing forms gave him 'the sense of shock or surprise which direct evocation could not possibly do'.[59]

Graham's first major venture in creating these objects was called *Two Standing Forms against a Palisade* (now in the Vancouver Art Gallery). They look like larvae emerging from the top of an urn-shaped carapace, and they stand on plinths, like sculptures, and bear some resemblance to an up-ended version of the *Articulated Forms* of the previous year. Mysterious they certainly are, but not sinister; after a time they are oddly engaging. Graham called them 'monuments and presences', and when accused of obscurity, he liked to quote some lines of Blake:

My spectre round me night and day
Like a wild beast guards my way
My Emanation far within
Weeps incessantly for my sin.

Their music was actually enhanced by their obscurity, he believed. So in painting it could be argued that obscurity preserved a magical and mysterious purpose.[60]

His preoccupation with standing forms lasted some four years and was to coincide with experiments in making sculpture as well as in painting these very sculptural 'monuments'.

After spending the summer in England, Graham and Kathleen returned to La Mignonelle in early November. On the boat from Dover they met, by chance, Henry and Irina Moore, who were on their way to an exhibition of Moore's work at the Musée National d'Art Moderne in Paris. They all saw the show together the following morning. The decade ended in a blaze of conviviality. Hans and Elsbeth Juda came over to Monte Carlo before Christmas, and they made a killing at the casino; they all dined together with Francis Bacon, who was still there, on Christmas Eve; and on Christmas Day Graham and Kathleen had lunch at the Villa Mauresque.

The setting symbolized both the substantial achievement of the portrait and the distance that Graham had travelled since 1945. Stylistically, he was trying to bridge the gulf between the English and Continental traditions, and in so doing he had greatly extended the range of his subject matter, even to the point of embracing portraiture. To a considerable extent, the celebrity which he was beginning to enjoy was a tribute to the individuality of the results. An era of financial anxieties was coming to an end, although stresses of a more subtle and emotionally taxing nature lay ahead.

7

Maximum Exposure

1950-3

THE STYLISTIC CHANGES of the previous five years suggest that after his late start as a painter, Graham felt that he had to make up for lost time. A period of consolidation seemed to be required. But, being a ferocious worker, he hated to seem to stand still and easily felt bored and dissatisfied with what he had done.[1] He was also reluctant to reject new projects, whether they were commissions, ideas for exhibitions, books or films. Insecurity played its part in this passion for work. How reassuring it must have felt to be swept along over the next few years by the full promotional machine of the British Council and Arts Council. Yet was their enthusiasm altogether desirable? Perhaps, in retrospect, the two organizations did him a disservice by giving his work maximum exposure when it was at its most hermetic and least accessible.

The next four years were to be the most turbulent of his career. Too much happened too fast. There were major exhibitions in Venice, Paris, London and elsewhere; a commission to design the largest tapestry in the world; a leading role in a row in the art world whose bitterness shocked even politicians; and a commission to paint the nation's hero, Sir Winston Churchill, which was to end in an even bigger rumpus.

Any one of these would have been enough for most people. Overlapping as they did in several cases, they constituted a major trial of strength. Fortunately, Graham had a remarkable resilience for such a thin-skinned man, which, coupled with Kathleen's unfaltering faith in him, saw him through.

As it happened, the first major commission of the new decade—in April 1950—provided an opportunity for precisely the sort of consolidation that seemed to be needed. It came from the office of the Festival of Britain, a celebration of all that was most 'contemporary' in British design that was due to open on the South Bank of the Thames in London the following spring. The theme was to be the 'Origins of the Land' (though Graham first called his work *Forces of Nature*), and it was to be a canvas measuring some 14 feet high by 11 feet wide, dwarfing even the Northampton *Crucifixion*.

Here was a chance to tackle the kind of primeval theme he loved. His mind must have gone back to those days in 1924 when he helped Clive Gardiner with his Wembley mural. First, he produced a series of small studies of the various themes which he wanted to bring together on the huge canvas: rock formations found at Tourette-sur-Loup, near Vence; a pterodactyl skeleton from a natural history museum; and one of his pupa-like standing forms. He then experimented with various ways of putting these together before producing a final working drawing, measuring $49\frac{1}{2}$ by $39\frac{1}{4}$ inches, in chalk and gouache. This he transferred to canvas, with the help of an assistant, introducing considerable compositional changes in the process (for instance, he enlarged and lowered the pterodactyl, which owed something to the influence of Max Ernst). The canvas itself was painted in a basement studio made available to him at the Tate Gallery, of which he had by now been a trustee for more than two years.

The painting, Graham explained later, was divided into layers, like a cliff face.[2] The standing forms in the foreground represented the principles of organic growth; the pterodactyl was a hint of prehistory; the rocks at the top represented the action of water and wind on the earth's surface; the flowers at the base were symbols of the heat of the earth's interior. Graham did not finish it till mid-March 1951, a month and a half after the deadline. The fee of £1000 was paid in instalments as the work progressed. While working on the final stages, he joined the Sign and Display trade union, in common with some twenty of the seventy-one painters doing work for the Festival, thus acquiring a union card and paying his dues of four shillings and one penny a week. But membership afforded him no protection against one unforeseen mishap: scarcely had the painting been fixed in place than it was wilfully slashed. 'The authorities are grossly to blame, since there are no doors to the building, into which anyone can walk,' he wrote to Kenneth Clark on 15 April. Clark replied soothingly four days later: 'You know that for those of us who have looked after old pictures, a slash or two means absolutely nothing.' The culprit was not caught.

No less than fifty studies for the painting were shown at the Redfern Gallery in November 1952. 'In a haze of yellow, pink, green, orange and red the organic and inorganic energies rise together and marry and put forth their strange progeny,' wrote the *Manchester Guardian*'s critic approvingly. *The Times*'s critic reckoned the finished canvas to be one of Graham's most successful and romantic works, with a 'genuine amplitude of form', but thought his talent was best seen in the 'small and rather slight' works at the Redfern, a feline compliment echoed by the *Listener*. The idea that studies for larger works might in themselves make a good exhibition had first been sown by Curt Valentin, Graham's American dealer, when he saw the preliminary work for the *Crucifixion*. It had by now taken firm root, and the sale of such 'preparatory' works—sometimes modified after the completion of the main work—became a regular, and not unprofitable, feature of Graham's output.

In September 1950, after a few weeks in Villefranche, Graham and Kathleen paid their first visit to Venice. With the exception of 1951, they were to stay there for a fortnight or more (usually a month) every summer for the rest of Graham's life. The man who first made it possible was Arthur Jeffress, of the Hanover Gallery. He had a house there, not far from the Ponte dell'Accademia. It was not grand, but it had four or five bedrooms, nineteenth-century furniture, works by the Belgian Surrealist Paul Delvaux in the dining-room, a competent staff and—a touch of ego-boosting luxury—a private gondola lined in costly red fabric and propelled by two handsome gondoliers accoutred in papal yellow and white. In general, Graham did not like cities. But Venice, riding peerless—and carless—on the water, is *sui generis*. He spent that first holiday absorbing its paintings, its churches and its mysterious recesses. Its social life came later.

That autumn saw the publication of the second book on Graham's work, after two years of far from painless preparation. It was published in November 1950 by Hans Juda's Ambassador Editions, with a text by Robert Melville, a critic whom Graham had met through Arthur Jeffress. Melville upset Juda by falling behind schedule with his text. Graham upset him by being prima donna-ish over some photographs which Elsbeth Juda had taken of him for the book. The one they planned to use was, he suggested, rather cold and depressing in tone. There seemed to be practically no 'modeling' (sic) between nose and mouth, and he seemed to be pursing his lips, 'which are naturally thick and sensuously full', he had written to Juda in September 1949. It was probably more perfectionism than vanity, but Graham could be maddeningly particular in his dealings. A photograph by Israel Shenker was used eventually.

The book, entitled simply *Graham Sutherland*, 'with an introduction by Robert Melville', was a tall, slim production with seventy plates (twenty-four in colour) and twenty-seven illustrations in the text, priced at £2 12s. Melville covered Graham's evolution as an artist, and in particular his imagery, but the plates were exclusively of his last five years' work. Included among them was a reproduction of a handwritten 'letter' from Graham to

Juda about his creative process, of a kind later to become familiar, sometimes clotted in style, sometimes wonderfully simple and revealing, as when he wrote: 'The unknown is just as real as the known, and must be made to look so.'

If Graham's prose sometimes suffered from over-compression, Melville's oscillated between brilliant insights and a facility bordering on auto-intoxication. Vividly, for example, he described the faltering and anxious quality of Graham's draughtsmanship, seeing him as 'one of the great diffidents, a virtuoso of inconfidence', one who touches on things 'barely ponderable'. Less convincingly, he saw some X-marks on the background of the Northampton *Crucifixion* as 'faint impressions of inarticulate emotions and undisclosed thoughts . . . a kind of abstract scrawling of Consummatum Est . . . terribly bitter in its implications', and so on. Melville detected a 'grave animal face' looming out from Christ's torso. (In the 1955 revised edition of his Penguin book, Eddy Sackville-West also found a face formed by Christ's nipples, rib-shadow and abdomen.) Graham himself dismissed such claims as nonsensical.[3]

The book was duly launched on 29 November. A party at Hans Juda's penthouse flat at Number 10, Palace Gate, Kensington, was attended—as a notice solemnly inserted in *The Times* next day recorded—by Sir Philip Hendy, who had taken over from Clark at the National Gallery in 1946, Sir Edward Marsh, Maugham, Herbert Read and a selection of friends and art critics. Graham was genuinely grateful to Juda for everything: 'over all these months (and years) you have put up with all my nervous reactions and criticisms with the best possible grace,' he wrote on 27 November. 'I am touched and encouraged by this mark of confidence in my work—the best possible tonic at moments when I feel despondent. It is *such* a beautiful book—and I hope it sells really well. My gratitude and thanks and love— Graham.'

It did *not* sell well. Two thousand copies were printed. The critics gave it a generally friendly welcome. But Juda was not a professional book publisher, and despite some help with distribution from the firm of Zwemmer, of Charing Cross Road, Graham found himself (even more often, perhaps, than most authors) constantly discovering that far from stocking it, bookshops had not heard of it.

In the spring of 1951 he was back in Cap Ferrat, staying in another rented villa in the same road as La Mignonelle and sketching Lord Beaverbrook, while Kenneth Clark opened a medium-sized retrospective of his work at the Institute of Contemporary Arts, in Dover Street, London W1. The ICA, very different in those days from now, had been founded in 1947 principally by Roland Penrose, Peter Watson, Peter Gregory and Herbert Read. All were well versed in French painting, and for the next dozen years the ICA played an important role in making British art more international and, like the British Council and Arts Council, in promoting those in whose work it believed.

The ICA retrospective drew heavily on the collections of such well established Sutherland admirers as Clark himself, who lent seven works, Colin Anderson (two), Wilfrid Evill (five), Frankland Dark, the architect (three), Raymond Mortimer, who wrote a catalogue introduction (three), Eddy Sackville-West (two) and so on. It ran to seventy items, a good cross-section, though early etchings and war drawings were minimally represented. In his opening address Clark spoke of the perils with which the South of France threatened British landscape painters—one could not imagine Constable on the Riviera, he said—but thought that after first losing a certain poetic suggestiveness, Graham's work had become more solid in construction, his compositions fuller, with something of the 'frontality' of classical art.

The exhibition provided the first public showing of the Maugham portrait, which Clark had helped to get out of France. Sutherland, he said, was now painting Lord Beaverbrook. He doubted whether many sitters would 'subject their mugs to such impartial scrutiny' and believed that in the next years the purpose of Graham's art would be to make objects more real. However large and brilliant Sutherland's canvases might be, he was primarily not a decorative painter but a painter of truth, revealed in moments of vision, he concluded. It was the gentlest admonition, advice wrapped in a tribute.

Graham thought Clark was on the right lines in speculating about a move towards realism. 'Without committing myself, I think that the day of the form that stands instead of the real form, *merely* as a symbol of it, is over,' he wrote from Cap Ferrat, on receiving the text of Clark's speech.[4] 'And that the transformed form must "look" in some way like nature. This can easily be misinterpreted and is difficult to explain, but I think *you* will know what I mean.' In fact, Graham continued to paint standing forms and even stranger objects for the next two or three years.

Capturing the likeness of Lord Beaverbrook, the Canadian-born newspaper proprietor, wartime Cabinet Minister and brilliant amateur historian, was meanwhile proving no light task. 'I have been working on the Beaver,' Graham told Clark.[5]

I found him very agreeable and amusing and entertaining. As a sitter he never keeps still, neither as regards the whole head, not the individual features on it, for, literally, one second. I had to crawl around his face to see what I was drawing a second before I made a lot of *very* indifferent drawings and one colour sketch. I think I have got most of the facts, though, and they now need sorting out and co-ordinating by the aid of memory, which at the moment is still very clear about his look. But he has a thousand 'faces', and it is difficult consciously to select one which seems to be the real person. Alternately he was blasting someone to hell on the telephone, or in retrospective contemplation, or allowing his face to light up with love of his granddaughter, who is the apple of his eye—or comparing the appearance of the Pope ('little rat') adversely with that of the Moderator of the Church of Scotland, or singing hymns![6]

The main sittings took place at Beaverbrook's Villa Capponcina at Cap d'Ail. This time, in addition to the usual pencil studies, Graham did an oil sketch in front of his subject and a fully worked painting of his head, also from the life, before tackling the portrait itself, most of which he did at his studio in Kent,[7] seeing Beaverbrook once more in the process.

He had finished a 'head', he reported to Clark on 23 April. 'I think it is a likeness, because I have analysed him very carefully, and I can now afford, without forgetting his physical and psychological personality, to leave him for a bit to gain some very necessary detachment.' But this second portrait proved far harder than he had expected. He was fascinated by the scissor-like way in which his subject crossed his short legs but could not get them on to canvas to his satisfaction, eventually destroying four versions before finishing the final one.[8] He was still grappling with it on 1 October, when he wrote to Milner Gray: 'I've been through hell over the Beaver's portrait and haven't finished yet. Completely demoralized.' Felix Man had taken photographs during the Cap d'Ail sittings, but these did not enable Graham to overcome his problems. Man recalled clearly the state of near-panic to which Graham was reduced by his struggles to get the Beaver right.

The portrait was finished in November, however, and showed Beaverbrook in a vivid blue suit, perched on a small chair against a predominantly green background of draped fabric and loosely holding some papers in his lap, his tanned features puckered in an ambiguous smile. Once again, it was an image of great vitality, bordering perhaps on caricature.

The portrait had been commissioned as a birthday present by a group of Beaverbrook Press executives, who had contributed to its cost out of their own pockets, but it was eventually to be handed over to the Beaver himself not by Graham, who had developed 'flu at the last moment, but by Kathleen, who took it in the first half of November to Beaverbrook's

London flat at Arlington House, behind the Ritz Hotel. 'Well, Kathy,' he said, after surveying it, 'it's an outrage—but it's a masterpiece.' Maugham, faced with competition from his Riviera neighbour and friend, commented: 'Now that he has done me and Lord Beaverbrook, I wish he would give up portraits.'⁹ Maugham had lent his own to the Tate after the ICA show, later giving it to his daughter, Lady John Hope (later Lady Glendevon), on the understanding that she gave it to the Tate—which she did, without taking possession. In January 1952 Beaverbrook joined Maugham on show there.

The reactions of the Beaverbrook Press were predictably sycophantic. Others were less convinced by the portrait. Could the odd power of folds, furrows and highlights carry the spectator's imagination over the weakness of the solid masses on which they should depend, the *New Statesman*'s critic, 'J. B.', wondered on 2 February. In the *Listener* of 14 February Quentin Bell gave the Beaver good marks for being happy to be shown 'looking very much like a diseased toad bottled in methylated spirit'. Sutherland was no flatterer: but the crucial diagonal running towards the top corner was feeble and uncertain; the head was divorced from the shoulders; and the left leg had not been understood. Taken with the sketch at the Tate for the Northampton *Crucifixion*, with its 'loudly shouted misquotations' from the Grünewald altarpiece, something was very wrong about Graham Sutherland, Bell concluded.

Graham now became, willy-nilly, the darling of the Beaverbrook Press, which was soon chronicling his comings and goings to the South of France, his every commission, even his indispositions. The critics, distressed perhaps, if only subconsciously, to see an indubitably 'modern' painter becoming the subject of popular interest and even acclaim, began to subject his work to a scrutiny possibly tinged with a desire to discredit. It was a very natural reaction. If the Beaverbrook Press, emulated by its rivals, was promoting Graham, there would always be those anxious to prick the bubble of his popular fame—for such it became. During the next decade the gap between his popular and his critical reputation was to grow. This hurt Graham considerably. It was a very difficult time in his career, and he expected more sympathy from the informed.

In July 1951 he faced his second one-man show at the Hanover Gallery. Although there was less excitement about it—his Mediterranean mode, and the gallery, now being established—it was commercially more successful than the first; twenty-five out of more than forty oils, gouaches and watercolours were sold. The strange but compelling standing forms, against a variety of backgrounds, predominated, yielding gradually to some overtly human figures seen at the ends of paths in bamboo plantations and to some attractive studies of roses and datura flowers, those rankly sweet trumpets to whose sensuous forms Graham often returned.

The Times's anonymous art critic (Alan Clutton-Brock) thought some of the paintings showed signs of effort (clearly un-British). In the *Sunday Times* John Russell, who had met Graham in the early 1940s through Sackville-West, welcomed his recent switch from thorn to rose and to a new sweetness of colour and content. The Arts Council paid £315, the top price, for a very fine *Standing Form against Hedge*, and the Vancouver Art Gallery gave £157 10s. for *Two Standing Forms against a Palisade*. The show yielded £1137 net, less £200 for framing costs.

If the critics were only moderately enthusiastic about the standing forms—and even Douglas Cooper, when most sympathetic to Graham's work, called them 'puzzling and somewhat artificial . . . expressions of a private visual and emotional obsession . . . fetish-like . . . essentially unreal', while conceding them a 'potent degree of pictorial reality'[10]—they were unlikely to be impressed by Graham's next portrait commission.

It was to paint the Queen, who had seen his portrait of Maugham at the Tate in early July. Graham accepted, no doubt with misgivings, given the Royal Family's patchy record of patronage. He suggested August or September for the first sittings, but the Queen traditionally went to Scotland then. To the annoyance of both palace and painter, the *Evening Standard* got wind of the project. 'Next year Sutherland may paint a portrait of the Queen,' it announced on 14 November. 'This would be Sutherland's first portrait of a woman.'

However, the health of King George VI declined, and in early February 1952 he died. That July the Queen Mother, as she now was, felt able to revive the project, and sittings were suggested for the autumn. Then Graham's father died, and other commitments pressed in. The plan was on again in 1953 and 1954. Graham was quoted in the press as saying he wanted to paint the Queen Mother in a hat because it 'added to the impression of Queenliness'. He had picked a hat with a shower of feathers and regarded the picture as 'a kind of challenge to my style of art'. But Graham continued to produce a range of excuses for postponing work on the portrait (the publicity, absence abroad, ill health, poor winter light), and the Queen Mother did not sit for him until 1961. Only a sketch, of some charm, finally emerged.

That autumn of 1951 he was faced with a far more challenging commission. In November he was invited by Basil Spence, then an only moderately well-known architect, to discuss with him the possibility of designing a tapestry to go behind the high altar of the new Coventry

Cathedral which Spence was to design. (That saga we will examine later.) When Spence came to see Graham in January 1952, he was in the throes of his experiments with sculpture. The Sutherlands were staying this time in a studio flat in Villefranche which belonged to some acquaintances, Ronnie and Charlotte Morris. It was up seven flights of stairs, in a street aptly called Descente du Marché, and Kathleen recalled helping Graham to haul sacks of plaster up the stairs. Sometimes they would break, leaving a fine powder and a trail of footprints.

One of the plaster casts, Graham wrote to Clark on 9 February 1952, took between three and four weeks to make: 'so far, among those done, there are alas only two pieces which satisfy me—even moderately: but it is no good forcing things.' It is believed that Graham made about six sculptures in all at this stage. But only one, *Standing Figure 1952*, was cast in bronze in about 1959, in an edition of six. It is a rather charming, faun-like little creature, wholly benign. Meanwhile, Graham's painting was to continue to have a strongly sculptural look for the next three or four years, as it had since 1949.

His hankering to do sculpture remained to the end. 'I would like to do very much more,' he said in 1978.[11]

I would really like to have been a sculptor. In some ways I much prefer sculpture as a medium, partly because when you've made something, when you've got to a certain stage, it's there. It's in front of you. You can touch it. You can put your hand around it, whereas a painting is a very ephemeral thing. It's true, you can destroy something that you've made in sculpture fairly easily by false moves, especially in carving, but in modelling there's no risk of that because you can just go on, you can scrape off again, but in painting you can destroy in five minutes or less. The whole thing can collapse.

That winter of 1951–2 Graham was anxiously accumulating work for a retrospective exhibition which promised to be decisive as far as his international reputation was concerned. He had been invited, in February 1951, to be the main painter represented at the British pavilion at the 1952 Venice Biennale. The Biennale had been founded by the Italians in 1895, no doubt partly as a showcase for Italian paintings, which continued to occupy a disproportionate space. Each country had its own pavilion, filled to best advantage by its cultural authorities; and there were numerous prizes for artists being shown, selected by juries of varying qualifications and impartiality.

When the Biennale was revived in 1948 the British Council had only three months' notice to find exhibitors. A travelling Turner exhibition was rerouted, and Moore, who had plenty of work available, was pressed into service, winning the main sculpture prize and greatly furthering his own international reputation and that of British art. Perhaps it was the Venetian light that killed interest in Matthew Smith's work in 1950, while Hepworth's was, unfairly, considered to be sub-Moore.

Graham had been unanimously selected by Philip Hendy, Herbert Read, John Rothenstein and Lilian Somerville. His stable mates were to be Edward Wadsworth, a veteran of the Vorticist, Futurist and other early movements, who had died in 1949, and a group of talented young sculptors: Robert Adams, Kenneth Armitage, Reg Butler, Lynn Chadwick, Geoffrey Clarke, Bernard Meadows, Eduardo Paolozzi and William Turnbull, not one of whom failed to make their mark sooner or later. A token Moore was also included but nothing by Hepworth, to her deep distress. Graham co-operated in the selection of his own work. No etchings, few 1930s drawings or paintings and no war drawings were to be included. Clark was to write an introduction to the catalogue.

Organizing such a show is a considerable task. The British Council had to write to several dozen potential lenders and arrange for the works to be packed, dispatched to London and collected, then transported to Venice. Tact was essential: to ignore a collector might alienate him for good. Should an impression of rich diversity or of underlying consistency be aimed at? At first, Graham thought that his large *Deposition*, owned by Evill, might make for disunity but eventually decided in its favour. Clark was keen that his *Red Tree* of 1936 be shown. It became the earliest exhibit.

Graham and Kathleen arrived in Venice on 8 June. Evill and his friend Honor Frost were already there, as were Robert Melville and wife, the painter and writer Michael Ayrton, the art historian J. P. Hodin and, naturally, Lilian Somerville, whose finest hour the Biennale was. The national pavilions—Britain's had been a restaurant—were in the Giardini, one of Venice's few green spots, and in the evening St Mark's Square and the city's restaurants became gathering places for artists, dealers and critics who gossiped about who was terrific, who dreadful and who merely mediocre.

In those post-war years, before cheaper air travel and freight had shrunk the Western world, the Biennale was, to a considerable extent, where reputations were made and where fascinated participants watched European art, and French art in particular, being toppled from its perch by the vitality of the New York school. That year Alexander Calder of the USA won the main sculpture prize. It was too soon to deprive French art of both main prizes, and the one for paintings worth some £800 went to Raoul

Dufy, presumably for earlier achievements. Graham had to be content with an 'acquisition' prize (the money went on one of his works) from the Museum of Modern Art in São Paulo, Brazil, worth some £300. It was better than nothing, and the British pavilion as a whole aroused tremendous enthusiasm. 'Even if the younger sculptors had not been influenced by Graham, they looked as if they had a good deal in common,' Lilian Somerville recalled.[12] 'Graham was all thorns and bristly things, and they were rather spiky too.'

M. H. Middleton, writing in the *Spectator* of 27 June, was one of those who regretted that Graham had not got the main painting prize. He thought it likely that his three rooms would confirm his reputation internationally, as Moore's had done four years before. The fantastic revival of Britain's international prestige in the visual arts deserved to be better appreciated at home, he said. That was a thrust against an article by Sylvia Sprigge in the *Manchester Guardian,* which attacked Graham's work for bearing no resemblance 'to anything we love, like or hate in nature or man', and the young sculptors for seizing on Eliot's image of the Hollow Men and peopling the Waste Land with their 'iron waifs'. She was rapped on the knuckles in the paper's letters column first by Herbert Read, who said that, as the 'commissario' of the British pavilion, he had been told again and again by foreign critics and others that the British pavilion was the most vital, brilliant and promising in the whole Biennale, and then by Alfred Barr, of the Museum of Modern Art in New York. 'Graham Sutherland's growing international reputation as the leading painter of his generation was confirmed,' Barr wrote on 3 September, while the young sculptors provided the biggest surprise of the whole Biennale.

Graham and Kathleen stayed on, *chez* Jeffress again, for a week after the Biennale's opening. Among those they met were Freya Stark, the writer and traveller, who lived not far off, near Treviso, and whose father had been a sculptor, and Renato Guttuso, the gifted Italian painter (and communist), and his aristocratic wife, who became good friends. Jeffress was there part of the time. Michael Wishart and his wife, Anne Dunn, both painters, came to dinner one evening. Talk turned to galleries, and Anne observed: 'Erica [Brausen] is the only good thing about the Hanover Gallery' — forgetting that her host owned it. There was a loud silence, after which she ran all the way back to their room in the Clock Tower of St Mark's Square.[13] The Wisharts were good friends at the time; they were for gambling, eating and drinking with, mainly on the Riviera, and had something of Bacon's wild originality.

The Venice show was, on balance, a considerable success and laid the foundation of Graham's reputation abroad, variable though that was always to be. Next came Paris, still the capital of modern art, even if in decline. In April Graham's friend Jean Cassou, Director of the Musée National d'Art Moderne there, had confirmed to the British Council that he would like the Venice exhibition to come to Paris afterwards. He was supported by Georges Salles, Director of the Louvre museums, whom Graham had met in March, also through the British Council's Frank McEwen. A similar request came later from Dr Willem Sandberg, then Director of the Stedelijk Museum in Amsterdam. All lenders thus had to be asked if they would extend their loans until April of the following year.

But first Graham returned to Kent for three months. There he worked on his first design of the Coventry tapestry; became more involved in growing tensions at the Tate Gallery; did some teaching at the Slade School of Fine Art, to which he had committed himself, on an occasional basis, at the invitation of William Coldstream, its head since 1949; visited the Queen Mother to arrange a portrait postponement; and worked on paintings for another New York show in March 1953. A tendency to overload his schedule was already noticeable. As if under-occupied, however, he returned to Venice in September to take part in the UNESCO International Conference of Artists with Stephen Spender, the playwright Benn Levy, the architect Ralph Tubbs and Henry Moore. A low-yield event, by all accounts.

Back again in Kent, Graham heard that his father was dying in Jersey. He and his brother Humphrey flew there on 2 October. Graham had been to see his father in June 1945, after he had had a heart attack, and he had returned in March 1952, when the arthritic hip from which his father had suffered for twenty-five years had led to a circulatory defect. Now the old man's suffering, aggravated by near-blindness, was painful to behold. 'I shall be glad when I die, because then I shall be rid of this beastly pain,' he told Graham and Humphrey, when they arrived after a hair-raising flight in a Dragon Rapide biplane, which had been flung upwards by air currents as they passed over Jersey's coastal cliffs. He died on 4 October at 3 p.m., aged 79, of 'cardiac infarction [and] generalized osteo-arthritis'. A talented man had gone to his grave without ever really fulfilling his potential. Graham's determination to make full use of his own gifts perhaps stemmed from a conscious desire to avoid a similar fate.

Although Henry Moore's sculpture had preceded him there, Graham was to be the first living British painter to be shown at the Musée d'Art Moderne. Frank McEwen believed that the impact Graham and some examples of his work had had on Georges Salles at a dinner he had given in

March for Graham (Léger was also there) had played an important part in securing the show. The French had even offered to print the invitation cards. Unfortunately, the six government bodies involved could not agree on the wording. Four days before the private views McEwen discovered that not one had been printed. Swift action by him averted disaster.

Graham arrived on 2 November, taking the opportunity to dine with Peter Watson, his old patron, who was back in Paris. Salles made an opening speech, and no less than 1500 people came to the private view. Attendance over the thirty days from 6 November was less impressive: just under 6000 in all, or 200 a day. But those who mattered had been impressed, McEwen reckoned, and a surprisingly warm press supported his view.[14] *Combat* described it as a 'magnificent panorama of the work of one of the most important British painters'—Sutherland made nature sing with luminous harmonies and an extreme sensibility. *Le Monde* said that Graham felt nature with 'a mixture of fear and veneration' and 'took the imagination under the earth into the obscurities of germination'. *Le Figaro* called him 'Sutterland' but was favourable. In *Arts* a most enthusiastic Bernard Dorival said Graham mingled dynasties and species, animated the inanimate, metamorphosed the universe and infused his most delightful imaginings with undeniable artistic life. Where was Parisian chauvinism? In abeyance, it seemed. (Only in Turin in 1965 did Graham ever again receive such sympathetic reviews.) Even French dealers now wanted to show his work. But he did not have enough in hand; everything was needed for New York. It was a matter of long-lasting regret to him, Kathleen recalled, that he was unable to catch a tide which in Paris never flowed so favourably again.

Graham's successes in Venice and the French capital had their effect in London. In his fiftieth year Graham Sutherland enjoyed an international reputation not accorded to an English artist since Constable showed at the Paris Salon of 1823, said a profile—anonymous, but redolent of John Russell, its art critic—in the *Sunday Times* on 23 November. He had dominated the vast, miscellaneous scene in Venice. Now his 'dramatic vegetables' were commanding attention in Paris. Detecting in Graham 'the eye of a coastguard and the heart of a Franciscan', the article said that he had been exalted, not altogether willingly, to the status of a 'roving, wary and uncockaded ambassador'. It was a fulsome tribute, which read ironically when Russell attacked Graham a decade later.

The Venice/Paris retrospective went on to Amsterdam and Zurich, spreading the message in only moderately receptive countries. Graham, after a brief return to England, headed south again, calling in at Paris once more; it was his sixth visit that year. On a visit to Vallauris after Christmas with Curt Valentin, they saw Picasso and his two vast murals ($15\frac{3}{4}$ feet by 34 feet) called *War and Peace* in a disused chapel, destined to become a Temple of Peace. A burst of work on the Coventry tapestry coincided incongruously—a form of reaction, perhaps—with a particularly intensive bout of gambling. For a spell Graham and Kathleen were at the roulette table almost every evening in Monte Carlo. Gambling reflected their rootless state there: rented villas or flats were not much fun in the evening. Often they went with the Wisharts, who were then living on the coast.

In early March they had moved briefly from an uninspiring house called the Cottage Dominic in Pont St Jean, at the less desirable end of Cap Ferrat, to the Voile d'Or Hotel, spectacularly situated on its tip. It belonged to an Englishman, Captain Frank Powell, and his son Michael, a successful film director and producer. From there Graham returned to the Villa Mauresque to take some fresh notes of Maugham's head: he had been commissioned by A. S. Frere to do a lithograph of Heinemann's moneyspinner for a special edition of *Cakes and Ale*, to celebrate the author's eightieth birthday in January 1954. Graham and Kathleen had remained on extremely friendly terms with Maugham, frequently eating at the Mauresque. Now, with a familiar subject and only a head to worry about, Graham produced one of his most sympathetic character studies: four heads, of which the finest was transferred to stone at the Curwen Press in London that July. Graham and Maugham signed all 1000 copies of the five-guinea edition of *Cakes and Ale*, which rapidly sold out.

The relentless sequence of exhibitions continued. On 10 March 1953 Graham's third one-man show at Curt Valentin's gallery in New York opened with twenty-nine works completed since 1950, of which fourteen were oils. A rather unappealing, Bacon-like monkey called *Cynocéphale*, done for Venice, was there, some standing forms and some reworkings of the 'path through plantation' theme. A new form of sculptural head made its debut at this show, not based on strange stone formations but rather resembling a hybrid of bird, insect human and vegetable. As Bernard Dorival had so justly said, Graham was mingling dynasties and species, the animate and the inanimate. The new heads were also on a little plinth. The result looked like a painting of a bizarre sculpture. Later in the year Graham first moved towards more overtly mechanistic forms, distillations perhaps of his memories of Derby and wartime factories, blended with organic forms. His interest in the inter-penetration of things was gathering pace.

The New York critics were marginally more favourable this time. The famous English painter invariably dealt with appearances as they became transfigured in his imagination, Stuart Preston wrote in the *New York Times* of 15 March. His creations were 'strange and wonderfully imaginative precipitations of organic shapes'. But although their unnatural naturalism fascinated, the critic claimed, he provided no more than its mask, and that was too laboured. In the *New York Herald Tribune* that day Carlyle Burrows found evidence of significant effort to dramatize evolution but little felicity of design or colour. Only rarely had the result seemed anything but obscure.

Bafflement predominated when a modified version of the ICA retrospective of 1951 was shown from coast to coast in 1953, first (in April) at Boston's own Institute of Contemporary Art and thereafter in Seattle, Los Angeles, San Francisco, Houston, Washington DC, Akron and Coral Gables, Florida. A small selection of Henry Moore sculpture was shown with it. 'After the first few days of the show, Boston seemed pretty cool in its reactions,' *Time* magazine reported on 13 April. Some visitors had complained about Sutherland's deliberately ungainly compositions and harsh colours, it reported, wondering 'what goes on in the head of a man who's always painting grasshoppers'. However, one student said it was like meeting a famous relative for the first time; and Aline Louchheim, in the *New York Times* of 12 April, found something very much 'of our time' in Graham's use of enlarged detail and in his awareness of organic forces in a world conscious of the fact that matter is energy and energy is matter. However, she found his later, invented images less vital and drier, more literary than his earlier ones.

This unusually sensitive critic mentioned Masson and Matta among other artists preoccupied by organic forces, but if any one influence seems to have predominated at this stage, it was Bacon's, though the traffic in ideas was not wholly one-way.

It is fascinating to compare the work of the two men.[15] One possible deduction is that in some cases Graham seemed to be painting Bacon-like works on a given theme *before* Bacon himself tackled it. For example, Graham's *Men Walking* of 1950 (of which he did two very similar versions) shows two men walking in strong sunlight against an archetypal Riviera landscape of palm trees. Bacon did three or four not dissimilar landscapes (for example *Landscape, South of France*), all of them dated 1952. In the right hand corner of Graham's 1950 work is a Bacon-like dog. Most of Bacon's dogs date from 1952. However, Bacon was painting monkeys in 1951 (*Figure with Monkey*); Graham's first monkey, *Cynocéphale* (shown in Venice), dates from 1952. It may be relevant to note that Bacon has always been a much slower worker than Graham, destroying a far higher proportion of his output: there may have been Bacons which Graham saw appreciably earlier than they were later dated or which never emerged from Bacon's studio.

Like most serious painters—Picasso being the prime example—Graham was enthralled by the whole world of painting. Influences pursued a mole-like path through his mind, taking some time to throw up a mound or two as evidence of their passage. However, as a friend, Bacon was now fading from Graham's life. Graham continued to admire his work, though later he thought it had become a shade too autobiographical. He came to find Bacon's drinking bouts tiresome, as also Bacon's denigration of those Graham admired, like Picasso, Braque and Matisse.[16] (In fact, Bacon rarely bothered to attack those whose work did not interest him.)

Bacon, for his part, was far from enthusiastic about Graham's growing friendship with the redoubtable collector and critic Douglas Cooper. Bacon had known Cooper in about 1929–30, and Cooper had bought a desk he had designed. They had resumed contact after the war, but Cooper, according to Bacon, then turned against him. Cooper, as we shall see, had a low opinion of most contemporary British artists at this stage—despite, or perhaps because of, his involvement in Unit One in the 1930s—and friends of Graham, like Bacon and Lucian Freud, felt that they were on some long black list of Cooper's.

None of this prevented Graham from producing a markedly Bacon-like work just in time for his next high hurdle: a full-scale retrospective at the Tate Gallery in May, part of a special programme of exhibitions marking the Coronation of Queen Elizabeth II. The last-minute addition was a large (6 feet by $4\frac{1}{2}$ feet) oil called *Christ Carrying the Cross*. It shows Christ stumbling under the weight of the cross, kicked forward by a thuggish, bloated and horribly grinning soldier, seemingly on the veranda of a Mediterranean villa.[17] Delicate brushwork heightens the savagery of the scene.

There were always distractions—in this case, more filming, in Kent, for the first BBC television study of his work, directed and written by John Read (son of Herbert), with research by Robert Melville. Although not without glimpses of the obvious ('From his studio have come many of his most important works'), it succeeded well in the difficult task of relating to Graham's work the sources of his inspiration in Wales, France and Kent. This time Graham did not return to Wales for filming. The programme was transmitted on 7 December 1953.

Retrospective exhibitions can be a severe test, sometimes revealing a monotony or repetitiousness in an artist's output not evident in a smaller selection. Alternatively, they may show an artist lurching from one influence to another, without any real individuality. Those who generally emerge best

...raham with his portrait of W. S. Maugham at Cap Ferrat, May 1949

Graham posing Churchill's fingers, at Chartwell, 17 October 1954

Churchill wanted to paint a portrait of Kathleen. Elsbeth Juda took this photo to help him

Graham in late 1950s

Graham and Kathleen with
Churchill at Chartwell,
17 October 1954

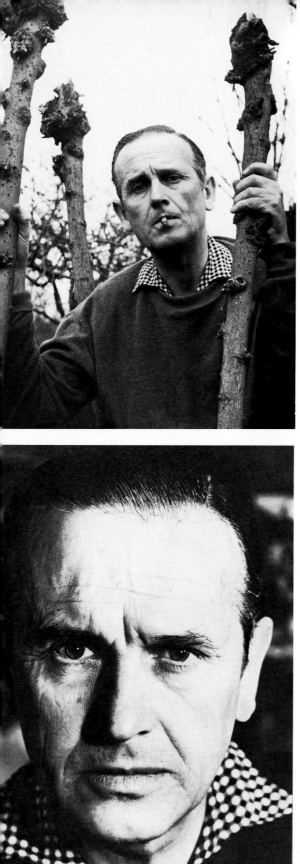

Graham with mutilated trees,
probably at Trottiscliffe, Kent, in
late 1950s

Graham in his late 50s: a piercing
yet troubled gaze

Graham in a temporary studio at Cottage Dominic, St Jean, Cap Ferrat, with a model of Coventry Cathedral. February 1953

Top) Objets trouvés at Graham's original studio at the Villa Blanche in Menton, 1966
Above) A working table in the same studio

Graham making an oil sketch of Lord Beaverbrook's head, at Cap d'Ail, 1951

Graham as 'standing form' behind reeds, probably in the Var valley, south of France, mid-1950s

Chimère I. Oil on canvas, 1946.
$78\frac{1}{2} \times 47\frac{1}{2}$ in (199.4×120.6 cm)

Thorn Trees. Oil on canvas, 1946.
50×40 in (127×101.6 cm)

Still Life with Gourds.
Oil on canvas, 1948.
$18\frac{1}{4} \times 20\frac{1}{2}$ in
(46.3 × 50.1 cm)

Head II. Oil on canvas,
1952. 36 × 28 in
(91.4 × 71.1 cm)

Three Standing Forms in a Garden II. Oil on canvas, 1951. $52\frac{3}{8} \times 45\frac{3}{8}$ in (133×115.2 cm)

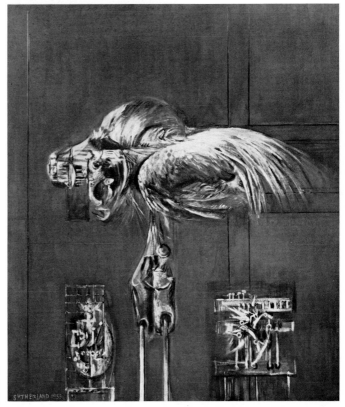

La Petite Afrique III. Oil on canvas, 1955. 56×48 in (142.2×121.9 cm)

Origins of the Land. Oil on canvas, 1951. $167\frac{1}{2} \times 129$ in (425.4×327.6 cm)

Apple Orchard III. Oil on canvas, 1955. 44 × 34 in (111.7 × 86.3 cm)

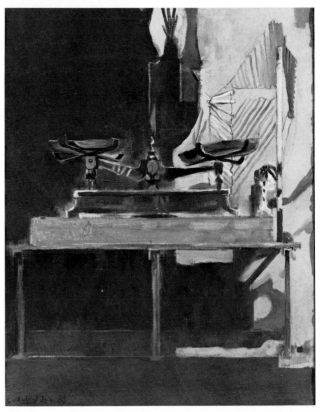

he Scales. Oil on canvas, 1959. 50 × 40 in (127 × 101.6 cm)

Study for lithograph of W. Somerset Maugham. Black and red chalk, 1953. $8\frac{3}{4} \times 5\frac{7}{8}$ in (22.2 × 14.9 cm)

Sketch of Lord Beaverbrook. Oil on canvas, 1950. 20 × 16 in (50.8 × 40.6 cm)

rtrait of Sir Winston Churchill (Destroyed). Oil on canvas, 1954. 58 × 48 in (147.3 × 121.9 cm)

Portrait of Arthur Jeffress. O
canvas, 1955. $56\frac{1}{2} \times 47\frac{1}{2}$ in
(143.5×120.6 cm)

Portrait of Dr Konrad Adena
Oil on canvas, 1965. $56\frac{5}{8} \times 48$
(143.8×123.2 cm)

are those with an underlying coherence and development. The Tate exhibition was to be the same as that which had started in Venice and had travelled to Paris, Amsterdam and Zurich. With its emphasis heavily on Graham's post-war work, it was not comprehensively retrospective: the early etchings, the early Welsh landscapes and the war drawings were still wholly or largely absent. Since he had been involved in the selection process, that must have been deliberate. Perhaps he wanted to avoid the old refrain that he had never done anything as fine as the early landscapes.

He spent three days helping to hang the show, assisted in turn by an old American friend from wartime days, Bill Roerich, who, through an introduction from the Clarks, had become one of the props of the ageing E. M. Forster. Graham and he had lunch with the novelist in London shortly before the opening. In the end, Graham was pleased with the way the show looked. The Contemporary Art Society gave one of its elegant parties, and on 20 May, a week before a Gainsborough exhibition, also at the Tate, it opened.

The catalogue contained three separate tributes to Graham's work. 'Gainsborough and Sutherland, for all their diversity, are both exponents of the true native tradition which springs from an obsession with the English landscape,' wrote Philip James, director of art at the Arts Council, which presented the show. But Sutherland's world of appearances reflected 'the harshness and doubts of a troubled age'. Kenneth Clark called Graham 'the outstanding painter of his generation' and predicted that he would continue to move a few steps ahead of his admirers. Herbert Read dragged in Henri Michaux, Wordsworth, Coleridge, Schelling, Novalis, Heidegger and Sartre to demonstrate the breadth of his cultural knowledge and concluded by saluting Graham as 'possibly the first painter since Turner to take up an independent position as an artist and to maintain it with conviction in the presence of his European contemporaries'; and Cyril Ray was all sensitive admiration in the profile of Graham in the *Sunday Times* of 17 May, finding him very English in his looks and in the shyness that he detected beneath the surface frankness—but commendably Latin in the lunch he offered. Graham used words like 'mysteriousness' and 'ambiguity' in trying to explain his standing forms, and was, Ray suspected, aware of the bones beneath the smooth, grassy skin of the Downs as they strode over them, post-prandially.

But again the British critics disappointed. *The Times*'s thought Graham had been drawing uncommonly near in style and sentiment to Francis Bacon in one or two recent works. He suspected that Graham's moments of 'vision' when he was out walking amounted to no more than spotting nature imitating art, then inserting them into a work in the modern style, setting up his forms, 'singly or in rows, with as monotonous a reiteration of vertical lines as the figures in a photographer's wedding group'.[18] For Bernard Denvir in the *Daily Herald* Graham's works were 'probably the most repellent pictures ever to be seen inside the Tate'. But this was the age of Belsen and the Bomb, he said; when men wanted to know what it was like to be living in 1953, they would look at his paintings. The *Manchester Guardian*'s critic (signed 'A.C.S.') regretted that Graham's transformation of the object first seen went so far, in recent work, as to leave 'little more than an unintelligible private fetish'. It was the smaller, earlier works that most pleased. . . .

The unkindest cut came, not for the first time, from Patrick Heron, a painter of the St Ives School.[19] 'Without doubt he has little ability for controlling strong colour, and even less for creating pictorial sense,' he wrote in the *New Statesman* of 6 June. 'He does not, and never has, understood pictorial form, that quality of plastic weight which unites the forms in a picture rather than separating them. . . .' He feared that Graham had become confused and eclectic since he had gone to the South of France. In the August issue of *Studio* magazine John Curtis also felt Graham should pay more attention to form and the constructive use of colour. Even the dignified *Apollo* magazine fired some barbed shafts in a commentary in its July issue. No one so well sponsored by the British Council, the Arts Council, the Tate Gallery and a cabal of art writers and civil servants with authority in the official art world could help having something of an international reputation, it said, claiming that the show had been launched on a wave of adulation.

Graham, ever hyper-sensitive to criticism, must have been deeply hurt by these attacks, particularly as the critics had no comparable reservations about a concurrent show of Henry Moore's drawings at the ICA. It was scant comfort that in *Time and Tide* his old friend Eric Newton said it was only superficially true that Graham was beginning to owe too heavy a debt to Francis Bacon. However, Kenneth Clark was quick to offer support — although he seemed to concede that the critics might have a point. He wrote on 12 June:

> It is really very nasty to be attacked, as I well know, and it is so difficult to do any creative work that any donkey or jackal can put one off. Of course your friends and all those who really understand what you are doing will not be in the least affected. I believed in your genius before Patrick Heron went to school. In fact I think your later paintings are a great advance (as I have said). Of course it is true that all considerable artists pass through a middle period, when they are developing a new style, and when their

early adherents get left behind. That you are in this position simply indicates that you haven't got into the usual doldrums of English painters. So please don't worry any longer, and do not for a second doubt the genius which it has been our privilege to recognize and acclaim for many years.

There was a good deal of food for thought in Clark's comforting if slightly ambivalent letter. As movement is frozen by a photograph, so Graham's critical reputation was to a large extent frozen by this not fully representative selection of his works. It had caught him in the middle of a very fertile but difficult 'middle period' in which—Clark was right—even admirers were in danger of being left behind. It was nine years before Graham had another substantial exhibition in London. Meanwhile, he became bigger and bigger news. The gap between fame and critical reputation grew wider.

Clark was also right in surmising that those who believed in Graham's work would not be put off by the sniping of the critics. Among those now anxious to purvey Graham's works were the hard-headed Bruton Street dealers, Arthur Tooth and Son, who seasoned a profitable line in Impressionists with some contemporary offerings. In June 1953 they asked Graham to join their modern stable, but he decided against. By now Arthur Jeffress was planning to set up his own gallery in Davies Street, London W1 and wanted to show Graham's work. (Francis Bacon remained faithful to Erica Brausen and the Hanover Gallery.)

Graham still had good relations with the Redfern Gallery, whose directors, Rex Nan Kivell and Harry Tatlock Miller, would make forays to Kent for watercolours and gouaches in particular, usually for stock. 'You had to step over them,' the latter recalled.[20]

> He seemed to work and throw them aside. Some would have coffee spilt over them. I thought he would be meticulous, but he wasn't. There was always a feeling of activity, of force and of power. Graham would simply state his price. That was it, no bargaining; but it would always be a fair price. It was all wonderfully comfortable: delicious food, and a wonderful feeling of sophistication and simplicity. Yet I was always conscious with Graham that he was in a sense tormented . . . it was as if he wore a crown of thorns himself.

Heinz Roland, of Roland, Browse and Delbanco, also in Cork Street, would go on similar missions to Kent, periodically mounting shows of Graham's drawings, all of which would find a buyer before very long.

Dealers were not affected by the critics; nor were the taste-makers of the art establishment or friends. Graham's framer, Alfred Hecht, was by now among these. He was an emigré German Jew who collected both paintings and people at his premises in the King's Road. There, over dinner, he mixed a series of intriguing human cocktails, which included politicians, actors and painters. At one such dinner, on 9 June, he introduced Graham and Kathleen to Aneurin Bevan and his wife Jennie Lee. Still under Clement Attlee's leadership, but in Opposition since 1951, the Labour Party was going through one of its bouts of strife between its left and right wings. Nye Bevan, the brilliantly gifted but temperamental Welshman, was the standard-bearer of the left, Hugh Gaitskell—his opposite in temperament and background—led the right flank.

Stalin had died recently. Bevan was pressing for high-level talks to help thaw the Cold War. There was plenty to talk about over dinner, and Graham, who did indeed have a core of shyness beneath his self-possessed manner, as Cyril Ray had suspected, responded to Bevan's warm-hearted geniality, charm and intelligence. Jennie Lee, since 1945 also a Labour MP, was slightly more doctrinaire in her views. Both were enthusiastic about modern painting, and collected in a modest way. They came to dinner at the White House in Kent in September, when Graham presented Bevan with a war drawing of a bombed house. In October they met again at Hecht's, this time with Francis Bacon too, and on Boxing Day were there once more. A friendship had been started which led to Graham's commission to paint Churchill.

Another friendship, of longer duration, was soon to bear equally interesting if less dramatic fruit. Ian Phillips had met Graham while studying architecture at Cambridge and lodging with the county education director Henry Morris. He was later involved in Morris's efforts, ultimately abortive, to raise enough money to commission works by Graham and Henry Moore for Impington Village College. Graham did a considerable amount of work for a mural before it had to be abandoned. Ian and Jane Phillips—she later became a Labour member for Hammersmith on the London County Council—saw Graham and Kathleen often after marrying in 1943. But it was the Phillips's friendship with Eddy Sackville-West that was to prove seminal. Jane Phillips had met him in 1939, when they were both working for the Red Cross. Both had trained as pianists, and they used to go to concerts and exhibitions together.[21] The friendship continued, and in May 1953 the Phillips went to the private view of the Tate retrospective.

The Maugham and Beaverbrook portraits were there. 'We wanted Graham to be able to paint someone he knew well, with whom he was in sympathy, with no time limit and no constraints,' Jane Phillips recalled. 'We went across the Tate Gallery and simply said [to Graham]: "Would you like to paint Eddy?" It was a commission between old friends.' Graham and

Kathleen went off the following weekend to Long Crichel, the eighteenth-century ex-rectory at Wimborne, in Dorset, which Eddy shared with Eardley Knollys and Desmond Shawe-Taylor. But the sittings proper did not take place until the second half of November, when Graham returned to Long Crichel for five days. Felix Man went down to take some photographs, and after five sittings Sackville-West retired to his white French bed, where he reclined for Graham, rather than sat, looking very elegant in a red flannel hospital robe.[22]

Much of the main work on the portrait itself was done the following spring in the South of France. But its completion was to be delayed by the Tate row and the Churchill portrait.

8

The Tate Affair

1952-4

NINETEEN-FIFTY-FOUR was the most unpleasant and the most testing year of Graham's career. Throughout it he was under pressure to finish the working sketch for the Coventry tapestry. In January he resigned as a trustee of the Tate Gallery, a move which provoked a storm of publicity, distressed many of his colleagues and friends by the manner of its execution and, far from providing the expected clean break from the imbroglio of the Tate Affair (as it was soon called), enmeshed him yet deeper as he sought to justify himself. In August, when the Tate Affair was still in full swing, he began his portrait of Winston Churchill, which was destined to cause more printer's ink to flow than any other in living memory. Yet, in between rows, he laid the basis of perhaps his finest portrait, that of Eddy Sackville-West.

Graham was deeply scarred by the Tate row. He was reluctant to talk about it. One should either tell all or nothing, he thought. Given the nature of Britain's libel laws and the secrecy of Whitehall, to aim for the whole truth would be both rash and lengthy. Silence on such a crucial episode is scarcely possible. The only account so far published is Sir John Rothenstein's, in his autobiographical *Brave Morning, Hideous Night*.[1] As Director of the Tate Gallery, he was at the centre of the storm. His account is inevitably partial, though perhaps unnecessarily emotional.

Graham kept no diary at any stage of his adult life. His general attitude was that his colleagues had ratted on him and that the Establishment had ganged up against him. His fellow trustees, by contrast, felt that he had failed them. Had Graham been a more rational creature, he might well have been a lesser artist, or certainly a very different one. His behaviour in the Tate Affair was not rational. It bore some resemblance to his comportment during the final phases of the completion of the Coventry tapestry. In both instances he handled a good case badly and allowed himself to be unduly influenced by others. In charting his emotional passage one wrings one's hands and thinks, if only he could have saved all that energy for his work. But he had a combative streak, and these battles were not without their anguished pleasures.

Unaccustomed as he was to thinking things through, he no doubt did not realize what he was letting himself in for when he accepted the invitation to become a trustee of the Tate in 1948. The Tate was a monument to the provincialism of British art and taste. The excitements of Roger Fry's exhibitions in the 1910s and the hectic internationalism of the 1930s had passed it by. Part of the trouble went back to its conception. The Tate was founded in 1897 as a branch of the National Gallery, with a mandate to house modern British art only. In 1917, following a report by a committee of National Gallery trustees, it became the national collection of British painting of all periods and of modern foreign painting and sculpture — with no clear definition of 'modern'. Its administration was placed in the hands of a separate board of trustees, its Keeper advanced to the rank of Director; but the collection remained the responsibility of the trustees of the National Gallery, who could (up to 1954) move any work of art from Millbank to Trafalgar Square.

The National Gallery trustees on whose advice such changes were effected were not of adventurous taste themselves. 'We have not in our mind', they said, 'any idea of experimentalizing by rash purchase in the occasionally ill-disciplined productions of some contemporaneous Continental schools, whose work might exercise a disturbing and even deleterious influence upon our younger painters.' One of the last acts of Rothenstein's predecessor, J. B. Manson, had been to advise H. M. Customs in March 1938 not to admit a group of sculptures by Arp, Brancusi, Duchamp, Laurens and Pevsner as works of art.[2]

When Rothenstein took over that year he was struck, by his own account, more by the gaps in the modern British collection — nothing by Wyndham Lewis, Ben Nicholson, Victor Pasmore and Henry Moore, for example — than by the much bigger ones in the modern foreign collection. His own enthusiasm for the more demanding works of modern masters like Picasso and Matisse was only moderate, though later he became a keen admirer of Bacon's work. From the beginning of 1938 to the end of 1948 (just after Graham became a trustee) the Tate bought 189 British works out of gallery funds and only fourteen foreign ones.[3]

It is true that the war did not encourage an international spirit, that some of the Tate's funds from bequests were tied to the purchase of British works and that it had no purchase grant from the Treasury until 1946, when £2000 was vouchsafed annually from the nation's coffers. But foreign works *could* be bought, as was proved by the acquisition of a modest Max Ernst in 1941 and a Juan Gris collage in 1946, respectively the gallery's first Surrealist and Cubist works; and wealthy patrons might have been persuaded to help.

Such was the distressing situation when Graham, with all his enthusiasm for Picasso, Matisse and other great innovators of twentieth-century painting, became a trustee. Coincidentally, that same year the Tate received its first major injection of funds: the Cleve Bequest of £27,000, then a useful sum. Graham helped to create the climate which led to the purchase in 1949 of two Cubist Picassos, a small early Matisse, a Léger, a Rouault, two Degas sculptures and two recent paintings and a sculpture by Alberto Giacometti, then little known. He was a particularly fervent advocate of the Picassos and the Giacometti, the Swiss-born artist having been a protégé of Peter Watson.[4] The following year Graham strongly recommended the purchase of Bacon's *Figure in a Landscape*.

Much of the credit for the wise use of the Cleve fund, which constituted a turning point in the collection's history, belonged to Douglas Cooper, who accompanied Rothenstein on the fruitful shopping trip to Paris. Graham had not had contact with Cooper since the latter's days in the 1930s as the backer of the Mayor Gallery. They met again over dinner at Cooper's London flat in June 1948, not long after Graham's first meeting of Tate trustees and just after the opening of his one-man show at the Hanover Gallery.

There are many myths about Douglas Cooper and the origins of his considerable wealth. It can reliably be said that in 1759 a certain Thomas Cooper went to Australia, whether voluntarily or otherwise it is not certain. His son, of the same name, went into business with a Mr Levi. They founded a trading company called the Waterloo Warehouse. It prospered greatly. On its profits the Cooper fortunes were founded.[5] Some of the proceeds were used to buy real estate in Sydney. Daniel Cooper, second son of the entrepreneurial Thomas Cooper, became the first Speaker of the New South Wales Legislative Assembly, and was made a baronet in 1863. He built a large pile called Woolahra House in Sydney. His son, the second Sir Daniel, left Sydney, settled in England at Newmarket, where he established a good stable of racehorses. After his death in 1909, a hideous drinking fountain for horses was erected there in his memory. The title passed to his brother, who had sold the Woolahra estate in about 1890 and had also moved to England. He was Douglas Cooper's grandfather, and under his will Douglas, the oldest of three brothers, inherited a substantial sum of money on reaching the age of 21.

Douglas's own father, whose elder brother inherited the baronetcy, became a major in the British army, took part in the Boer War and the First World War, married the daughter of a Dorset baronet, Sir William Smith-Marriott, and lived a life of leisure in Belgravia and the country before becoming assistant county welfare officer for Middlesex in the Second World War.

Douglas Cooper studied at Repton and at Cambridge, which he disliked. He left after a year, repairing to the Sorbonne and then to the university at Freiburg-im-Breisgau, Germany, where he acquired fluent French and German, later adding Italian. Having sunk a fraction of his fortune into the Mayor Gallery, he learned much from Freddie Mayor's experience and even more from trips to Paris, where he came to know Picasso, Braque, Léger and others and laid the basis of his collection of Cubist works and of his formidable erudition. The war found him living in Paris, having severed connections with the Mayor Gallery. After various adventures in the RAF, he ended it as deputy director of the monuments and fine arts side of the Allied Control Commission for Germany. When Graham met him again, he had studies of Klee, Gris, Léger and Turner in the pipeline—all were published in 1949—and was preparing the catalogue of the Courtauld Collection. Later he became Slade Professor of Fine Art at Oxford.

What made Cooper so formidable, even (to many people) frightening? It was not the depth and range of his knowledge, impressive though they were, nor the clarity of his critical mind. He had developed a low opinion not only of modern British art but of Britain as a whole. He expressed his views extremely strongly, sometimes in the anonymous columns of the *Times Literary Supplement*, sometimes in his loud, penetrating voice. He had a notable capacity for ridicule: he was sometimes very funny indeed, sometimes devastating. He was physically a big man. The whole effect could be overpowering.

Given Cooper's acknowledged scorn for British painting, which had earlier embraced his own work, Graham must have known that he risked alienating some of his old friends by becoming identified as a Cooper protégé. There was also some surprise in the art world at the fact that a critic who had championed the classical strain in modern painting against the expressionist, the formal against the poetic, should support an artist who was so clearly a descendant of the Romantics. There could scarcely be a larger gap than that between Léger and Sutherland.

With some justification, Graham doubtless believed that Cooper could help him to secure a durable international reputation. For more than twenty years Cooper was indeed to be a redoubtable advocate of his work, and

Graham benefited also from his contacts among the museums, collectors and the rich, from his friendship with Picasso and from his high-spirited company, exhausting though that could be. Cooper, in turn, was attracted by Graham's intelligence and charm, as well as by his qualities as an artist.

As their friendship developed, Graham and Kathleen took to making the detour, on their way south, to the handsome Château de Castille, near the Pont du Gard, in Provence, to which Cooper moved in 1951 and part of which was later embellished with a design by Picasso. Cooper periodically descended on the Riviera or called in on them in Kent on the way from Dover. Graham was impressionable. He came to lean so heavily on Cooper's advice that, rightly or wrongly, people regarded him as Cooper's *deus in machina* in the Tate Affair.[6]

Cooper had no formal link with the Tate, but he had a keen and, initially, a friendly interest in its deficiencies, to the point of lending some of his own collection in the earlier days of Rothenstein's stewardship. His relations with Rothenstein remained good, as did Graham's. Rothenstein recalled a dinner with Graham at the White Tower in February 1951, at which Graham warmly denied a suggestion that he was critical of the gallery's policies. Shortly before, when Graham was painting the *Origins of the Land* in the Tate's Poynter studio, Rothenstein lent him the key of his flat there so that he could rest or have a coffee or a drink. Graham gave him a study for the work that autumn.

Rothenstein's troubles, in which Graham became so embroiled, were initially, as he himself admits, largely of his own making. On a visit to South Africa in 1948, his official host was the Director of the Pretoria Art Centre, a tall, stoutish man in his thirties, with a voice of compelling warmth, called LeRoux Smith LeRoux. LeRoux had become friendly with Lord Harlech, former British High Commissioner in South Africa and a trustee of the Tate from 1946 to 1953. He now winkled his way into the credulous Rothenstein's favour, and the long and short of it was that in 1949 Rothenstein pressed on an unenthusiastic board of trustees the appointment of LeRoux as a temporary deputy keeper of the Tate. He took up his post, with special responsibility for publications, in March 1950.

In October 1951 Sir Jasper Ridley, the patrician chairman of the trustees, who had got on well with Rothenstein, died. He was succeeded by Lord Jowitt, the former Labour Lord Chancellor, a handsome, engaging but complex man, described by some ex-trustees as a 'whited sepulchre'. By the spring of 1952, troubles were beginning to brew at the Tate. Two vacancies among the trustees were coming up. Graham, Henry Moore (who had been re-elected in 1949 after a gap) and others were keen that one of them should go to Kenneth Clark, who was not yet chairman of the Arts Council. Graham wrote to him on 28 April 1951:

> The question of you becoming a Tate Trustee is exercising *all of us*. It is vitally important—particularly just now. But there are, it appears, some queer 'goings on'. But it is my belief that things will sort themselves out soon—I hope that when they do you will still be prepared to come on the Board!

In the event, one vacancy went to Colin Anderson, the other to Dennis Proctor, formerly of the Treasury. Rothenstein believed that the artist-trustees, who also included Edward Bawden and William Coldstream, held Clark's non-appointment against him. It was, he said, a Treasury decision. Brilliant and sympathetic though Colin Anderson was, he did not carry the same weight as Clark in the art world or among the Establishment.

Rothenstein's long, largely self-imposed Calvary began in earnest in the autumn of 1952. At the September or October trustees meeting[7] LeRoux, who attended as the director's right-hand man, rose and read out a long attack on Rothenstein's character and administration, delving into the past and accusing him of behaving with inhumanity to himself and to others who had left.

A number of senior staff had indeed left. Among them was a good friend of Graham's, Humphrey Brooke. Graham and Kathleen had made him welcome at the White House in the spring of 1943, when he was doing a pre-officer's training course at Wrotham, near Trottiscliffe.[8] In 1946 he had been appointed a deputy keeper at the Tate. Before long, he discovered some serious malpractices in the publications department, only to be told that he was interfering in a sphere outside his competence. In the spring of 1949—well after Graham's appointment—he had a nervous breakdown and was not permitted to return to the Gallery as a staff member. A Treasury inquiry that autumn confirmed his suspicions about the publications department. Eventually Brooke became a very successful Secretary of the Royal Academy.

Graham felt that Brooke had been victimized. LeRoux's accusations therefore fell on fertile soil. The South African was a plausible and engaging rogue. Graham believed to the end that, in his way, LeRoux was quite efficient and might help to wield a new broom in the Tate's administrative areas. Certainly, LeRoux was keen to find evidence with which to damage his benefactor.

Rothenstein made the task all too easy. As he himself relates, there followed a series of incidents which LeRoux used skilfully to undermine the

Director's standing with the trustees. The first two were trivial. That autumn of 1952 Rothenstein gave permission for the actress Zsa Zsa Gabor, then taking part in a film about Toulouse-Lautrec, to be photographed at the Tate for a magazine article. When this appeared in November there were questions in Parliament about this 'cheesecake tour' and the use of the Tate for publicity purposes. LeRoux made sure, anonymously, that many MPs and people both in the art world and at court received copies of the offending article.

The second incident, equally ridiculous, concerned the shooting of part of a film, called *The Fake*, in the Tate Gallery. Rothenstein had written the script. It was all part of his desire for art to reach a wider public, he explained in his memoirs. But LeRoux whipped Lord Jowitt into a frenzy with his insinuations about Rothenstein's relationship with the film company. Other trustees, like Graham, simply saw the episodes as indicating the Director's basic lack of seriousness.

The third, more serious charge concerned the recent purchase, for £9000 from Marlborough Fine Art, of a well-known Degas bronze, *Petite Danseuse de 14 Ans*, complete with muslin tutu. The accusation this time was that Rothenstein had misinformed the board about the price, and the insinuation—as he recorded in *Brave Day, Hideous Night*—was that he had pocketed a large commission. Graham and his fellow artist-trustees Henry Moore and John Piper expressed disquiet about the price: they had heard from their New York dealer and friend Curt Valentin that he did not think it should cost more than £5000.

There matters stood when Graham returned in mid-November 1952 from his successful Paris opening. The evening after his arrival LeRoux came down to Kent to brief him. The trustees' meeting on 20 November was to be the crucial one. Rothenstein, not unmovingly, recounts his numbed shock as LeRoux attacked him over the Degas bronze in particular, with Graham following suit. It was decided, principally by Jowitt, that the Treasury, which still shared ultimate responsibility for the Tate with the trustees, should examine the whole complex of questions which had been raised. The inquiry was eventually conducted by Sir Edward Ritson, deputy chairman of the Board of Inland Revenue.

At this juncture Graham decided to return to Paris, pick up his car and head for the Riviera. He thus missed Ritson's meetings with the trustees. Jowitt warned Rothenstein that some trustees—he no doubt had Graham in mind—would resign if LeRoux were forced to go. In fact, LeRoux was reprimanded and Rothenstein was criticized in fairly mild terms and told by Jowitt that the curtain was now 'locked down' over the events of the past.

Graham was disgusted and decided to offer his resignation. To Colin Anderson, who had kept him abreast of events, he wrote on 7 January 1953:

No, Colin, I cannot come to any conclusion but that the whole thing has been a horrible travesty of justice. . . . all along there has been a bias towards face-saving—and an attitude of distortion, for that reason, wholly opposed to British justice. . . .

I can only say that this—and it sounds really too pompous—is a matter of conscience; and finally, I would really like to see the Tate efficient— not just in the running of it but the finding of the right pictures—in effect, a broad, progressive policy. If we all resigned, it would be a gamble. It is just possible that the Treasury would yield. They hate, above all, a scandal. If LeR agrees to work with JR I shall reconsider my own position. But how I hate injustice and expediency, above all in a world so dear to my heart. Civil Service logic and calm is so often a cloak for the basest casuistry. It *is* logical—it *is* calm—it must be or it wouldn't exist. It must be kept beyond criticism! You will disagree with me, no doubt. My attitude is not 'steady'!!

Graham felt it was quite wrong for the trustees to bow to the findings of the Treasury investigator, of which they were—as he later assured Kenneth Clark—'almost unanimously critical'. But both he and Lord Harlech, who also wanted to resign, were persuaded to remain 'on the understanding that there would be reorganization—that duties would be clarified and harmony and co-operation reign'.[9]

Thus far one feels a good deal of sympathy for Graham's position. He was genuinely upset by what he considered to be a miscarriage of justice and by the deficiencies in the Tate's management. He felt strongly that his fellow trustees should not have accepted the Ritson report. On the other hand, LeRoux's cuckoo-like behaviour was not attractive; and Graham's absence abroad when most needed weakened his case.

So he fought on. At this stage (early 1953) a fresh issue of some significance became interwoven with the coarser strands of the Tate Affair. It concerned the National Gallery and Tate Gallery Bill, then reaching the later stages of drafting. The aim of the Bill was to give the Tate Gallery its own separate legal existence, with responsibility for its collections vested in its own trustees.

Its terms, eventually announced in November 1953 but already known to those interested, contained three controversial provisions. One was to permit the loan of foreign works of art abroad, until then forbidden. Another was to enable 'second-class' works to be lent to the Ministry of Works for display in public buildings and official residences at home and abroad. The

173

third, and most contested, concerned the sale of works of art. Under the 1856 National Gallery Act, the trust could sell works but must — discouragingly — hand the proceeds to the Treasury. The new Bill would permit such proceeds to be retained by trustees, though Treasury and Parliament must be consulted about proposed sales. This was rapidly suspected to be a Treasury device to avoid the need for proper purchase grants: the Tate's increased to £6250 from £2000 only in 1953. Equally, it was seen to oblige trustees to stand in judgement on what part of the nation's pictorial heritage should be sold or lent to another government department.

Pictures might be cleared out just because they were out of fashion. Among those sensitive to this danger was Denis Mahon, collector, specialist in seventeenth-century Italian painting and later a trustee of the National Gallery. 'The real question', he recalled, 'was: were the staff of the two institutions such as to merit the very remarkable powers being given to them? If they weren't, how could this fact be brought out?'[10] The National Gallery seemed to have an indifferent board, and Philip Hendy was overworked. 'Then it suddenly emerged that the administration of the Tate left much to be desired, and this was highly relevant to the passage of the Bill.' It was in this way that people from the Old Master side, like Denys Sutton, then sale-room correspondent of the *Daily Telegraph*, and Benedict Nicolson of the *Burlington* magazine, came to be involved. This was for Mahon the first of many campaigns to save the nation's heritage, as he saw it. 'Reason is never sufficient, alas, when you are dealing with the Treasury. There has to be a row, and for that you need press and Parliament,' he said.

In June 1953 Dennis Proctor, an ex-Treasury man, was chosen by his fellow trustees to succeed Jowitt as chairman. 'You can imagine how that put shivers up our spine,' Mahon recalled. Proctor had, in fact, had enough of the Treasury and had gone to work for the Danish shipping magnate A. P. Moeller. None of the artist-trustees wanted to become chairman, and Colin Anderson was over-committed elsewhere. A strange situation arose when Proctor was invited, and accepted, to rejoin the Civil Service in 1953, as Deputy Secretary at the Ministry of Transport. But as his duties there seemed not to overlap with Tate affairs, he became chairman that June. A slight, lively and humorous man, he shared Graham's concern about the cumulative failure of the Tate to buy available work by the masters of modern French painting. He had met Cooper and got on with him rather well.

The second phase of the Tate Affair was ushered in by Cooper, who wrote a letter to *The Times* of 21 December 1953 posing a whole series of questions about the unexplained disappearance of Renoir's *Nue dans L'Eau* from the

Tate's collection. It had been bought from the Courtauld Fund and sold, it soon transpired, with the full permission of Sam Courtauld, who wanted no publicity. A Picasso and a Matisse had been bought in 1949 with part of the proceeds, Proctor explained in the same columns.

Although Cooper's main target had been the trustees' putative powers of sale under the new Bill, the use of bequests now became the central issue, and on 26 January 1954 the trustees published a list of thirteen purchases made between 1939 and 1951 which did not fully square with the terms of the fund used. Most of these errors had been leaked *seriatim* to the press. Some £2750 was to be paid back to the incorrectly depleted funds.

Did it matter frightfully that a Léger had been bought with Courtauld funds when he was not on Courtauld's list? Opinion varied. In the House of Lords Lord Kinnaird was always asking questions about the Knapping Fund. This was intended for the purchase of work by living artists or by those who had been dead not more than twenty-five years. A Constable had been bought from it. A Moore sculpture had been bought from the Kerr Fund, intended solely for paintings. It was all very regrettable. Trustees were supposed to be just that: trustees. The impression of inefficiency revealed by each 'defalcation' was damaging, though many had taken place long before.

Graham, who had become obsessive about the whole Tate business, took it all very seriously indeed. Once again, however, he decided to adhere to his plans. On 1 January 1954 he and Kathleen again headed for France, this time to La Souco, a very pleasant villa on the road to upper Roquebrune belonging to the French painter Simon Bussy and his Bloomsbury wife Dorothy Strachey, author of *Olivia*. They arrived there on 18 January, after a fortnight in Paris and a visit to Douglas Cooper at his château, where Sonia Orwell was visiting.

The Tate's problems must have seemed a long way away as they enjoyed the view out to sea and over to Monte Carlo (less like Manhattan then than now) from the villa and its terraced garden. A week later Cooper and his friend of those days, John Richardson, joined them. The next two days were spent composing letters to the press and to Dennis Proctor. Graham also wrote to Colin Anderson and Kenneth Clark. The burden of all the letters was the same: he had decided to resign from the Tate's trustees, and explained why. To Kenneth Clark he wrote on 27 January: 'A line to tell you that I have severed myself from the Tate. Things have got too bad to be supported'—and he listed his reasons, concluding: 'I hope you may feel I've done right. I write to you as my friend and oldest supporter.'

On receiving Graham's letter, Proctor wrote back immediately—as did

Colin Anderson—assuring him that he felt exactly the same about the whole situation and begging him to stay. But well before Graham received these pleas, his decision was announced: first, without explanations, in the Londoner's Diary of the *Evening Standard* on 29 January, then fully in the Sunday papers of 31 January.

To them he explained that he had offered his resignation to Lord Jowitt in 1952 but had been persuaded to withdraw it: his colleagues had hoped that the causes of his discontent, with which they sympathized, would soon be eradicated. They had not been. Graham listed four reasons for now feeling obliged to 'lay down his trust'. There was the misuse of bequest and trust funds. Public money had been wasted because the board had been misled over the current value of modern works of art. Too many opportunities had been missed to buy works of reputable modern artists at reasonable prices: an important work just bought could have been had for just over half the price paid. He had not agreed with the recommendations following official investigations into the administration of the Tate. For these and other reasons—which, he said, would involve a breach of confidence—he had resigned, in no spirit of animosity but after mature reflection.

Proctor issued a statement that Sunday evening. Sutherland, he said, should have resigned to the Prime Minister, from whom trustees received their appointments. Sutherland had set out his reasons for resigning more fully to the press than to him. Sutherland had been present at the meeting when the spending of moneys from bequests and trusts was discussed and had concurred with the agreed corrective action. He had, however, missed the last three board meetings and could not be fully aware of all the steps taken to deal with the situation. Proctor regretted that they had not been able to discuss the matter fully together before he decided to resign: Sutherland had given no indication of his intention before leaving for the South of France.

Graham tried hard to counter this lethal broadside. Further irregularities had come to light since the discussion of misapplied funds, he told the *Daily Telegraph* next day (though the three he listed had been mentioned in the later statement by the trustees). As for the missed meetings, he regretted having had to miss the first. The second was 'routine', he said. The third, the important special meeting, he had not been told about. But why had Graham not warned or consulted his colleagues about his intention to resign? 'I think in a way he felt he wanted to get out, for selfish reasons, really,' Colin Anderson reckoned.[11] He held that Graham should have joined with other trustees in trying to put matters right. 'I think he felt his reputation was being assailed by being mixed up with all those awful things people were saying. All he did really was to join the critics.' That, to Graham, was the Establishment reflex: standing together above all, no breaking of ranks. Denis Mahon, who had been closely in touch with Graham and remained so through 1954, thought Graham felt that 'if he had consulted them first, the thing would have been smothered, and pressure put on him not to resign'.

Certainly, the manner of Graham's going adversely affected his relations with Anderson, Moore and Piper. All three said that they found it quite unacceptable, as well as regretting Graham's friendship with the combative Cooper. Piper, whose term as a trustee had in fact ended in 1953, had a letter in *The Times* on 3 February. He was certain that the motives of 'my friend Graham Sutherland' in resigning had been excellent, he wrote. But he believed the purchasing policy of recent years had been sound and right.

What really irritated Graham's friends on the board was that they shared his dissatisfaction with the failings of the past, but they felt it better to stay and to try to redress them. In an immediate sense, Graham's move was counter-productive. There was a dramatic late-night meeting in the Pre-Raphaelite room in Colin Anderson's spacious Admiral's House in Hampstead. Holman Hunt's painting *The Awakening Conscience* looked on.

It came to a vote, Proctor recalled. Four favoured sacking Rothenstein, four were against—which left him with the casting vote. John Freemantle, later Lord Cottesloe, a trustee since 1953, stood up and told Proctor: 'Whatever your vote is, it's obvious we can't sack the Director of the Tate on a divided vote like this.' Proctor would have voted against anyway. 'Graham and Douglas had built up this appalling vendetta in public, and we simply couldn't have thrown him to the wolves.' he said. 'If Graham hadn't resigned, the whole course of events might have been different.' Rothenstein, he believed, owed his survival to Graham's resignation. Proctor's wife, Barbara, summed it up well, he thought: 'Graham has kicked the ball through his own goal,' she commented at the time.

Meanwhile Graham wrote to Sir Winston Churchill, then Prime Minister—with whom he was soon to have rather different contact— expressing his willingness to explain himself further, should he desire it, and pointing out that at the trustees' meeting on 22 January (which he had missed) several trustees had expressed views far from unsympathetic to his.[12] Graham had still not grasped, and indeed probably never did, that it was *because* his colleagues agreed with his views that they were annoyed at his action.

As if all this were not enough, he had trouble with the *Daily Mail* on another score. On 2 February it reported that he had been commissioned by a wealthy foreign industrialist to paint a portrait of the Pope. Some such portrait had been mooted, Kathleen recalled, but secrecy was essential. A close friend had blabbed. Through Avilda Lees-Milne, who had a house in Roquebrune, Lord Rothermere, the newspaper's owner, was wheeled into action. Graham met him in Monte Carlo.

Next day the *Daily Mail* was obliged to print a qualified retraction of the story. Shortly afterwards Graham and Kathleen left the coast for three days *chez* Cooper in Provence, no doubt to rehash the whole Tate business and to plan tactics. The Russian-born painter Nicolas de Staël, who lived not far away at Ménerbes and killed himself a year later, came twice to meals. Cooper was to write a brilliant study of his work.[13]

They returned to La Souco, where Graham found an understanding letter from Clark, to which he replied on 9 February:

> Coming at a time when the winds of criticism blow coldly around my legs, your letter gave me new courage. . . . It is obvious of course that my action was premature. But I doubt if much more would have been done. Most members would cover up murder to preserve the façade!

He repeated his (illogical) view that the 'irregularities' sprang largely from the trustees' failure to take action after the Treasury investigation: in fact, most had taken place well before it. He was now 'determined to have no further part in it'; nor could he condone what appeared to be three separate instances of grave injustice to three staff members, on which he held some evidence, he said, as on the question of prices.

> But I want to keep out of it all now: my reasons satisfied *me*, and I made my gesture. But I will defend my position to the hilt. . . . Pray for me please! I feel out of touch and unreal—so much so that I can't work yet, and sometimes wonder whether I shall be able to. *Why* is one born *tough* AND *vulnerable*? I'll send a more cheerful letter later. . . . Eternal gratitude and love to you both. Graham.

Vulnerable yet tough; anxious to have no further part in it, yet determined to defend himself: Graham was torn between two sides of his nature. He decided he must concentrate on justifying his behaviour, and on 13 February he and Kathleen left for London by train. They were welcomed there by Graham's kindergarten classmate Lord Amulree, a gentle and delightful physician who was an old friend of Douglas Cooper and had been loyally playing his part in the Lords with questions about misapplied funds. They dined that evening with Humphrey Brooke, who had helped the cause with information about bequests.

Graham spent the next fortnight in London—which was most unusual—putting together a dossier on the background of his resignation. In this he was helped by Cooper, also now in town, LeRoux, Mahon and Denys Sutton. On 5 March it was posted to R. A. Butler who, as Chancellor of the Exchequer, still had some titular responsibility for the Tate's affairs and happened to be married to the daughter of the biggest donor of all, Sam Courtauld (she died that year).

That same day LeRoux—still on extended probation—was handed a letter of dismissal by Dennis Proctor. Proctor stressed that the trustees did not connect him with trust-fund troubles, nor did they wish their decision to be construed as a reflection of his competence, but they had unanimously concluded that he was not suitable for permanent employment as a deputy keeper. At the same time Rothenstein was told by letter that the board was not prepared to bear indefinitely with the consequences of his 'personal embroilments' when they involved the good standing of the Gallery.

To the informed, the trustees' decision to be rid of LeRoux did not make Graham's case look any stronger. He became 'very low and depressed', Kathleen's diary recorded on 11 March. Consultation with Mahon and Sutton continued: they achieved their chief aim—which Proctor had all along fully supported—when in April it was announced that neither the Tate nor the National Gallery should have the power to sell works of art, and that only the Tate should be able to lend them to certain listed institutions.

LeRoux stayed on at the Tate for several weeks. On 13 May Graham, Mahon and Lords Jowitt, Harlech, Methuen and Kinnaird went as a deputation to R. A. Butler to urge that LeRoux should be allowed to resign. 'Jowitt did the speaking', Mahon recalled. 'The argument produced was that if LeRoux were sacked at that stage, it would look as if he had been inculpated over the misuse of trust funds'—which had occurred mainly well before his time. LeRoux's dismissal was withdrawn, for safety's sake, only after he had resigned.

The news of his departure in early June was hailed by the press as another sign of crisis at the Tate. LeRoux explained that he had wanted to leave eighteen months earlier but had yielded to an 'urgent appeal' by the trustees to stay. This had proved to be an error, he said. Consulted by the *Daily Telegraph*, Graham said: 'I think the fact of his resignation does bear out a good many of the contentions which I made in my memorandum to the Chancellor of the Exchequer, Mr Butler.' In the same way, Graham's allies had contended that the resignation of so distinguished an artist as Mr Sutherland had borne out *their* contentions. For a time, the bitterness flickered on in London. Not for nothing had the Liberal MP Jo Grimond spoken in the Commons of the courage needed to enter the lion's den of art controversy by MPs living in 'the comparatively calm and impartial atmosphere of party politics'.

Probably as a result of Graham's advocacy, LeRoux went straight from the Tate to work for the Beaverbrook organization in Fleet Street and, later, in Beaverbrook's native Fredericton, in New Brunswick, where the many-sided Beaver was establishing an art gallery. In London LeRoux helped to organize a *Daily Express* Young Artists' Exhibition, which Graham, Herbert Read and Anthony Blunt were to judge next April. LeRoux lasted two years with Beaverbrook, resigning hurriedly in 1956 and leaving for medical consultations and treatment in Europe. Later he worked in London for Wildenstein's, the art dealers. He died in 1963.

Graham, for his part, had returned to France on 20 March, initially to La Souco, then back to the Voile d'Or Hotel, where the Powells had lent him an old garage as a studio. There he made progress on the Sackville-West portrait. On 29 April he invited Willie Maugham to come and have a look at it.

No doubt largely as a reaction to the Tate affair, he and Kathleen now began to look seriously for a house in the area. Before long their interest began to focus on one rather far away—in the hills behind Menton—conceived and owned by the British designer Eileen Gray. Beaverbrook, with whom they dined several times in these still troubled weeks, took a keen interest in their search for a base in France.

In London public interest in the Tate Affair was briefly rekindled in October 1954, when the trustees produced their first report since 1938. It listed acquisitions made since that year but was, as *The Times* commented, 'in no sense a controversial document', making no allusions to criticisms which had appeared in the press, but providing some relevant factual information. The *Daily Telegraph* thought something more might have been said about the resignations of people like Graham Sutherland and LeRoux Smith LeRoux, if only to show that nothing was basically wrong. On 8 October the *Spectator* called for an end to the whole 'campaign' against Rothenstein. The following week it carried a letter from Graham calling the article 'seriously misinformed'. He reiterated that his colleagues had shared his disquiet and insisted there was all too much truth in rumours about staff troubles. On 9 October the *New Statesman*, whose editor, Kingsley Martin, Graham saw periodically, described the trustees' report as very reticent and asked if there was to be no reply to Mr Sutherland's criticisms.

The harsh fact was that these did not carry much weight, since they concerned matters which his colleagues had been trying to put right. They were helpful only in increasing the pressure for reform. Furthermore, sympathy had begun to swing towards Rothenstein. The criticisms had become terribly repetitive. The Tate's diminutive Director did himself some good by punching Douglas Cooper on the jaw on the evening of 2 November.

The fracas took place at a reception for a Diaghilev exhibition at Forbes House, by Hyde Park Corner, attended by Ingrid Bergman and Dame Edith Evans, among others. Cooper and John Richardson had been to lunch at the White House in Kent that day. They came up with Graham to London for the Diaghilev party (Kathleen stayed at home). According to Cooper's account, printed in the *Daily Express*, he had seen Rothenstein nearby while talking to a friend and had said: 'There is that poor little man they are all persecuting. I do feel so sorry for him.' Sir John had then waved his arms around like a windmill. According to Rothenstein's memoirs, Cooper followed him from room to room, shouting taunts. Eventually Rothenstein stood and faced him. The big face loomed closer; anger welled up; and he punched it hard. (Graham did not, Kathleen believed, see the incident.) The punch was celebrated in cartoons and verse, including a ballad in the *News Chronicle* by Percy Cudlipp, hailing

> Battling Rothenstein
> Master of those contrasting arts
> The 'noble' and the 'fine'. . . .

Shortly afterwards Cooper and Proctor lunched together. A truce was agreed. The final victory of the removal of Rothenstein had not been vouchsafed, but time, Cooper thought, was on their side. He was wrong. Rothenstein served another ten years at the Tate.

Graham had no time to tot up a balance sheet: he was working furiously to finish the Churchill portrait. But he emerged wounded from the battle and believed to the end that he had been betrayed by the Establishment. With hindsight, it is all too easy to see that he handled his case badly. He had good reason to feel unhappy about the Tate's record, on both the administrative and the purchasing sides. Even though many of his colleagues shared his dissatisfaction, resignation was a legitimate way of showing that he thought the pace of reform too slow. His resignation undoubtedly did speed the movement to reform. If he had consulted Proctor before resigning and then left well alone, he would probably have emerged with credit. But his desire to justify the way in which he had resigned led him to magnify the reasons for his resignation. His continued involvement, largely through misplaced loyalty to LeRoux—whose behaviour many found deplorable—was a triumph of emotion over reason.

The whole episode revealed how emotional, and in some some ways how confused, Graham could be beneath that courteous and charming exterior. The complexity is apparent in his paintings, as are the anxieties and insecurities. Yet just how well he could conduct himself under heavy pressure emerged from his not much less traumatic encounter with Winston Churchill.

9

The Churchill Portrait

1954

WHAT ON EARTH does one give the world's most famous living statesman on his eightieth birthday? The informal, all-party committee of MPs appointed to select and organize a suitable present for Sir Winston was not to be envied. Despite doubts about his fitness, the great wartime leader had become Prime Minister in 1951, following Labour's defeat at the polls. The birthday was on 30 November 1954. A Birthday Presentation Fund was also being organized: it eventually collected £259,000.

The committee's chairman was a Labour MP, Frank (later Lord) McLeavy. According to Jennie Lee, who was a committee member, he suggested: 'How about a good likeness?'[1] It was agreed that a distinguished artist should be commissioned to paint a portrait of Churchill as a House of Commons man, which could later find a permanent home in a suitable corner of the Palace of Westminster. Various artists were suggested, including James Gunn, who was considered too expensive.[2] Jennie Lee proposed Sutherland. The suggestion was warmly received, the decision to give him the commission unanimous.

Graham's portraits of Maugham and Beaverbrook had cast their spell. No one, seemingly, considered whether Churchill would welcome similar treatment. The decision was lightly taken, and Jennie Lee, as a friend of Graham's, was deputed to sound him out. After some initial reluctance, he accepted. Charles Doughty, the Conservative MP, barrister and secretary of the committee, wrote to Graham to clinch arrangements on 14 July.

The portrait would be presented on the birthday itself, Doughty said. Sir Winston had agreed to give the necessary sittings, which should start as soon as mutually convenient. 'The portrait required will be full length,' Doughty wrote. 'Details of it, costume, location and other matters, must of course be arranged between Sir Winston and yourself. We certainly would not attempt to interfere in a technical matter of this kind.' The committee had noted Graham's charges (1000 guineas), and his very fair statement that any difficulty in collecting the amount (from MPs) would not prevent him from giving of his best. He suggested that Graham should let him know when a first sitting would be convenient; later sittings could be arranged direct with Sir Winston.

The seeds of controversy had been sown. Twenty-three years later Graham was to write to Churchill's daughter, Mary Soames:

> I think it only fair that I should tell you of the conditions of the commission. I was myself present at the original meetings of the inter-parliamentary [sic] Committee when I was by this body commissioned [curiously Teutonic grammar]. My memory is perfectly clear on two points raised: 1. I was instructed to paint your father in his normal parliamentary clothes; 2. that the portrait was to be given to your father by both Houses on his 80th birthday *for his lifetime*, and that after his death *it would revert to the House of Commons*. I was even shown places where it might hang.[3]

Of this last point, Doughty made no mention. McLeavy said later that the presentation was made with no strings attached, though some committee members hoped that the Houses of Parliament would be its ultimate destination.[4]

Once again, the *Evening Standard*'s Londoner's Diary had first news of the commission. It gave the bare facts on 24 July, with the inevitable plug for the Beaverbrook portrait. Willie Maugham, although he had said that he hoped Beaverbrook would be Graham's last portrait, welcomed the news. 'I think you will find him extremely pleasant himself, but a difficult subject. If you can bring it off, it will be a real triumph,' he wrote on 3 August. As for the Beaver, Graham wrote to him:

> I remember—when I was painting you, that you mentioned that I ought to do it. Now I'm going to have a try—at least, and know you will keep your fingers crossed!! It won't be an easy thing at all especially in the very short time they are allowing me. You remember what a time you had to wait for yours to be finished.[5]

In fact, Graham considerably shortened the time available by being in Venice from early July to early August, staying with Arthur Jeffress (Alfred Hecht was also there at first). Churchill returned in early July from a taxing trip to the USA and Canada, so might have been available. Graham arrived in England on 7 August, and his first meeting with Churchill was arranged for 26 August: lunch at Chartwell, the Churchill country home near

Westerham in Kent. 'If you arrive around 12 a.m. I will take you down to my studio in a detached building,' Churchill wrote on 14 August.

> Here there is a very good light arrangement as the blinds can be pulled down from the top or from the bottom. All the lights can be cut off and there is also a movable platform for me to put my chair on. Oswald Birley found it very convenient to paint his picture of me here. I thought after showing you this studio I would leave you to get your tackle in order and then after we had lunched I might come and sit for an hour or so. I hope this will be convenient to you. In case, on inspection, you do not find the studio suitable we must make other plans.

No doubt Graham was feeling highly nervous as he approached Chartwell that day in his new Hillman Minx, after the drive of some 20 miles from Trottiscliffe. It was the first time he had met Churchill. It was not very encouraging to know that the Prime Minister had been consulting Rothenstein about his own painting. According to Rothenstein, Churchill had asked him that March: 'What can you tell me about Mr Shingleton . . . the man who's been making such a nuisance of himself to the Tate trustees?'[6] Any lingering doubts Churchill had about Graham's identity were about to be removed.

Graham arrived at the grey Victorian mansion, which commands magnificent views of the Weald of Kent. He was shown up some stairs to Churchill's study and left there, alone. He recalled:[7]

> Suddenly I saw a nose appear around the corner of the door—just the nose alone, and it was Churchill. With that slightly sort of bent, peering look which he put on—I suppose partly to intimidate the person he was meeting—he shook hands, and showed me his hands, his mother's hands, which he had modelled: he thought his mother's hands were very much like his own.

They talked about conditions, how the sittings should be done, how many there should be and so on. Churchill wanted to be shown wearing the robes of the Order of the Garter, but Graham believed his mandate was to portray him in his parliamentary garb of black coat, waistcoat, striped trousers and spotted bow tie. Then they walked down to the studio. 'All the way he was making comments on the buddleia bushes, because he had a passion for butterflies,' Graham said. And then there were the famous goldfish.

> He would throw some rather expensive food into the pond, and I would say: 'But the ones at the back aren't getting anything at all, you're just throwing it in the front.' And he said: 'Well, that's life, you see. We can't all be communists, we can't all be equal.'[8]

In another version, Churchill said: 'Their turn will come if they try hard enough'—a robustly Conservative sentiment unlikely to have appealed to Graham.[9]

Churchill showed Graham some of his paintings in the studio; dozens lined the walls. They were very nearly first-rate, he told Kathleen, but had a touch of vulgarity about them.[10] 'He had a natural gift, and he was always very humble about his painting, really. He would be very good with certain teachers. . . . if a teacher was bad, he would turn out some pretty vulgar stuff.'[11]

Not long after Graham arrived, Churchill asked: 'How are you going to paint me? As a cherub, or the Bulldog?' To this Graham replied diplomatically: 'It entirely depends what you show me, sir.'[12] To Beaverbrook he said:

> Consistently . . . he showed me the Bull Dog. For better or for worse, I am the kind of painter who is governed entirely by what he sees; I am at the mercy of my sitter. What he feels or shows at the time, I try to record.

That was perhaps a slightly disingenuous self-justification: what Graham saw was not necessarily what he was shown, since he was likely to have formed his own conception of so famous a sitter, through which the reality would have been filtered. In fact, he admitted shortly after the portrait's completion: 'I was thinking of the Churchill who had saved England, who stopped the enemy and so on.'[13]

The first three sittings, all at Chartwell, were on 26, 29 and 31 August. 'The whole conversation was very friendly,' Graham recalled.[14]

> I had said I didn't want to show him my day-to-day progress, and he said: 'Come on, be a sport. Don't forget I'm a fellow artist.' So I had to be a bit dishonest, really, and juggle with something I didn't mind showing him, and something which I was really doing. . . . one day he would say: 'This is going to be by far the best portrait I have ever had done—by far.' Next day he would look at the same drawing, almost, but he would say: 'Oh no, this won't do at all. I haven't got a neckline like that—you must take an inch, nay, an inch and a half off.'

On another occasion Churchill was furious at having been given a double chin: he had not got one, he said, and must look 'noble'.

Churchill was also proud of the lack of lines on his face, though Graham was quite surprised to find that at close quarters he was not as unwrinkled as recent photographs suggested.[15] There were a few laughter lines around the eyes, a slight scar on his forehead from a cut he had sustained when he was knocked down by a New York taxi, small bags under his eyes, two creases from nose to mouth—and his mouth slightly drooped at one corner.

While thinking he was being very co-operative, he was a very restless sitter, smoking cigars, dictating letters and posing rather than relaxing. After lunch he tended to become 'torpid', as he called it. Once he told Graham that they were really engaged in a duel: perhaps they should paint each other simultaneously. Seeing Graham drawing with his usual pencil stub, he told him he had not got the right gear, showed him his own paints from Switzerland and promised to have some sent. He even suggested that they should go sketching in the South of France together: there was nothing he liked better, he said, and described how he would sit back to back with his detective, Sergeant (Edmund) Murray, and say, 'A little more yellow ochre, please, Sergeant Murray,' and Murray would squeeze a little more on to his palette.[16]

Both Sir Winston and Lady Churchill were favourably impressed by Graham. Churchill got Graham to sign a copy of Robert Melville's book on his work. Confronted by those mysterious yet passionate forms, he said he found what he saw 'difficult', but he thought he knew what Graham was after. Both were surprised that Graham seemed so normal. 'Mr Graham Sutherland is a "Wow",' Lady Churchill wrote to Mary Soames on 1 September.

> He really is a most attractive man, and one can hardly believe that the savage cruel designs which he exhibits come from his brush.
>
> Papa has given him three sittings and no one has seen the beginnings of the portrait except Papa and he is much struck by the power of his drawing. . . .[17]

Graham soon realized that external factors were shaping his sitter's demeanour. 'All this time, there were unfortunate complications of a political nature,' he told Beaverbrook.

> Repeatedly I was told: 'They (meaning his colleagues in the Government) want me out. But'—and this is a paraphrase of the actual conversation—'I'm a rock'; and at that the face would set in furious lines and the hands clutch the arms of the chair.

Prominent Conservatives were concerned about the Prime Minister's flagging powers. After a minor heart attack after Pearl Harbor and a minor stroke in 1949, he had had a seemingly serious stroke in June 1953. He made a remarkable recovery, but logic pointed to an early resignation in favour of his heir apparent, Anthony Eden. Churchill felt that he still had much to give in the new climate created by Stalin's death in 1953 and the testing of the American H-bomb. The Conservatives were divided over the withdrawal of British troops from Suez. A new leader might help to pull the splintering factions together. But Churchill's intentions remained a mystery; he did not retire until the following spring.

Graham was privy to some of these affairs of state. 'He was very frank about everything, even foreign policy and so on,' he said.[18] On one occasion Churchill asked whether Graham would mind if he dictated a highly confidential letter. 'While I went on with my studies, his words were mouthed silently; then the dictation commenced, every comma and semi-colon included—a perfection which I'm never likely to hear again.'[19]

Graham was still trying out different ideas for the portrait. Perhaps as a favour to Churchill, he borrowed some Garter robes—possibly Churchill's own—and asked his bulky solicitor, Wilfrid Evill, to sit in them on a visit to Kent on 1 September. The resulting studies were later incorporated into a sketch of Churchill as a Garter Knight, which was shown to Sir Winston after the birthday presentation, then finished and sold to Lord Beaverbrook.[20]

With the main portrait the first hurdle was the head. 'There are so many Churchills,' he told Churchill's doctor, Lord Moran.[21] 'I have to find the real one.' Gathering that Graham intended to paint a lion at bay, Moran tried to sound a warning note, he later claimed. 'Don't forget', he admonished Graham, 'that Winston is always acting. Try to see him when he has got the greasepaint off his face.' But the artist, he lamented, paid no heed, and painted the Prime Minister as he pictured him in his own favourite part, accepting the legend for the truth.

Graham found Churchill's face all too variable. Sometimes it was a young man's face, reminiscent of earlier photographs or portraits which he had studied, the Churchill of Omdurman; sometimes it was the face of a tired old man.[22] Graham worked late in his studio, trying to fuse the essences together.

The September sittings were on the 2nd, 4th, 9th and possibly the 17th. In all Graham made from life about twelve pencil or charcoal studies, six oil sketches and numerous drawings of details of the sitter's hands, eyes, nose, mouth, shoes and so on. The 9 September sitting was unusually fruitful. Churchill at one stage sat by a window dictating a letter. The setting sun lit up one side of his face, seeming to render the skin translucent. He was in a 'sweet melancholy and reflective mood', Graham later told Beaverbrook. He used that glimpse of the melancholy cherub to lay the basis of two oil sketches. One—a minor masterpiece—he later gave to Alfred Hecht; the other he sold to Beaverbrook.

Graham took his photographer friend Felix Man along twice. He recalled:[23]

I had photographs made to my precise directions from the exact positions from which I was drawing, also from all round the head as if it were to be a piece of sculpture, as it soon became clear that Sir W. was going to prove an unusually restless sitter and that I must use every means I could to enable me to gather information.

On one occasion Churchill arrived a good hour late, in a bad mood and with a sore throat. He was called to the telephone several times during lunch: there seemed to be trouble with the Cabinet, Man remembered.[24] Lord Moran was summoned to paint the prime ministerial throat. He wanted to send his assistant, but Churchill insisted he come himself.

While the sittings were on, life was hectic. 'I've been working every second of the time,' Graham wrote to Beaverbrook on 12 September, 'and in the evenings I have rushed home to try and put down on canvas what I remembered of the face and expression while I retained it in my mind. . . . now, having finished the preliminary sittings, I am much more free. . . .' Life resumed a semblance of normality as he tackled the portrait proper. The canvas he chose measured almost 5 feet by 4 feet. The shape was part of the conception: 'I wanted to paint him with a kind of four-square look—Churchill as a rock,' he explained later.[25] The first head did not seem quite good enough, and he washed it out, much to the regret of some who had seen it, he said. 'In painting, you have to destroy in order to gain. . . . you have got to sacrifice something you are quite pleased with in order to get something better. Of course, it's a risk. . . .'[26]

Graham and Kathleen dined with Beaverbrook, who was planning his Fredericton gallery and wanted advice. Arthur Jeffress came to see the sketches Graham had done of him that summer in Venice, and the start of his portrait. On 28 September, Graham went up to London to report progress to Charles Doughty, the presentation committee's secretary. The Tate Affair was still rumbling, and he lunched that day with Kingsley Martin of the *New Statesman*, Denis Mahon and LeRoux.

By 9 October the portrait was sufficiently advanced for Graham and Kathleen to take it in a borrowed truck to Saltwood Castle to show it to Kenneth and Jane Clark. Clark, according to Kathleen's diary, said it was like a late Rembrandt, and that it was a privilege to be alive in an age when anyone could paint such a thing. They took the portrait back to Trottiscliffe, and next day Winston Churchill's only son Randolph and his wife June came to lunch: they had met Graham in wartime London. Randolph was no connoisseur but shrewdly remarked that Mama would not like the portrait, since it made Winston look disenchanted. On 17 October June Churchill wrote to thank Graham for the meal and for a drawing he had given her: the nicest present she had ever had.

> Your picture of my father-in-law seemed to me *brilliant*, really quite alarmingly like him, and so alive one feels he might suddenly change position and say something. But something pretty beastly I should think; I wish he didn't have to look quite so cross, although I know he quite often does. But please don't change this one anyway, because you might ruin it and make it look more ordinary, and I think it is *wonderful*. I never imagined it could be so good.

There was a further sitting on 17 October, when Graham—by arrangement—took along Kathleen and Elsbeth Juda. He had decided that Man's photographs needed supplementing. Churchill was in a good mood, and was rather taken by Kathleen. He insisted that Elsbeth should take some photographs of her for him, so he could paint a portrait of her. 'If Mr Sutherland can work from photos, so can I,' he said. Some of Elsbeth Juda's photographs of Churchill taken that day show him looking cheeky and benevolent; others show him with exactly the expression Graham portrayed. There was a sitting after lunch. Churchill's torpor soon set in. He kept on slumping forward, Elsbeth Juda remembered, and Graham would courteously suggest: 'A little more of the old lion please, sir.'

The drawings and sketches which Graham did at these sittings were sometimes worked up into a more finished form: the process helped him to gain insights for the large canvas. Some were re-done later, he told Beaverbrook, who at the end of November contracted to buy everything available. One of the studies of Churchill's hands included a cigar with a spiral of smoke, and a cigar was briefly included in the actual portrait. Graham then decided that as it was to some degree a state portrait, the cigar had better come out. An oil sketch of Churchill's right profile showed a long cigar jutting from his lips—and virtually no neck.

> For weeks I painted in an atmosphere of cigar smoke. I was plied with gifts from the box; and I used sometimes to give one to a friend, saying 'This is one of Winston's,' and the friend would keep it under the pillow for weeks. But there was no cigar in the portrait—by agreement.[27]

Meanwhile another commission got away. Haile Selassie, the diminutive Emperor of Ethiopia, was on a state visit to England in October. He was looking for a painter to undertake his portrait and was shown Graham's Maugham and almost complete Sackville-West portraits while in London.

The fee was to be £5000. But the Lion of Judah decided Graham's style was not official enough for a state portrait. 'I would say that is perfectly true,' Graham told the *Sunday Express*.[28] 'I would like to have painted him. He has a remarkable face.'

On 30 October, Alfred Hecht came to measure the canvas for framing, and next day Graham and Kathleen went to lunch at the Clarks. Lady Churchill was there, as were Mary Soames and Willie Maugham. But it was a purely social occasion; the portrait stayed in Graham's studio. There Douglas Cooper saw it on 2 November (Kathleen recorded that he said he liked it very much) before going up to London to attend the bruising Diaghilev function. Two days later Cooper, Graham and Lord and Lady Harewood lunched together in London: an idea for Graham to design an opera was in the air, but nothing came of it.

Gloom over the portrait was now setting in. It was deepened on 6 November, when Jane and Kenneth Clark came to lunch in Kent: Jane said she had liked the eyes more the first time. Clark was silent, eventually saying: 'It's the best portrait Graham has done, really'—scarcely a ringing endorsement by his standards.[29] Then Jane felt that she had been too critical and left in tears. For the next two days Graham was deeply depressed and longing to give it all up. Kathleen helped him to lay a new canvas and to square it up. But he soon reverted to the old version, darkening the right side, getting the face more in tone and introducing some mauve (later eliminated) into the background.

Graham was to have one more extended sighting of his elusive, many-sided quarry: a weekend at Chequers, the official residence of the Prime Minister near Wendover, in Buckinghamshire. Lady Churchill had written on 29 October to invite them for the weekend beginning 13 November. But on 10 November she had to write excusing her absence: plagued by sleeplessness, she had to stay in bed. Her daughter Mary would represent her. When, she asked in a postscript, was she going to see the portrait? 'Jane Clark says they both think it brilliant and powerful. Could I motor over and see it the weekend after next, when we shall be at Chartwell?'

Graham's heart must have sunk. But first came Chequers. They arrived there in time for lunch that Saturday. Also present: Mary Soames and her husband Christopher, then Conservative MP for Bedford; Antony Head, then Secretary of State for War, and his wife Lady Dorothea, Lord Shaftesbury's daughter, both of whom the Sutherlands liked immensely; Lord Cherwell ('the Prof'), the half-Alsatian, half-American physicist and Churchill adviser; the Speaker of the Commons, W. S. Morrison, and wife; John Colville, the Prime Minister's joint principal private secretary; and

Oscar Nemon, the sculptor, who had been commissioned that February to do a bronze of Churchill for Guildhall.

Kathleen noted that Churchill was on good form but was disappointed that Graham had not brought the portrait. Nemon later remembered his reaction as stronger than that. Sir Winston, he said, told Graham he had been assured at the previous sitting that he would be shown the painting.[30] He asked Graham when he would be allowed to see it. Graham said he was not ready to show it. Sir Winston, clearly angry, wanted to know how he was looking in the portrait. 'You are sitting in an armchair and have your head looking up,' Graham replied. Sir Winston showed concern that that would expose the 'fleshy' part under his chin. Two months later, on 31 January 1956 (after his retirement), Churchill was to write in response to a perhaps fence-mending letter from Graham:

> Dear Graham Sutherland, I was vexed at your not keeping what I thought was your promise to show me the picture before presentation. The expected opportunity presented itself when you came to Chequers in November 1954. In vain I asked for it. In consequence I had no opportunity of commenting upon it or of giving you the extra sittings which you might have agreed were necessary. I am much obliged to you for the assurances which your letter contains. Yours sincerely, Winston S. Churchill.

The Prime Minister did not allow his annoyance to cloud the weekend, however. Graham had another shot at drawing his eyes when he was playing bezique with Soames or Colville. 'He was wanting to win, determined to win. . . . I caught the look, the expression I wanted,' Graham recalled: it was a combative look.[31]

> Then, I remember, we went off and dined with the ladies, after which he entertained us with a marvellously graphic account—full of gesticulations and sound effects—of the Battle of Omdurman. As the drinking and the talking and the smoking went on, until two or three in the morning, he gained in vitality, while we, though fascinated, were ready to drop.

There was speculation over the dinner table about the danger of atomic warfare, and over Soviet attitudes to Berlin. After dinner Churchill recited poetry.

Churchill was teed up to do his portrait of Kathleen. 'He has my photograph ready in a slide thrown on to canvas to paint,' she noted. Not for him Graham's tedious technique of squaring up for transfer.

Graham and Kathleen left on Sunday night, in time to be home by

*Portrait of
W. Somerset Maugham.*
Oil on canvas, 1949.
54 × 25 in
(137.2 × 63.5 cm)

*Portrait of the Hon. Edward
Sackville-West.*
Oil on canvas, 1953–5.
$66\frac{3}{4} \times 30\frac{3}{8}$ in (169.5 × 77.1 c

midnight. The critic (and friend) Eric Newton was coming next morning. It was a visit, Graham later told Newton, which 'gave me the strength to continue over the last lap'.[32] A bare week remained for Graham to work on the portrait before Lady Churchill came to see it on 20 November—a week walking the tightrope between improving and wrecking it. To soften the tension of the occasion, Graham had invited his first victim, Willie Maugham, Alan Searle, his secretary and companion, and Hecht, in a sense the *fons et origo* of it all. Sportingly, Maugham agreed beforehand to accompany Lady Churchill up the narrow stairs of the White House to the studio.

Together they surveyed the old warrior, looming black and white against a background of yellow ochre stained with umber, chin up, heavy with years and good living but still tough and pugnacious, a slight warmth permeating the flesh tints.[33] Maugham had said he would whistle down to them if Lady Churchill liked it. 'He did, and when I arrived, Lady Churchill was in tears, and said: "I can't thank you enough",' Graham recalled later.[34] Kathleen noted in her diary: 'She liked portrait very much. . . . she was very moved and full of praise.' Maugham told a similar story later, adding: 'I liked it, and so at the time did she.'[35] She asked for a photograph to take back to Winston, and Graham gave her one. Maugham and Searle left around 3 p.m. Lady Churchill stayed another half-hour, and Hecht stayed to dinner, later bearing off the sketch of Churchill's head which Graham had given him (and which Beaverbrook later said should have gone to him as part of his deal with Graham). In short, the evidence is overwhelming that Lady Churchill at least appeared to like the portrait at first sight. Politeness may have played its part. She had been somewhat conditioned to react favourably by Kenneth Clark, whom she liked and admired. Deep down she may have been dismayed, but her pleasure seemed genuine.

All seemed to have gone well as they retired to bed that night, and the sight of a large, palpably prime ministerial limousine arriving the following afternoon, as Graham rose from his siesta, aroused no sense of foreboding. 'A letter of praise, perhaps,' Kathleen thought; and Graham, she believed, had the same comfortable expectation. The driver brought in a largish, white envelope. Inside Graham found two type-written sheets.

My dear Graham Sutherland [written in Churchill's hand],
    Thank you for sending me the photograph.
    Personally I am quite content that any impression of me by you should be on record. I feel however that there will be an acute difference of opinion about this portrait and that it will bring an element of controversy into a

function that was intended to be a matter of general agreement between the Members of the House of Commons, where I have lived my life. Therefore I am of opinion that the painting, however masterly in execution, is not suitable as a Presentation from both Houses of Parliament. I hope therefore that a statement can be agreed between us which will be accepted by the Committee.

About the ceremony in Westminster Hall. This can go forward although it is sad there will be no portrait. They have a beautiful book which they have nearly all signed, to present to me, so that the ceremony will be complete in itself.

It has been a great pleasure to me to make your acquaintance and to meet your wife. When the present pressure has abated I should like to talk over the portrait with you as I have some suggestions to make if you invited them. Yours very sincerely, Winston S. Churchill.

Graham sent back a note expressing great regret, but saying that he had painted honestly what he saw.[36]

It was a deeply wounding rejection from a man Graham greatly admired and, in its prediction of controversy, eerily accurate. 'The worst day of our lives', Kathleen called it, tempting providence perhaps. Yet Graham doubtless sounded calm as he rang Charles Doughty, the committee secretary, to tell him the appalling news. Doughty (Eton, Magdalen College, Oxford, and the Coldstream Guards) was a man of action. He said he would go straight to Chartwell.

His wife Adelaide—she became Dame Adelaide in 1971 for services to the Conservative Party—went too, and had a chat with Lady Churchill while her husband talked to Sir Winston in his study. Lady Churchill told Mrs Doughty: 'I think it's a very fine portrait myself'—and she pointed to a portrait by Sir William Orpen, done after the Dardanelles débâcle and commented: 'When I first saw it, I didn't think I could bear it, he looked so defeated and sad. Now it is one of my most treasured possessions.'[37]

'Then my husband and Churchill came in to tea,' Dame Adelaide recalled.

Churchill was in his boiler suit, and pretty grumpy. 'Your husband says I have got to accept the portrait,' he said.

I don't think my husband had any difficulty in persuading him. I think he explained people would be very upset and hurt if he rejected it. The MPs had contributed towards it out of their own pockets, not all of them terribly willingly.

Her husband told her later that when he had gone into Churchill's study, the latter had pointed to a little painting of the young Napoleon on his desk and had said: 'Now that's what I call art. This other thing'—pointing at the photograph of Graham's portrait—'How do they paint one today? Sitting on a lavatory!'

During Doughty's rescue mission, Hans and Elsbeth Juda arrived at the White House. On hearing what had happened, Juda immediately offered to buy the portrait. But he did not, of course, get the chance: at about 6 p.m. Doughty rang and said: 'Forget it. The ceremony goes on.' Juda advised Graham to tell no one about the letter, and for many years it remained a secret.

So now the programme agreed with Doughty could get into gear. Next morning, Monday, the portrait went to London to be framed by Hecht, who gave a small dinner party that evening to celebrate. Peter Wilson, the suavely forceful chairman of Sotheby's, Arthur Jeffress and the actress Kay Walsh and her husband were present. They were all, Kathleen noted, 'knocked sideways' by the portrait.

On Tuesday it went to Downing Street. Confronted by the portrait itself, Churchill is said to have remarked: 'It makes me look half-witted, which I ain't,' and 'Here sits an old man on his stool, pressing and pressing.' When John Colville saw it, he turned to Churchill and said: 'The portrait of Dorian Gray?' Churchill said nothing, smiled and turned his back on it.[38] Colville had a point: the portrait did seem to have an uncannily strong impact on its subject. 'The days leading up to the presentation were a nightmare,' Mary Soames recalled.[39]

> I was in and out of the house a lot, but I do know my mother was having a most harassing time of it. I do remember her saying: 'It's too awful. I don't know if your father is going to turn up. He's so upset about it.' I think it was during those days that her own hatred worked up.
>
> I now see that they did both deeply feel that they ought to have been able to see the picture sooner than they did. This is something no artist may agree about. He would say: 'I wouldn't change it anyway.' But they did feel a fast one had been pulled on them, and that they had been taken for a ride. I think they didn't have the slightest idea it was going to be like what it was.

Graham's own personal charm compounded the sin. Sir Winston was deeply wounded that this 'brilliant painter with whom he had made friends while sitting for him should see him as a gross and cruel monster', Lady Churchill later wrote to Lord Beaverbrook.[40] The experience amounted to a culture shock for her father, Mary Soames believed. Graham had completely ignored an image of himself which Sir Winston had come to accept and which had become an international symbol: that was Kenneth

Clark's theory, and she thought it was correct.

Probably, Graham subsequently believed, Churchill saw the portrait as part of a plot to get rid of him. 'Though it is supposition, I think probably the view is correct that he thought depicting him in his feebleness was a malicious conspiracy to do him down,' he said later.[41] 'I don't know if he realized that I've always voted Labour. But he knew I was a friend of Nye and Jennie. I think he probably thought I was employed to undermine his image.' When, in a Canadian television broadcast in March 1961, Beaverbrook suggested that Graham might indeed have been influenced by Nye Bevan, Graham told him that the only contact with the Bevans at the time was before the portrait was commissioned, when Jennie Lee sounded him out, and after.[42]

> *No one*, I can say categorically, influences me in my renderings. The only danger to me sometimes is the charm of the sitter. Churchill often showed me the greatest charm and could not have been kinder. Nevertheless, he was self-conscious and ill at ease during the actual time of the sitting. I was seduced by his charm at other times, and wanted so much to please him. But I draw what I see; and 90 per cent of the time I was shown precisely what I recorded. . . . I would not like to go down in the small history I may create as being a person who obliterated or unconsciously malformed a face at the dictate of another.

If Graham felt there was a gap between Churchill's true personality and what he showed when sitting, was it not his job as a portrait painter to bridge it? And if charm was an important part of that true personality, should he not have shown some of it in making the final synthesis? The answer is perhaps that Graham was not, for all his protestations, just painting what he saw; he was also recording a conception he had of Churchill—as a rock, not as a charmer.

The portrait went from Hecht's to the Ministry of Works, so that the necessary dispositions could be made for the ceremony, and then to a locked committee room at the House of Commons, where it could be inspected by presentation committee members, members of the Cabinet and so on. On 25 November the Bevans rang Graham to say how much they liked it. It was also officially photographed by *The Times* for the rest of the press. Graham was appalled by the result and had a terrible time trying to get newspapers to use ones taken by John Underwood and Elsbeth Juda. Only some complied.

There was a lull before the presentation on 30 November. Graham gave some interviews. 'I expect criticism of this painting, because my idea of Sir Winston is probably nothing like the idea of the ordinary man in the street,' he told the *Daily Mail* in a pre-emptive strike. 'I don't paint pretty pictures just to win applause.'[43]

The dreaded day came. Probably every newspaper in the country, and many abroad, carried a reproduction of the portrait. The exposure was overwhelming. Graham must have felt naked. *The Times* that morning also carried the first critical assessment: advantage had clearly been taken of the photographic session. Its art critic found the portrait more successful than those of Maugham and Beaverbrook, both in composition and in treatment of form, and summed it up as a 'powerful and penetrating image'.

It was a sunny morning. Graham and Kathleen took their places for the presentation ceremony—being televised throughout the country—in Westminster Hall, on a platform reserved for special guests, just behind and to the right of Churchill himself. Lady Churchill shook hands with them as she and Sir Winston arrived. The portrait, standing on an easel at the top of some steps, loomed over the proceedings: in the eyes of Sir Beverley Baxter MP, 'its grim, uncompromising quality dominated the setting and almost obliterated the sun.'[44] The Opposition leader, Clement Attlee, spoke gracious words. Sir Winston rose. 'This is the most memorable occasion of my life,' he said.

> I doubt whether any of the modern democracies abroad has shown such a degree of kindness and generosity to a party politician who has not yet retired and may at any time be involved in controversy [laughter]. . . . the portrait [and he turned to look at it] is a striking example of *modern* art [laughter, applause]. It certainly combines force and candour. These are qualities which no active member of either House can do without or should fear to meet.

A roar of appreciative and understanding laughter greeted the gibe at modern art in which the old man cleverly disguised his bitterness. 'I felt sick with disgust,' Kathleen wrote in her diary, but she and Graham managed to exchange smiles.[45]

After the ceremony MPs and peers pressed around the portrait for a closer look. Nye Bevan said he thought it 'a beautiful work, wonderful'. Sir Walter Monckton, then Minister of Labour, found it 'jolly good'. Sir Richard Acland felt that it gave Churchill a big Roman nose. George Thomas, later Speaker, thought that of the many Churchills, Sutherland had caught 'one we have often seen in the Commons'. Captain Henry Kerby, a right-wing Conservative, said that he had the highest respect for Graham's work but was 'profoundly shocked' by it.

The attack was led, with characteristic impetuosity, by Lord Hailsham, who was heard to say:

> If I had my way, I'd throw Mr Graham Sutherland into the Thames. The portrait is a complete disgrace. . . . if I did my work the way Mr Sutherland has done his, I would never get a brief. . . . I have wasted my money—we have all wasted our money. . . . It is bad-mannered; it is a filthy colour. . . . Churchill has not got all that ink on his face—not since he left Harrow, at any rate.

In general, with notable exceptions, Conservatives disliked it, while Socialists liked it—thus fuelling Churchill's conspiracy theory.

Graham heard the barrage of protest as he walked by, grim-faced.[46] When he was introduced to some official guests, people turned to him and said loudly: 'Look, Sir Winston's got a dirty face,' and 'What a terrible tribute to our greatest man.' It was a searing experience. To an *Evening Standard* reporter he said only: 'Opinion is bound to be both ways.' Then he went off with Kathleen to a lunch given by members of the presentation committee, who were all reported to be in favour of the portrait.

Alfred Hecht sprang supportively into the breach again. Graham and Kathleen retired to his place in the King's Road for a rest, followed by dinner. This time the Nye Bevans were there, Sonia Orwell (a good friend of Francis Bacon, Peter Watson and so many others) and Andrew Shonfield, then foreign editor of the *Observer*, and his Polish-born wife.

Next day the morning newspapers were full of the Churchill Portrait Storm, as the *Daily Express* called it. Fleet Street was deluged with letters and telephone calls. 'Throw the thing away,' urged a *Daily Telegraph* reader. 'It must be burned,' sobbed a female caller to the *Daily Express*—little suspecting that Lady Churchill herself would come to share her feeling. In the Commons the Labour MP Emrys Hughes, who sat opposite Churchill, said that it was an excellent portrait of a depressed-looking old man thinking of the atom-bomb, a remark that was greeted with laughter. A fellow Socialist, Henry Usborne, thought it might come to be regarded as the greatest portrait of the century, but believed most members wanted to give not a great painting but one Churchill himself would like (a fair point).

Late that evening, 1 December, after dining at the Antony Heads with Lady Diana Cooper and Lords Salisbury and de L'Isle and Dudley, Graham and Kathleen went to a reception which Churchill was giving at 10 Downing Street. Churchill was very amiable and said to Graham with some generosity: 'Well, Sutherland, although we may not agree on artistic matters, we can still remain friends.'[47] It was not to be. Graham and Kathleen were told the portrait was not being shown to avoid spoiling the occasion. Since seeing it, they gathered, Churchill 'looks in the glass all day at his neck'. Mary Soames was again full of praise for the painting. There was champagne, caviar sandwiches and a toast to the Prime Minister proposed by General Lord Ismay.

Willie Maugham was among the guests. He wrote shortly afterwards:

I am afraid you are very much upset by the adverse criticism you have had to put up with over your portrait of the PM. I beseech you not to let it affect you. You have had an immense deal of praise, and justly, for your work in the past, and now that you are a public figure, which means that you attract the attention of masses of ill-instructed people, you must be prepared to suffer from their ignorant reaction. . . . I know that criticism is wounding, but believe me, it is very soon forgotten, and the work remains. I am convinced that posterity will receive your portrait as a convincing and powerful representation of the man who will have become a great historical figure.

In this case, as we know, the work did not live on, and posterity was denied its chance to make its judgement.

Colin Anderson also wrote comfortingly, calling it 'an unforgettable image, which is also jolly *like*, whatever people may say'.[48] Graham replied: 'However much one says one "doesn't mind" this unfortunate kind of publicity, one does, of course, a bit, and notes such as yours *do* fortify.'

On 3 December, at very short notice, a motley group of art critics and others was invited to inspect the portrait in the Churchills' old home at Hyde Park Gate. 'It's very much better than the photographs, isn't it?' William Coldstream was heard saying to Ben Nicolson of the *Burlington*. Nicolson later summed it up as a prodigious *tour de force*. The public had grown so used to flashy, elegant portraits that it was shocked by the representation of the loose stomachs, scraggy necks and pudding cheeks old gentlemen were apt to develop, he wrote.[49] In the *Spectator* M. H. Middleton felt that it would remain (oh, irony) 'by far the best record of the Prime Minister which we shall bequeath to posterity', but regretted that it should have been painted so thinly and questioned the Baconian fading-out of the legs in such a presentation work.[50]

Graham himself showed magnanimity that day, when he sent Lady Churchill a sketch of Churchill's hand. 'My dear Mr Sutherland,' she wrote on 4 December, 'I am touched that you should have given me the sketch of Winston's hand. Thank you very much indeed. Yours very sincerely, Clementine S. Churchill.' Graham may have hoped for some equivalent gesture. It did not come.

For perhaps a few weeks the portrait remained at Hyde Park Gate. It was then crated by Messrs Bourlet, sent to Chartwell and uncrated, but never hung.[51] Within a year, as the world learned in January 1978, Lady Churchill ordered its destruction.

'The question of painting a national hero is a very special thing,' Graham said ruefully, in a radio interview three days after the presentation.[52] Perhaps, he mused, it should not have been done in the hero's own lifetime. Photography, he said three years before his death, had made people much more aware of what they and other people looked like—or thought they looked like.[53]

> I think it is true that only those totally without physical vanity, educated in painting or with exceptionally good manners can disguise their feelings of shock or even revulsion when they are confronted for the first time with a reasonably truthful painted image of themselves. . . .
>
> Many people have the fixed idea that my portraits are cruel. I do not aim to make them so . . . but I do *look* at the person whose characteristics I try to record. I don't always succeed . . . and, from my own point of view, hardly ever do so. I want neither to flatter nor to denigrate. Least of all do I want to soil and mortify.

Churchill did seem to have felt both denigrated and mortified. We may think that, for a great man, he over-reacted. Nevertheless, by the terms of his stated aims, Graham had failed on that particular count. The portrait's impact depended heavily on the Abraham Lincoln-like posture and angle of presentation, which also helped to underline Churchill's physical debilities. Therein lay the seeds of its destruction. Graham had seriously under-estimated his sitter's sensitivity. As a portrait, his work was masterly; as a gift, it was a dismal failure.

10

The Coventry Tapestry

1952-62

THE COVENTRY TAPESTRY was to occupy Graham off and on—more off than is generally realized—for ten years. Was it all a colossal mistake? The spectrum of opinion is broad. There are those, like Dr John Hayes, Director of the National Portrait Gallery in London, who feel that it was the 'central event' of Graham's career and 'the work for which he will be most generally remembered'.[1] Others, like Francesco Arcangeli, the Italian author of another critical study, feel that it was alien to his main activity as a painter of nature.[2] An intermediate view—to which I incline—is that Graham should not have undertaken it, but the end result largely justified the effort. There is much to be said for Graham's own comment when he saw it *in situ*: 'Well, it could be worse.'

In its freakish way, it is even rather magnificent. But there was always something suspect about the emphasis on its being the biggest tapestry in the world. When the cathedral's architect, Sir Basil Spence, pointed this out to the Duke of Edinburgh on a private visit, adding that it weighed three-quarters of a ton, the latter not unreasonably commented: 'I hope that is not its only quality.'[3] Certainly, it is a strange work of art, which started as a painting, became a huge photograph and ended up as what the *Observer* called 'the biggest single sheet of woven wool in the world'.[4]

In all, Graham did three cartoons or finished sketches (sometimes also called maquettes) for the tapestry's design. They were successively approved by the cathedral authorities in late 1953, early 1955 and the autumn of 1957; the last was heavily revised. Weaving proper began in 1959 and finished in early 1962. It involved nine visits by Graham to the workshops in central France and much tedious correction of the photographic enlargements which guided the weavers. France was periodically in a state of political semi-paralysis, followed by the near-revolution of May 1958 which brought

General de Gaulle back to power. The aftermath of the Algerian war was bitter, and strikes on the railways and elsewhere sometimes complicated Graham's contacts with the weavers.

The tapestry's origins went back to November 1940, when the German Luftwaffe destroyed most of Coventry's cathedral. An open competition for the design of a new one was eventually organized. In 1951 Basil Spence, an Edinburgh-based architect with a growing reputation, especially for exhibition design, heard that he had won. He had been much impressed by Graham's Northampton *Crucifixion* and, latterly, by his 1949 tapestry, *Wading Birds*, which Spence saw at an Arts Council exhibition, together with others commissioned by the Edinburgh Tapestry Company. Later he bought *Wading Birds*. If he won the Coventry competition, he decided, he would ask Sutherland and the same company to design and make a vast tapestry to hang behind the high altar.[5]

Thus it was that he wrote to Graham on 22 November 1951 to ask whether he would be interested in tackling the vast tapestry, 65 feet high by 44 feet wide. There would be many restrictions, he warned. The tapestry should depict our Lord in Glory, supported by the twelve apostles. The central figure would have to be about 30 feet high, with the hands and feet showing signs of the Passion. The tapestry should communicate directly to the ordinary man, whose worship this modern cathedral was intended to help. 'From the first moment that I conceived this tapestry I thought of you as its designer,' Spence wrote. Graham cannot have been insensitive to the compliment.

At 44 years old, Spence was four years Graham's junior, and appreciably less well-known. Graham was by now painting standing forms and experimenting with sculpture. He had painted Maugham and Beaverbrook. The wider fame fostered by the Tate Affair and the Churchill portrait was yet to come, however. He sent Spence a guarded reply, suggesting a visit to Villefranche in January. His natural caution about taking on so vast a project had probably been increased by Kenneth Clark, who disliked what he had understood of Spence's plans: 'I do not see why a cathedral should look like a mixture of factory and a cinema simply because these have become more usual forms of architecture,' he wrote to Kathleen on 27 December, before knowing of Graham's possible involvement. 'I believe that association and function are indissoluble, and that the new cathedral is not functionally adapted to Christian worship.'

Spence arrived in the South of France on 5 January 1952 and spent five days discussing the tapestry and the cathedral and doing some relevant sight-seeing: the Matisse chapel in Vence, the Picasso museum at Antibes, where they saw some remarkable tapestries woven in France from designs by Picasso, Rouault and Dufy, among others. Spence took to Graham and Kathleen and found Graham sensitive and charming.[6]

He had brought with him a set of plans, photographs of his perspective drawings, and a painting he had done of the interior showing his own rough idea of the tapestry. He was an able artist, and Graham was undoubtedly influenced by it. Spence explained that he wanted a majestic Christ figure surrounded by the four beasts symbolizing the Evangelists. They read from the Book of Revelations, which describes the beasts as like a lion, a calf, a man and a flying eagle respectively and Christ as 'to look upon, like a jasper and sardine stone' (a symbol perhaps best ignored).[7]

Graham thought the proportions of the proposed tapestry a trifle squat and was worried by the colour restrictions imposed by the pinky-grey sandstone of the interior (then also being quarried for the new *Financial Times* building in London). Spence noted these reservations; the tapestry was duly elongated to some 78 feet by 39 feet, and the stone was eventually abandoned inside. He made an important suggestion: that the cartoon or sketch should be done fairly small, perhaps 7 feet high, then magnified photographically to full size, thus saving much labour and preserving the vitality of a smallish design (but creating many new problems, it transpired).

Spence left, fairly confident that Graham would accept the task. Writing to Clark six days later, Graham said he found the shell of the proposed building tolerable but was worried about the projected embellishment, font and sculpture, within. He had accepted to design the tapestry, he said, 'if I can be assured that the interior decorative and religious details meet with my approval.... I tried to influence the architect, whom I found modest, humble and sensitive, but lacking in perspicacity.' Clark welcomed the news: 'if it is to be built, then it can only be saved if you and others like you will generously co-operate,' he wrote on 19 January; 'if you do enough, it may end up as a masterpiece.' But why a tapestry? he wondered — 'Surely a mural painting would be far more expressive of your intentions, as well as being cheaper.'

The official commission came from the Reconstruction Committee in mid-January.[8] Graham wrote a letter of provisional acceptance, pointing out that he had plans for a New York exhibition in March, although this could be postponed (and was, by twelve months), and planned to paint the Queen, subject to her plans.

Apart from these matters, I shall give you every priority that is possible. But this is a great and important work. I must proceed slowly and naturally, after many studies and much care, and I know you would not wish me to bind myself in any way to a schedule of time.

He noted that the committee agreed to the proposed fee of £4000 and asked for a couple of weeks to 'think around the subject'. It was the first of many letters to the secretary of the Reconstruction Committee, Captain Norman Thurston, MC, who turned out to look every inch the retired officer: polished shoes, moustache, military bearing, tweedy clothes.

Whereas with the Northampton *Crucifixion* Graham had had a free hand, he was now bombarded with suggestions and stipulations. 'This tapestry will be the dominating feature of the cathedral for all the centuries to come,' trumpeted a daunting brief drafted by the cathedral's provost, the Very Rev. R. T. Howard, and approved by the bishop, the Rt. Rev. Neville Gorton. 'The congregation will have no choice but to see it all the time by night as well as by day. . . .' It must, he stressed, be theologically sound, and he listed four main themes: the Glory of the Father ('light unapproachable'); Christ in the Glory of the Father (Christ to be shown either standing, sitting, blessing, helping, ruling, giving the Sacrament or drawing humanity up to Himself); the Holy Spirit and the Church (represented by some symbol and by the apostles); and the Heavenly Sphere (represented by angels or saints). 'These four themes will afford the artist almost infinite scope for creative imagination,' the Provost concluded. 'It will be for him to unite them into one composite whole.'

Spence, rather less confusingly, had suggested that the main Christ figure should be surrounded by the symbols of the four Evangelists: lion (St Mark), eagle (St John), calf (St Luke) and man (St Matthew): hence the title *Christ in Glory in the Tetramorph*. Graham clung to this. He decided fairly early on that he wanted to create a central figure of 'great contained vitality', as he later put it: not a Jehovah, but a figure

> with something of the power of lightning and thunder, of rocks, of the mystery of creation generally. . . . My idea, then, was to make a figure which was a presence, and to surround that figure with the traditional layout of the four symbols of the Evangelists.[9]

It should be a formal yet realistic presence, with a face which looked at one.[10]

Graham had naturally looked at a great deal of religious art—mainly in books—when doing his Northampton *Crucifixion*, his *Deposition* and his *Christ Carrying the Cross*. He now widened his quest for a figure which was at once decorative and hieratic. He was much impressed by the quality of 'pent-up force' he found in Egyptian sculpture in the Louvre and felt he should do a large figure like a Buddha or something in the Valley of the Kings.[11] He was deeply impressed, while in Venice in 1952, by the mosaics of the cathedral of Santa Maria Assunta on the island of Torcello, one of the crowning achievements of Byzantine art in Europe, he felt. He also wanted to convey something of the stillness of the rather frightening Pantocrator half-figures of Christ found in Greek churches and in Sicily. He examined equally the great Romanesque and early Gothic French cathedrals, including Vézelay, Autun, Rheims and Chartres.

Aesthetically, a single, dominant figure ran the danger of being excessively or insufficiently symmetrical. Graham at first, and finally, decided to enclose it in the traditional mandorla, an almond-shaped frame found in Romanesque renderings of the theme, tying the symbolic beasts to it with brass-coloured tape, like that binding early Egyptian mummy portraits to coffined figures.

The challenge was to make an impact with something a little outside, or different from, what had been done before. Graham thought that perhaps a new vocabulary of gestures might emerge from the old ones, and filled a whole notebook with them—finding that they had little to offer, however. This 'clearing of the ground', as he called it, went on intermittently in 1952 and early 1953. Right from the start, his two or three early sketches from this period show, he was playing with the possibilities of three alternative poses for Christ: with arms raised, horizontal or lowered. In between work for the various retrospective exhibitions, his mind was focused on the tapestry by meetings with Spence, which took place, for example, on 30 May, 10 July and 24 August 1952, in London or Kent.

Spence wanted to test the capacities of the Edinburgh Tapestry Company with a sample piece. Graham did a sketch of the calf and, on 13 October 1952, went up to see the trial piece. It was his first and only visit to Scotland, remarkable self-denial in one so proud of his Scottish origins. The result was 'absolutely bad', as he later put it.[12] The 'drawing' was bad, and the colours did not match. Spence agreed.

Late January 1953 found Graham experimenting on the Christ figure in the rented Cottage Dominic, in a burst of sustained concentration on the tapestry. 'It *must* look vital, non-sentimental, non-ecclesiastical, of the moment, yet for all time,' he wrote to Spence, welcoming the news that he had decided to remove the wall behind the altar and to place the tapestry at the end of the cathedral.[13] He was still doing work for the New York show and gambling a lot.

With no evidence of progress by June, Spence and Thurston began to grow restive. Graham wrote Spence a long letter to explain.[14] First came an idea, he said, then many small sketches, then the drawing and redrawing of the various parts: 'All this is a kind of testing period.' For the Christ figure he wantd to make little sculptured models as well. Time was a factor. After a month, a drawing which had seemed all right might seem to lack truth. When all the bits were done, he started on a more final, and eventually *the* final, design. 'All great monumental designs have been done this way—from Michel Angelo to Picasso, and I make no apology for working this way,' he said. 'This is not a mere *decorative* effort: but must contain some spiritual intensity and essence. . . .' To call for a finished maquette before he was sure that the *drawings* were authentic was putting the cart before the horse. Given the sense of urgency hanging over the work, 'I have very seriously considered telling you that I cannot continue with it under these circumstances. . . . You may feel the same. . . . [I] would look forward to continuing, if I can work in peace—but I can't work in an atmosphere of rush—like commercial art.'

Much of the rush was of Graham's own making: as usual, he had too much on his palette. Spence, too, was under various pressures. Some members of the committee, including the chairman, E. H. Ford, had seen Graham's show at the Tate that May and had reacted with stunned incomprehension. When they spoke to Spence about it, their eyes said, 'Let it be on your head,' he recalled.[15] Graham's dilatoriness did not make him easier to defend.

Only after a meeting of artist and architect on 1 July 1953 in London did Graham get down to the first cartoon in earnest. It was to be about the size of a door (a tenth the size of the tapestry itself), in oil and gouache. Graham gave it a dullish green background, like old velvet, a yellow mandorla and a bearded Christ: for the head he looked at sources as varied as his own *Paris-Match* photographs of cyclists, Rembrandt, Egyptian art, and a Romanesque fresco at Tavant in France, found in a book. Here too he did not lack guidance. 'Victory, serenity and compassion will be a great challenge to combine,' Provost Howard told him.[16] 'Just as the Italians boldly conceived an Italian face for Christ and the Spanish a Spanish face, it may come to you to conceive of an English face, universal at the same time.' (He was disappointed, Kathleen recalled, when Graham gave Christ brown rather than blue eyes.)

This first Christ was a rather resigned-looking Redeemer, arms down at his sides, wounded palms turned outwards, seated, but not unambiguously so. The overall design was not unlike the final one. He was surrounded by the Evangelists' symbols, in the design of which Graham had striven hard to avoid the dusty, heraldic connotations of eagle and lion. Between Christ's feet he placed a tiny man to give a sense of scale: it was just man-sized in the tapestry. Underneath was a little dragon in a chalice, another St John symbol. At the bottom he sketched in three panels showing a *Pietà* (the Virgin Mary and others mourning the dead Christ—a tragic note to balance the risen Christ above) and, on either side, an Annunciation and a Visitation, which he later painted out.

Bishop, provost, Ford and Thurston came down to inspect this slightly sentimental but rather successful first effort at the White House on 30 December 1953, almost a month before Graham resigned as a Tate trustee. The provost later called it a day of many powerful impressions.[17] One was that Graham, a Roman Catholic, had erred in portraying a *Pietà*. This was not within the Anglican tradition, Bishop Gorton wrote to tell him, slightly apologetically, on 8 January 1954. The Lady Chapel (in which that part of the tapestry would be seen) would be used for Mothers' Union meetings and such like, he explained, and they would associate Our Lady with Christmas and the birth of Our Lord. The two side panels were all right. They wanted Graham to give up the *Pietà* and to show the Mother of the Lord in whatever surroundings he felt were right.

Graham was not sure after this whether the committee wanted another cartoon or not. He would like to feel free to develop and change his design gradually and for some time to come, he told Spence.[18]

Indeed, thereupon—at La Souco—he started a second version, this time with Christ's arms outstretched. But the repercussions of his Tate resignation seriously delayed progress. 'I had thought that the fact of my resignation would end there!' he rather naively told Thurston, when he was back at La Souco on 31 March and hard at work on the design again. In mid-August Thurston nagged again: four and a half months had passed, he wrote. Graham was all apologies. He had had three weeks' holiday in Italy and had then been struck by 'flu, he replied on 3 September. 'You must understand that in work of this magnitude I cannot work absolutely continuously without a break.' He needed to hang it in his studio to contemplate it for two or three weeks at a time. Furthermore 'now, out of the blue comes the work for this Churchill portrait. . . . I was not told to go ahead until recently—this in terms not unlike a Royal command!' But the maquette was nearly finished, he said.

By this stage Spence's patience was beginning to fray. Graham's tapestry was only a part, albeit a very important one, of a massive team effort which he, as architect, was co-ordinating to a tight schedule. Reading of Graham's portrait commissions—Sackville-West and Arthur Jeffress, as well as Churchill—he wrote angrily to Thurston on 16 September: 'As I see it,

Graham Sutherland is rapidly turning into a fashionable portrait painter with lucrative commissions and social engagements, which all detract from his doing what we want him to do with the tapestry.' Spence was also worried by Graham's lack of liaison with his office. 'I think he is probably our best artist,' he told Thurston, 'but the success of the tapestry rests on the collaboration between himself and myself, as if it is in the slightest degree out of key, it may destroy all that we have worked for over the years.'

Then came the storm over the Churchill portrait, and Graham had to confess to Thurston that his frame of mind 'was not such as would best serve work of a religious nature'.[19] but he recovered in time to get the second cartoon (in an uncompleted state) to Spence's office in London in time for a meeting on 20 December 1954.

Like the sketch which Graham had started at Roquebrune that January, it showed Christ with arms outstretched horizontally, vestment sleeves greatly enlarged to fill the space created. The arms looked curiously foreshortened; there was no mandorla, but instead some strange flashes (of heavenly light, perhaps) at Christ's waist and ankles; and the four symbols—eagle and lion looking unsteady—were in frames or boxes. At the bottom were three panels showing a Madonna and Child flanked by an Annunciation and, on the right, St Michael wrestling with the Devil. It had a new intensity but looked rather messy beside Mark 1, which Graham also brought along for comparison.

The committee, which included prominent laymen, as well as bishop, provost and other clerics, seemed to prefer the second cartoon and made one or two suggestions. On 12 January 1955, Graham took both cartoons to a meeting of the cathedral chapter in order to have them vetted on theological grounds.

1955 was marked by uncertainty over the future weaving of the tapestry. The strain of waiting for the huge contract had proved too much for Spence's friends, the Bertie family, who owned the Edinburgh Tapestry Company, and a new management and chief weaver had taken over. Graham suspended work while a further sample piece was awaited, feeling that he might need to modify his technique when he saw it. In June, while in the South of France, he gained the impression that the tapestry could be executed in the Aubusson area for less than half the projected £20,000. Spence duly sounded out various firms, and in August Graham wrote to Madame Cuttoli, the greatest living authority on modern tapestry, for her advice, reminding her that they had met in Paris and Cap d'Antibes (in March and December 1952). She promised to see what could be done, but she warned him about the coarse threads and simplified colours currently in use in Aubusson, cheaper though they were.

Various trial panels produced that autumn by the Edinburgh firm showed steady progress towards the fulfilment of Graham's intentions. But he and Spence had lost confidence in its capacity to handle so unprecedentedly vast a project. In January 1956 Graham and Kathleen visited Madame Cuttoli in Cap d'Antibes. She said that it could be done for £13,000 in eighteen months.

In May 1956 Madame Cuttoli gave Spence a more considered estimate. The tapestry could, she said, be woven *in one piece* if the width remained within 12 metres (just over 13 yards). That would give a vastly superior result. Weaving would take approximately thirty months. She would act only as artistic and technical adviser. The matter was more or less clinched when the Edinburgh Tapestry Company suggested that it should be woven in about fifteen pieces, then stitched together, with a coarsish weave of four or five stitches to the inch. Madame Cuttoli meanwhile produced a first-rate sample for Graham, with some twelve stitches to the inch. He and Spence agreed that it was much better, and the price was lower. A 25 per cent import duty was a danger, but it was eventually waived by the Treasury. Finally, Madame Cuttoli revealed the name of the firm she had in mind: Pinton Frères, of Felletin, near Aubusson, right in the centre of France. They had worked with Matisse and Léger, among others, and were the best, she considered.

In between various portrait commissions in 1956 (Paul Sacher, Helena Rubinstein, Mrs Eaton), Graham found time to start a third cartoon. As it transpired, it was no bad thing that he had spun out the creative process for so long. On 20 November 1956 Spence wrote to say he had decided to replace the pinky-grey sandstone of the interior with white or a very light colour. The tapestry would certainly look better, and the change would save some £100,000, he told Graham. Furthermore, an anonymous benefactor had given £20,000 for the tapestry.

The change enabled Graham to switch to a brighter palette with a vivid green background. He did not fail to point out that, had he taken less time, the weavers might have started before the design changed, 'with what disastrous results I leave to your imagination', he wrote to Thurston on 15 March 1957, when again under pressure to produce his final ideas.

The cathedral's Reconstruction Committee had meanwhile undergone some drastic changes. Its chairman, E. H. Ford, a local businessman, had died in 1955 and had been succeeded by Sir Fordham Flower, of the brewing family, a man of greater panache. The following year Bishop Neville Gorton had retired, to be succeeded by Cuthbert Bardsley, who was something of an amateur painter. Graham had taken to him on a visit to Coventry in January 1957. On 8 April that year Bardsley came down to lunch in Kent with the provost and Thurston and to inspect progress on the third cartoon.

The provost—who made the running in these matters—thought that the new design was a considerable advance on the old one, but once again Graham was in trouble over the lower panels. When the previous ones were cleared, he had undertaken not to make any 'doctrinal' alterations without referring to bishop and provost. Now he had restored something resembling a *Pietà* in the central panel, which was not 'scriptural'. But to accommodate Graham's feeling that it should show a scene connected with the Passion (as a counterpoint to Christ in Glory and as a reflection of the horrors of our times), they would agree to a Standing by the Cross, the provost wrote nine days later.

Graham found it all very confusing and suggested to Thurston he should be paid an additional fee of £300–£400 for extra work caused by 'differences between the ecclesiastic authorities'. That was agreed in July 1957. Consulted by telephone, the bishop said he favoured a Deposition, but 'without too much horror'.[20] The doctrinal quibbles 'have taken away some of my confidence—have made me diffident, if not afraid', Graham told Spence. The matter was resolved when he had lunch with Bardsley at the Athenaeum Club in London on 15 August: Graham should paint a Crucifixion, a theme which he had all along felt would admirably balance the Risen Christ above.

That is what he did (in time, even) for a gruelling series of committee meetings he had undertaken to attend in Coventry on 17 and 18 September. '11 DAYS TO FINISH TAPESTRY,' he wrote in capitals in Kathleen's diary on 6 September.

The third cartoon showed Christ with forearms raised close to His body, hands parallel to cheeks, head sitting perhaps a trifle uneasily on shoulders. A patterned border ran down the middle of the garment, dividing the composition painfully into halves. His expression is serene, almost amused. The Crucifixion in the single central panel was much less contorted than the Northampton one and hung more vertically.

The cartoon was seen and approved successively by the Reconstruction Committee, the Chapter and the Council of the cathedral. But no sooner was the seal of official approval on it than Graham realized that he heartily disliked it. He recalled:[21]

I then started to make not another cartoon, but to strip this one of its inconsistencies, and to redraw some of the panels: the St Matthew panel, for instance, at the top left-hand corner. A great deal was done, and the lower part of the central panel was entirely recast.

Christ's arms were slightly lowered and his expression was made a great deal more melancholy yet enigmatic: Graham was striving for the tenderness he had discussed with Bacon. The central division and decoration of the garment were removed, the shape reverting to an oval leaf form which Graham had sketched early on. 'I think it is *very greatly* improved,' he told Spence on 20 October. 'Without altering much ... it is much more "realized" in the parts which I thought lacked tension.' Graham was altering something which had been approved as more or less final, 'but I think it will be thought the same as that seen by the committees,' he said.

He put in two or three weeks of solid work on the cartoon in January 1958 in his Kent studio. Understandably, after six years of spasmodic bursts of concentration, he was reluctant to say: it is done. His mind was now being concentrated by the prospect of the cartoon's being photographed for the gigantic enlargements from which the weavers at Felletin would work.

A Wimbledon industrial photographer, W. A. Cook, had quoted £592 for this all-important operation. It involved photographing the cartoon in horizontal strips, which had then to be blown up to the size of the tapestry. The end product would be twenty-four strips, each 39 feet long and 3 feet deep. For work requiring such precision and high definition, Cook wanted to use his own studio. But he was prevailed upon to come to Graham's in mid-February—to minimize wear and tear on the cartoon—and had to adapt it as best he could. When Cook came to process his negatives, he found that the definition was very successful but the scale not absolutely consistent. The difference was only one-sixteenth of an inch but would have produced a cumulative discrepancy of almost a foot in the enlargements. He spent weeks trying to devise ways of eliminating the inconsistencies, but in vain.

In April he asked if he could have the cartoon at this studio to do the job again, but by then it had been taken to France for the weavers. The Fourth Republic was on its knees and was approaching the Algerian *coup* of 13 May. It was too risky to try to get the cartoon back, so the work was entrusted to a Paris firm. This time the scale was right but the definition greatly inferior to Cook's—with serious repercussions for Graham.

At the end of February 1958 Graham, Spence and Thurston went to Paris to meet Jean Pinton, head of the weaving firm to which the great labour was being entrusted, his son Olivier and Madame Cuttoli, to discuss all the technicalities and the details of the contract. Pinton was about 60: bright blue eyes, very erect and courteous. Olivier spoke good English. Like Jean Pinton, Madame Cuttoli had been active in the resistance. Her husband, a senator, had died six years earlier. She had known Picasso for twenty-five years and had more than thirty of his works at her Paris flat, where they met, and in her villa at Cap d'Antibes.

The meeting was followed by the release to the press of official photographs of the cartoon, of which virtually every national newspaper carried large reproductions. 'This is it—Sutherland's Christ', trumpeted the *Daily Express* of 4 March, above a large close-up of Christ's top half. The release was thought to have gone very well.

The contract with Pinton Frères, agreed on 1 September, stated that the tapestry would be executed within thirty months for 20,060,000 francs (£17,000), subject to wage increases, and 'in exact accordance as to form and colour with the painting by Mr Graham Sutherland which is in your possession, and also to the satisfaction of the artist and architect', who were also to approve samples of the weaving. Graham was later to lay much stress on his contractual rights.

Basil Spence was the first to get to the Pinton works at Felletin, calling in there in September 1958 on the way back from a family holiday in Spain and Portugal. Anthony Blee, his son-in-law and partner, recalled:[22]

> Down by the River Creuse there it was like an old Emett drawing, with steam issuing from boilers and vats full of colour. Inside the factory were the tins of German dyes, and the chap in charge of dyeing, wearing an old beret, would go along casually dipping a long-handled spoon into this pot and that one, and spooning the dye into the vat. He got the colours spot-on every time, and he knew exactly how long to leave the skeins of wool bubbling in the vats. Then the wool would be hung in the river to be washed. The German dyes had been tested with an accelerated light machine, and were known to be fast.

The question of the dyes had caused anxiety when the decisions over the contract were being made. Some colours, notably yellow, are more fugitive than others: the blue look of many old tapestries is caused by the yellow leaving the original green, not by some antique predilection for blue. Pintons were known to use the best German dyes, and the Creuse, being lime-free, was ideal for fixing them.

Most remarkable of all, here was the widest tapestry loom in the world, made of two great tree trunks weathered by time, just wide enough to fulfil the Coventry commission with 6 inches to spare. Twelve weavers could sit in a row across the loom's width.

By now the French photographic enlargements had been completed, but they had not been put together to see if they fitted. Only a field was big enough to hold them all, and some cows had to be shooed off one first, Blee recalled. The photographs did match up.

The strength of a tapestry derives from the robust warp threads, the design from the interwoven weft. The weavers, using a shuttle or *flute*, pass the coloured wool weft in and out of the warp as it moves from side to side on the loom. The strips (*bandes* in French: the word came to have nightmarish overtones) were placed under the warp to guide the weavers. Each separate area of colour had first been outlined on them in chalk by a specialist, so they resembled a map with colour references. For the colours—some 900 were eventually used—the weavers referred to the cartoon. This was fixed to a pulley behind the weavers, so that it could be passed up and down when needed. The whole weaving operation was done upside down, with the back of the tapestry uppermost: how otherwise could the weavers tie the knots? Only about 5 feet of the tapestry could be seen at any one time during weaving, and then only from underneath the loom.

Graham was surprised to learn from Spence in November that the weavers needed his guidance to interpret the *bandes*. The English ones could have been used without redrawing, he told Spence: 'Alas, that they were not right in size!!'[23] He planned a first trip to Felletin in late November. But Pinton *père* decided that it would be better for him to wait until they had finished a sample—part of the eagle panel—which Spence had ordered. From that Graham could deduce what guidance was needed.

In mid-January 1959 Felletin's town crier was able to announce: 'A sample of the Coventry tapestry is coming off the loom!' After close inspection by Jean Pinton, the eagle symbolizing St John was hung above a restaurant door in the main square so that the populace could admire its glowing colours.[24] It was later taken to Paris, where Graham saw it *chez* Cuttoli on 27 January. 'Look at that wall,' Mme Cuttoli urged a *Daily Express* reporter who was there too, pointing to a seven-floor building. 'The finished tapestry will cover it. It will be the eighth wonder of the world.'

Graham was very pleased indeed with the sample, he told Pinton.[25] But he stressed the importance of keeping to the tonal variations of the original, and suggested how gradations of colour could best be achieved without geometric stylization. He was worried next day, however, when they adjourned to the basement of the Garde Meuble Nationale to spread out the photographic strips and to decide which areas needed revision. Some 'clarifying' additions had been made which bore no relation either to the photographs or to his style.

Poor definition was not the only difficulty. Magnifying the brush stroke ten times was rather like putting a butterfly's wing under a microscope. The grain of the negative became too strong, and tiny flecks of black or white were emphasized. Some created a pleasing effect; others he had to eliminate. Equally, some areas seemed unsatisfactorily drawn when enlarged, and he redrew them, sometimes even making new studies. More usually, a part had become so vague it needed to be delineated afresh.

A pattern of work now began to emerge. The weaving was to start at the bottom, and therefore with the Crucifixion and its brilliant green flanking areas. First, Graham did the necessary rectification of the photographic strips for that section and dispatched them to the weavers, usually by train. The weavers pressed on with this guidance, while Graham did the next section, and so on, working upwards. Sometimes Graham got behind and received an urgent appeal for the next *bandes*. Sometimes he was well ahead.

A major difficulty was finding somewhere to pin up the 39-foot-long strips. The mayor of Menton, Francis Palmero, who was a friend, came to the rescue by making available a disused department store in the town. There Graham could pin five strips on top of each other and could even get a 'cathedral' distance away from them. In his Menton and Kent studios it was very difficult.

He paid his first visit to Felletin on 5 October 1959 and was much impressed by the long traditions of the weavers and by their colour sense. As work progressed, he discovered that some were better than others. Three principal weavers were responsible for the most obviously difficult parts, like the central figure and the four panels. He returned there on 12 December, on his way to England, bringing more completed strips with him. All seemed to be going well, if slowly. On his way through later, heading south in April 1960, he found little progress and only just forestalled a disastrous interpretation of the upper part of the crucified Christ.

Spence became anxious about progress in May 1960, but Pinton was reassuring: there had been labour problems and the initial work had been very delicate. Anxieties increased in July, when a detachable bit of the cartoon—a piece of brown paper on which Graham had redone the Crucifixion panel, sticking it over an earlier version—was stolen during a lunch break, probably by one of the tourists who poured through (all approach roads had posters announcing 'La Plus Grande Tapisserie du Monde'). Graham was not informed and was very annoyed. Madame Cuttoli, who seemed to be doing nothing, tried to soothe: that bit had been done, she told Graham, and was no longer needed ('ne servait plus'), which was scarcely Graham's attitude to his working sketches.

In all, he went to Felletin twice in late 1959, twice in 1960 (in April and December), four times in 1961 (in February, April, May, October) and finally in February 1962, when it was finished. Sometimes he was pleased with the progress that he could see, sometimes distressed at some minor failure of interpretation. Corrections were possible, and he ordered a number. Relations with Jean Pinton, at whose château overlooking the village he stayed once for two nights and at which he was entertained several times, remained cordial.

During the fourth visit, in December 1960, Jean Pinton mentioned an idea of Madame Cuttoli's: that the finished tapestry might be shown at the Louvre on its way to England. The Reconstruction Committee's chairman, Sir Fordham Flower, caught wind of this plan and asked Thurston to nip it in the bud. Time would be very short, Thurston wrote to Graham on 27 January 1961, and everyone in Coventry felt very strongly that the tapestry should first be seen in its rightful setting.

Graham replied on 30 January—disingenuously, perhaps—that he felt quite neutral. It could be argued that a showing at the Louvre would lessen the tapestry's first impact in the cathedral, but it might arouse wide enthusiasm and interest, and no painter asked to show in such a place could remain *entirely* unmoved. He had the feeling that he was thought to have cooked up the idea with Pinton: 'This is entirely the reverse of the truth.' No more was heard of the subject for a while.

He spent a great deal of time over the photographic *bandes* in 1961 and, in February, had to borrow back the lower half of the cartoon for a week to rework the skirt. All this was far more than he had expected in the way of 'supervision', and in May he wrote to Thurston to suggest a further fee of £1500. In all, he reckoned, he had put in seven months' exclusive work on the tapestry since finishing the maquette.[26] Once again, the committee turned out to be sympathetic to his request, but he was asked to wait until the final financial position could be considered. It is not clear whether he received the extra £1500.

Up to the spring of 1961 Graham's relations with Spence had been extremely warm. He had lent Spence the villa they had bought behind Menton for a holiday. Spence had given Graham some wine and a coffee table he had designed. Spence had shown understanding for Graham's dilatoriness, Graham for Spence's changes in the design for the cathedral interior. Now, when the weavers were half-way through, the friendly tone of their correspondence changed.

Graham seems to have criticized part of the cathedral floor, possibly in the

Unity Chapel.[27] Spence wrote a hurt letter back. Then, in November, Graham grew anxious about how the tapestry would look when removed from the loom. He was particularly worried about Christ's hands, which he had not seen since he had improved and redrawn them. What he wanted to insist on, he told Thurston, was his contractual rights to be the final judge of the quality and to see the finished work 'in its entirety, preferably hung, of course, in France'.[28] Small parts could then be reworked if necessary. He asked Thurston to underline to Pinton his right to see the tapestry before binding arrangements were made about transport and other matters.

Spence told Graham that he was 'hurt and surprised' that he should have written direct to Thurston on this, since everything to do with the building was in his hands: 'Time is woefully short now, but I understand your anxiety and will discuss these points with Pinton and let you know what can be arranged.'[29] Spence had not told *him* about the transportation arrangements for the tapestry, Graham countered. He wanted to exercise his rights before these became a *fait accompli*.[30] Spence replied by return that Graham obviously could not or would not understand that his responsibility as architect was to

> dovetail every scrap of work in the Cathedral into a whole, requiring a great deal of careful organization and pre-planning to see that all the craftsmen, workmen and artists do not get in each other's way and the Cathedral is ready for Consecration.

All other artists had recognized he was aesthetic as well as works co-ordinator for the cathedral, 'which after all is my design and my reputation hangs by it'.

Briefly, relations took a better turn. Spence wrote to Pinton, with a copy to Graham, explaining Graham's anxieties and the need to have the tapestry in position in time for rehearsals of the consecration service because of its acoustic properties, concluding: 'We can only hope Mr Sutherland will find little to alter in the final tapestry when he examines it.'[31] Graham was slightly mollified. 'I am not expecting all will not be well,' he replied, but 'in a tapestry of this size . . . it is absolutely essential to see the total effect. . . .'[32] There must be some place, perhaps in Paris, where it could hang, since seeing it on the ground would give little idea, he feared.

'Believe me, I understand your concern,' Spence replied on 22 November. 'You must know that I too am deeply involved, as I have given you a wall of the cathedral, and a bad tapestry can be extremely serious from my point of view.' But the tapestry could not be hung before delivery, on two grounds: time and cost. The last possible date for delivery was the end of February 1962. Hanging would take six weeks, if all went well—the supporting structure alone had cost £1000. Then Harrison would start tuning the organ: the tapestry would materially affect its sound. That would take a month, leaving three weeks for rehearsals. But he agreed that Graham must see the tapestry off the loom and could not see why small adjustments should not be made if necessary.

The argument so far was confused, and it became more so. Graham wanted to see the tapestry that he had designed hanging vertically before it passed the point of no return for correction. That was a reasonable demand. Something might just have gone terribly wrong. Had he maintained that position and concentrated the search on the environs of Felletin, his case would have been watertight. But would Paris really be a good place to hang it? Once hung—a major undertaking, in however temporary a form—could it be easily got back to Felletin for corrections? It was hard not to think that other considerations, mainly of prestige of one sort or another, were influencing him.

For Spence a whole timetable was at stake. He deserved sympathy, though it was not wholly Graham's fault that the tapestry was behind schedule: Pinton had been laggardly early on. Timing aside, the Reconstruction Committee's insistence on having the first showing of the tapestry at Coventry was, if understandable, more debatable. Had there been time enough, to have shown the tapestry in the country where it was woven would have been an imaginative gesture, a point which Graham was to make cogently, even if not wholly altruistically.

Graham, who was in Kent, now brought in a heavy calibre support weapon: Douglas Cooper himself, co-veteran of the Tate campaign. Cooper came down to the White House on 3 December and drafted—in azure ink on pink paper, with red ballpoint emendations—a magisterial letter to Spence. Graham followed this very closely when he wrote five days later. He could not allow the tapestry out of France until he had seen it hung vertically, he told Spence. It was unfair to suggest that he should look down on it from above. Why should the artist, 'who will bear responsibility to the end of time for any shortcomings in the execution of his design', give his approval under conditions differing greatly from those in which the public would see it, disadvantaging him in relation to critics and congregation? He was, he said, keen that an offer to hang it in Paris, which seemed to be imminent, should be accepted. It seemed only fair that this great example of French workmanship should be shown publicly in France, even if only for a few days.

Spence, returning from an enforced rest, said he was 'very alarmed' by

Graham's letter.[33] Sir Fordham Flower was arranging an emergency meeting of the Reconstruction Committee, which owned the copyright of the tapestry. He admonished Graham not to forget that he too was responsible, contractually, for approving the tapestry and was convinced that no judgement could be made until it was in the right context, 'in other words, at Coventry'.

Graham and Kathleen headed South, spending Christmas with Cooper at the Château de Castille. Cooper visited them in Menton a few days later. The Clarks were also in France, and they lunched with them on New Year's Day. Only now did André Malraux, de Gaulle's Minister for Cultural Affairs, come up with his offer to hang the tapestry in the Sainte Chapelle in Paris, a Gothic jewel near the Palais de Justice. He had been prodded by Madame Cuttoli, Kathleen's diary indicated.

By now the Reconstruction Committee had met. They felt very strongly and unanimously, Sir Fordham Flower wrote to Graham on 12 January 1962, that the tapestry should not be seen by the public until it was in its final position on the cathedral wall. They were utterly against any public exhibition, anywhere, prior to consecration. But they wanted to be helpful and suggested that it should be unfurled by Pinton on to another roller, so it could be examined section by section. Graham's cabled reply was drafted with the aid of his Nice solicitor: 'This really will not do,' it said. 'Must clearly insist on my contractual rights to inspect and approve the work in its entirety before permanent hanging.' Nobody was questioning that right. The Paris offer had confused the issue.

Graham followed up his cable with a long letter to Sir Fordham.[34] No building large enough could be found to hang the tapestry, he said, and he rehearsed his worries about the weaving. His friend Picasso, he said, had told him: 'Up to 25 square feet you can rely on the weavers—but 70 feet! You will be mad if you do not see it hung before acceptance—no weavers, however good, can be expected to produce with certainty on that scale what you want!' Malraux's offer was a great honour for England; he could have seen the work hanging for some days; the workmen would have received well deserved acclaim; national friendship would have been cemented; the wools were easily available from Felletin for small adjustments. . . .

> For my part I may say that I have never been treated so badly before. . . .
> it would seem that you are breaking the contract between us. . . . should I
> be dissatisfied, even in part, with the final result, I shall have . . . to make
> clear . . . that I have been denied opportunity to judge.

It was not a very potent threat. He went on to plead: 'One is not an inanimate object producing a machine-made cloth merely to act as a baffle plate for the organ! Sir Basil . . . perhaps would be content to get anything on that blank wall' —a childish thrust, but Graham's blood was up. Emotion prevailed.

The tapestry would, it transpired, be available for inspection on the floor of the gymnasium of the Building Trades School at Felletin from 17 February. Logically, Graham should have rushed there; instead he suggested that he should come on the 22nd. That would be rather late, Pinton wrote: it must be packed on the 28th.[35] Even the *Daily Telegraph* beat Graham to it. He first saw the gargantuan fruit of his labours in several fine photographs in its 19 February issue.

He got to Felletin two days later, with Cooper, to find that the tapestry had been turned face-down for work on the back. With ill grace, the twenty-odd workers agreed to turn it over, after much expostulation. A ladder was procured. From this inadequate vantage point Graham could see one or two unsatisfactory patches. Cooper drafted a telegram to Spence, which was sent next day from his local telephone exchange, Vers.

Have today seen tapestry under most adverse conditions. Believe treatment excellent in general but some major rectifications necessary in hands and feet. Contrary your letter Pinton says these cannot be done in Coventry and will take eight days. Exercising contractual rights have ordered him complete these revisions before shipment. Rely on you implementing my instructions and modifying timetable as Pinton says three weeks for hanging Coventry grossly exaggerated. Regards Sutherland.

Spence cabled back tersely: 'Agree faults in tapestry should be rectified immediately', and cabled Pinton confirming the instruction. How much was in fact done? On 26 February, the *Daily Telegraph* reported that the giant tapestry was back on the looms for minor alterations requested by the artist. Jean Pinton, however, could recall no adjustments to hands and feet: 'In any case that would have been impossible, since once weaving is finished, one cannot go back on it,' he said.[36]

The row seeped into the newspapers via Graham's *Evening Standard* friend, Sam White, in Paris. 'There never has been and I hope never will be a row between ourselves and Mr Sutherland,' Thurston commented on 24 February.[37] Two days later Graham told the *Coventry Evening Telegraph*: 'I think the translation from my design was magnificent.' He was reported to be 'disappointed' that the tapestry could not be hung first in France. The delay was caused by minor retouches to Christ's left ankle, the report said.

The tapestry arrived in Coventry on 1 March. On the 5th Sir Fordham

Flower, who had been away, at last answered Graham's wounded outpourings. The Sainte Chapelle offer had been most handsome, he said. But the committee was utterly convinced that it had taken the right decision. He hoped Graham's unhappiness, which he sincerely regretted, would be mitigated by the sight of his glorious work in its final and proper setting and by the popular acclaim which it would undoubtedly and deservedly receive.

Graham was not to be placated. He had only wanted to see the tapestry hung vertically and in such a way that corrections could be done if necessary, he replied on 6 March. The Sainte Chapelle was one of the few places where this would have been possible. 'I can only thank you and your committee for their lack of consideration,' he ended gracelessly.

Over the next few weeks he gave several interviews, very much the artist harshly treated by uncomprehending patrons but keeping a stiff upper lip. 'It's all over now and I'm sure it will be all right, and I don't want to say or do anything to upset anybody,' he told Noel Barber,[38] a friend and *Daily Mail* journalist who had a house at Cap d'Ail. 'And I would hate anybody to think that I wanted the tapestry shown in Paris for publicity reasons.' Just a few days' delay, mused Barber, would have meant peace of mind to a great artist who for ten years had given heart and soul to the creation of this great work.

It took two days to get the tapestry up but a month to make it hang perfectly square. It was several inches longer than planned at either end. Most tapestries spring back when liberated from the loom; contrary to calculations, this one was too big to do so. The original plan was to keep it under wraps till consecration, but after some unauthorized press photographs had been printed, it was shown to critics and cameramen with the rest of the cathedral in April.

Reaction to the tapestry was by no means as unequivocally enthusiastic as Sir Fordham had foreseen. *The Times*'s architectural correspondent (J. M. Richards) said that it dominated the interior space but was 'in some ways a disappointment. The eye focuses on a rather nebulous patch of white in the centre, and the degree of stylization varies uncomfortably between one part and another.'[39] But it did furnish the intended climax of glowing colour, he conceded. The *Observer*'s respected architectural pundit, R. Furneaux Jordan, said that the cathedral was, in general, brilliant; however, 'that Sutherland, a painter in oils, was almost bound to fail when designing in wool, might have been foreseen'.[40] Why he had failed he did not say.

Was Christ sitting or standing up? People were irritated that they could not tell. Graham was not greatly worried about that. 'I didn't want to make it specifically sitting,' he said later. 'In fact, I didn't mind a hint of ambiguity.'[41]

Spence felt sorry for Graham. 'I am shocked at the press the tapestry is getting,' he wrote on 22 May. 'I think the criticisms are spiteful and ignorant. . . . I think it is a triumph.' A month later he admitted to Graham that he had been disappointed at first but had come to like it more and more.

Graham and Kathleen genuinely wanted to attend the consecration, along with the Queen and various notables, on 25 May. But, behind schedule as usual, he was working furiously in Menton for his first major one-man show in London for nine years and decided he needed the time. He wrote a long letter to Bishop Bardsley expressing his acute disappointment. He would hate it to be thought that he was absent out of pique, he said, and feared the press would put the worst light on it. John Gordon, the *Sunday Express*'s curmudgeonly columnist, did so. Only two seats were unoccupied in the triumphant service: those allotted to Graham Sutherland, who created the tremendous tapestry, he wrote on 27 May. How sad that men could not combine in magnificent achievement to God without petty squabbling, he moralized smugly.

On 20 August Graham went to see the tapestry *in situ* for the first and only time. He was determined (perversely, or impishly?) to see it incognito and even thought of pencilling on a moustache, Kathleen recalled. But after queuing for an hour with her and their friends Andrew Revai and Robin Chancellor of the Pallas Gallery, he was spotted, whisked in and conducted around by the Rev. Simon Phipps, then the diocese's industrial chaplain.

At last, and in absolute silence, he saw it hanging vertically. Afterwards he told journalists: 'It is beautifully done. I never had any doubt that the actual weaving would be anything but very good.' However he was worried that the rippling effect, caused by weight and humidity, altered the tones here and there. Was he satisfied? he was asked. 'One always thinks one can do better. There are a lot of things that could have been improved, but then one could go on for ever.'[42] To Kathleen and friends back in the car he said simply: 'Well, it could be worse,' and he never went back to look at it again.

Was it all worth it? To this day, as any informal sample of opinion among visitors to the cathedral and its official guides will show, the tapestry arouses enthusiasm and antipathy and remains by far the most controversial aspect of the interior. It is all too easy to criticize. Christ's feet and the figure between them are, to me, unsatisfactory. The very lively symbols of the Evangelists—the eagle owl is splendid—balance and support the Christ figure very effectively. But Christ Himself, although a haunting presence, has slighly mawkish, pre-Raphaelite overtones. Perhaps Graham overdid his researches. The doctrinal stipulations were oppressive, but a less knowledge-laden approach might have made for a more 'modern' central image.

Financially, it was by no means a disaster. Graham had given the preparatory drawings to Kathleen, who had salvaged many of them as he cast them aside. With his agreement, she decided to sell them. The Redfern Gallery, having helped to gather together 127 drawings and paintings, including the first two cartoons, secured them for £30,000 and planned to show them in May 1964, when Andrew Revai's book on the genesis of the tapestry—mainly an extended interview with Graham—was to be published.

In March that year Lord Iliffe, the Midlands newspaper proprietor and publisher, offered to buy them through a family trust. He had been alerted to their availability by the Duchess of Leeds. Kenneth Clark, whom he knew slightly and who thought the tapestry 'a great work of religious art',[43] told him they were important and should be kept together.[44] Iliffe bought them for £80,000 and presented them to the Herbert Art Gallery and Museum, hard by the cathedral, where they continue to offer fascinating insights into the creative process.

11

Mainly Portraits

1955-9

GRAHAM'S BEHAVIOUR during both the Tate Affair and the row over the Coventry tapestry suggests that he positively needed an element of tension and drama in his life. Some people, creative and otherwise, find drama in sexual adventures. That was never his way. He realized that Kathleen was the cornerstone of his life, and was devoted to her. Consciously or otherwise, he sought drama in his semi-public life. Without thinking very clearly about the issues, he made up his mind on the rights and wrongs and then pressed his case in an obsessive way—an approach which usually proved counter-productive.

What link was there between these semi-public crusades and his work? From his glowing, sometimes brooding Welsh landscapes of the 1930s onwards, it was suffused with a sense of drama, which lent urgency to his war drawings and to his religious works, and permeated those frontally presented, almost theatrical standing forms, monstrous heads and hybrid machines of the late 1940s and early 1950s. Yet a direct association between the traumatic incidents of his life and the more anguished of his paintings is not easy to establish. Cooper's theory is not persuasive: he claimed that those thorn studies executed after 1954 derived their (to him) 'more violent, spiky yet formalized appearance' from Graham's 'mental and moral anguish' over the Tate Affair.[1] It is broadly true, however, that around that time Graham was producing some of his most tortured images, yielding to serener ones in late 1955.

It was a happy coincidence that, in the spring of 1954, while still in the throes of the Tate Affair, he should find himself painting his friend Eddy Sackville-West. The anxious features of the frail heir of Knole reflected his own troubled spirit. As early as 11 June 1954 Sackville-West wrote to Graham to complain that he would evidently be the last person to see the

223

portrait: the chorus of praise from those who had seen it in Graham's studio had assumed 'the monotony of a bell tolling for Matins'. Then came the Churchill episode. Not till mid-January was the portrait safely delivered to Ian and Jane Phillips, who had suggested this wholly trouble-free commission. Sackville-West saw it at their home at Charlton Mackrel, near Yeovil, on 6 March, after recovering from 'flu. 'I must say at once that I think it is absolutely masterly (so does Raymond [Mortimer]),' he wrote to Graham on 8 March.

It is the face I see when I look in the glass, but the expression is very different. I always expected you to find me out, and of course you have. The picture is the portrait of a very frightened man—almost a ghost, for nothing is solid except the face and hands. All my life I have been afraid of things—other people, loud noises, what may be going to happen next—of life, in fact. This is what you have shown. There is, of course, much more; but I should say that was the keynote of the portrait, which reminds me (partly because of the method of painting the clothes, only in highlights) in the oddest way of Fuseli.

When one looks closely at the face, one is fascinated by the beauty of the paint. You must not touch an inch of that part, though perhaps the chair, and my left foot, might be made a shade more solid.

Well, dear Graham, I am profoundly impressed. I am quite sure it is a work of genius, which will continue to interest people long after I have been forgotten. You have got the essence of me in the picture, and the vividness is terrifying.

I think Jane—and even Ian—really do appreciate the picture, though Jane must be very tough (indeed, we know she is!) to be able to live in the room with so anxiety-ridden a figure! Ian talks of building a grotto in the garden and putting the picture in it, lit from above. I see his point.

Writing back from a flat they had been lent on Lord Beaverbrook's estate at Cap d'Ail, Graham said:

You relieve my apprehension and fill me with pleasure with your letter. I am *delighted* and proud that you approve, and thank you for going to such a great deal of trouble in writing to me so charmingly and generously of your reactions.

Of course I don't see you as you describe yourself *at all*. For what you write as applying to yourself is really *exactly* applicable to ME!! That is to say, if one leaves out the ghost-like element. *I* saw you as tensed, quick, appraising, slightly shy at being examined, but in return slightly mocking, in the final reckoning, detached, poised (even in pyjamas) and by the same token elegant, critical, tempered (even at croquet) mercifully with mercy

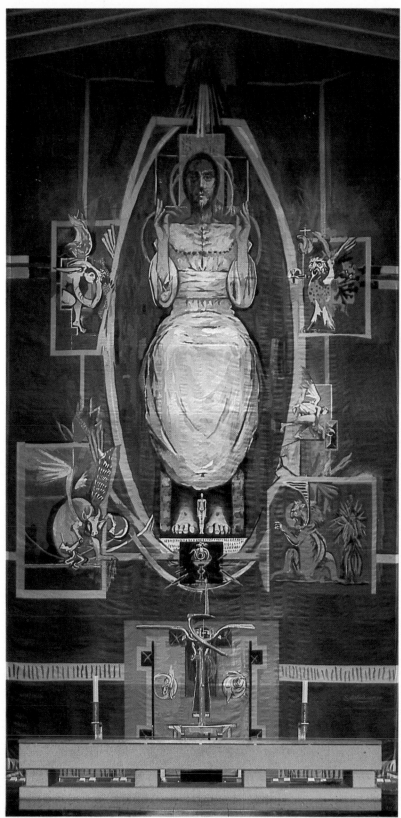

Christic in Glory.
Tapestry, 1962.
74 ft 8 in × 38 ft
(22 m 76 cm ×
11 m 58 cm)

Study for *Wild Nest* in the sequence of aquatints 'The Bees'. Watercolour, 1977. $15\frac{1}{2} \times 12\frac{1}{2}$ in (39.4×31.7 cm)

Large Interior. Oil on canvas, 1965. $102\frac{3}{8} \times 114\frac{1}{8}$ in (260×289.9 cm)

and slightly (to me a Francis Baconism) 'sick of the whole thing!!'. . . .

He said he hated the idea of the grotto and was suspicious of working on the left foot 'because for all your very real tangibility there is an ethereal quality I should hate to have lost. The chair is another matter and could be worked on a bit: but not much, I think.'

When Sackville-West wrote back on 6 April, he said he found Graham's letter 'amusing and informative' and interesting for posterity to ponder, 'but I still think I look frightened'. He hoped Graham would allow him to buy a sketch. Normally, Graham was most generous in this way. But he had promised Lord Beaverbrook the only two he thought adequate for his new gallery in Canada. Later, using his old source material, he reworked two heads of Sackville-West. One was for Beaverbrook; the other is now in the Birmingham City Art Gallery. Sackville-West was annoyed, his friend Eardley Knollys recalled. Graham's actions raised various questions. Should the price of the portrait (£1000 again) include the sketches? With Graham it never did. Could a portrait painter go on profiting from sittings?

The portrait was generally seen as a marked advance in subtlety and penetration on Graham's studies of Maugham, Beaverbrook and Churchill, and many people believe it to be his finest. Sackville-West's cousin, Benedict Nicolson, called it 'a magnificent image of controlled distress', when it was shown at a Royal Academy exhibition in January 1957.[2]

It was a good start to what might in other respects be called the Year of the Beaver. Lord Beaverbrook had taken a close interest in the Churchill portrait, persuading Graham to sell him all available related sketches. Later he tried to persuade Lady Churchill to give him the portrait itself: in October 1957 he told Graham he had 'every reason to suppose' that he would get it. Was he misled or just over-optimistic? Theoretically, the portrait had been destroyed for at least eighteen months by then. He wanted, he told Graham, to make his Fredericton gallery 'the great Sutherland Gallery', and in all he bought forty of his drawings and paintings, mainly portrait studies. 1955 was the high point of this traffic; in May Graham sold him six Churchill studies (including the Garter robes study), two of Maugham and two of Sackville-West for a total of £3180. He threw in four more Churchill studies and the original study for the Maugham lithograph as a bonus and asked only £200 for a further oil sketch of Churchill. Beaverbrook was distressed to find that one oil sketch of Churchill had got away—to Alfred Hecht, whom he knew—and bullied Hecht to sell it to him. When the Beaver died in 1964 his son Max Aitken felt that Hecht had been hard done by, and Hecht got it back.

Graham confided to Beaverbrook the problems he was having with Churchill over the copyright of the portrait, which had been assigned to Churchill by the parliamentary committee: 'I am not allowed to have a reproduction even for a comprehensive book on my work appearing next summer, and I am not even allowed to have the "studies", of which I hold the copyright, reproduced,' he wrote on 12 February 1955. Later he said he had been against reproducing the sketches himself, 'because I did not want to hurt such an admirable man'.[3]

Perhaps as a form of reaction to being bullied at Epsom, Graham admired power. 'With those who have been in political power . . . or run great empires of chemicals or whatever, I find there is . . . almost a sort of spiritual gloss, a sort of power gloss, which I find very interesting indeed,' he said once, when explaining his choice of portrait subjects.[4] Beaverbrook, who could be immensely charming, was a shameless power-monger. He used the columns of his newspapers—news as well as opinion columns—to pursue his causes (like Commonwealth trade) and his vendettas (against the British Council, Lord Mountbatten and so on). Beaverbrook was also genuinely interested in pictures, however. He doubtless enjoyed playing patron to the best-known living British painter, and his newspapers helped to ensure that he remained the best-known. In addition to his purchases of portrait studies, he now took an interest in Graham's search for a Riviera home.

From the very modest flat he had lent them at La Capponcina, Graham and Kathleen continued their house-hunting. Eileen Gray's house, which they had seen almost a year earlier, was still on the market. Lord Beaverbrook had advised against it: he thought it too isolated. But it was relatively cheap (£4800); the surroundings were beautiful; and there was a studio in the garden. They decided it was, after all, the best bet. There remained the difficulty of obtaining the necessary foreign currency, no light task, given the exchange control regulations of the time. Lord Beaverbrook had offered to make some dollars available. There had been consultations with the Bank of England, and now, despite his reservations, the necessary arrangements were made. The house was theirs by mid-May 1955, and Graham was able to pay back his benefactor immediately.

Their new Riviera home—called Tempe a Pailla, but soon rather uninspiringly renamed La Villa Blanche—was a small, austere monument to its designer, Eileen Gray, who was to die in 1976, aged 97. It was only her second house, and she had designed most of the furniture and fittings as well. Completed in 1934, it had been successively vandalized during and after the war by Italian, German and American troops. Miss Gray returned to it and made good the damage, but she had decided to sell when poor eyesight prevented her from driving.

The house stands on the left edge of a steep, twisting road about 3 miles both from Menton and the hilltop village of Castellar. It is tiny (three small bedrooms) and designed with the economy of a ship: circular skylights like portholes, shutters set in tracks, chests with drawers pivoting sideways, a metal wardrobe with rounded, sliding doors. The main joy is the view from the side away from the road—straight out over a valley to the sea. The hills around it are ravishing, filled with nightingales in due season. The studio was a small cottage in the garden, too low-ceilinged to allow Graham to get a large canvas on to an easel but at least his own. He laid the foundations of an arthritic knee, he believed, by standing large canvases on the floor and kneeling to do the lower portions.

Perhaps relief at having acquired a firm base in France contributed to the serenity of several studies of fruit-laden apple trees which he did that summer, back at the White House in Kent, which now also formally belonged to the Sutherlands: Kenneth Clark had handed over the deeds to Graham in the spring. It was also a 'very rich, mysterious and lyrical' summer, as he told a new patron, Maja Sacher.[5] 'I don't remember one like it in England for about twenty years.' Two of the apple studies were shown in September in a mixed exhibition called 'Critic's Choice' at Tooth's, in Bruton Street, the critic being their perceptive friend Eric Newton.[6]

For the last thirty years of his life, Graham's work could be divided into three main categories: 'free' paintings (nature, still lifes, machines and so on) and graphic work, religious commissions and portraits. Leaving aside the Coventry tapestry, the ten years from 1955 to 1965 were a period of consolidation in all three fields, although the 'free' work moved gradually towards a more accessible, less private imagery.

The portraits too can be divided into three main groups: 'sacred monsters', friends and the very rich. He had started with three *monstres sacrés*, Maugham, Beaverbrook and Churchill, old men whose struggles were to some extent written on their faces, reminding Graham of weather-beaten objects in a landscape.[7] Sackville-West was a friend. So was his dealer Arthur Jeffress, whose portrait he finished in May. If the hands and legs were a bit fudged, the head wonderfully caught Jeffress's humour and exotic quality. Jeffress thought it marvellous and showed it in early June, with a mixed bag of twenty-one early and more recent Sutherlands, at the gallery in Davies Street, London W1, which he had opened the previous year. Each time he looked at it, he felt posterity gazing down at him, he wrote to Graham on 8 June. He was to kill himself six years later.

During September and October, Graham started and completed a head of another friend (and patron), Hans Juda. It had been commissioned for his fiftieth birthday in 1954 but had fallen behind schedule. 'When Hans's portrait first came, I couldn't stand it,' his widow Elsbeth recalled. 'Now I find it marvellous. It is Hans saying something absolutely outrageous, and no one can tell if it is serious or a joke. It is one facet of him—not a deeply searching portrait, or a resumé, like Rembrandt.'[8]

Graham reckoned that he turned down roughly as many commissions as he accepted, about four dozen. One such came from the film producer Alexander Korda in January 1955; it was to paint the actor Laurence Olivier in the costume of Richard III. Graham's sense of drama did not extend that far.

His seventh portrait opened a Swiss chapter. Paul Sacher was extremely rich, but he and his wife Maja became close friends as well as good patrons. Her first husband, who had been killed in a car crash, was a Hoffmann; his father had founded the Swiss pharmaceutical company Hoffmann-LaRoche. Paul Sacher was a young conductor, and together they built up a private orchestra, the Basle Chamber Orchestra, for which Bartok, Stravinsky, Hindemith and Tippett, among others, composed pieces.

Maja Sacher had written to Graham in early 1953, suggesting that he paint her husband. The artist wrote to explain his terms: 'For a full-length portrait I charge 1000 guineas, 700 guineas for three-quarter-length, 500 for a head and shoulders. . . .' The commission was regarded as an experiment: if neither the sitter nor he liked it, there was no charge. If he liked it but the sitter did not, he charged £150 for loss of time, expenses and so on. If both liked it, he charged his fee.[9] And so the terms remained, except that the £150 became 10 per cent in advance, and the charges rose fairly swiftly.

They first met in the summer of 1955, when Sacher was conducting Stravinsky's *The Rake's Progress* at Glyndebourne, and in November Graham and Kathleen drove from Menton to Pratteln, a village outside Basle where the Sachers' house, Schönenberg, stood on a hill. It was modern in an austere, Swiss way, with fine modern paintings, including Picassos and Braques, lots of house plants, a gloomy butler and excellent food.

Graham went into Basle several times to watch Sacher rehearsing. He was fascinated by the intensity in his face and his blazing blue eyes. Michael Tippett came to stay one night. After eight days, studies completed, they returned to Menton. It was a savage winter. Burst pipes delayed progress on the portrait. Graham worked on two versions, a profile and a three-quarter face: 'the idea of Paul, so it seems to me, varies more than most people I have seen, according to whether he is in profile or not,' Graham wrote to Maja Sacher on 25 February 1956. He was feeling harassed by the pressure of time and was having difficulty with his legs in April. She urged him to take all the time he needed.

They first saw both versions in July 1956, when Sacher was back at Glyndebourne, conducting Mozart's *Die Entführung aus dem Serail*, and liked them so much that they asked Graham to do Maja too. Graham kept the portraits for some final touches and delivered them to Basle in September, having called in at Colmar in Alsace to see the Grünewald *Crucifixion* for the first time.

The Sacher portraits were an uncontroversial and private success. By the time he had completed them, Graham was sketching another sacred monster, this time a female one: Helena Rubinstein, who from modest Polish-Jewish origins had risen to become queen of her world-wide cosmetics business. Cecil Beaton had had a hand in the commission, as a friend of Madame's entertainingly camp right-hand man, Patrick O'Higgins. Graham and Kathleen first called on her at her flat on the Quai de Béthune in Paris on 26 April 1956. She lived, with a fine collection of primitive carvings, above the future President Pompidou. There were several sittings over the next few days and some meals together (which Graham found almost equally useful for observing his subjects). He took a number of photographs after a Sunday lunch at her country home, a converted mill outside Paris.

At first he could not get any feel for his diminutive sitter. He tried a head on canvas in Kent that July, but only when he returned to the Quai de Béthune in early September did he find the key. Madame was on very good form and mentioned she had bought a new Balenciaga dress. Would she be prepared to put it on? Graham asked. It was red and enormously richly embroidered with gold thread. Suddenly as she stood against some white panelling in it, sporting an enormous amethyst ring, he realized that she was an empress, an old empress.[10] More sketches, more snaps. She even allowed him to snip a piece off the hem as a colour guide.

Back to the easel in Kent. On 15 December the portrait was almost finished. Graham decided he wanted to change the background, Kathleen recalled. 'Don't I smell burning?' she called up. 'I'm just burning the bloody studio down,' Graham called back, and the canvas went out of the window. Some glowing ash from his cigarette had ignited the highly inflammable cleaning spirit.

There was nothing for it but to start afresh. Graham's insurers eventually paid £2600 but seemed convinced that he had done it deliberately. During the first quarter of 1957 he worked in short, intensive bursts on two new versions, one seated, one standing, producing in the same period two paintings for Buckingham Palace and working on the third Coventry tapestry cartoon.

The two Rubinsteins were finished by mid-April. On 14 April the *Sunday Times* scooped the Beaverbrook press with a Felix Man photograph of Graham at work on the sitting version, taken some time earlier. Cecil Beaton commented: 'It looks superb, a staggering likeness of the old bird. She's pretty marvellous, and you've given her the proper treatment, and not cheated on her baldness or grandeur.'[11] Graham was anxious to know which version Beaton preferred and urged him to inspect them at Hecht's, where they were being framed. Beaton replied that he found them both remarkable likenesses:

> the colour dazzling, the use of paint very exciting and alive, and the portrait conceived as a painting is a rarity. . . . Upon close study I came very definitely to the conclusion that I *much* preferred the sitting picture. It has more depth and vitality, more solidity, and the face is more vibrant. . . . the whole exercise has been a *tour de force*, and I'm sure the old bird will reap great rewards from her cleverness in inveigling you into the project.

In fact, Madame was far from thrilled by what Graham had done to her. First he sent off some photographs of the portraits to O'Higgins, who wrote back to suggest that the 'sagging' chin line might be softened; he said she needed, for business reasons, to be made to look 'ageless' (she was over 80). 'I have *never* made a practice of altering my portraits once finished,' Graham wrote back from Venice on 3 June.

> My portraits are objective—neither idealized nor caricatured, as everyone knows. If I start softening etc. etc. it is the beginning of the end. To say nothing of the fact that I cannot 'invent' new necks without spoiling the paintings. On the other hand I grew very fond of Madame while working, and I would like her—from her business point of view (because I know she is *far* too intelligent to mind otherwise, for reasons of personal vanity) to be happy.

On his return, he would look to see if anything could 'honourably be done'.[12]

On 24 June Madame herself made the pilgrimage to Hecht's place to see the two life-sized portraits. She was at a loss for words at first, she recalled afterwards,[13] and hated this view of her as an 'eagle-eyed matriarch'. She found them both bold, domineering interpretations of what she had never imagined she looked like. Later, when she saw them at the Tate Gallery in the autumn, she had to admit—while still scarcely recognizing herself—that as paintings they were masterpieces and nearly overpowered everything else there. But her first reaction was to reject them both. O'Higgins did it tactfully. Madame was very *impressed* by their power and impact, he wrote on 27 June. She had great respect for Graham. . . . forceful works of art. . . . did not want to cause him distress. . . . if he considered softening certain lines. . . . alarmed at their scale. . . . several museums wanted to buy them — how did he feel about this?, and so on: a qualified thumbs-down.

The Nye Bevans greatly admired the portraits when Graham and Kathleen, back in England, dined with them at the Hechts on 1 August, and on 13 August they heard from O'Higgins that Madame had decided to accept the seated version after all. The fee was £2000. Beaverbrook soon snapped up the standing version and some preliminary drawings for £3500. She hung hers eventually in the entrance hall of her New York apartment; his went to Fredericton. But first both went on show at the Tate, and Beaverbrook's scribes were soon asserting that his version was superior. The pose of defiance was more effective, the Londoner's Diary said, explaining fatuously: 'A seated figure with hands folded on her lap cannot look so striking as a person standing with a hand on hip.'[14] They got a very good press; *The Times* called them Graham's most confident and unambiguous portraits to date.[15] Beaton, it could be argued, had put his finger on their essence: to an unusual extent, Graham had used his sitter as an idea for a picture, which was more interesting than the reality.

While Graham had been in Paris for his first sittings with Helena Rubinstein, he heard the tragic news that his old patron Peter Watson, the financial backer of *Horizon*, had died in his bath in London, aged only 48. Back in Kent, Graham contracted jaundice, a result, he believed of kissing goodbye a friend's wife, coincidentally one of the few women for whom he felt a physical aversion. Then Kathleen fell down the back stairs of the White House, bruising herself badly. It was a trying period for them both, and Graham's work came to a temporary halt.

Once he had recovered, he tackled another woman, Mrs Signy Eaton, whose husband John owned a chain of department stores across Canada and was a good friend of Lord Beaverbrook. When the Beaver heard that they were thinking of commissioning Pietro Annigoni to paint her, he persuaded them to use Graham instead. As a favour to his patron, Graham complied — and raised his fee to £3000 for a three-quarter-length portrait.

Mrs Eaton, a handsome woman of middle age, came down to the White House seven times between 17 and 28 June. Towards the end Graham showed her the head he was working on. She said she would like the mouth to look less sour. They dined together in Venice in June 1957, and Graham took her to visit Peggy Guggenheim, the collector and former wife of Max Ernst. He delivered the finished portrait to a villa she had hired in Antibes in early July that year, when three of her boys were present. Graham, with whom she had established no great rapport, regretted that he had not seen her in a family atmosphere before, she recalled.[16]

Madame Cuttoli, whom she had met through a friend, came to see the portrait. 'She remarked that although it did not look like me, it one day surely would.' In Toronto her husband disliked it intensely, as did most of their close friends. They solved the problem by sending it to the Beaverbrook Gallery in Fredericton. 'I was relieved to take it down, because in some uncanny way, when I looked in the mirror I saw a reflection of myself as Graham had depicted me,' she said. The portrait's shortcomings stemmed, she felt, largely from herself: it had not been a good time for her emotionally. She remains the happy owner of two 'free' Sutherland paintings.

As for the royal commission, it came just before the first Rubinstein canvas caught fire, from Graham's friend at court and Kent neighbour, Patrick (Lord) Plunket. He lived in Offham, near West Malling, at The Mount, a large Victorian house which he had decorated with flair. Orphaned by an air disaster in 1938, when he was 15, he had spent a good deal of his childhood at court—his mother had been a friend of the Queen Mother, and he was King George VI's godson. Later he became equerry first to the King, then to the young Queen, and finally a Deputy Master of the Household, playing an important part in the conception and construction of the Queen's Gallery and a significant role as the Queen's confidant and unofficial adviser.

Graham had first met him in Kent while wrestling with the Churchill portrait. On 10 December 1956 he telephoned to ask whether Graham would do a smallish picture for the Queen to present to President Craveiro Lopes of Portugal on a state visit the next spring. It should symbolize the common interests of the two countries: exploration, trade and so forth. Graham went off to the National Maritime Museum in Greenwich in late January 1957 for inspiration and on 5 February finished two versions to submit for approval. The one that the Queen chose ingeniously and attractively incorporated grapes (port), an armillary sphere on which two white doves settled uneasily, Drake's Dial and a (British) rose, a sailing boat and an (exploring) eye. It was a sunny and happy work. Prince Philip later said how much he liked the other one. Graham took the hint and offered it to him, since when it has hung in his rooms at Buckingham Palace.

1957 was to be a busy year for portraits. In addition to finishing Rubinstein and Eaton, he started two others, both also of women, and initiated a fifth. In late July and early August, while her husband was conducting Mozart's *Magic Flute* at Glyndebourne, Maja Sacher sat seven or eight times for Graham, to be followed almost immediately by Mrs Ramsay Hunt.

Mrs Hunt was a rich New York socialite, seemingly a friend of a friend (Herschel Carey Walker, who was later to sit for a portrait himself) of Graham's New York dealer, Curt Valentin. She was also an admirer of Osbert Sitwell, an often absent fellow Tate trustee in Graham's time. She was handsome but no longer young. As was the case with Churchill, her image of herself was crystallized some years back, and she did not like what Graham did (probably just a head). 'Don't let's quarrel,' Graham said, and she swept out of the White House. It was the only outright rejection he is known to have suffered.[17]

Maja Sacher was not easy either, for very different reasons. She had a pleasant, intelligent expression but a difficult mouth and teeth. Graham showed her three-quarter length, seated, and from his favourite angle: three-quarter face, looking to the spectator's left. He did not eventually deliver it until late 1958. She was not, he later believed, altogether happy with it, though initially, out of friendship, said she was.

In an art as delicate as portraiture some element of hit and miss is inevitable. Graham later spoke memorably of the 'quilted atmosphere of silence, as when it snows' when a subject first saw his work.[18] Generally speaking, the better he knew his subject, the better the portrait. Portraits which displeased were not always the least successful artistically, but usually they were, and the least successful aspect—often the legs—was the most disliked. There were exceptions. Rubinstein was no friend, but the portrait was brilliantly successful—yet she disliked it. Graham's next subject, also started from a cold canvas, so to speak, was to produce another triumph with melodramatic overtones.

Max Egon, Prince von Fürstenberg, was a tall Bavarian landowner and founder of the music festival at Donaueschingen, where he lived in a castle surrounded by relatives. His picture curator and cousin, Christian Altgraf zu Salm, had earlier met Graham's friend Felix Man and raised the question of Graham doing a portrait. Graham and Kathleen called in for lunch at Donaueschingen in July 1957. A fee was negotiated: the prince found Graham's suggested £4500 for a three-quarter-length portrait 'for our idea rather high', he wrote on 16 August. They settled for £4000. The sittings took place the following summer, when Graham and Kathleen stayed at the castle. The prince, who was 63, looked rather like a retired colonel. Effortlessly he adopted exactly the same pose, with left leg crossed over right almost at a right angle, day after day. Man took some photos. Graham thought he detected a streak of the philosopher in Fürstenberg when he said one day: 'You know, I'm never really happy until I'm alone in my hunting lodge',[19] and was struck by his air of brooding and melancholy.[20]

It was this look that he caught to good effect in the portrait, which he and Kathleen arrived to deliver on 6 April 1959, after a pleasant drive through spring blossom. The prince and his wife Minzi saw it in privacy after lunch, then hastened to the guest apartment to express their delight. They embraced Graham and Kathleen, and all went back to look at it. Together they contemplated Graham's magnificently solid yet subtle composition. Then the prince pointed to a spluttering candle which Graham had placed near the right-hand edge of the canvas. 'Does it mean that I have just one year to live?' he asked, with a smile. Graham assured him that he had just thought it would look right there.

That evening, over a high tea of frankfurters swimming in a watery soup, they were told the prince was indisposed. Graham and Kathleen retired to their rooms. It was a *Wuthering Heights* night; rain thrashed the windows. Breakfast was brought in at 7 a.m. by two maids with red-rimmed eyes, dressed in black from head to toe. The prince, they said, was dead.

Graham and Kathleen were profoundly shocked, fearing that the portrait had contributed to his demise. They crept downstairs like assassins, Kathleen recalled, and said goodbye to an old uncle who had acted host the previous evening. Princess Minzi was at prayer in the chapel. Later she and Count Salm wrote to Graham to assure him that they had known for some time the prince was very sick. Graham's portrait had given him 'a last great joy' and was a great consolation to her. Graham thought it was the best portrait he had yet done,[21] and it is generally held to be among his finest.

Excluding Sackville-West, Graham had painted eight portraits since 1955. He started two more before the decade was out. The first was of Herschel Carey Walker who was an elderly New York collector with, *inter alia*, some fine Cubist works. He came to sittings, and usually lunch too, in Kent in July 1958, insisting on being painted in a lemon-yellow mandarin jacket which assorted oddly with his weather-beaten face. They met again on the Lido in Venice. When Walker first saw the portrait in Kent in September 1960, he suggested that the cheeks should be less full and the eyes bigger. Perhaps Graham obliged, since it was not delivered till April 1961. In May they received a long letter from him, saying he was thrilled with it. The fee was £2000.

Finally, there was A. S. Frere, whose half-length portrait Heinemann had been persuaded to commission for a modest £1500. Graham needed only two sittings in the South of France in May 1959; 'I know your battered old mug backwards,' he told Frere.[22] Kenneth Clark called it 'stunningly full of life' when he finished it the following spring.[23] Frere bought it for himself when he left Heinemann in 1962, but in 1975, on giving up his Albany flat, he decided to sell it, eventually sending it to Christie's for auction. 'Cats and pigeons ensued,' he recalled. 'Graham was palpably upset, so I withdrew it and, on his advice, let his dealer have it.' The 'battered mug', as portrayed, remained unsold.[24]

There were other commissions which Graham either turned down or gradually slid out of. Sometimes his choices seemed arbitrary, although it was understandable that, in the year of the Suez fiasco (1956), he should postpone a decision about whether or not to paint the Prime Minister, Sir Anthony Eden, for Christ Church, Oxford. Graham's brother Humphrey, the college curator of pictures, first mooted the idea. Then Sir Roy Harrod took over and tried to persuade Graham. Kenneth Clark did his best to help, and in 1959 Beaverbrook asked Graham whether he was interested. But the project held no appeal for him, and the torch passed to William Coldstream, who submitted Eden to between thirty and forty sittings (he worked straight on to canvas in front of the sitter). The result, only moderately successful (Coldstream agrees), hangs in the college. On the other hand, Sir Allen Lane, the founder of Penguin Books, which had published the first book on Graham's work, might have been thought a sound proposition. Sir William Emrys Williams, still a director of Penguin as well as Secretary-General of the Arts Council (of which Kenneth Clark was then chairman), asked Graham if he would tackle the King Penguin in February 1959. Graham said no.

He was, by contrast, very keen to paint his old friend Nye Bevan. The idea was mooted in 1955, and Hecht eventually commissioned the portrait. They had kept in touch, dining together at Hecht's, for example, on 13 January 1959, a week before Graham and Kathleen dined with Hugh Gaitskell at the home of Lady Pamela Berry. Later it was suggested that Bevan should spend part of his convalescence, after his major stomach operation of December 1959, at the Villa Blanche, where Graham would do his sketches. [25] But Bevan's health declined too swiftly, and in July 1960 he died, to Graham's great grief.

In the spring of 1958 Graham had found a rather different but very rewarding sitter—an enormous frog or toad, which he spotted crossing the road near the Villa Blanche. He scooped it up, popped it into a large glass jar and spent a whole day drawing it. Before returning it to the same spot, he called in Felix Man, who had rented a cottage nearby, to take some photographs. The beast served Graham well. He did endless variants on the theme over the next ten years, in all media. Douglas Cooper showed one to Picasso in September 1960. The great man put on his spectacles, studied it closely and finally pronounced that he liked it very much, calling it a very serious and sensitive painting and praising Graham's independence. Cooper passed on the message.

Graham and Kathleen had some direct contact with the great man. They lunched at his large, ugly villa at Cannes, La Californie, in March 1958 and visited him at the Château de Vauvenargues in May 1959, afterwards eating at a Spanish restaurant in Aix. Picasso sat between Kathleen and Alice B. Toklas. His Spanish accent was a problem, as was their modest French, but Picasso's eyes were extraordinarily expressive, Graham found.

At this stage Douglas Cooper was a copious source of advice about important decisions affecting Graham's dealers in New York and London. Curt Valentin, whose chief love was sculpture, had wonderful judgement and excellent contacts with museums. 'A few mumbled words—almost under his breath—"beautiful"—rarely more—set one up for months, for one knew his standards,' Graham later wrote of his old friend.[26] In an unfavourable climate, and with not much profit to himself, Valentin had done pretty well in getting Graham's work into some fine public and private collections in the USA. But towards the end he drank rather too much, and in August 1954 he died. Two years later Alexandre Rosenberg, whose father, Paul, had put on Graham's first one-man show as a painter at Rosenberg and Helft in London in 1938, wrote to ask whether Graham would like to resume the pre-war relationship. Having fled the Nazis, Rosenberg père had opened in New York in 1941 and now wanted to give a more vigorous emphasis to contemporary painting.

Advised by Cooper, Graham eventually agreed to a contract giving Rosenberg first choice of his work and an obligation to buy ten paintings a year, of certain sizes, for a guaranteed sum of $7500. Graham sent him six in May 1957: a very beautiful and impressive group, Alexandre Rosenberg called them. In January 1959 Graham sent transparencies of twelve more. Alexandre Rosenberg said they would like them all, and some more, for an exhibition in November, if possible. Graham sent six more by October. It was a great feat, Rosenberg said, to have executed a group of such quality, invention and diversity.

Graham's work had by now become much more accessible. There were several frogs, a Coventry-like eagle-owl, a Matisse-like palm, some new variants on the 'entrance to lane' theme, called *Path in Wood*, some serene and beautifully painted *Scales*, which Kenneth Clark had bought and lent, a bat and a fine Gothic heron taking wing in front of an arched, quasi-Venetian gateway, called *Dark Entrance*, as well as a few more cryptic works.

The show ran for a month from 9 November. 'I am back from New York and saw your pictures at Rosenbergs, and they looked *magnificent*,' Kenneth Clark wrote on 14 November. 'Everyone who had seen them was enthusiastic, including Duncan Phillips, who showed signs of buying the melancholy bird.' *Dark Entrance* duly entered the famous Phillips Collection, a privately owned museum in Washington DC. (Maja Sacher had bought a *Path in the Wood* earlier that year, for £800, displacing a Picasso to hang it; and a fine *Hanging Form* (for £1000), which she presented to the Kunstmuseum in Basle.)

Almost as if to show he was keeping his feet on the ground, that year Graham designed some fabrics for the Hungarian-born textile manufacturer Miki Sekers (whose novel idea for a fee was to have some clothes designed for Kathleen in Paris by Balenciaga), and a couple of ceramic-tiled tables—one dining, one occasional—for a firm called Dennis M. Williams. These tables featured a black-and-white, thorn-related design. The wrought-iron legs of the dining table had a decorative feature with 'a very definite "skirt-ripping" characteristic', as Williams put it, which Graham was asked to modify. They ate off a Sutherland table in Kent from then on.

Around 1955 Graham had begun to look around for more prestigious representation in London. Latterly he had had groups of paintings and drawings on show at Arthur Jeffress's gallery in 1955, 1957 and (the biggest) January 1959, when the critics mauled two largish oils, executed in 1957 and 1958, of Santa Maria della Salute in Venice and St Mark's at night. Jeffress was a good friend, but his gallery was regarded as light-weight. In February 1959 Harry Fischer of Marlborough Fine Art, in Old Bond Street, put out a feeler. The gallery was well on its way to establishing an ascendancy in the London gallery world (which later declined somewhat). Both Fischer, a man of charm and erudition and a great flatterer, and his partner, Frank Lloyd, were of Viennese origin; they had met doing kitchen fatigues in the British army. Lloyd was a tough financial wizard, even if, eventually, too sharp for his own good—as was shown by the Rothko affair. The third member of a well-teamed trio was David Somerset, handsome, upper-class and friend of royalty and the ultra-rich (the Agnellis, the Kennedys, Niarchos, among others).

Fischer and Lloyd realized that the 'blue-chip' Impressionists would become harder to find as museums stopped them turning over and started taking on leading living artists like Moore, Bacon, Pasmore and now Graham, some on a shared basis, and also some slightly lesser lights. Some artists found the financial stability that Marlborough gave a blessing; others found it stifling and left. Fischer, who had been helpful to Graham over the casting of his little sculpture, *Standing Figure*, by Noack in West Berlin, suggested a deal whereby Jeffress should in general handle his watercolours and gouaches and Marlborough his oils. It was clinched with a celebratory drink with Fischer at the Grand Hotel in Venice on 15 June 1959. Marlborough and Jeffress agreed to buy paintings and drawings to the value of £5000 a year for three years, prices to be reviewed after two. Should not enough pictures be available in one year, the difference would be held over to the next. Portrait commissions, unless procured by Marlborough, and lithographs were excluded. Foreign sales, unless covered by the agreement with Rosenberg, were included. Graham could now face the 1960s with the backing of powerful dealers in both London and New York.

12

Acclaim and Hostility

1960-5

NINETEEN-SIXTY was the year in which John F. Kennedy was elected
President of the United States, the Israelis snatched the Nazi war criminal
Adolf Eichmann from Argentina, the South African police shot sixty-seven
blacks at Sharpeville, the *News Chronicle* ceased publication and Princess
Margaret married the photographer Antony Armstrong-Jones. Harold
Macmillan had led the Conservatives back to power in the 1959 general
election, and the materialism and hedonism of the coming decade were to be
reflected in the advance of Pop Art, just as the Kitchen Sink school had
mirrored the social concern of the 1950s. By 1960 the gentle, landscape-
related abstractions of the St Ives School were giving way to more bracing
transatlantic influences.

Graham was rising 57, handsomer than ever and—theoretically, at
least—at the peak of his powers. In practice, the next five years were to be
rather patchy. Fate seemed alternately to smile and to scowl, and, by
comparison with the previous half-decade, a certain loss of momentum was
detectable. The two troublesome years of the Coventry tapestry's weaving
(1960-1) were at hand, and a first exhibition at Marlborough Fine Art in
1962 loomed.

Like most serious painters, Graham regarded his work as his life. Even
social life tended (except in Venice) to be work-related, friends being in the
main other painters (especially in the earlier days), collectors, writers and
sometimes portrait subjects. Travel, for its own sake, Graham avoided. It
stopped him from working and therefore did not interest him. (At one stage
he and Kathleen had planned to go to the São Paulo Biennale of 1955, at
which the British Council was showing twenty-six of his post-war works,
but eventually Graham decided he had too many commitments.) It was
therefore an event when, in late January 1960, they decided to go with

239

Alfred Hecht to the French ski resort of Mégève for some sunshine and
walking. But it rained much of the time, and the trip was a failure.

Graham's mother had died in 1957, not long after Graham had given a
family dinner party to celebrate her eightieth birthday at the Dorchester
Hotel. Now, in February his last link with Derby was severed when Uncle
Budge died after falling on to an electric fire. Graham and his brother
Humphrey went up with their wives to sort through the house at Arboretum
Square. Nothing had ever been thrown away, Humphrey recalled: 'It was
like cutting into a cake baked fifty or seventy-five years ago. . . all his mother's
dresses were still there, wrapped in tissue paper.'

In early April, to Graham's astonishment, he was asked whether he would
agree to become a member of the Order of Merit when the Queen's birthday
honours were announced later that month. The award, instituted in 1902 by
Edward VII and in the gift of the monarch, is restricted to twenty-four holders
and is generally considered the most distinguished available. Other holders
included Winston Churchill (did he, one wonders, approve of the choice?),
the scientist Lord Adrian, the Poet Laureate John Masefield, T. S. Eliot, G.
M. Trevelyan, Bertrand Russell, several famous soldiers and Augustus John,
RA, the only other painter. Basil Spence joined in 1962, the year of Coventry
Cathedral's consecration, Henry Moore in 1963, Kenneth Clark not until
1976: they had both become Companions of Honour in 1955 and 1959
respectively, thus delaying their OM. Clark and his wife Jane hastened to add
their congratulations to the hundreds flowing in by post and telephone. To
Jane Clark, Graham wrote on 5 May: 'That K's "advice" is responsible for
this rather extraordinary thing that has overtaken me I can have no doubt!
. . . *what* friends you have been to us. . . . I am moved beyond words.' Two
days later he wrote to Clark, recalling his

> vital financial help at all the difficult times, the care always, the
> criticisms—not always acted on, I fear, straightaway—but which were
> assimilated deep in me. I particularly remember at Belle Vue [Clark's
> house at Lympne in the 1930s] you saying: 'Use huge canvases and
> enormous brushes,' and realize that it was not until a good deal later that I
> did in fact do so. . . . had we lived at the time of the Renaissance, I like to
> think that we would have been a typical example of the relation between
> artist and patron. . . .

Among the many others who sent congratulations were Hardy Amies, H. E.
Bates, Joan and Basil Spence, the Henry Moores ('It's the very top of all'),
Julian Huxley, Eardley Knollys, Eric Newton, Tristram Hillier, Judy
Montagu, Ashley Havinden, Vita Sackville-West ('How much more satis-

fying than being given the Garter'), Sir Gerald Kelly, Roland Penrose, Herbert Read (who saw it as the final canonization of modern art), Helena Rubinstein, LeRoux Smith LeRoux, Hecht and the West Malling Branch of Westminster Bank. Typically, Lord Beaverbrook felt that his gallery in Fredericton, as the possessor of many of Graham's works, shared in the honour. Graham's letter of thanks to Colin Anderson showed the conflicting emotions it had aroused in his breast:

> I've never been a great chap for wanting honours. I am certain it is intended as a mark of awareness of the work and direction which many of us have been obsessed with over a number of years. That does not mean to say that I am not glad to represent all this. One would be hardly human not to be pleased. I can only pray that I will not be thought respectable.
>
> I can assure you that the old neuroses and paranoia still envelope me like a cloak, and however much one may groan at one's products, I hope there are a few signs of madness — I'd like to presume to call it innocence (for that is what we all want to preserve) — left.

Above all, he told his friends, it was Kathleen who deserved to be praised for bearing the brunt of his 'neuroses' over the years.

It was a remarkable award. Graham was not only a modern painter but also a controversial one. Behind him lay the Tate Affair, the Churchill portrait, advocates like Douglas Cooper. Perhaps Clark did have a hand in it (it was pleasant, as he told Graham, to imagine the lips pursed in disapproval at the Queen's choice); perhaps Plunket had dropped a word of guidance. Whoever had proffered the advice, it was an imaginative decision.

Graham and Kathleen did not stay in Kent waiting for plaudits but left for France the day after it was announced, calling in at Felletin on the way. A few weeks after they had settled in to the Villa Blanche again, a visit from Walter Hussey, who had commissioned the Northampton *Crucifixion*, spurred Graham to action on a painting for Chichester Cathedral, of which Hussey was now dean. It was to be a rendering of the Risen Christ appearing to Mary Magdalen for a chapel to be re-dedicated to the latter. The challenge was to paint something which, although of modest size (32 inches by 21 inches), would make an impact both from the far end of the 100-yard south aisle and from close at hand.

Graham sought the answer in brilliant, jewel-like colouring, mainly turquoise blue and red, against which a hatted Christ figure, poised half-way up a ladder, holds out a hand — *Noli me tangere* — to the kneeling Mary. He did not finish it until shortly before the dedication ceremony on 5 April 1961. On that occasion Colin Anderson deputized for Kenneth Clark, who was recovering from pneumonia, reading Clark's speech praising Hussey's 'extraordinary artistic perception' and congratulating the Friends of the Cathedral for paying. Not all of these rejoiced at Graham's contribution: one called it 'bizarre' and another 'sinister'.[1]

It was probably not so much Christ's straw hat (the model was borrowed from Trottiscliffe's vicar) as the strongly Jewish features of Mary Magdalen which upset them. Graham asked a modest £550 for the work. Like his *Origins of the Land* at the Festival of Britain in 1950, the painting was to attract a vandal. In February 1963 a woman defaced and punctured it with a ballpoint pen, later telling a Chichester court that it was obscene and filled her with loathing. Unstable though she seems to have been—she also signed her name on the stone altar—it was a tribute to the power of Graham's work, though not in the same class as Lady Churchill's.

As was by now their habit, Graham and Kathleen had spent part of May and most of June in Venice: two weeks as Arthur Jeffress's guests and four as paying tenants, the payment being two small oils. Thanks largely to Jeffress's connections (he had a weakness for the aristocracy), they were penetrating the upper stratum of Venetian society. Friends they saw there every year included Brando Brandolini and his wife Cristiana (who was Gianni Agnelli's sister), and Anna Maria Cicogna, a daughter of Count Volpi, who played host most summers to Nancy Mitford. They often foregathered at the Lido. After Nancy Mitford had read *The Times*, she would stand in shallow water, arms on hips, gossiping to Graham out of reach of inquisitive ears. Among other summer friends there were Renato Guttuso, the communist painter, and his aristocratic wife; Teddy Millington-Drake; and Peggy Guggenheim, with whom Graham tended to quarrel.

Graham loved Venice, the sea and swimming. It was not so much the fantastic architecture and the setting of the city that attracted his imagination as its more private, hidden aspects: muddy ripples against a canal's edge, remote bridges, street lamps reflected in water, a gate barring an abandoned shed for gondolas, water dripping from the silted mouth of a drain pipe. Some of these themes gradually penetrated his painting. Generally, however, he worked there on his existing commitments, always heavy, painting only in the morning, swimming in the afternoon and relaxing at Harry's Bar or, often, entertaining at Jeffress's house in the evening. Venice was above all a place for unwinding and relaxing.

The following year, 1961, was to be their last at Jeffress's pleasant house. That September Graham and Kathleen heard that he had killed himself in a Paris hotel.

Jeffress, like many very amusing people, had a deep streak of melancholy. He used to wear a ring with cyanide in it—his key to the emergency exit from life, he called it.[2] The cause of his death was found to be a heavy dose of poison or barbiturates. Gradually, the mystery of his suicide was explained. From Corfu, where he had spent a holiday that summer, he had arranged the sale of his famous gondola, the sacking of the gondoliers and the ordering of a motorboat. The final straw with the unruly gondoliers had come when, after a dinner at the house of Anna Maria Cicogna, the Duchess of Windsor had expressed a desire to return home in the gondola, which she had so often admired. Neither gondolier could be found. One was drinking, the other making love. When sacked, one or both denounced Jeffress to the authorities (there was a purge against homosexuals at the time), and on his return from Corfu, he was not allowed to land. Anna Maria Cicogna managed to put him on to a train to Paris, where he killed himself at the France et Choiseul Hotel. Thus did Venice devour one who truly loved her.[3] Graham gave a moving address at his old friend's memorial service in London.

In late 1960 he returned to the rigours of portraiture, first with two lithographic studies of Helena Rubinstein at the Curwen Press. However, it transpired that Madame—they met again over dinner at the Mirabelle restaurant in December—wanted them largely for publicity purposes, and he abandoned the almost completed venture.

Now the ten-year-old project to paint the Queen Mother was on again, thanks in part to London University. She had become its Chancellor in 1955, and in 1959 the university had asked for a portrait of her. The Sutherland project sprang to mind. In 1960 the university agreed, and a price and other terms were discussed.[4] On 13 December Graham went to see his first and only royal sitter to discuss his requirements, and he found her very charming. Perhaps to please the university, she asked him, as Churchill had, to paint her in the robes of the Order of the Garter. But Graham managed to dissuade her, explaining that he was no good at that sort of official portrait.

After spending much of January, in Kent, and February, in France, struggling with Christ's skirt in the Coventry tapestry, Graham returned to Clarence House for a first sitting on 22 March. There were five more sittings in the next week. At first the Queen Mother appeared in a tiara and white dress. Graham persuaded her to sport instead the ostrich feather that he had originally selected and a plainer dress. He found that her flow of conversation made concentration difficult, and he was not used to coping with a face so relatively cherubic and unlined.

Graham eventually reached the conclusion that he would not be able to produce the sort of picture that the university wanted to hang at Senate House. The university accepted the decision. He did complete the oil sketch on which he had been working, however, although not until April 1967 (Kathleen's diary indicates), by which time, Plunket told them, his sitter found that it made her look pleasantly young. It showed her almost full face, with a quizzical, amused look, right forefinger raised to right cheek, and wearing, in addition to the whimsical hat, a white, short-sleeved dress and three rows of pearls. Unlike most royal portraits, it suggests her intelligence. The sketch, which Graham offered to Her Majesty, made a good impression when it was shown, with many other portraits of the Queen Mother, at a National Portrait Gallery exhibition marking her eightieth birthday in August 1980.

Graham spent part of August and most of September 1961 painting one of his very rich sitters, Arpad Plesch. Plesch, who was over 70, and his much younger wife Etti were friends of Douglas Cooper and lived at La Leonina, a large, unlovely villa at Beaulieu with one of the best cooks on the Riviera.

Plesch was Jewish and had left his native Hungary as a young man, studied for a time at Edinburgh University, then worked in Germany—part of the time for IG Farben, the chemical colossus, which he left well before its evil flowering in the Nazi era, proceeding first to France and then to Switzerland. Etti, then married to another Hungarian, Count Palffy, had had the poor taste to shoot with Goering in the 1930s, near Berlin.[5] Although some of Plesch's fortune came from the post-war sale of a large sugar company in Haiti, which he had bought in the 1930s, it was over his activities as a financier in Switzerland before and during the war that a cloud hung. He had a somewhat sinister reputation, but with the help of Lord Beaverbrook and the success of a stable of racehorses—his wife's Psidium won the Derby in 1961, as did Henbit in 1980—he became socially accepted. He also collected rare plants and botanical books and some erotic literature.

Plesch had suggested the portrait in 1956, but the first sittings did not take place until late 1959, first at Beaulieu, then at Claridge's Hotel in London, where he was staying, and finally, in May 1961, in Menton. Graham brought the finished product to La Leonina on 28 September. Perhaps there ensued one of those 'quilted silences'. He had shown the shrewd old man, head and shoulders, against a fawn background, staring outwards, full-face, with hard-boiled eyes; strangely accentuated fingers clasped a symbolic book, presumably botanical.

Plesch made suitable noises about its being a work of genius but said that he would prefer a brighter background. By contrast Etti Plesch and her daughter by a previous marriage, Bunny Esterhazy, liked it as it was. Graham decided that it would be better to do a fresh version rather than meddle with the first, so he worked on a very similar one, with a red background, and then took both versions to dinner one December evening that year at Lord Beaverbrook's London flat when the Pleschs had also been invited: Plesch had met the Beaver through a Monte Carlo bookdealer, and Beaverbrook found him fascinating. Arpad Plesch preferred the red version and settled for it eventually, for a fee reduced from £3500 to £1500. When Plesch died in 1974, aged 85, after suffering for several years from Parkinson's disease, Graham—with characteristic generosity in such matters—gave his widow the fawn version she had always liked. She kept it, giving the red one to another daughter.

It was proving to be a distressingly dramatic year. On 25 October, barely a month after Jeffress's suicide, Douglas Cooper was attacked and stabbed three times in the stomach not far from Nimes. A North African soldier was later held. Skilled surgery and Cooper's constitution pulled him through.

Cooper's monograph on Graham's work, due out that autumn, was by then in the later stages of production. Its birth pangs had been long and painful. The book had been conceived in 1954 by Peter Gregory, the former chairman of Lund, Humphries, the publishers and printers. Originally, Robert Melville, author of the Ambassador Editions study of Graham's work of 1950, was to compile the list of plates, and a more prominent art historian, probably Kenneth Clark, would be asked to write an introduction of some ten pages. A much better plan was adopted in about 1957–8: Cooper would write a fullish critical and analytical study, with some biographical material as well, while Melville would continue to work on the plates. Then Gregory died in 1959 and was succeeded by his right-hand man, Anthony Bell. Cooper and Graham laboured long over the text and illustrations. Inevitably, Cooper found much to criticize in Melville's efforts; eventually, the latter withdrew and asked for his name to be removed from the title page. He was paid but received no other credit for years of work.

Graham had spent many days that spring trying to execute a lithographic design in black, red and green for the cover, spine and back of the book. He always found designs involving lettering exceedingly difficult. When the cover was first printed by Lund, Humphries at their Bradford headquarters, he rejected it. The colours were not right. Anthony Bell called in the Curwen Press to help. They devised a method by which Graham could draw on grained plastic foil, which worked, but he was still not satisfied with the intensity of the green and red when he saw proofs. Fresh inks were found, fresh proofs submitted. Graham was still not satisfied. Yet other inks were found; in late October he agreed that printing could go ahead and expressed satisfaction with the outcome.[6] Such perfectionism did produce wonderful results, but sometimes at a high cost in human terms. His relations with Herbert Simon, then chairman of the Curwen Press, were never the same again.

As for the text of the book itself, Anthony Bell was himself in a difficult position. Mounting production costs were making his first major undertaking a hopeless commercial proposition. Within the closed community of the art world his firm might sustain damage of a different sort if Cooper's known prejudices proved hurtful. But since an author is entitled to strong views, and since Kenneth Clark had given the text his blessing, he suggested only some modest pruning.[7] Bell sensed that Graham was somewhat in awe of Cooper and half-prepared for a volte-face in the text.

There was none: but its polemical tone, replete with slighting references to other British artists, aroused predictable antagonisms when the book was published, at four guineas, on 30 November. Cooper's opening barrage set the tone. 'Graham Sutherland is the most distinguished and the most original English artist of the mid-twentieth century,' he said. Fifteen years before, that statement would have seemed surprising. But since then Sutherland had transcended the weaknesses and provincialism of the English school and had emerged as a painter of international standing, Cooper asserted.

The critics hastened to dispute this. Precisely the reverse was widely believed today, Alan Bowness, who was later to become Director of the Tate Gallery, wrote in the *Observer* on 26 November. Sutherland's reputation was now rather less secure than fifteen years before. Parts of the text read like a moral fable: poor little English painter, struggling for a place among the greater, triumphs over every obstacle; driven from English public life by his valiant crusade about affairs at the Tate Gallery, he works best only away from the artistic backwater of his native land. Bowness suspected, very plausibly, that Cooper's enthusiasm was more for the symbolic role in which Graham could be cast than for his work. To Ronald Alley, later Keeper of the Tate's modern collection and organizer of the 1982 Sutherland retrospective there, the idea that Graham's work had been immature until fifteen years before and had since steadily improved was 'individual to the point of eccentricity', he wrote in the *Burlington* magazine.

The book's production standards were widely praised, as were Cooper's insight and lucidity. But several critics, including Eric Newton, disliked his use of the text and footnotes to belabour other British painters, like Nevinson and Wyndham Lewis, for 'aping the Futurists and Cubists';

Matthew Smith, for 'trying to be a Fauve'; Paul Nash, for flirting with Surrealism; Henry Moore, for letting his work become 'bloodless and academic'. Cooper's conclusion, that Graham was 'recognized in European circles as the only significant English painter since Constable and Turner', was widely disputed.

Graham suffered by association. He had nailed his colours to Cooper's mast and was presumed to have collaborated on the text. He was upset by the critics' shafts. 'Filthy article by Alan Bowness,' Kathleen noted in her diary. 'V. depressed.' An interview linked to the book's publication was my own first contact with Graham. I was very inexperienced and nervous but dazzled by his charm. '*Evening Standard* reporter Roger Bertoul [sic]. V. hostile and unpleasant,' Kathleen commented, though the article was rated 'v. good' (it was not) and prompted a telegram of congratulations from Graham—a minor example of his tendency to over-react.

Douglas Cooper had recovered sufficiently to come to London in early December, and he, Graham and the theatre critic Ken Tynan lunched at the Ritz Hotel on 14 December. The following day it was lunch with Ian Fleming, whom they had met, with his wife Anne, at Cooper's Château de Castille earlier. It was a Fleming phase. The creator of James Bond had taken to calling in at Trottiscliffe for a sausages-and-mash lunch on a Friday on his way to play golf at Sandwich. He and Graham, who shared an interest in cars, speed and gambling, got on very well. Fleming died three years later.

In general, men took to Graham more warmly than women. He was attractive to homosexuals, but heterosexuals and the happily married also frequently felt emotionally attracted to him. Graham in turn, dependent as he was on Kathleen's support, generally found men more interesting as companions than women, on the intellectual and conversational planes. Boring or tiresome wives were a frequent cross.

Graham had scarcely swallowed the bitter-sweet medicine of the reaction to Cooper's book than he was in the thick of the row over the hanging of the Coventry tapestry, and then working frantically for his one-man show at Marlborough's New London Gallery in June 1962. No fewer than seventeen of the thirty-five oils in this first major London exhibition since the 1953 Tate retrospective were painted in the first half of the year. It was a very characteristic mixture of animals—ram, toad, bat—a fine *Scales*, two or three wood interiors, some suspended forms, which were curious hybrids of machines and vegetable forms, and some brutally pollarded trees found in Mereworth Woods in Kent, which were perhaps subconsciously symbolic. Some of the recent works had a slightly rushed look, and the critics were—yet again—divided in their opinions:

'The colour is often strident, even crude,' Terence Mullaly, normally an enthusiast, wrote in the *Daily Telegraph*, though for his *Sunday Telegraph* colleague, William Gaunt, colour remained 'one of Mr Sutherland's great assets'. *The Times*'s critic, by now David Thompson, thought Graham had 'come back fighting', and David Carritt in the *Evening Standard* sensibly saw both defeats and triumphs in the show. John Russell, in a centre-page feature article in the *Sunday Times*, decided to wade in. There was nothing odder in the recent history of English reputations than the ascendancy of Graham Sutherland, he wrote on 10 June 1962. Neither Ben Nicholson, who for lifelong achievement and international acclaim had no rival among living British painters, nor Francis Bacon, currently drawing 5000 people a day to a Tate retrospective, nor Ivon Hitchens (showing at the Waddington Gallery) was a public figure in the sense that Bardot, Hemingway or, latterly, Graham Sutherland were, he said. Graham's new public associated him with 'an atmosphere of adulation from which puffery and pietism have not always been absent'. His recent paintings involved a broadening and coarsening of style which, Russell implied, was tailored to the 'big-spending economy' in which his work was fighting for its life.

Enter Kenneth Clark on white charger the following Sunday. It was a cruel misrepresentation, he wrote in a letter printed under the headline 'The Sutherland Controversy', to suggest that Sutherland was a publicity hunter who had vamped together an exhibition to cash in on the gullibility of rich and vulgar people. Russell countered that he had said no such thing: 'These must be projections of the anxiety with which the artist's friends awaited the exhibition.'

The *Observer* had also sinned. There were some feline touches in a generally sympathetic profile it had published of Graham on 22 April, prompted by the Coventry tapestry: for example, a reference to the 'faintly cloistered atmosphere' of the Sutherland household ('no children, no dogs'), and another to Graham's images of thorns, yucca leaves and rotten trees as 'symbols of sterility and frustration'. Harry Fischer, of Marlborough Fine Art, told Graham he thought people were envious of Graham's social success in the Riviera sunshine.

The New London Gallery show was commercially a huge success, virtually selling out within a few hours. Top prices were between £2000 and £3000, of which the gallery kept half as commission.

When an artist shows his work, he exposes himself to attack more nakedly than other creators. In Britain, moreover, the public is probably less sympathetic to, and less interested in, modern art than in most comparable Western countries: we are more of a musical and literary nation. Graham needed all his resilience to withstand these see-saws of fortune.

The see-saw moved upwards again in June 1962, when he joined Charlie Chaplin, Dean Rusk and Yehudi Menuhin in being made an honorary doctor of literature at Oxford University. Chaplin stole the show, inevitably, but it was good for morale, and Graham's brother Humphrey proposed the toast at a dinner given that evening for all honorands at Christ Church.

After all this, Venice beckoned relaxingly. Jeffress's house being no longer available, Graham and Kathleen took a ground-floor flat at the Cipriani Hotel, beautifully situated on the Giudecca. The hotel then belonged to the Guinness family, and the flat to Lady Honor Svejdar, elder daughter of the head of the family, Lord Iveagh, and formerly married to Sir Henry 'Chips' Channon. Again, Graham paid with pictures: painting is the most tradable of the arts.

Some time earlier he had been asked to paint a portrait of Daisy Fellowes, one of those tiresomely legendary social figures of the time. Initially, she had telephoned to suggest that he should paint her black servant in a greenhouse. Graham explained that was not the kind of commission he undertook, and she suggested he painted her. Mrs Fellowes's mother had been a Singer sewing-machine heiress, her father the Duc Decazes, her first husband Prince Jean de Broglie, her second Reginald Fellowes, who died in 1953. She was variously held to be wonderfully amusing and generous, or horribly bitchy and rude, and no doubt could be all four and more. Graham and Kathleen had first visited her villa, Les Zoraïdes, at Cap Martin in 1956. She also had homes in Paris and London—where she entertained Graham and Kathleen—and in Berkshire and Venice. To this last, the Palazzo Polignac, Graham now repaired for sittings.

He and Kathleen stayed a few nights there, hiding the drawings under the carpet when they went out, since they suspected her of slipping in to see them. Graham started on the portrait on his return to Menton, while she was fresh in his mind. She died that December, aged 72. 'But I haven't finished the portrait,' he said on seeing the small announcement in the *Daily Telegraph*. The finished work, showing the redoubtable lady reclining in a chaise-longue, went to her daughter, Emmeline de Casteja, in early 1964, and was reproduced in the *Daily Express* shortly afterwards.[8] Graham complained to Lord Beaverbrook about the reproduction. 'Here is a Graham Sutherland letter complaining, complaining, complaining, complaining,' the ailing Beaver dictated. 'Send it down to the archives at Cherkley.' It was probably their last contact. Beaverbrook died in early June that year.

Graham was due to go to Tunisia in January 1963 to paint President Bourguiba, but it seems there was a threat to Bourguiba's life, and the project lapsed. The artist used the time to tackle his first and last commission for a Roman Catholic church.

James Ethrington, parish priest of St Aidan's in the unlovely London suburb of East Acton, wanted an enormous painting of a Crucifixion for the new parish church. It was to go high above the altar, on the end wall of grey, whorled concrete, in a church of extreme (though not inspiring) simplicity. Ethrington, a tall, pink-faced bespectacled man, was just the kind of gentle, sensitive soul Graham liked as a patron. Contacts had opened in 1959. The idea came from the architect, John Newton, but Ethrington had seen Graham on television and had been impressed, even though his own taste in pictures was not adventurous.[9] The church's consecration in July 1961 passed without Graham's producing anything: 'My life is bedevilled by false optimism, always thinking that things will go more easily and more quickly than they do,' he apologized to Ethrington almost a year later.[10]

Now here was a chance to get down to it. Graham had sent Ethrington some sketches the previous September. Ethrington's diocesan authorities thought Christ's loin cloth too brief, he recalled. 'I had to write an extremely delicate letter to Graham about it, and it caused him a lot of extra work. He did another one which was even briefer, but I had done my bit.'

Graham painted the vast canvas (18 feet by 10 feet) in a single burst of sustained activity in Kent between 15 January and 10 February 1963. He left it to be fixed to the wall next day, then returned for several consecutive days to work on it *in situ*, from a tall ladder. It had been impossible to judge the effect of so large a work from close at hand, and he decided to make the colour bolder. He and Ethrington lunched together every day. Sometimes the priest saw Graham praying and wondered if he had come to a particularly difficult bit and was seeking guidance.

Graham's last word on the Crucifixion theme, with its grey, awesomely emaciated Christ against a vast background of vermilion, is a work of sledge-hammer impact and yet derives a certain serenity from Christ's resigned expression. Graham insisted that he wanted no fee. 'But I was over-insistent,' Ethrington recalled, 'and he got £1000 right away. Normally he had to wait for a long time, and that took him by surprise.' The painting was consecrated on 17 February; Graham was present.

It was the year of the Great Train Robbery. Graham rather admired its ingenuity. However, his attitude changed a fortnight after it—24 August, his sixtieth birthday—when they came back from a modest meal *à deux* in Menton and found the beds strewn with clothes and all Kathleen's jewellery, a cigarette box, radio, camera, even some cheeses stolen. He drew all the jewellery for the police, but the burgled property (estimated value

£2400) was not recovered.

It was also the year when Graham painted the West German Chanceller, Dr Konrad Adenauer. The portrait's origins went back to the 1950s. 'You ought to paint Adenauer,' Felix Man had observed one day.[11] Man put the idea to the West German ambassador in London, Hans von Herwarth, who passed it to Bonn. The unpromising reply was that Graham now lay eighth among applicants. It was uphill work: Adenauer thought little of 'modern' art. Then, in Bonn, he was shown Graham's portrait of Fürstenberg and was impressed. But had Fürstenberg not died a few hours after receiving the portrait? 'Supposing that happened to me?' he asked with a twinkle.[12]

Sweeping such intimations of mortality aside, he gave his approval in spring 1959. Sittings in Cadenabbia, on Lake Como, where he habitually took his holidays, were suggested for April. The London embassy announced in its bulletin that the eminent portrait painter Graham Sutherland was to paint the Chancellor. The *Daily Express* rang Graham. He, having had no formal invitation, said he had not been officially approached — it had been spoken of by friends as a possible idea. 'But no one told him,' said the *Express*'s headline next day, 18 April. The Parliamentary Press Service in Bonn improved the story: Sutherland had been surprised by the embassy announcement, it reported, and said he would be busy for the next six weeks with 'wallpaper designs' for Coventry Cathedral!

The portrait was called off by State Secretary Globke because 'apparently Mr Sutherland himself has never uttered the wishes to paint the Chancellor'. Graham explained matters to the ambassador, and all was smoothed out. On 12 November Graham was summoned by telegram from France to have lunch with Adenauer at the embassy in London, where the Chancellor was on a visit. It was a small occasion. Graham sat on his right, and greatly enjoyed himself.

There were further delays, caused mainly by the political situation in Germany. Like Churchill, Adenauer was clinging to power; a crown prince — Ludwig Erhard, the chubby architect of the economic miracle — waited in the wings. The Spiegel affair in the autumn of 1962, in which Franz-Josef Strauss resigned as Defence Minister, underlined the strains in his coalition.

A date was fixed in April 1963 for Graham to start, but he contracted 'flu two days before it and cancelled on the day itself. All was well, however, and on 1 September they finally arrived in Lugano, reporting to the Villa Collina at Cadenabbia for the first sitting next day. It stood in large grounds, on a hill looking over the lake and out to the Alps. Adenauer struck both Graham and Kathleen, who came along that day, as extraordinarily well preserved: a tall, upright, rather stiffly held figure, with a calm, reflective, seemingly immobile face.[13] Since Graham spoke no German, he tried French. No, said Adenauer's elder daughter Ria, if you speak English, I will translate. On other occasions the Chancellor's secretary, Dr Anneliese Poppinga, or Felix Man acted as interpreter.

A sitting was arranged for 5.30 that evening. Thereafter they took place regularly at 10.30 a.m., and there were nine in all. Adenauer, who was 87 and due to retire at last the following month, soon loosened up, and conversation ranged over literature, music, painting—he particularly liked Giotto, Grünewald and Titian—the new Pope Paul and the international scene (he showed himself to be still bitter about the way the English had sacked him as Oberbürgermeister of Cologne in 1945).

Graham did not feel he had glimpsed his sitter's deeper character until the sixth day, when there was a fiesta on the lake, with fireworks and thousands of paper boats bearing flickering candles on the water. Adenauer took some twenty family members and friends out in a motor cruiser. Graham saw his host/prey sitting at the prow, bare-headed, alert, reflective, and asked if he could join him. In those moments, watching him, he saw Adenauer not just as a cool statesman but as a contemplative, even a visionary.

On the Sunday, a week after they had arrived, they went to mass in Cadenabbia. There was clapping from a large congregation as the old man took his place in a seat draped in red. Next day Kathleen came along to the sitting in her 'sternest critic' role, and on Tuesday, the day of the last sitting, Graham took presents she had bought for some of the twenty-three grandchildren. Adenauer seemed genuinely touched and said goodbye most cordially. He had been a very good sitter and accepted Graham's desire not to show him his sketches.

Graham tackled the portrait proper straightaway, in Menton, achieving a good facial likeness on the third day. In October they returned to Kent. Graham started a fresh version—and Adenauer retired. 'You will understand, I know, my feeling that I cannot let the hour of your resignation pass without writing to you,' Graham wrote, in the ceremonious style of his youth.[14]

It would be unbecoming for me to add my voice to those who have praised your achievement.

On the other hand, during the hours in which you submitted to my 'peerings', I was able to see something of the motives behind your 'grand design', and to admire the character which had produced it and to understand something of the intellect and courage which had sustained it.

History will record that it was you who delivered Germany after the war. I only hope that I can deliver the face which did this!

It is not an easy face to do. The variety of emotions are too great. But I am working away at the portrait, and hope that I shall not have to trouble you for further sittings again at Bonn, as you kindly suggested I might do. . . .

Graham worked on the main portrait, and a smaller one, off and on during 1964. In late June he decided to abandon the second version, but since the head was rather successful, he (exceptionally) cut it out and stuck it on the new canvas, moving the figure well to the left, and later adding a background of leaves to mark his sitter's love of gardens. Only a knowing eye can spot the cannibalization. Not until 12 January 1965 could he write to tell the retired statesman that the portraits were virtually finished. 'It has taken a long time, I know, to do them, but I think that the results justify the long time spent on them,' he said.

A showing was arranged for 9 March, in Bonn. It was a most unusual situation. Marlborough Fine Art, rather than Adenauer, had commissioned the portrait, with Man as intermediary. Adenauer was under no obligation to buy. Graham was to get a fee (£6000 had been mooted) and Man a percentage. Graham was keen to go to the showing, but Kathleen contracted bronchitis. There was no direct flight from Nice to Bonn, and he did not feel that he could leave her for more than a day. Eventually, those present in Adenauer's office in the Bundestag building in Bonn were Harry Fischer of Marlborough, Felix Man and ex-ambassador von Herwarth, now back in Bonn.

The large canvas (almost 5 feet by 4 feet), showing Adenauer in contemplative pose, stood on an easel. Adenauer studied it in silence. Then he said: 'Yes, I like the pictures. Herr Sutherland has shown me as a thinking man'; and he took the smaller picture, showing him in half-profile, right hand raised to temple, and gazed at it by the window. He asked to keep them both for up to a week, so that his family could see him portrayed in this seemingly unusual thinking role.[15] Two days later he wrote to Graham:

My feeling about the pictures is now firm: they are two excellent portraits, and with both you have expressed my spirit very well. That is the most important thing with every portrait. I admire your art, and am very pleased that you have spent so much time working on a picture of me, and see in that a great appreciation (*Anerkennung*) for me personally.

The smaller of the two, the sketch, seems to me the better of the two. [Graham cannot have liked that.] The expression shown there catches my personality particularly well when I am working—and work is after all my daily bread. I thank you also for the drawing [which Graham had sent as a present via Fischer] . . . which corresponds to the smaller painting. . . . It would please me very much if we could meet again.

Graham replied fulsomely on 3 April:

> To know that you like my portraits of yourself is a great pleasure to me. You were right to keep them so that you could see them in different lights. It is the only way to judge. Naturally being a connoisseur yourself, you understand this. May I say that it was a real privilege to be able to make these paintings, and I have the warmest and liveliest memories of the hours at Cadenabbia. . . .

The head-and-shoulders study, based on an oil sketch done at Cadenabbia, is very 'like' and strikingly free in execution, even if the right arm does not quite work. It was acquired by the *Land* of Baden-Württemberg and hangs in the waiting room of the state's elegant offices in Bonn. The full-length portrait was acquired by Dr Adenauer's daughter, Ria Reiners, who is married to an engineer, and it hangs in a large room of their home at Mönchen-Gladbach.

The rather funereal, laurel-like leaves which Graham used as background to the larger portrait had begun to feature in his work in 1963. They were prominent in the strange, simian *Crouching Figure* of 1963–4 and in several of the darkly sensual fountains, inspired by one not far from the Villa Blanche, which became a favourite theme for several years. *The Captive* (also 1963–4) was another striking image of this period: a gruesome, rhinoceros-like creature with manacled front legs deriving from a shape seen in the woods above Trottiscliffe.

There is a powerful sense of melancholy in the work of these years, and it was reflected in Graham's second show at Rosenberg's in New York in May 1964. This time Alexandre Rosenberg, who had at last met Graham and Kathleen over dinner in Kent in 1960 and had been deeply impressed, offered to pay for their tickets—and they decided to make the trip at last. There followed twelve hectic days, based at the Stanhope Hotel, during which they whirled around meeting collectors and looking at pictures. The first weekend they spent in grandeur, as guests of the newspaper proprietor Jock Whitney and his wife Betsy, a trustee of the Metropolitan Museum. Her sister, Minnie Fosburgh, was there too; she put to Graham the idea that he should paint a posthumous portrait of Jack Kennedy, assassinated the year before. They met Jackie Kennedy before leaving and saw a film about Kennedy's life, but Graham did not like the idea of painting someone he could not see and hear, and the plan was dropped.

For the rest, it was a mixture of museums (the Metropolitan, the

Cloisters, the Frick); collectors (Mary Lasker, Joshua Logan, Richard Rodgers, the Rosenbergs themselves); old friends (Carey Walker, who gave a splendid party for them, Jack and Dru Heinz, who had a villa near Antibes, Helena Rubinstein, Michael Wishart, then living in New York); and some sightseeing in and around the city, which they surprised themselves by liking. 'Really unexpectedly—for we are the most chauvanist [sic] of chauvanists!!—we enjoyed it all,' Graham told Maja Sacher later.[16] However, some critics were cutting about the exhibition, and it sold less well than the one in 1959.

As compensation, the *New York Times* of 17 May carried an admirable interview by Brian O'Doherty, in which Graham vividly described his encounters with subject matter.

> I often go for a walk in a big tract of land, half cut down, half forested [no doubt Mereworth Woods, where Spanish chestnuts were grown for fencing]. Suddenly I see something like a figure or an eagle sitting there— it can look like an insect or even a piece of machinery—and then you get up to it and see it isn't. This momentary flash, this glimpse of the thing, one gets for a very short time, very often, but sometimes long enough to draw it. For I'm very long-sighted; I can see detail in the distance. I've always liked to see things very near or very far. Often I draw things from long distance, just for themselves, without recognition. . . .
>
> I walk down a road. . . . I see something exciting and extraordinary. There's a welling up of interest, and a shiver down the spine. . . . by walking, one is able to catch things unawares. One is very relaxed, and one sees things even when one's not looking for them.

As we have seen, Graham avoided any such displacements of identity in his portraits: the dexterity of his hand concentrated on the exterior, while eye and mind probed for the interior. What task could be more delicate than to paint two very close friends, both deeply versed in the history of portraiture? Kenneth Clark and Douglas Cooper were the friends in question, both with enlarged critical faculties.

Graham had started Clark's portrait in 1962, with sittings mainly in the Trottiscliffe garden. 'I am very proud you are painting me at all—added to which it has been a real joy to have uninterrupted talks with you,' Clark had written on 11 September 1962. By October, Graham had done a preliminary oil, which he thought a very good likeness, but (Adenauer intervening) the Clarks saw the finished portrait only on 4 December 1964, when they came to lunch in Kent. Clark tactfully expressed pleasure. But later he commented: 'The portrait makes me look like a snooty dictator—which I'm not at all.'[17]

255

Not altogether charitably, Graham had confronted his old benefactor and friend of thirty years with the less attractive side of his manner, which did not—Clark may reasonably have thought—correspond to his deeper character. He did think it was well painted, however, and hung it for a time at Saltwood Castle; but that began to seem 'ego-maniac' and he eventually gave it to his son Colin. Alan, another son, acquired it from Colin, but as he already owned a fine sketch, he sold the portrait to the National Portrait Gallery. Lord Clark took his second wife to see it there in early 1981 and thought it looked better than he remembered, and less snooty.[18]

There were also difficulties over the price. The portrait was a head-and-shoulders study, showing Clark in open-necked shirt and, most unusually for Graham, in full profile. It was a good deal smaller than most—only $21\frac{1}{2}$ inches by 18 inches. Graham wanted £2000 for it: not excessive, but perhaps high for one's oldest and staunchest supporter. The relationship survived the strain.

The portrait of Douglas Cooper was full-length and showed him sitting against more laurel leaves, in shirtsleeves, legs apart, stomach prominent, wiping his spectacles on his lap with a handkerchief, with a ladder on the right. It was finished in 1967, shown in the Munich retrospective which Cooper helped to organize that year—and destroyed after Cooper's rupture with Graham and Kathleen.[19] The portrait made him look uncharacteristically stiff. If the seriousness of an act of vandalism is based on the value of the object vandalized, his was not a heinous crime, though it would have been an item of some historical interest.

At this time Graham was also involved in one of his most interesting religious commissions, which was to suffer a more public but less fatal rejection. Its origins went back to 1962, when the Dean and Chapter of Ely Cathedral asked Louis Osman, the architect and goldsmith, to design and make a silver cross for the high altar. It was required, unrealistically, to make an impact both from the west door, more than 100 yards away, and against an intricate nineteenth-century reredos (behind the altar), designed by Sir Gilbert Scott. A Crucifixion figure was to be included, unusually.

Osman made three suggestions: that the screen should be removed; that a major artist, chosen by himself, should design the Crucifixion figure; and that the latter should be in gold (which would greatly increase the cost). Osman had decided Graham was his man, thinking it would be his first sculpture. He sent him his preliminary drawings for a cross some three and a half feet high, leaving a blank for the figure—and in the spring of 1962 went out to Menton.

His full-size drawing was spread out in the garden. Osman recalled:[20]

Citizens of Felletin admiring the sample of the tapestry woven by Pinton Frères, displayed in the village square in January 1959

Weavers at work on the Coventry Tapestry, January 1959, with the cartoon behind them on its pulley

(*Left*) Douglas Cooper at the Villa
Blanche, probably early 1960s
(*Above*) Eardley Knollys in his 40s
(*Below*) Graham and Kathleen at a
Riviera restaurant, February 1953

(*Top*) Kathleen, Maugham, Graham and Alan Searle at a restaurant in the south of France, in early 1960s

(*Above*) Graham and Kathleen with Pier Paolo and Marzia Ruggerini at a restaurant, in late 1960s

Graham with Prince Egon von Fürstenberg and his portrait at the family castle in Donaueschingen, 6 April 1959, a fateful day

Standing Figure (Bird).
Bronze cast from plaster
model done in 1952. An
edition of six was produced
by Marlborough Fine Art

A photograph of Lord Airlie,
taken by Graham in June
1978, and squared up for use
in a subsequent sketch, or the
portrait itself

(*Top*) Elder statesman: Graham with Walter Scheel, then the West German President, at the 'Sutherland Paints Adenauer' Exhibition near Bonn, September 1978
(*Above*) Graham as doyen of the Order of Merit, on H.M. the Queen's right at the Buckingham Palace luncheon on 17 November 1977 to celebrate the order's 75th anniversary, with some of the other members: included in the back row are J. B. Priestley, Sir Isaiah Berlin, Harold Macmillan, Lord Clark, and Sir Frederick Ashton, and in the front row William Walton, Professor Dorothy Hodgkin, Graham, H.M. the Queen, H.R.H. Prince Philip, Henry Moore and Lord Mountbatten

Top) The sitting room of the new Villa Blanche, finished in January 1970
Above) The new Villa Blanche, with studio at left overlooking the valley

Graham at the Villa Blanche, in early 1970s, in one of a set of chairs made from vine branches

(*Left*) *Helena Rubinstein*. Lithograph, 1960. $10\frac{1}{2} \times 9\frac{3}{8}$ in (26.6 × 23.8 cm)
(*Below*) *Study for portrait of Maja Sacher*. Oil on cardboard, 1958. 12 × 13 in (30.5 × 33 cm)
(*Bottom*) *Unfinished sketch for portrait of Max Egon, Prince von Fürstenberg*. Oil on canvas, 1958. 20 × 17 in (50.8 × 43.2 cm)

Toad I. Lithograph, 1967.
$26 \times 19\frac{7}{8}$ in (66×50.4 cm).
Published by Marlborough F
Art as part of the 'Bestiary'
series in an edition of 75

The Captive. Oil on canvas,
1963/4. 55×48 in
(139.7×121.9 cm)

he Braziers and a Monument. Oil on canvas, 1967. $71\frac{1}{2} \times 56\frac{1}{4}$ in (181.6×142.8 cm)

(*Top*) *Forest and River*. Oil on canvas, 1971. $34\frac{1}{2} \times 42\frac{7}{8}$ in (87.6×108.9 cm)
(*Above*) *Forest with Chains*. Oil on canvas, 1971/2. $44\frac{1}{8} \times 66$ in (112×167.6 cm). The chains were
those found on the beach at Benton Castle

Form in an Estuary.
Oil on canvas, 1972.
$37\frac{3}{4} \times 39\frac{1}{8}$ in
$(95.8 \times 99.3$ cm).
The painting was
presented by H.M.
Queen to President
Pompidou on her
trip to France

Study for *Landscape
with Setting Sun.*
Watercolour,
gouache and ink,
1969. Dimensions
not available

Portrait of Lord Clark. Oil on
canvas, 1963–4. $21\frac{1}{2} \times 18$ in
(54.6 × 45.7 cm)

*Portrait of Mrs Reginald
Fellowes.* Oil on canvas, 196
$51\frac{1}{8} \times 65$ in (129.8 × 165.1 c

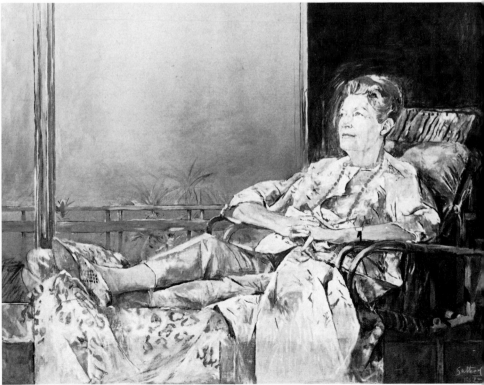

Portrait of Max Rayne. Oil on canvas, 1968/9. $71\frac{3}{4} \times 43\frac{1}{4}$ in (182.2 × 109.9 cm)

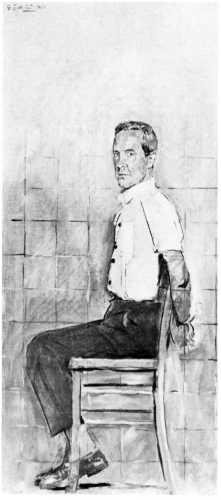

Portrait of Giorgio Soavi. Oil on canvas, 1968. $47\frac{1}{4} \times 23\frac{5}{8}$ in (119.6 × 60 cm)

Portrait of Lord Goodman. Oil on canvas, 1973/4. $37\frac{3}{4} \times 37\frac{3}{4}$ in (95.9 × 95.9 cm)

Graham found two pieces of twisted and eroded olive wood, some rabbit bones, and took wax and began to model his cross and figure. He dropped his glasses, picked up the two pieces of a broken lens, and with these formed the rib-cage of his figure, pressing them into the wax softened in the sun. We then dipped the composite object in molten wax heated in Kathleen's best kitchen saucepan, and the first maquette was complete.

Osman was particularly impressed by Graham's appreciation of the nature of fine gold, which throws back light in a unique way. 'Throughout we had the attitudes of composer and soloist: Graham wrote the cadenzas,' he said.

Osman took the fragile object back to England, had it cast in bronze, and gilded it. Graham thought the legs weak, cut them off, remodelled them and made a few other adjustments. Osman took this second version of the Crucifixion figure—also cast and gilded—to Menton in April 1964, where it was positioned on a three-dimensional design of the entire cross. Osman had placed square terminals at the head, foot and arms of the cross. Graham modelled fingers for these, which they agreed should also be in gold. Cutting a heart shape with scissors from a tin box, he placed it behind the Crucifixion figure to increase its isolation. The contrast was to be further heightened by a coating of matt black silver niello, an enamel-like alloy, behind the gold parts.

In all there were forty-five separate pieces of the cross to be variously cast, forged, burnished and assembled. Some 1250 ounces of 'fine' and 'Britannia' silver were used, and some 60 ounces of 'fine' gold: in 1964 fine silver was around £5 an ounce (roughly £20 in 1981), and fine gold £21 an ounce (up to £300 in 1981). That made £7500 worth of bullion at 1964 prices. The Goldsmiths' Company had generously contributed £1750. The rest was to be raised by public appeal through the Friends of Ely Cathedral. Since it seemed unlikely that either Osman or Graham would receive any fee, Graham suggested a limited edition (of nine) in silver of the Crucifixion figure with its heart-shaped backing. Marlborough Fine Art handled it, and they shared the profits.

On 7 May 1964 the completed cross went on show at the Goldsmiths' Hall in the City of London, where its poignant impact—deriving partly from the way Graham had pierced Christ's eye right through His semi-profiled head—could be felt at close range. 'The whole thing was a co-operative effort . . . with no defined spheres of activity!' he wrote to Colin Anderson ten days later.

All through Osman and I worked harmoniously, and all through I had the benefit of his special knowledge of the silversmith's craft, together with architectural advice governing size and readability. But for good or ill, the thing was designed and made for casting by these two hands which write to you . . .

—as we have seen, a slight overstatement.

After being shown later that month at the Redfern Gallery along with Graham's Coventry sketches, the cross went to Ely, with a basic figure for its cost. There it was seen by the Dean, Chapter and Friends against the reredos and without the lighting Osman had recommended. That autumn it was shown at the David Jones Art Gallery in Sydney, Australia, as the main feature of a Goldsmiths' Company exhibition.

Ely Cathedral's Friends were not impressed, and seem to have made little effort to raise the necessary funds. Osman suspects they found the cross disturbing. He, Graham and the Goldsmiths' Company were contacted, and in an agreed statement it was announced in May 1965—a year after its completion—that it had been rejected. 'Because of the way its surface is broken up, it becomes almost invisible,' the Dean, the Very Rev. Cyril Hankey, told journalists on 27 May (begging numerous questions); he added that it had been intended that the cross should dominate the cathedral right to the west end—a tall order for an artefact just over a yard high. The Goldsmiths said that if they could have their contribution back and the cross, they would pay off the costs.

Among those who read the press reports were Graham's friends Emery and Wendy Reves, who had seen and loved the cross at the Redfern. Reves was a Hungarian emigré of anti-fascist and internationalist views, who in 1930 had started a features agency, the Co-Operation Press Service, syndicating commissioned articles by some 120 leading statesmen across the world from his Paris office. Churchill was among them. In 1945 Reves published a book called *The Anatomy of Peace*, which Albert Einstein recommended to his listeners in his first interview, on radio, after Hiroshima. It subsequently sold 800,000 copies in thirty languages. Later Reves secured the foreign language rights of Churchill's war memoirs and an interest in their American publication.

All this enabled him in 1954 to buy La Pausa, a mansion built in upper Roquebrune by the Duke of Westminster for Coco Chanel in 1926-7. He filled it with a finely chosen collection of Impressionist and post-Impressionist paintings, furniture, porcelain, old glass, Renaissance jewellery and carpets. Few museums have one sixteenth-century Spanish rug as good as the eight or nine at La Pausa, and visitors either had the soles of their shoes wiped by a major-domo or were given slippers to wear.

Wendy Reves came from Texas and had helped make fashion modelling socially respectable in New York. She had a warmly effervescent personality and pert, slightly boyish good looks. Reves maintained contact with Churchill, who found Wendy engaging; the ex-Prime Minister spent some 400 days at La Pausa between his retirement in 1955 and 1960, usually accompanied by a private secretary, one or two other secretaries, a Scotland Yard man and a butler.

Douglas Cooper had taken Graham and Kathleen to lunch at La Pausa in August 1959. A friendship burgeoned, and in 1965 Graham was going to paint Reves's portrait. Meeting at a party shortly after the rejection of the Ely cross, Wendy said she would love to buy it. Graham thought it a marvellous idea. Reves moved swiftly. The Goldsmiths' Company named a figure (around £7500), and by the end of June the cross was installed at La Pausa, on a grey stone, seventeenth-century socle in the entrance hall, against a white wall. 'Isn't it just lovely?' Wendy would say to Graham in later years. 'It's really quite something,' he would murmur.[21]

Emery Reves was to be Graham's third sitter that year. The second had been Charles Clore, the vendor of shoes and property whose name became synonymous with a certain type of capitalism. Rather feebly perhaps, Graham had agreed to do him after persistent badgering. Clore came for sittings at the Villa Blanche in May, and Graham found him boring and philistine. Enthusiasm tapered to such a point that he did not finish the portrait until 1975, after another sitting that year.

Graham started drawing Emery Reves in June 1965. In January Graham had spent a week in Oxford, staying with Humphrey and sketching the Dean of his college, Christ Church, Dr Cuthbert Simpson, sometime Professor of Hebrew, who was a Canadian-American of both worldliness and sanctity. The portrait, completed in 1967, was in large measure a kindness to Humphrey, but it gave satisfaction all round—even though, through illness, Dr Simpson had rather changed shape by then. Graham gave Humphrey a second version. (Some years later Lord Butler, then Master of Trinity College, Cambridge, asked Graham whether he would paint *his* portrait. Graham replied on the back of a postcard: '£8000 — G.S.' 'I was sorry because I pointed out he had painted the Dean of Christ Church and might therefore paint the Master of Trinity,' Lord Butler recalled.[22] Graham could behave arrogantly.)

While he was in Oxford, Churchill was dying, and Graham was interviewed about his experiences when painting the portrait by Donald McLachlan, editor of the *Sunday Telegraph*. Ten days later he and Kathleen attended the memorial service at St Paul's sitting with the Henry Moores and the Basil Spences, the men sporting their OMs.

The Reves portrait turned out to be a very revealing example of Graham's use of colour in this genre. 'I often use colour arbitrarily, but very much with a view to the subject's own "colour",' he once explained.[23] Wendy Reves was commissioning it, and they discussed it over lunch one day at La Pausa. 'I must say Emery is looking very well,' Graham observed. Reves was wearing a heavy, white silk jacket and a big yellow bow tie. Wendy suggested Graham should paint him in that outfit.

When the sittings started, in the garden of the Villa Blanche, it was very hot. Reves suffered severely in his heavy clothes but Graham was keen he should keep them on: it became something of a joke. He did several gouache and oil sketches—one of them a masterpiece—as they talked about Reves's pre-war and wartime experiences. 'I knew Graham didn't like anyone to see what he was painting,' Reves recalled. 'It was almost like a religious dogma with him, so I didn't ask.' Thereafter Kathleen kept them in touch with Graham's painful progress with the portrait, which he started four times. Then, in June 1966, Graham said it was done and brought it over.

> As he took the canvas out of the car, I was absolutely shocked, because it was a dark, dark painting, like a late Rembrandt—not a trace of the colours I had worn or of the surroundings where I had sat. I had been done in a dark brown suit which I never had; and I had no tie, but a pinkish scarf, which I sometimes do wear; and behind me was a window with railings, which gave the impression of a prison, and there were some dark green leaves, as in the Adenauer portrait.

Wendy asked Graham why he had done it like that. 'I couldn't see those other colours on him,' he confessed. 'There is a big background of tristesse, of melancholy there. That's the mood of Emery.' He had needed, they surmised, to see Emery in bright colours, just as—inversely—the father of a friend of Reves, called Blot, had seen Cézanne painting a sunny still life of fruit from a table covered with rotting brown apples and pears. Reves thought the head superbly well done, the body less so, and hung it opposite his bed. As he gazed at Graham's version of himself, he began, like Oscar Wilde's Dorian Gray, to feel that he was becoming more and more like it.

Another of Graham's subjects at this time might have been even more shocked by what Graham had done to him, had he not been dead 160 years. Lord Nelson had long been a hero of Francisco de Assis Chateaubriand, a Brazilian Beaverbrook of part-French extraction who had crowned a career as self-made proprietor of newspaper, radio and television station and founder of the Museu de Arte de São Paulo by becoming an outstandingly energetic ambassador to London from 1957 to 1961. He had met Graham through his old friend Hans Juda and in about 1959 suggested—directly or via Juda—that Graham should do a portrait study of Nelson who, Chato (as he was known) believed, had saved Latin America from isolation by establishing the Royal Navy as the Atlantic power. Graham thought it an amusing idea at first, then went off it and had to be nagged. Finally, in 1965, he produced a striking double portrait, based on the supposed life mask of Nelson at the National Maritime Museum in Greenwich. It showed the hero of Trafalgar full-face and in profile (side by side, head and shoulders only, on the same canvas), looking tired, gaunt and lank-haired, with cobalt-blue eyes.

Having got this far, he thought it was not good enough and was reluctant to part with it, Elsbeth Juda recalled. So her husband rang him in Menton to say they were coming to collect it. When they arrived on 8 June—Graham had been trying to finish it off—they visited the casino in the evening and won handsomely. But the croupier refused to pay. They finally had a row with the manager, who told Graham: 'Vous insultez un chevalier de la Légion d'Honneur.' To which Graham, no doubt bafflingly, countered: 'Et moi, je suis OM.' Winnings or no winnings, Nelson was delivered·to Chateaubriand in September and has since commanded a place of honour in the São Paulo Museum.

13

The Italian Connection

1965-70

THE FORTY-FIVE YEARS that elapsed after Graham found himself as a painter in Pembrokeshire may be divided very roughly into three main periods.

The first, from 1934 to 1946, was of predominantly Welsh inspiration. His reputation reached its peak with his fellow artists and within the art world (including critics), and he was widely acknowledged as the leader of a new, romantic movement in modern British painting. These years of flowering were relatively happy and free from controversy.

The second period ran from 1947 to 1965-7. Although Graham spent a good deal of time in Kent, the South of France was his main focus as an artist. In these 'Continental' years, his critical reputation at home declined as his popular fame rose — both excessively. He produced his best portraits, but his free work, although highly inventive and often beautifully painted, frequently appeared cryptic and private in its imagery. His life was marked by major commissions, much controversy and a good deal of unhappiness.

In the third period, from 1965 to 1980, Graham found a new public in Italy, and returned not just to Wales but to graphic work, his original love, as an important activity. The circle was completed. During these autumn years he faded from the headlines at home and there were modest signs of a critical revival. Portraits tapered off in quality, with exceptions; but in his smaller, 'free' works in particular he found again much of the lyricism of the first Welsh period. The old neuroses remained, but life was marginally more serene.

Few things are more difficult for a painter than to maintain a sense of momentum. He must navigate between the Scylla of repetitiveness and the Charybdis of unsuccessful experimentation. 'My worst moments in painting are twofold, I think,' Graham said late in life.[1]

One is when I am trying to assess what I've done, so as to judge in my own opinion whether the thing is going in the right direction or has come in the right direction. The other is the feeling that one's powers of invention may dry up. It happens that I feel that quite frequently . . . at the end of a fairly long stretch of painting on a similar theme, I think that, well, I shall never invent again.

By 1965 a certain repetitiveness had indeed become noticeable in his work: in particular, he had wrung the fountain theme dry. A new stimulus was needed. It was provided, not wholly expectedly perhaps, by a major retrospective exhibition of his work which opened at the Galleria Civica d'Arte Moderna in Turin in mid-October of that year. This show not only brought him into contact with a new set of Italian patrons but also led to his return to Wales. It was therefore a turning point in his later career. The loving enthusiasm which the Italians felt for him and his work touched a resonant chord in this proud and deeply sensitive man: 'my Italians' he would call his close friends among them. They gave his life an Indian summer.

The Italian connection had in a sense been initiated by Graham's very successful showing at the Venice Biennale of 1952 and was sustained by his annual summer holidays there from then on. High-society Venetian friends, like the Brandolinis and the Cicognas, bought a few works. The Guttusos, whom Graham and Kathleen had met at the Biennale, had become friends and advocates from their base in Rome; and even before the Biennale, another painter, Ennio Morlotti, had come to know and to collect Graham's work on visits to London.

Morlotti became a considerable enthusiast, and when, in the later 1950s, a Milan dealer, Beatrice Monti, put on a mixed show of paintings chosen by Italian critics and painters, he selected several Sutherlands. Mario Tazzoli, of the Galleria Galatea in Turin, was another admirer from the 1950s. As a result, there were almost three dozen works from Italian collectors and dealers among those lent for the Turin exhibition. Five belonged to Sophia Loren and Carlo Ponti, and of the rest, a majority came from Tazzoli and his clients in Turin.

Geography played its part. As Menton was on the Franco-Italian border, collectors and dealers—who usually warmed to Graham's personality as well as to his work—could visit his studio; sometimes Graham would have a meal with them on the Italian side of the border, at La Mortola, a beautiful restaurant looking out to sea with a notable selection of *hors-d'oeuvres*. It was also a favourite spot for entertaining, or being entertained by, portrait sitters and for signing original graphics intended for the Italian market.

The Turin show had been organized by Douglas Cooper, Franco Russoli and Vittorio Viale. Russoli, like many Italians but few English, was an expert on Old Masters who loved modern ones too. He was director of the Pinacotheca di Brera in Milan and strikingly good-looking. Vittorio Viale was the Director of the Turin gallery of modern art, where the exhibition — of 160 items—was being held. Early works and war drawings were adequately represented; and the Ely cross (lent by the Reves), more than a dozen lithographs and the *Wading Birds* tapestry were included. Only three portraits, however: Sackville-West, Fürstenberg and the Hecht sketch of Churchill; and there were no early etchings.

When Graham and Kathleen arrived in Turin on 16 October, they were greeted by a banner across the street near the gallery proclaiming the Sutherland exhibition. It was a good start, and the next day a lavish lunch was given in a beautiful house outside the city by Gianni Agnelli, the handsome head of the Fiat empire. He wanted Graham to paint his portrait but could never pin himself down to a timetable for sittings.

The day before the opening, Graham went along to the gallery to check that all was well. Noticing that the pinkish background of *Chimère I* (of 1946), belonging to Lilian Somerville, had faded, he decided—against all the rules—to touch it up without consulting her. At this moment Pier Paolo Ruggerini, who was to contribute so much to his happiness, came into his life.

Graham was up a ladder, Ruggerini recalled, jacket off, wearing a silk shirt and red braces. Next to him was a very elegant lady (Kathleen) in a black Balenciaga dress, holding against her chest a can of paint, into which he was dipping a brush.[2] Viale, the gallery's Director, spotted him at work and came rushing up, protesting that since the painting had been lent, he must do nothing to it—the museum would get into terrible trouble. (Indeed, Mrs Somerville disliked what Graham had done so much that she later sold it.) Ruggerini was introduced to Graham and asked him whether he would consent to be interviewed for a television programme. He was much struck by the impact of Graham's work, of which he had previously seen only a few examples, and by Graham's personality. 'He was *d'une gentillesse incroyable*. He took my catalogue, asked if I was a Catholic, and I said yes. He drew a Crucifixion—*très simple*. His intelligence also greatly impressed me.'

On first impact, Ruggerini himself was not particularly striking: he was of medium height and well built, with curly brown hair and unremarkable features, and he spoke no English. He led a curious double life. His family had owned farmland, then had gone into business, and with his brother and two cousins he ran two companies. One was a transport business, with a fleet of lorries; the other distributed state-imported domestic and industrial gas in two regions of northern Italy. He was rich, though not in the first rank of wealth. He was also a man of considerable culture, who made films on painters and writers for RAI, the state broadcasting company: Caravaggio, Giorgione, Manzu, Manzoni and Montale have been among his thirty-odd subjects. The short slots, like his first venture with Graham (and Douglas Cooper, who provided comments), were more journalistic. But so struck was he by Graham and his work that he soon wrote suggesting a full-length film. Ruggerini was to become the most enthusiastic collector of all of Graham's work and, through the Galleria Bergamini in Milan, in which he had a stake, and in other ways, the most active promoter of his reputation in Italy.

In Turin Graham and Kathleen also met Giorgio Soavi, a writer and talented photographer who became a friend and influential protagonist. He had married a daughter of the Olivetti family, of typewriter fame, and was employed by its advertising department 'to invent things which could be a support to this strange and famous Italian company', as he put it.[3] Among these were lithographs by artists such as Chirico, Manzu, Moore and Tamayo. He came to Turin to ask Graham to do three, and not long afterwards went to Menton to try to get the project under way. 'I had difficulties convincing him,' he recalled. 'His character was so uncertain. He said yes, but next day he realized he had to produce something else. He was absolutely adorable, but never started any job. So we came to see each other more frequently—I had to follow him around.'

Graham and Kathleen came to enjoy this gentle persecution. Soavi is a shortish, perky fellow, full of laughter and humour, neat in his movements; he also speaks good English, and is a talented mimic. In 1968, the year in which Graham painted his portrait, he published *Storia con Sutherland*, an anecdotal collage of his friendship with Graham. This was later revised, and incorporated with similar material on another friend, Alberto Giacometti, in *Protagonisti*. His talent as a photographer produced in 1973 a pictorial biography of great sensitivity,[4] showing Graham in Menton, Kent and Wales; some early family photographs were included. All these initiatives did a considerable amount to further Graham's reputation in Italy.

The Turin exhibition, in addition to providing a well chosen tour of Graham's work, contained a notable new work called *Interior 1965*. Graham had painted this huge canvas (almost 8 feet by 9 feet) in seventeen days in Venice a few weeks earlier. It was inspired by an enormous boat builders' shed near the Cipriani Hotel, which he had been lent as a studio. Knowing that the Turin show would need a big picture as a climax, and learning that *Origins of the Land* would not be available from the Tate because of its condition, Graham ordered a large canvas to be delivered, completing it in a quarter of the time he would normally require. 'It illustrates . . . the way my greatest bursts of inspiration come from accidental encounters with places or situations which have something peculiar to communicate with me,' he recalled not long afterwards.[5]

It was the marvellous quality of the light filtering through a beautifully proportioned, ivy-festooned window that fired Graham's imagination. On the left a spiral staircase provides a jagged counterpoint to the regular harmonies of the window, in front of which stands a typically complex and cryptic machine. On the right sits a cat, whose original, Kathleen recalled, became spotted with Graham's paint. This major work was later bought, through Maja Sacher, for the main foyer of the Basle headquarters of Hoffmann-LaRoche. In 1966 Graham painted a second version, slightly smaller, in which the staircase is on the right, the paunchy figure of a man can be seen peering through the window and a large fan hangs from the ceiling.

The show provided Graham with the unqualified success which he had not enjoyed since the 1938 and 1940 one-man shows in London. Some thirty Italian publications reviewed it, and even British critics who saw it were deeply impressed. 'Sutherland stands revealed as the greatest living British painter and one of the very few artists of our time whose works will unquestionably live,' Terence Mullaly wrote in a convincingly enthusiastic notice in the *Daily Telegraph* of 25 October. To an anonymous correspondent of *The Times* the show revealed 'a still developing artist becoming, in the most recent works, even more personal and more powerful'.[6]

Thanks in part to the good offices of Maja Sacher, the Turin exhibition was shown in February 1966 at the Kunsthalle in Basle (not to be confused with the Kunstmuseum, which Graham considered to be the best museum of modern art in Europe).[7] Some of the heavyweight German newspapers reviewed it there, with modest and much-qualified enthusiasm.

In January 1966 Graham and Kathleen had further strengthened their Italian links by spending a few days in Rome, where they dined by the Tiber with Judy Montagu and her American husband, Milton Gendel; visited Balthus at the Académie Française, and the sculptor Giacomo Manzu—who later did two bronze heads of Kathleen—at his studio; dined with the Guttusos, where they also met the novelist Alberto Moravia; and saw St Peter's and the Sistine Chapel. Later Graham made arrangements for one of his Northampton *Crucifixion* studies to be presented to the Vatican's gallery of modern art.

After struggling with the Reves portrait for much of April, he was struck by whooping cough, which was, as Kenneth Clark (a former sufferer), put it, 'immensely disagreeable and alarming'.[8]

Morale sank to a low ebb as injections, inhalations and medicines were tried. Even in late June he was only just fit enough to go to a party given on the coast by A. S. Frere, at which Charlie Chaplin told him that he would be honoured if Graham would immortalize him. This modest approach to a portrait commission had considerable charm, but Graham did not succumb, no doubt appreciating the difficulty of competing with the cinematic image. But while finishing the portraits of Dr Simpson of Christ Church and Douglas Cooper in 1966, he did agree to tackle Max Rayne, the financier and patron of education, medicine and the arts.

Rayne entertained Graham and Kathleen at his Hampstead home in September (also present: Lord Goodman, the Maxwell Frys, the Henry Moores and Richard Crossman, Leader of the House of Commons since the Labour Party's return to power that March), and sittings began in France in late October. The portrait had been commissioned by Darwin College, Cambridge, of which Lord Rayne is an Honorary Fellow. 'I was only interested in being painted if Graham were the artist, while Darwin were most enthusiastic about the idea of having a Sutherland painting,' he recalled.[9] Both Rayne and his wife Jane felt an immediate rapport with Graham and Kathleen, and Rayne was struck as much by Graham's 'shrewdly penetrating mind' as by his intelligence, sensitivity and keenly observant eye.

Graham finished two versions in 1969–70. In the Darwin version, which is rather brightly coloured, the emphasis is on Rayne, the dynamic entrepreneur, to a point which could seem flattering—though Rayne himself felt it was penetrating 'and in a curious way anticipated my appearance by several years'. (The fee was £10,000.) The other, rather subtler in colouring and expression, he acquired for himself when informed of its existence by Alfred Hecht.

More portraits, including those of Maugham, Adenauer, Daisy Fellowes and Douglas Cooper, were added to the Turin selection for an even larger retrospective which opened in Munich in March 1967, with Graham and Kathleen in attendance. It attracted 16,000 visitors in eight weeks before going on to museums in The Hague, West Berlin and Cologne, all in 1967.

The Munich show was to feature in a BBC film profile directed by Margaret McCall. It was not a very happy exercise. Graham had the bad idea of getting Soavi, whose English was not *that* good, to do the interviewing. When the film was screened on 7 May 1968 the *Daily Mirror*'s reviewer accused Soavi of practically pawing deferentially before him. As soon as the BBC's film unit had finished with Graham in Kent that August 1967, in came Ruggerini's. After a year's silence, he had had a positive reply to his letter suggesting a proper filmed study of Graham's work. It was to be called *The Mirror and the Mirage* and was being shot in colour.

Ruggerini had suggested to Graham that he should give him some addresses in Pembrokeshire: looking through his work, it was clear that Wales had been very important. But Graham said: 'No, I think I should come with you.' And so, on 28 August 1967, he returned to the scenery which from 1934 to 1946 had been his most potent inspiration. 'It's extraordinary,' he commented to Ruggerini, 'the light here is as intense as it is in the South of France.' They spent two exploratory days there, showing Ruggerini Sandy Haven, with its reddish rocks, exposed oak roots, rotting shipwreck projecting from the mud, dazzling yellow lichen and the golden evening light; Solva, perched on the sea by the heather-covered Gribin; Clegyr-Boia; and the grey romance of the crumbling Bishop's Palace. Graham soon realized, as he said later, that the long and regrettable gap since 1946 had been an error and that he had been 'sadly mistaken' in thinking that he had exhausted what the countryside had to offer both as 'vocabulary' and as inspiration.[10]

After filming in Menton, Kent and London, they returned to Pembrokeshire in May 1968, where they were joined by Douglas Cooper and Franco Russoli, who were collaborating on the Italian script and commentary. They all stayed at the Lord Nelson Hotel in Milford Haven, which they had discovered on the previous trip. It was run by an intelligent and very competent ex-nurse, Margaret White, who could see that the Sutherlands needed to be cherished. Henceforward it was their third home, and Mrs White became very fond of them.[11]

The rediscovery of Pembrokeshire was not reflected immediately in Graham's work, though, curiously, it had been anticipated in 1965 by a purely Welsh-looking oil, *Trees by a River*, just as the Mediterranean colours of the Welsh thorn studies had anticipated the first visit to the South of France. Portraits aside, lithography rather than painting was the main preoccupation of much of 1967 and early 1968.

Graham had done some thirty lithographs since 1948, reflecting a cross-section of most activities except religious commissions: sundry standing forms in the 1950s, heads of Maugham, Rubinstein and Adenauer, some animals, insects and roses (one of these being for Olivetti). The printers he used included the Curwen Press in London, Fernand Mourlot in Paris and various Swiss and Italian firms. In about 1961 Harry Fischer of Marlborough Fine Art had suggested a series of lithographs to illustrate a theme—something from Goethe, perhaps.[12] In the Cloisters museum in New York Graham had seen a medieval bestiary and he had also studied a catalogue of these compendia of real and fabulous beasts, called *Constant Companions*, from an exhibition in 1964 in Houston, Texas. Such a subject, he thought, might lend itself to his preoccupation with the affinities between men, animals and machines.

He got down to the project in earnest in March 1967, scarcely needing to look further than his own work for a rich store of suitable material. Slightly sinister birds, animals and insects had long been part of his pictorial vocabulary, from the pterodactyl of *Origins of the Land*, through the grasshoppers, cicadas, monkeys, toads and frogs of the late 1940s and 1950s, the lions and eagles of the Coventry tapestry, to the bats and beetles of more recent lithographs.

Most of these were to be reflected in his Bestiary, with support from a pinkish armadillo and a fine army of black ants crawling over a cross. Bats produced Graham's finest effort in the series of plates: *Chauve Souris (Interior)*, showing half a dozen of them swooping around in Gothic gloom, teeth bared, was a virtuoso performance. He sent off a first batch of zinc plates (on which the work was done, as an alternative to working on a lithographic stone or on transfer paper) in June, spending five days working in Mourlot's Paris atelier in September and a further six in February 1968. On his way to put some finishing touches to the plates in April 1968, he left the original drawings in a roll in a taxi. The police traced it to Orly airport, where Graham had to collect them.

Lithographs can be big business. The twenty-five plates of the Bestiary were to be published in an edition of seventy, each print costing between £85 and £125. At an average of £100 each, the total potential revenue was thus £175,000, less the cost of printing (roughly 10 per cent) and, of course, the galllery's overheads and profit. Then there were the preparatory studies, forty-seven of which were shown at Marlborough from 9 May 1968.

Half of the drawings were sold at the private view. The perfect dealer's show, Edward Lucie-Smith called it in the *Sunday Times*—'if you have an aversion to bats, take a look at the lion or the monkey or the owl'—though he did concede it was 'one of Sutherland's most interesting and most convincing exhibitions for some time'.[13] David Thompson, in the *Listener*, was not sure if Graham was 'a major artist working in a minor way, or a minor artist working fitfully in a major way'.[14] But Bryan Robertson, in the

Spectator, thought it all 'magnificent. . . . the gallery glows and flames with a variety of mood and complex gradations of light and darkness.'[15]

Meanwhile Graham's portrait painting was swinging towards captains of industry and commerce. First came Baron Elie de Rothschild, who had an engaging Austrian wife, Liliane, and became a friend. Sittings took place at their Paris home in the rue Masseran in June and September 1967; work on the portrait began in June 1968. Pressure to complete it increased that August, when the sportive merchant banker and collector lost the sight of one eye playing polo. The portrait thus became something of a symbol of his past self. In the event Graham sent off two versions by train from Menton in December 1968: a frontal view, for which he asked £10,000, and a smaller, three-quarter-face for £7000, which included an oil sketch. The increased prices reflected those of his other work.

'It was Graham who decided to do two portraits and asked me to choose which I preferred,' Baron Rothschild recalled.[16]

> Since I have three children, I bought both. I very much liked what he did of me, and have particularly pleasant memories of the sittings, which with other painters are torture. Graham liked one to move around, and above all to talk. His conversation was a delight.

In January 1969 the Rothschilds gave a lavish party to celebrate the portraits, to Graham and Kathleen's great delight.

Graham was such a complex blend of the straightforward and the oblique, of innocence and shrewdness, that it was sometimes hard to know at what level of seriousness he intended to be taken. Did he really mean it when he said that portrait painting was 'not a profitable occupation at all, far from it. For three-quarters of the portraits I have hardly got £1000 for each sitter, and mainly they have taken a very long time . . .'?[17] Only for the first seven was the fee £1000 or less. It is true, however, that he sometimes charged friends well below the going rate and, in some instances, nothing (Soavi was a case in point). Some portraits (for example, that of Reves) took a great deal longer to paint than it might have taken to earn the same money from 'free' paintings, and often Graham refused to do portraits for which he could have charged high fees. All that can safely be said is that there was a large element of the arbitrary in his choice of sitters; that he charged roughly what he thought the sitter could afford in relation to the current level of his prices and took account sometimes, but not always, of the degree of friendship involved; that, had he been mercenary, he could have made a great deal more money from portraiture than he did; and that in his last decade his portrait prices lagged behind those of his 'free' paintings.

Most of Graham first eight sitters—Maugham, Beaverbrook, Sackville-West, Churchill, Jeffress, Juda, Sacher and Rubinstein—had genuinely interesting faces. It was perhaps a pity that few of those who followed offered equally promising subject matter. Certainly Graham's next sitter, Dr Adolf Jann, President of Hoffmann-LaRoche, looked like a studious lawyer and banker, which was what he had been. Maja Sacher had arranged the commission, and the sittings took place at Dr Jann's office in January 1968 and, a few weeks later, at Graham's Menton studio. Two portraits resulted, in 1970 and 1971. What lay behind the spectacles? Graham provided no real answers.

In between the Jann sittings came Cecil King, then chairman of the International Publishing Company. Hugh Cudlipp, his deputy, had met Graham at a dinner party given by the Judas at their Palace Gate penthouse.[18] When a portrait of King was mooted for the *Daily Mirror* headquarters in Holborn, the name Sutherland sprang to mind. Cudlipp was told that Graham asked £5000 from the waist up, £10,000 for a full-length portrait. Who wanted to preserve Cecil's pants for posterity? he asked himself, and they settled for half-length.

Early 1968 represented the nadir of Harold Wilson and his Labour Government's fortunes. Sterling had been devalued in November 1967. The British press was bent on hounding Wilson out of office, with Cecil King and the *Mirror* making the running. 'Making a new start with a Coalition Government? Mr Cecil King leading the soundings', a *Guardian* headline proclaimed on 14 February, the day King arrived in Menton. He telephoned through a rebuttal, pointing out that he had been merely sounding the leaders.

Graham and Kathleen were much struck by King's gloom about Britain. King, for his part, recorded in his diary that he liked Graham and his wife but found it curious that the best portrait painter of the day should not really like doing portraits or regard himself as a portrait painter. Graham thought his best was of Adenauer, he noted.[19] There were five sittings. In May King was held to have overreached himself in calling for Wilson's departure, and on the 29th he was sacked. Nevertheless, the portrait went on and was duly hung in the boardroom, probably at the end of 1969.

However, in 1970, when the International Publishing Corporation merged with the Reed Paper Group and Lord Ryder became chairman, 'he did not wish to hang the picture and gave it to me. So it hangs here,' Mr King wrote from his home in Dublin.[20] 'Personally I think it is a standard boardroom portrait, and no more. But my wife [Dame Ruth Railton] rates it higher than that.' Some years after the portrait was finished, he said,

Graham wrote to her offering her the sketches he had done. She wrote gratefully accepting, but they never arrived. The portrait, a very good likeness, shows King full-face, looking suitably sombre, all three jacket buttons done up.

In terms of quantity, 1968 was the high-water mark of Graham's activities as a painter of portraits. In all, he was involved in seven: he was finishing Rothschild, continuing Rayne, and starting Jann and King, and there were also Mark Longman, Giorgio Soavi and William Paley.

Longman was chairman of the family publishing house, as it then was, and a friend of Patrick Plunket. He was 51 and, Graham found, rather conscious of his good looks. The portrait, finished in 1970, showed him seated in half-profile. It is a fluent work, though for me marred by the highlights which had first crept into the Rayne portrait, perhaps to indicate nervous energy.

Graham sketched both Soavi and Paley that July in Venice, then had five more sittings with Paley there the following July. If anyone had a 'power gloss', it was Bill Paley, whom Graham and Kathleen had come to know over the years in Venice. The son of a prosperous cigar manufacturer, he had won control of the Columbia Broadcasting System in 1928, when he was 27, expanding and controlling it for fifty years with more than a touch of autocracy and perfectionism. Here, in short, was a genuinely interesting, pioneering entrepreneur. But he was not an easy man to please, and his relations with Graham ended with a disagreement — 'minor in nature', according to Paley[21] — when the portrait was completed in 1971. According to Kathleen, Paley wanted a second portrait, which Graham did not have time to do. Presumably, Paley would have been less annoyed if Graham had not at some stage indicated that he would do another one.

In the latter part of 1968 Graham's enthusiasm for new projects, not always long-lasting, found a new outlet. Wendy Reves wanted a tomb designed for her mother, who had died that year, and had found a good site in Menton's cemetery. She recalled:

> The idea was to have a kind of chapel, with her body in the middle, and room for me and Emery later. Graham was immediately enthusiastic. He said: 'I think every artist should create one tomb.'. . . He had very definite ideas about how he wanted the light to come in. He wanted to play with the sunshine, so that it created interesting blends of colour inside as it filtered through the windows.

It was not the first such venture. In 1964 Graham had designed a narrow, arched stained-glass window commissioned for St Andrew's (Anglican) church in Zurich's Promenadengasse. Made in Paris and formally 'handed over' in March 1971, it showed in brilliant colours a large passion-flower above a crucifix design in the form of a medallion, creating a radiant effect above the font. To help him with the tomb/chapel, he called in Tom Wilson, an architect and son of Peter Wilson, the chairman of Sotheby's, who lived near Grasse. Together they evolved three different designs. But in mid-February 1969 Graham became disenchanted with the venture and dropped it. The Reves were distressed, and it was several years before relations were resumed.

Tom Wilson had become a friend, and Graham now turned to him for help with a less esoteric project: the design of an extension to the Villa Blanche—or, rather, a new house-cum-studio rather larger than Eileen Gray's severely functional original. The contract was signed in March 1969 and the work finished by January 1970.

Graham had remained financially fairly hard-pressed until he was nearly 50. In the mid-1950s, with growing fame, the patronage of Lord Beaverbrook and others, and more remunerative portrait commissions, his income improved, and by about 1960 it was clear that his potential earnings were high enough to attract the penal British tax rates then prevailing. Graham took advice and, after much discussion over several years, a Swiss company was formed in the mid-1960s, controlled by a trust. This company employed Graham's services as an artist outside Britain, of which he continued to be a resident while spending roughly half the year in France. Around 1969–70, when Graham had been thinking of moving the centre of his activities to France, the Inland Revenue decided that the income of the Swiss company was to be treated as his own for the purposes of taxation, and he lost an appeal against this ruling. With some reluctance, he therefore ceased to be a British resident. From then on all his work was carried out for the Swiss company, which paid him a salary (an arrangement that continued until his death), and his time in England was limited to ninety days a year.

For the most famous painter in Britain, as he was in the 1950s and early 1960s, Graham had lived modestly. The White House in Kent was very pleasant but far from grand. The Villa Blanche was tiny. The new extension, in essence a flat-roofed rectangle of concrete jutting out of the hill towards the sea from just below the Gray bunker, was by no means grandiose. It was dominated by a handsome sitting-room some 40 feet long, with port-hole sky-lights echoing those in the original house. The floor was of honey-coloured Travertine marble, and the left-hand wall (largely sliding glass doors) gave on to a balcony overlooking the garden. The slightly austere effect was softened by a scattering of rugs, white sofas and arm chairs, some curious chairs made of twisted vine branches and a handsome selection of Graham's paintings, drawings and *objets trouvés*.

Leading off this, successively, were two small bedrooms, the first of which doubled as library (art books, biographies, Graham's beloved P. G. Wodehouse, Kathleen's Proust, Balzac, Thomas Mann, Henry James, Arnold Bennett, E. M. Forster, Graham Greene). Finally, there was Graham's first proper studio, with an entire wall of window overlooking the valley and the sea beyond and untreated concrete walls for the minimum of distraction. Standing on the black-tiled, eventually paint-stained floor were three easels with spotlights trained on them from the ceiling; two chests of drawers for drawings; a cupboard covered with twisted roots, dried wood, pieces of stone (mainly from Wales) and some old bones; and, above a bed where Graham often slept, a bookshelf with more art books and a rack with metal drawers filled with his photographs of portrait subjects and objects-in-landscape, some squared up with a sharp point for use in his drawings.

A large sign advertising Sutherland Spreads (fish paste and so on) was pinned to the wall, and there were paints (mainly Rowney's) and paint brushes everywhere, the latter in a selection of jam jars and mugs. Although meticulous when off-duty—he dressed in a casually elegant style, with an occasional suit from a tailor in Cork Street—Graham was far from fastidious in his studio and would sometimes transfer paint from his working trousers to the white sofas in the sitting-room. Such habits (another was to dab at paintings with his handkerchief) would bring mild protests from Nenette Ferrari, a former secretary, married to a taxi driver, whom Kathleen had taken on as housekeeper in 1956. She was intelligent, resourceful and loyal, and in addition to doing some housework and much of the shopping at Menton's market, was good at dealing with local tradesmen and officials and spoke fluent Italian. If relations with employees are a test of character, Graham and Kathleen passed with an alpha: both Madame Ferrari and their 'daily' in Kent, Lily King, were devoted to them.

A secretary from Monte Carlo came in periodically to help with correspondence. Kathleen dealt with a good deal of this, in addition to doing the cooking and some light housework, fielding telephone calls and gardening. Apart from its situation, the garden was the house's great glory. Over the years Graham had, with some difficulty, negotiated the purchase by the Swiss company of five or six adjoining plots of land belonging to local smallholders. In all there was eventually 38 acres, forming a horseshoe shape below the house, with a small portion across the Castellar road.

The main garden included an old olive grove, carpeted with violets in spring, a copse of young oak, at whose feet Kathleen had planted wild primroses and, among other trees, cherry, mandarin, mimosa, almond, avocado (yielding about 100 pounds of pears a year) and cypress. There was also a vegetable garden. Over the paths near the house there were pergolas fragrant with jasmine and roses; mimosa and hibiscus bloomed; and red and white datura—which Graham loved to draw—hung their sensuous trumpets.

Much of the garden was semi-wild, and it was there increasingly that Graham took his afternoon walk, thus avoiding the risk of being stopped by those who recognized him in the roads nearby. Occasionally such a walk would yield an 'encounter' with a theme, and Graham always carried sketchbook and pencil, sometimes a small box of watercolours. But from 1968 onwards most of his inspiration came again from Wales, sketches made there producing more than enough material.

Whether Graham and Kathleen were in Menton, Kent, Wales or Venice, they were likely to be visited by Pier Paolo and Marzia Ruggerini. She was slim, pretty, warm-hearted. 'Mes enfants!' Graham would say, greeting them with an embrace. Arriving with caviar, a truffle or some other gift, they gave him a wonderful sense of being loved, understood and appreciated and indeed became almost members of the family. Occasionally, the Sutherlands would visit their small 'castle'—more a large, fortified house— at Valle Lomellina, in the rice-growing part of the Lombardy plain.

Il Castello, as it was rather unsubtly called, had belonged to Marzia's family and is comfortable, even cosy inside. Gradually, all other paintings were removed from the walls, and it became a Sutherland shrine, containing more than fifty oils and a great number of gouaches, watercolours and lesser memorabilia, beautifully framed and hung throughout the house, which was guarded by some notably fierce Alsatian and Doberman dogs. Some works bore inscriptions by Graham, but many Ruggerini bought from Marlborough Fine Art and other dealers.

Soavi too was active in Graham's interests, in 1969 commissioning a dozen gouaches for one of the desk diaries which Olivetti sent as a Christmas gift to valued clients and friends around the world. The fee was £6000. 'I asked him for twelve, and he did about thirty-five,' Soavi recalled. Almost all were of Welsh inspiration.

Then he called me and said: 'You can come.' He had arranged a show of these things in his studio in Menton. Every drawing had two or three variants. He said: 'You have to make your choice, then I will make mine.' When I had done so, he said: 'Not bad. But don't you think maybe this is better than that?'—and so on. The diary was superb, and 70,000 copies were sent *hors commerce* around the world.

Later Soavi printed two or three thousand copies of the gouaches with photos he had taken in Wales and poems by his friend Raffaele Carrieri, which probably pleased Graham more than the diary.

It was strange, perhaps, that Italians should have been so enthusiastic about the work of an English artist living near their border, inspired mainly by the landscape of the most distant part of Wales. But if the British could admire Giotto, Bellini, Titian and a hundred other Italian painters, why should not the Italians admire Sutherland?

14

The Graham Sutherland Gallery

ALTHOUGH GRAHAM could behave in a petty way, he was at heart a man of generous impulses. He was constantly giving away his work to friends old and new, and sometimes to help good causes. From the later 1940s he had — initially, it seems, at the suggestion of Peter Watson — given Kathleen a part of his output so that she would have something solid to support her in the event of his death.

In about 1970 he had the idea of passing on his house and studio in Menton, with some paintings, to the municipality after his death and also suggested that he should design a memorial chapel. Some tentative arrangements were made and reported in the press. But when his relations with the Menton authorities deteriorated with a change of mayor in 1977, his enthusiasm for the plan evaporated. Another idea, which also came to nothing, was to build some small houses in the grounds of the Villa Blanche and to create a refuge where artists and writers could work.

A further inspiration, sparked by his return to Wales each year from 1967 onwards, was to burn with a more enduring flame. It was that, as he later put it, 'having gained so much from this country, I should like to give something back.'[1] Over the years, perhaps with some such project at the back of his mind, he and Kathleen had kept a body of his work directly inspired by Wales. The problem was where to house it.

Graham was not actively looking for a site when, in 1971, a possible solution presented itself, thanks to the generosity of Hanning and Lady Marion Philipps, the owners of Picton Castle. Graham and Kathleen had visited the castle in the mid-1940s, when it was owned first by Sir John Philipps and then by his sister Sheila, Lady Dunsany. In 1947 she sold it back to the senior branch of the large and complex Philipps family, in the shape of Lord Milford, one of the four sons of Canon Sir James Erasmus

Philipps, twelfth baronet, three of whom had become peers. He in turn had handed it over to his son Hanning, for many years chairman of Schweppes and Lord Lieutenant first of Pembrokeshire, then of Dyfed.

Armed with an introduction from a relative of Lord Plunket, Graham and Kathleen had first met Hanning Philipps and his wife in the spring of 1968, while filming with Ruggerini, and a friendship soon developed. Hanning Philipps is a tall, austerely handsome man with a kindly expression and a gentle manner who is also an amateur painter of some attainment and a discriminating collector. His wife, Lady Marion, daughter of the twelfth Earl of Stair, is a passionate gardener and a very able farmer, the first woman President of the Royal Welsh Agricultural Society. Hers is a strong, sometimes volatile personality.

'Graham was always saying that one of the things he would really like would be to leave a collection of his pictures to Pembrokeshire, where he had derived so much inspiration,' Hanning Philipps recalled.[2] 'We had these disused buildings. We said: "Would you like a building if we could find some way of financing it?" He jumped at it.' They first discussed the idea in the summer of 1971. Philipps put his offer of some rooms in a wing of the castle more firmly in late 1972. 'Your IDEA thrilled me a lot, and we both think it wonderfully warm and generous of you to think of it at all,' Graham wrote on 2 January 1973.

I am going through the Welsh items that are in the Bank, and also my Welsh studies in France. These—even if they amounted to 100 works (mostly small) would have to be supplemented with at least 6 or 10 important oils, and I think that for the future I shall do a 'version' of every Welsh-inspired subject. In fact I do this now, but with your idea in mind, there is all the more incentive!

Graham was delighted both with the concept of a Sutherland gallery and its woodland setting, not far from the remarkable oaks and rocks of the Eastern Cleddau estuary which the twelfth-century castle overlooked, one of his happiest hunting grounds. He had always felt that work done in one area was best seen in that area (he was keen on decentralization) and liked the idea that a substantial, coherent body of his work would be on view there.

In mid-August 1973 Graham and Kathleen inspected the disused laundry, in a courtyard behind the castle, which the Philipps thought might make a suitable site. Graham discussed the project with a Haverfordwest architect of the Philipps' choosing, who was instructed to submit a survey for the design of a gallery with warden's flat above.

All went smoothly. Graham, at his own suggestion (via Kathleen), painted a portrait first of Lady Marion—a very fresh profile study of her head against some leaves—and then a more conventional head of Hanning Philipps, finished in 1974 and 1975 respectively. The portraits were understood to be a generous return for the help over the gallery, though Philipps made a token payment towards his own.[3]

In July 1974 Philipps outlined the project to representatives of the three local councils: Dyfed County Council, South Pembrokeshire District Council and Preseli District Council. They eventually provided some £5000 each towards the capital costs and £500 each per year towards certain annual costs. The Wales Tourist Board chipped in a generous £22,500 for the building, and Graham and Hanning Philipps contributed £7500 each, over and above the building and the collection respectively. There were further contributions from the Max Rayne Trust, the Monument Trust, Lloyd's Bank and the Ruggerinis (a Sienese marble floor). Rebuilding costs came to about £83,000.[4]

The idea was that the National Museum of Wales in Cardiff, which had been brought into the consultations, would provide the management and administrative costs of the gallery. The collection would be vested in a trust, finally set up in February 1976, on which the local authorities, the tourist board, the museum, Graham and the Philipps would be represented. But for the museum to nominate trustees turned out to be against its regulations.

Some 40 acres of gardens were to be opened to the public at the same time. The Philipps believed that the garden and the gallery would be complementary, teaching country lovers something of Graham's art, and art lovers something of the countryside.

Graham began to work on paintings specifically for the Picton Castle gallery in the autmn of 1974, eventually producing ten, to which five earlier ones were added. These fifteen oils, fifty-three early drawings in mixed media and some sixty graphic works were on show when the gallery was finally opened in mid-June 1976. The ceremony was performed by Lord Goodman, the trust's first chairman, whose portrait Graham had been painting, and who had become a friend.

With its cool yet cosy interior, and with Graham's work skilfully hung (the big paintings had been tailored to their spaces), the gallery made a very attractive impression. Graham had come to hope that it would become in its way a cultural centre, with facilities for exhibitions of other artists' work, poetry readings, lectures, films and quiet study. A small lecture theatre/cinema was part of the premises, and he hoped expansion would be possible.

An enterprise involving so many parties—three local authorities, a distant museum, a private owner, a busy London chairman, a sensitive artist living mainly in France and a secretary who, from early 1977 onwards, moved to Suffolk—was not lightly brought into being and sustained as a going concern. Two problems proved to be particularly intractable. One concerned the car park, the other the environmental properties of the converted building.

The cost of the construction of the car park and its services was borne by the gallery's trustees. The car park itself was to serve both the gardens and the gallery, which shared a single access road and could effectively be reached only by car. Admission to the gallery, it was eventually decided, was to be free, and was advertised as being so. But the Philipps, like any stately home owners, wanted to recoup some of the heavy cost of maintaining the gardens and decided—as opening day approached—to impose a car park charge of 50p per car. The National Museum of Wales felt this amounted to an admission charge. Graham was against it on principle, and also because it angered visitors who had seen the gallery advertised as free. It became the subject of much bitter debate among the trustees, and at one stage Graham seriously considered starting afresh on a new site. His relations with the Philipps, who had in some ways been so generous, deteriorated sadly.

As far as the building was concerned, it was natural that the National Museum of Wales should demand that certain criteria for light and humidity levels should be met. All too soon it became evident that the conversion of the old laundry had not been wholly successful in excluding water and damp. There was also the matter of security, in which the museum demanded a standard at odds with the informal rural environment. Taking these various factors into account, the museum did not feel able to sign a management agreement of more than very limited duration.

A number of issues related to these two main problems were resolved at a meeting of trustees in October 1979, for which Graham flew over specially from France. The car park was to display a notice saying it was private and had nothing to do with the gallery. Funds were to be provided from Graham's trust for the building to be brought up to standard. Hanning Philipps was to make available an additional, adjoining site for an extension of the gallery. The National Museum would enter into a long-term management agreement. But the underlying question of the control of the pictures remained, and after Graham's death the trustees decided to go it alone without the not always kindly tutelage of the Cardiff museum. Lord Goodman became president; Basil Alexander, Graham's accountant and friend from Kent, took over as chairman; Sir Norman Reid, former Director of the Tate Gallery, became a trustee; and Gordon Bennett, the gallery's custodian, became secretary. Plans for an extension to increase facilities and to provide more hanging space for an enlarged collection were agreed and before long went ahead.

Meanwhile the gallery itself proved to be a tremendous success. Attendance figures were as follows for the first four years:

	1976	1977	1978	1979	1980
Adults	8254	9329	14621	11128	10157
Children	1914	1647	2847	2287	2094

The record was in August 1978, with 4464 adults and 1311 children. During these four years the gallery was closed in winter for a total of nine months. The monthly average for visitors when it was open was 1092 adults and 220 children. Some visitors were locals; many were tourists, often from as far afield as Australia, the USA, Japan and, frequently, Germany and Holland.

It was an extremely satisfactory record, particularly given the 'difficult' nature of Graham's work. Reactions ranged from disgust to intense enthusiasm. In general, the smaller works proved more popular than the big oils, some of which were not among Graham's strongest. He himself particularly cherished the remark of two labourers who had at first been foxed by the pictures. They came back a second time after working for a while, and said it had 'dawned on them'. He loved the idea that he might have helped things to 'dawn': not so much pictures as objects in nature. A local farmer was heard to comment: 'I don't know what it means, but the colours are Pembrokeshire', while an elderly woman took one look and said: 'I'll come back when I'm feeling stronger'—and did just that. Even those who knew Graham's work well saw it in a different light so near the scenery which had inspired it. Suddenly, it seemed more of a distillation of reality than they had realized.

Between 1968 and his death in 1980, Graham generally visited Pembrokeshire twice a year, for a month in summer and a fortnight around Christmas time. He and Kathleen always stayed in the same rooms, overlooking the car park, at the Lord Nelson Hotel, sometimes eating at Chez Gilbert, a restaurant in Haverfordwest. Graham spent much of the morning and late afternoon sketching and taking snaps in his favourite spots, the foreshores at Sandy Haven and near Picton and Benton castles. He particularly loved St Ishmaels and the walled wood by Monk Haven, and there were trips to Wolf's Castle, Porthclais and other old haunts.

Kathleen would go with him, reading in the parked Jaguar (long Graham's favoured car—he liked the most highly powered ones) after a walk, while he sought out an old theme or a new juxtaposition of forms which might unlock the door to a painting. His theme once found, he would settle on a little canvas folding stool to sketch it, wearing a hat against the flies and wellingtons in which to wade through the mud. Sketching was an absorbing but exhausting activity, and sometimes he would come back from those trips looking drained.

Social life was kept to a minimum. Apart from the Hanning Philipps at Picton Castle, there were Jack and Betty Sulivan, the owners of Benton Castle. Benton—a 'small but almost perfect castle', Graham liked to call it—consisted mainly of a circular, white-washed tower, gloriously situated above the main Cleddau estuary, surrounded by an imaginatively sculptured garden and a wood of twisted oaks. Down on the foreshore their boughs hung so low over the water that the receding tides left seaweed hanging from them, and gnarled roots laid bare the struggle for survival. There Graham found a pile of chains, formerly used to tie boats to the overhanging oak boughs, now refreshed and protected from rust by tidal baths of salt water. He used them in many late works, like *Forest with Chains* of 1970.

Jack Sulivan is a tall, upright, deceptively conventional-looking ex-Royal Artillery colonel, who had become general manager of the Milford Haven Conservancy Board: a major responsibility after the controversial decision of 1957 to make Milford Haven Britain's main oil port. Since then four refineries had been established on its shores by Esso, Texaco, Gulf and Amoco, and BP had built a major terminal. Their giant tankers came under the Board's jurisdiction. Betty Sulivan had been a pupil of Graham's at Chelsea. She too is intuitive, behind a bubbling manner, and saw that Graham and Kathleen needed affection without fuss, and certainly without being shown off to local friends. So they would dine *à quatre*, at Benton, at the Lord Nelson, or Chez Gilbert. Graham and Kathleen spent Christmas each year between 1972 and 1975 at Benton Castle. It was a rather unexpected friendship, which gave much to both sides. Around 1973 they fell so deeply in love with the castle and its situation that they offered £300,000 for it; but the Sulivans pointed out that they had two sons who were equally besotted with the place, as indeed they themselves were.[5]

Castles or no, these six or seven weeks in Wales each year were lived at a simple level, enabling Graham to immerse himself in the curiously charged atmosphere of 'his' estuaries, taking back to France sketchbooks and memories from which he recreated their strange magic.

15

The Last Decade

GRAHAM'S FINAL DECADE was a period of great activity, yielding gouaches and graphics in particular that were among the most lyrical and accessible works of his career. Marked as it was by a complete break with Douglas Cooper, Kathleen's near death in a fall, the Picton gallery saga and news of the destruction of the Churchill portrait, the period was not without its dramas too.

Portraiture continued at much the same level as during the previous decade. There were fourteen new subjects. After William Paley and the Philipps, Graham painted Lords Bath and Plunket. The Bath commission, originally for a head and shoulders (fee: £7500) came via David Somerset of Marlborough Fine Art, son-in-law of the mildly eccentric but entrepreneurial owner of the stately home of Longleat in Wiltshire. Half-way through the sittings in Menton in October 1970, Graham suggested that he would like to do a full-length Bath. The latter recalled:[1]

> I naturally somewhat wavered, as I knew he charged £12,000 for a full-length portrait, but he quickly assured me that he would do it for the same price, which I accepted, I think rather regrettably now, as the head down to the waist is excellent, but the scenery and torso, etc., is, to my mind, not up to the delicateness or preciseness of the head and shoulders.

Most unusually, Graham put in some background scenery showing a road with cars on it and some trees, possibly, Lord Bath surmised, to indicate his commercialization of Longleat, but none of it, he thought, was very good or enhanced the portrait artistically. Like its subject, the portrait was tall and narrow and has hung, since it was completed in 1971, in the Ante-Room at Longleat.

Patrick Plunket came to Menton for sittings in March 1971 and stayed with the Sutherlands (a privilege granted to close friends only) at the Villa Blanche. Graham finished the portrait with unusual dispatch that August. (Could he have sensed that his friend at court had not long to live? He died of cancer in 1975, aged only 51.) It was no doubt Plunket who, in 1972, suggested to the Queen that Graham should submit a painting for presentation to President Pompidou on a state visit to Paris that May. Graham sent transparencies of four works, at the same time offering any one of them as a present to his old friend and ally from Marlborough Fine Art, James Kirkman, who had set up on his own. The Queen and Kirkman plumped for the same one: *Form in an Estuary*, a fairly typical Welsh scene. Graham insisted on doing a new version of it for Kirkman. Contrary to his fears, it was just as fresh as the first.[2]

The Pompidous were keen amateurs of contemporary painting, and their pleasure was evident, according to an eyewitness, when the painting was presented to them on 18 May. Kathleen and Graham flew to Paris from Menton for a British Embassy reception that day, and talked to both the Queen and the President.

It was a time when Graham was rather more sensitive than usual about his standing in Paris. Francis Bacon had had a large and very successful retrospective at the Grand Palais there between October 1971 and January 1972, which Graham had seen and admired, and his reputation was probably at its peak, while Graham's had fallen. A comparable exhibition in Paris became a target. Equally, Graham found it hard to understand why Bacon's prices were rather higher than his (in 1970 up to £30,000 for a large Bacon, up to £18,000 for a large Sutherland). The explanation was simple: regardless of their comparative rating, Graham produced numerous paintings and many gouaches, watercolours and graphics. Bacon produced only a small number of largish oils, and anyone who wanted a Bacon had to buy one of these. Graham would protest that his output was not *so* much greater, but of course it was.

His next sitter was Sacheverell Sitwell, travel writer, poet and brother of Osbert and Edith. They had met from time to time in Venice, and Graham started and completed a head and shoulders in 1973. Sir Sacheverell believes his wife paid £1000 for it: 'expensive in my opinion. . . . I doubt if I have made £1000 in the whole of my life, writing some sixty or seventy books and reams of poetry since 1918. But there it is.'[3] He was 'not so mad' himself about the result, which hangs at his home, Weston Hall, Towcester; it seemed to him 'more the portrait of a footballer than the portrait of a poet'. Local footballers must be an unusually intellectual-looking lot. Graham's next portrait was an undoubted triumph, however. Lord Goodman's spectacular bulk, his reputation and the quality of his mind and personality all conspired to elicit from Graham one of his finest efforts in this field. That the portrait was destined, through a then anonymous benefactor (Lord Rayne), for the Tate Gallery must also have been a stimulus.

The ubiquitous lawyer and conciliator came to sit for Graham in Menton in April and May 1973. Graham started five different canvases, then worked in parallel on two of them, a frequent practice which he found enabled him to make helpful comparisons[4] (and sometimes to sell two rather than one). The main portrait was finished in 1973, and its subject judged it a 'very fine, penetrating and sympathetic study'.[5] That was the general verdict. It showed him seated, an ample monolith against an orange-red background, hands clasped on knees, head sunk in half profile on chest, sparse hair flying. Above all, it seemed to catch the inner melancholy of a brilliant man of many—perhaps too many—commitments. Lord Goodman has the second canvas: the remaining three Graham destroyed.

After a gap of two years, he returned to the very rich, in the form of Pierre Schlumberger, the French geophysicist, whose father and uncle had made a fortune from oil-drilling equipment. They had been introduced by Rory Cameron, who had sold his Clos Fiorentina at Cap Ferrat to Madame Schlumberger. Since Schlumberger was not really the type of subject Graham would normally have agreed to paint, he indicated to Cameron over dinner in Monte Carlo that the price would have to be high (it was £22,000). Schlumberger, a quiet man, emerged smiling and holding a cigar in Graham's elegantly executed portrait, which was completed in March 1976 and was hung in the sitter's Paris home.

Lord Iliffe, although no pauper as the grandson of the founder of the largest trade and technical publishing house in Britain, was a friend and neighbour; he and his French wife had a house in old Roquebrune. 'My reaction when we started off was that I was a most difficult subject: my mother used to say I had no likeness,' he recalled modestly.[6] 'I couldn't imagine what a portrait could possibly be like.' When he saw the result, he thought Graham had been very kind—and also very reasonable, charging only £5000, partly because he felt indebted over Iliffe's purchase, through the Redfern, of the Coventry tapestry studies.

Iliffe believes that he helped to persuade Graham to do the self-portrait which he executed at the last minute, in May 1977, for the exhibition of his portraits which opened that June at the National Portrait Gallery in London. You really must do one, he told Graham, and promised to ring up periodically to ask if he was working on it. Graham complained that it was 'such a fag—you have to rig up mirrors and so on'; yet in the end he did not

one but two, the second in 1978, selling it to an Italian admirer, Gianni
Tinto, for a substantial sum.

For the same exhibition he also decided to do a new head of Charles Clore
'for his own satisfaction', as he told the National Portrait Gallery's Director,
Dr John Hayes. He felt that the first portrait had not been wholly successful,
but was perhaps not overwhelmingly surprised when Clore bought the
second that November for £8000.

A reproduction in the *Daily Telegraph* of Graham's self-portrait helped to
revive an old project. It had been suggested, when Graham finished Emery
Reves in 1966, that he should paint Reves's wife, Wendy, but Graham said
that he never tackled anyone so pretty. She must age first. In 1977, when
they offered to buy the self-portrait, they sent a picture of a hideously lined
old peasant women. 'This is how Wendy looks,' they wrote on the back.
'You really must paint her.'

Graham agreed that perhaps he could now try, and he and Kathleen went
to dinner at La Pausa. Wendy was wearing a strapless dress with a black and
white feather boa and a black beret. 'That's how I'm going to paint you,'
Graham said. 'But you're such a great colourist,' Wendy protested, and later
she laid out a selection of clothes for Graham to choose from. 'Nonetheless,
he painted me in the black and white boa,' she recalled, 'but instead of a
black beret, which was really rather chic, he painted me in a white beret,
which was less chic. It was all black and white and grey, except he put in lots
of little yellow lightning things around my head.'

The large canvas (fee: £14,500) was finished on 5 June 1978, just three
months after the first sitting. When they went to see it at Graham's studio,
he explained that the white beret gave her spirit more accurately and made
her brighter. 'I had been expecting to look like an old bag,' she said to
Graham. 'You have made me young.' Graham replied that he had painted
what he saw. When she commented on the size, he said gallantly: 'But you
are larger than life.' 'It just sparkles,' she commented. 'Yes,' he said, 'my
yellow touches.' Her only criticism was that because Kathleen had stood in
for her once or twice, he had taken a foot or so out of her body (Wendy was
much taller). To match the portrait's size, he planned a large study of Emery
standing in a doorway in a long overcoat, but he did not live long enough to
undertake it.

Only three days after Graham had finished Mrs Reves, David Ogilvy,
thirteenth Earl of Airlie and elder brother of Angus Ogilvy, arrived for
sittings with his wife and Alfred Hecht, at whose King's Road home they
had met several times over dinner. Probably in 1977 Graham had said on
such an occasion: 'If you would like to have your portrait done, I would be

happy to do it'—a rare initiative. Airlie said he felt flattered. 'I was conscious it might involve me in quite a large sum of money, which I wasn't mad keen to part with,' he recalled,[7] 'but he managed to brush that aside, no doubt in typical manner, and said he thought he could come to some happy conclusion.' A figure 'between £10,000 and £15,000' was eventually agreed.

It was very hot when they arrived on 8 June. At his wife's suggestion, Airlie had brought his kilt. Graham was delighted by the idea of a kilted subject, and Airlie was made to change into it. The sittings were very enjoyable. Graham showed a keen interest in Airlie's financial world (he was then chairman of the City merchant bank, Schroeder, Wagg). He also took a lot of photographs of Airlie walking ten or a dozen times up and down the iron stairs from studio to garden. 'I want to see how you walk up and down hill, how it goes, your position, what you do with your legs,' he explained.

One evening the Airlies asked Graham and Kathleen to dinner at the Hôtel de Paris in Monte Carlo, and waited for them in the corner of a huge bar room. The Sutherlands made the most stylish entry imaginable. 'She was dressed from head to foot in green: green stockings, green dress, green hat. He was all in white—I don't say a white tie—and with a cane. Everybody looked up. It was stage-managed. He had enormous charm, to both sexes, I think.'

In the first week of January 1980 Airlie heard that the portrait was finished and at Hecht's. He had no idea whether he would be shown standing, sitting or walking, and was not expecting to be immediately pleased. He was surprised first by the size—some 5 feet by 3 feet 6 inches—and found that Graham had shown him, most unusually, walking through a Sutherland-ish landscape (lots of green) in bright red kilt. The head had been given less prominence than usual but seemed 'rather good'. It struck Airlie as an unusual portrait, 'a sort of modern picture with rather an establishment kind of portrait in it. . . . the more one sees it, perhaps, the more one likes it. . . . one leg just isn't right, you notice it. . . . in a way, you know, one rather wished he had done just a head and shoulders.' The portrait, finely framed by Hecht, hangs on the staircase at Cortachy Castle, the Ogilvy seat in Angus.

In September 1979 Graham had finished a head-and-shoulders study of Milner Gray for the Society of Industrial Artists and Designers' London headquarters: Gray had been a founder member and president and Graham a member. By now rather bald and faintly Pickwickian in appearance, Gray arrived at the Villa Blanche for sittings in May 1979. The society had only £1000 available and expected only a sketch. Graham decided he deserved an oil, which they got for the same price.

Graham's penultimate sitter was Dorothy Hodgkin, fellow OM member and winner of the 1964 Nobel Prize for chemistry. With her husband Thomas, an expert on West Africa and Fellow of Balliol College, Oxford, she came for sittings in Kent in August 1979. The portrait was to be for the Royal Society, to which she had belonged since 1947. Graham completed only a sketch, which Kathleen gave her after his death.

The last portrait on which Graham started work was to be of Alfred Hecht, whose own image was at last to go into one of his gold-leafed frames. He arrived in Kent on 1 January 1980. Graham did some drawings but was never able to complete work on his old *copain*, who had so often helped him and Kathleen.

Honours, some more glittering than others, and exhibitions strewed Graham's last years. In July 1972 he followed Matisse, Dufy, Rouault, Villon, Braque, Picasso, Chagall and Dali as the guest of honour at the Menton Biennale, with a substantial retrospective of his post-war work. It was organized by a local painter and friend, Emile Marzé, to whom Graham had periodically shown his work, watching him closely for a reaction. 'One didn't really need to say anything,' Marzé recalled. 'He could tell.'[8]

In May that year Graham had been made an honorary member of the (privately endowed) American Academy and Institute of Arts and Letters, other new honorary members including Kenneth Clark, Louis Aragon and Rebecca West. In August the French government made him a Commandeur des Arts et des Lettres, the senior of three ranks of this specifically cultural order, though a far cry from the Légion d'Honneur.

In the USA, despite the American Academy honour, Graham's reputation had fallen disappointingly behind Bacon's. For all Alexandre Rosenberg's regard for Graham as artist and person, he was not considered to have been very active in pushing his interests or, indeed, in keeping his American prices up to European levels. In about 1972 Graham's arrangement with him lapsed, and it was understood that Marlborough Fine Art, which had opened with a splash in New York in 1963 as the Marlborough-Gerson Gallery, would henceforward represent him there. Although Graham kept to himself the Italian market, increasingly his biggest—thus saving himself the 50 per cent dealer's commission—his dealings with Marlborough were always very amicable. But he never managed to bring himself to the point of having another New York exhibition.

Between 1971 and mid-1973 Graham produced more than forty oils of almost exclusively Welsh inspiration. It was his estuarial phase. Although no works seem to have been actually duplicated, there was a good deal of overlap; the background of one picture would appear, substantially unaltered, in another.[9] Some two dozen were shown at Marlborough's newish gallery in Zurich in October 1972 and were then transferred, in March 1973, to its Bond Street premises, where the show virtually sold out on the opening evening. Even some critics were enthusiastic. The total effect was of 'an important artist at the top of his bent in a productive period', Nigel Gosling wrote in the *Observer*.[10] In the *Financial Times* Denys Sutton saw the radiance of Graham's palette as proof of his belief in life.

In May 1973 a second crop of recent oils was shown at the Galleria Bergamini in Milan, in which Ruggerini had a stake. He and Marzia gave a gigantic dinner party at their home in the Lombardy plain the day after the opening. Only fine château-bottled wines were served for several dozen guests. That exhibition too was an enormous success. Put together, with medium-sized oils fetching a good £10,000 each, these shows brought into Graham's Swiss company sums undreamed of during those hard years of teaching.

In this second Welsh phase Graham's imagery once again took on some richly erotic overtones, of which he was fully conscious. One pink, erect column of rock that he had sketched rather startled Greta Garbo when she called at the Villa Blanche with Cécile de Rothschild one September day, just after Graham, Kathleen and the Ruggerinis had returned from Venice.[11]

Speaking in his by now quite good French, Graham asked La Divine whether she would like to look at some sketch books. 'O, la la,' she said, when she came to the penile monolith. Graham peered over. 'Oh, madame, c'est un peu phallique,' he conceded apologetically, and explained that he was not guilty—the rock really looked like that and was that colour too. 'Mais je l'aime!' said Garbo. 'C'est fantastique.'[12] From then on the phrase 'un peu phallique' became something of a joke. Another was Graham's 'c'est une possibilité', used, for example, when being asked to paint some wholly uninspiring Italian industrialist. It meant that there was absolutely no chance of his ever doing it.

In May 1974—he was now 70—Graham became the first British painter to be awarded the annual Shakespeare Prize for outstanding achievement by a British citizen in the arts. The money—£4200, plus a scholarship of £1000 for study in West Germany by a student of the winner's choice— came from the president of the FVS Foundation in Hamburg, Dr Alfred Toepfer, a grain importer and shipowner. The jury was Anglo-German. Graham chose a Maidstone School of Art student, Robert Ward, as his beneficiary.

From Graham Sutherland, O.M.
La Villa Blanche
Route de Castellar
Menton AM
TÈL. 35·81·19

14·V·73.

Dearest Marzia and P.P.

Your party for us was <u>wonderful</u>
— thank you!

M = marvellous matchless miraculous
A = acme of perfection
R = refined — beautifully reticent
Z = full of ZIZZ!
I = invigorating idolisable (you both)
A = assemblage (wonderful)

P = personal thought fulness
I = Individual ('original) emulate
E = exquisite (impossible to emulate)
R = rejuvenating
P = precious (occasion for us)
A = adorable (thought)
O = out pouring of Kindness
L = loveable (full of things)
O = out of this world.
R = rarefaction (finesse)
U = ultra (ultime)
G = grand style & GENEROSITY
G = gratitude (ours)
E = elegant (such elegance!)
R = Ritornello (what a refrain!)
I = Incommensurable
N = melodic "NUTS about you"!
I = Inborn thought ful ness.

P.T.O

And this is to say how very much we
appreciated & enjoyed it all & how
grateful we are for all you have both
done over the past months of preparation.

* I must apologise, I believe that at the
end of dinner I had to speak to G.
Lloyd. It was arranged the evening
before that he should have a word with
Franco & I had to prompt G. about
my wishes. It was only intended to be
a talk of a few minutes. But I was
punished for my bad manners in being
made to feel like a dog being called to
heel!!! No doubt you & K. were
protecting me I am sure — as I
suffer from;

G = gout
R = rheumatism
A = acne
H = hysteria
A = anaemia
M = morbid fears
S = renal calculus
U = ulcerated leg
T = trembling.
H = halitosis
E = enteroptosis
R = rictus
L = liver (bad)

From Graham Sutherland, O.M.
La Villa Blanche
Route de Castellar
Menton AM
TÈL. 35·81·19

A = alcoholism
N = tinnitus aurium
D = debility (general)
   & need protection!

Finally :— all the little touches which
you contrived did not escape un-noticed
For so many things it is impossible to
find the real words by which to say
'thank you' — but I expect you know
the feelings in our hearts.

Your devoted
Graham

Letter from Graham to Pier Paolo
and Marzia Ruggerini, dated 14 May 1973

The ceremony, held in Hamburg on 30 May 1974, called for a major speech, less easy perhaps for Graham than for some previous winners, like Peter Brook, Paul Scofield, Harold Pinter and Graham Greene. He spent several days writing it on Picton beach and called it 'The Nature of Poetry and Some Affinities'. Imagery which condensed was at the root of all poetry and painting, he told his audience; it created a new world out of the same world. And he quoted a favourite image from Aeschylus, 'Dust is mud's thirsty sister', which he found precise, economical and stirring to the senses. He dwelt on his love, since student days, of German art: first Dürer, then Altdorfer, Baldung, the mysterious Cranach and the supreme Grünewald, who had continued to astonish and transport him. And Bach, to whose tightly knit musical architecture he owed more than he could realize, was his favourite composer.

There followed a *laudatio* for Graham from Douglas Cooper, replete with quotations from Schiller, Goethe and Hebbel and some typically felicitous touches: Graham's pictorial metaphors were, he said, like bridges helping our imagination to move between the different realms of the human, the organic and the mechanical.

No one could analyse and interpret Graham's work with the same penetrating clarity as Cooper. His catalogue introductions were notable for their insight, crispness and elegance. For more than twenty-five years Graham and Kathleen had enjoyed his stimulating (if sometimes exhausting) company, benefited from his gallery, museum and social contacts and his vast knowledge, listened—too closely sometimes—to his advice, and reaped the mixed harvest of his protagonism.

Hamburg turned out to be his last fling as Graham's champion. The great breach came seven months later. Its origins went back to a waspish article by Patrick Thévenon, published in the 9 September 1974 issue of the French magazine *L'Express*, entitled 'Le Choix Insolent de Douglas Cooper'. Which paintings of the first half of this century would be left in 150 years' time? One man thinks he knows, wrote Thévenon: Douglas Cooper. His list was so surprising and so 'insolent' that an exhibition was to be made of it at the Musée des Arts Décoratifs in Paris. Of the fifty-four paintings chosen, ten were to be by Picasso, eight by Matisse, six each by Braque, Gris, Léger and others. Critics would compile their own lists of those omitted, Thévenon said, and would criticize some choices which were not obvious, like Beckmann, Robert Delaunay, Boccioni, Schiele, 'and, above all, the Englishman Sutherland'.

Eventually this article percolated through to Graham and Kathleen. Their French being imperfect, and Thévenon's not pellucid, they were struck by the juxtaposition of the word *omis* ('omitted') and the name of Sutherland. Kathleen, who habitually did most of Graham's less agreeable tasks for him, not always very delicately, sprang to Graham's defence with a letter to Cooper.[13] It was her sorrow, she said, that he was excluding Graham from the exhibition, though Graham did not care, as he was used to not having a real supporter. Most of the press cuttings she had seen said that he, Cooper, was an arrogant snob for having left out this one and that one, and *surtout Sutherland*, and so on, and she signed off with love from an 'outraged wife'.

Cooper replied to this rash and not altogether coherent outpouring with a long and withering diatribe, which he circulated to at least one of Graham's close friends.[14] She had, he wrote, no accurate information about his exhibition 'Masterpieces by European Artists 1900–1950' but had had plenty of chances to ask about it. She had decided he could be written off as a snob and not a real supporter, and had obviously decided to break a long and intimate friendship. She should have her way. To show how she could harm her husband professionally, he would withdraw the painting by Graham that he had planned to include in the exhibition (which, in fact, never took place).

A lull followed. There was an awkward confrontation at a grand lunch *chez* Plesch for the Rainiers—Princess Grace admired Graham and invited him and Kathleen occasionally to the palace—in early March 1975. Cooper simply nodded at them. Hostilities were resumed later.

It was all very sad. Cooper decided to sell thirty-seven paintings, drawings and lithographs by Graham, and they were exhibited at the Redfern Gallery in September 1976. The Redfern had consulted Graham, who did not seem upset, and the affectionate inscriptions on many of them did not put off buyers.

Graham later admitted that the cause of the row did not reflect much credit either on him or on Kathleen, or on their command of French. 'Eventually we wrote him a letter of apology, and the nearest we ever got to a *rapprochement* was a letter from him saying that it was a step in the right direction,' he recalled.[15] Somewhat later, Wendy Reves had the idea of trying to effect a reconciliation. Cooper did not seem opposed to it, and a date was fixed for a dinner. Then Graham rang to say that it was sweet of her to think of it, but Douglas had always wanted to guide and steer him. He felt he now knew what he wanted to do, and wanted to do it alone. He did, however, seem to regret the personal side, she recalled.

Had Cooper decided that he had overestimated Graham's work, and had he used Kathleen's letter as a pretext? In a letter to *The Times* of 28

February 1980, prompted by a tribute to Graham by myself which referred to his own role, Cooper said that for a 'short period' before 1970 he had thought he saw in Graham Sutherland a gifted painter and a creative artist who was misunderstood and inadequately appreciated. He had attempted, through a few exhibitions and essays, to explain what he understood to be Sutherland's special value. Subsequently, Sutherland's work had become progressively weaker and more repetitive, and he had lost interest in it. He had never believed or claimed that Graham Sutherland was, in the historical perspective, an artist of major stature, he said.

The latter claim may be literally true, though as recently as 1974, in his Hamburg *laudatio*, Cooper had described Graham as 'the only major artist who has emerged in Great Britain since the death of that nowadays much overvalued Turner', adding that he was 'internationally recognized as a significant 20th-century artist' and the only British artist to have contributed to enhancing and enriching the European tradition. Cooper was not a careless man with dates, and it was perhaps significant that in his *Times* letter he marked 1970 as the end of his 'short period'—still more than twenty years—of appreciation. Possibly the second Welsh period, from 1968 onwards, was too 'English' for his taste. He had never fully shared in the general enthusiasm for the first one.

With Cooper's friendship, as with the landscape of Pembrokeshire, there had always been the feeling of being 'on the brink of some drama'. Like the Crucifixion theme, it had an element of the 'precarious balanced moment, the hair's breadth between black and white', of the deep blue sky which could almost be, and now definitely was, black. Perhaps that had been part of its attraction.

Meanwhile, in 1973, Nancy Mitford and Picasso had died. Picasso had continued to take an interest in Graham's work, and they had met periodically through Cooper. In 1961 he had given a tea party for Graham's fifty-eighth birthday, on 24 August, at Mougins. Among other friends, Patrick Plunket and Hans Juda died in 1975, Jane Clark in 1976.

The cycle of life went on. The Italian connection was strengthened by the addition of a new and wealthy admirer, a Turin machine-tool manufacturer called Gianni Tinto. They met in July 1975, through a Genoese dealer called Rinaldo Rotta, over lunch at La Mortola, on the Italian side of the border, near Menton. Thereafter Tinto and his attractive wife, Rosanna, came periodically to the Villa Blanche. He spoke no English or French but had a consuming desire to fill his apartment with Graham's paintings, preferably very large, and with his gouaches. Altogether he collected some fifteen oils and twenty-five gouaches,[16] including some of the most striking of the last works. Sometimes—about a dozen times in all—he made available to Graham a plane in which he had a share for quick hops to Wales, Rome or Venice. Graham thanked him with gouaches, worth some £2000 each by then.

Italian critics were taking over in the book field too. First came Francesco Arcangeli, former director of the museum of modern art in Bologna, with a very sympathetic critical study of Graham's work, beautifully produced by Fratelli Fabbri in 1973. Arcangeli died soon afterwards, and an English version came out in New York in 1975. With 230 illustrations, including 117 in superb colour, it is an indispensable volume for Sutherland admirers, though unfortunately the language of Italian art criticism is not easily rendered into English.

Then there was Roberto Tassi, a learned and delightful man who typified what Graham considered to be the great virtue of Italian writers on art: they really tried to understand what he was doing, and if they did not like it, they did not feel it worthwhile to express their lack of sympathy. He contributed a long introduction to a comprehensive survey of Graham's graphic work published in 1978, the quality of reproduction of which, unfortunately, was well below that of Felix Man's authoritative earlier study. Tassi also introduced a selection of Graham's war drawings, first published in 1979, which helped them to be recognized as one of his most moving achievements. Graham was rather less happy about another Italian study published in 1979 by Roberto Sanesi, but it did include reproductions of some recent work.[17]

The last major component of the Italian connection was a husband-and-wife team of master printers: Valter and Eleonora Rossi, with whom Graham first established a working relationship in 1973, visiting their Rome workshop for the first time in 1974. They interested Graham in the aquatint process, to which they had brought various technical refinements which made it possible to achieve more subtle tonal gradations than before. It was a happy but exceedingly demanding return to Graham's first love. Aquatint is a form of etching enriched with a watercolour effect. To achieve this, either in black and white or in colour, the etched copper plate is heated, then placed in a special revolvable box (with which Graham was equipped) full of fine resin particles. These, when agitated, are fused to the plate by heat, forming an 'acid-resist', which leaves tiny holes between each particle through which the acid bites.

Guided by the Rossis, who had great charm, he was to use the process to brilliant effect in his two series of aquatints, the 'Bees' of 1977 and the Apollinaire bestiary of 1979; but he started the partnership with three black and white aquatints, of which *Man Smoking* is the most striking. Meanwhile he continued to use Mourlot of Paris and Teodorani of Milan for lithographs, the latter handling a suite of six Welsh landscape studies called *La Foresta, Il Fiume, La Roccia (The Forest, the River, the Rock)*, shown at the Galleria Bergamini in Milan in 1972.

In that year Graham had established a printing room at the Villa Blanche, at first under the new studio, then in a small cottage within the grounds. There he installed his old etching press from student days, a modern electric press and an old hand press, the last two for lithographs. These were invaluable for experiments and trial proofs, but the final editions were always printed professionally.

By now Graham was the semi-exiled elder statesman of British painting (though the more hermit-like Ben Nicholson might have disputed the title). Although, with exceptions, the British critics did not share the Italians' enthusiasm for his work, there were signs of an impending reassessment. William Packer of the *Financial Times*, for example, felt that while Graham's professional reputation had ebbed inexorably to the present 'low point of general indifference', and while he had probably never been as good as popular opinion still supposed him to be, yet he did not deserve total critical neglect.[18] He was reviewing a show at Marlborough in London of Graham's sketchbook drawings and related paintings in June 1974, which went on to Bergamini in Milan that October. A fine facsimile sketchbook was also available in a limited edition.

At the other pole was the *Daily Telegraph*'s Terence Mullaly. 'Graham Sutherland's reputation stands as high as that of any other living artist,' he wrote in his declamatory style on 12 April 1975, à propos a retrospective selling exhibition of his work at the Lefevre Gallery in Bruton Street. The very fine *Lane Opening*, which Michael Balcon had bought in 1945 at the same gallery for £105, was in this show; its asking price was now £25,000, an indication of how dramatically Graham's prices had increased with Italian patronage. In this instance, since artists do not benefit from the resale of their work, he saw not a penny of the profit. At the same time, Colnaghi's of Old Bond Street showed a selection of his early etchings which they had rounded up, now fetching up to £240 each.

Throughout his life Graham only very rarely travelled anywhere without Kathleen. It was on one such rare occasion that she had a terrible accident, though it could have happened as easily had he been at home. He had left Menton for Wales on 3 May 1976 to see how the Picton Gallery, due to open in six weeks, was shaping. Two days later Kathleen was strolling in the garden after a convivial lunch with a female friend. Coming up over a small bridge towards the house, alone, she stumbled slightly. She put out her left hand to grip an ivy-covered rail but clutched only ivy and fell some 15 feet on to a spiked gate below the bridge. One spike impaled her armpit; another went into the top of her chest, just below her neck.

Seen with clinical detachment, it was a case of life imitating art. Graham had called several of his paintings of the 1950s *Suspended Form, Hanging Form* or *Poised Form*. Mercifully unconscious, Kathleen hung there for several minutes until spotted by Louis Judice, the smallholder who had refused to sell out and lived near Graham's graphics studio. He raised the alarm. Nenette Ferrari came rushing out of the house, and they lifted her off. Had she not been impaled, she might have broken her neck or her skull on the stone steps by the gate.

Madame Ferrari rushed her to hospital. The neck wound was a millimetre from Kathleen's vocal chords, the doctor said. Nenette contacted Graham in Wales, playing down the seriousness of the accident to avoid alarming him, and then, on Graham's urging, moved Kathleen to the best available clinic.

Since the police arrived to ask what had happened, the accident reached the press and was widely reported in Britain the following day. Graham immediately hired a private plane for £1200. 'When he came in and saw her, his eyes filled with tears,' Madame Ferrari recalled.[19] 'It was as if he had seen the Holy Virgin.' The spike which had entered the armpit had touched the pleura, and the wound had to be reopened. Madame Ferrari spent fourteen nights beside Kathleen—Graham insisted on buying her a softer mattress—and Kathleen returned to the Villa Blanche on 19 May. 'It seems I was fated to survive,' she said later. Madame Ferrari told her once: 'Vous êtes grande comme trois pommes, mais vous avez la force d'un lion.' There were no serious after-effects, once an initial tendency to choke on food had been overcome.

Kathleen's life in France was not as enviable as it might seem. There had been, it is true, some glamorous social life among the very rich, which she enjoyed more than Graham: he, half-fascinated, half-repelled and perhaps conscious of the need for patrons, would keep more of himself back. But basically hers was rather a lonely life. Graham worked largely office hours in his studio, and he had a siesta and took a walk after lunch. She could not drive; her French was not good enough for intimate conversation; and Graham preferred her to be on hand. He liked to ask her view of his work and became jealous if she went off with friends, male or female—he saw lesbians everywhere. So Kathleen was, in a sense, a cherished prisoner, sacrificing a great deal to sustain the man she had loved so long. He was very conscious of this, though like most creative people he had his black moods.

He devoted a good deal of the second half of 1976 to work on the 'Bees', and also helped John Hayes with preparations for a show at the National Portrait Gallery the following June of a selection of his portraits. It had first been mooted by Hayes's predecessor, Dr Roy Strong, and Cooper was to have catalogued it. When Strong moved to the Victoria and Albert Museum as Director, Hayes—a Sutherland enthusiast—happily took it over.

He was a gentle, rather shy man, well versed in the history of British landscape and portrait painting, whom Graham had backed to write an up-to-date study of his work which Phaidon wanted to publish (and did, in 1980, after Graham's death and with a text he had approved). Graham at first favoured a small show at the gallery, but Hayes managed to persuade him to expand its scope. Eventually it ran to 101 items, including two dozen finished portraits, studies and 'comparative' works like thorn heads, standing forms, tin miners and so on. Graham wanted neither Daisy Fellowes (too 'pretty') nor Lord Beaverbrook included: perhaps he feared the critics would again attack the composition of the latter. Like the missing Churchill, the Beaver was represented by sketches.

Hayes had an almost Italian certitude about Graham's stature: 'Graham Sutherland stands in the front rank of the great British portrait painters of all time,' he said in his catalogue preface; and the hagiographic tone was maintained with a series of references to Old Masters from Bellini to Ingres and Goya, intended mainly to indicate possible influences. When the show opened on 24 June 1977, the critics were less respectful.

'His drawing can be very bad,' wrote Packer on 30 June, and he instanced the feet of Maugham and Rayne and the hands of Maugham, Rubinstein, Plesch and several others. He concluded by wondering whether the 'quilted atmosphere of silence, as when it snows', to which Graham had alluded in a catalogue interview with Hayes, might have less to do with personalities than with 'the natural surprise, which we share in these galleries, of someone confronted, from the hand of an important and respected artist, by so much bad painting'. Some other critics, like John Spurling (*New Statesman*) and John McEwen (*Spectator*), were also severe, though Bryan Robertson (later, in the *Spectator*) was generally enthusiastic.

The 'Bees' provided Graham with a happy blend of the general and the specific. Their lifecycle had been suggested to him in 1975 as the theme of a suite of etchings by Bernhard Baer, a director of the Ganymed Press. Baer supported his idea with engravings by the seventeenth-century Dutch naturalist Swammerdam and some modern photographs.[20] Graham was not enthusiastic at first. Although bees were interesting in a literary way, he did not find them as appealing as many other insects as forms or objects.[21]

Perhaps it was because the bees were *not* visually exciting that the series was so successful. Rather than underline an exoticism of appearance, Graham had to draw out the inherent poetry in the bee's strange life, overcoming the relative ordinariness of its appearance.

He began drawings in August 1976, catching a few bees in the Menton garden and dissecting them. Three weeks in Venice in September were interspersed with earth tremors. One day he noticed that the Cipriani's barman, Elso Giacomello, looked very downcast. What was wrong? Graham asked. Giacomello replied that his son's house, into which he had put all his own life savings, had just been levelled in the Friuli earthquake. The thought preyed on Graham's mind. On returning to Menton, he did a gouache which he asked Ruggerini to sell and to send the proceeds (some £2000–£3000) to Giacomello, whose letter of thanks touched him deeply.

The Rossis spent several weeks staying in a hotel in Menton, coming daily to Graham's print studio to work with him on the plates. It was a very tricky process, and the costs were to be very high. In all, he did fourteen plates showing the bee's life from egg, larva, pupa and hatching, through courting of the queen to the dance, nesting and fighting. The edition of 100 of each plate was divided up for sale between the two small galleries that the Rossis had in Rome and Milan, the Galleria Bergamini in Milan, and the Marlborough in London, where the show opened on 21 June 1977, just before the portrait exhibition. Milan and Rome followed in the autumn. Commercially, the 'Bees' were an immense success, the more lyrical plates selling out very quickly. The London critics were, as usual, divided: the bees were 'for the birds', according to the *Spectator*'s McEwen, and 'right up Sutherland's track', in the view of Spurling in the *New Statesman*, for example.[22]

Of greater import than the London critics' views was the transmission, on 2 October 1977, of a beautifully wrought film on Graham's work, written and directed by John Ormond of BBC Wales. Ormond, twenty years younger than Graham and an accomplished poet, had been a good friend of Josef Herman and Ceri Richards, among other painters. He combined enthusiasm and a poet's intuition with a gentle, cherubic appearance, and he and Graham understood each other immediately. Indeed, Graham came to feel that Ormond had as good a grasp of what he was trying to do as anyone in Britain, and before the artist's death a friendship of great warmth had been established. The film, linked to the Pembrokeshire gallery, found Graham at his most persuasive, and fine camerawork avoided the glib cutting from landscape to related painting which can be so irritating in art films. It must have won many converts.

At 74, Graham was now slightly bowed by the years and using a stick to offset his arthritic knee. He suffered from varicose veins, probably induced by long periods of standing up to paint, and sometimes from sciatica. But those grey eyes were alert as ever as they probed a slightly hostile universe over the gold-rimmed half-spectacles. In this last decade he allowed himself and Kathleen a few luxuries—like staying, en route for Wales, at the Connaught Hotel in London, a cosily expensive place with some of the best food in Britain; the occasional Balenciaga dress for Kathleen; a silk shirt or two from Charvet's; some Gucci shoes; and, in France, special meals (when the Ruggerinis came, for example) cooked by Abel, who had been chef to the Duchess of Windsor and was Madame Ferrari's brother-in-law. It was all done with a great sense of style. Proud, prickly and sensitive on many issues, he remained at heart a modest, in some ways even a humble man, and the charm was never dimmed.

Although still far from ancient, he now found himself *doyen* of the members of the Order of Merit. As such, he was placed on the Queen's right when she gave a luncheon for members and their wives at Buckingham Palace, on 17 November 1977, to celebrate the order's seventy-fifth anniversary. Kathleen sat between Lord Mountbatten and Lord Penney, the physicist. Mountbatten expressed admiration for Graham's portraits of Maugham and Schlumberger, and Harold Macmillan recalled Graham's grandfather, James Foster, at the family publishing house. Also present, down the table, were Kenneth Clark and Henry Moore. Graham later sent the Queen a boxed set of the 'Bees'.

It was twelve years since Graham's most famous sitter and fellow OM, Winston Churchill, had died, and on 12 December 1977 Lady Spencer-Churchill, as his widow had become, joined him, quite suddenly, aged 92. When Graham and Kathleen had Christmas lunch with Alfred Hecht a fortnight later, they must have wondered whether there would now be any news of his portrait's fate. The answer awaited when they arrived at the Lord Nelson Hotel on 28 December: a letter from Mary Soames, dated 20 December, informed Graham, with some tact, that the portrait was 'no longer in existence'.

As he knew, she wrote, both her parents had unfortunately deeply disliked it. It was never hung but was stored at Chartwell. At some time in 1955-6, her mother had given instructions for it to be destroyed. Shortly after her father's death in 1965, her mother had told her and her husband about this decision, saying that she had been greatly distressed to see how much it had preyed on Churchill's mind and she had promised him that it would never see the light of day. Mary Soames was sorry to be the bearer of such unpalatable tidings, 'although perhaps you may have already guessed what happened', but she wanted him to know the true story before it became public knowledge. The very small number of people who had known the picture's fate had agreed that the facts should not be revealed in her mother's lifetime. To protect her mother from controversy and criticism, they had been forced from time to time to be 'less than candid' when questioned about it.

Graham replied on New Year's Day 1978.

> You are right in thinking that I may have guessed what happened, and I was prepared for it, since during the sittings, he (your father) had told me of an occasion when your mother, disliking a portrait by Walter Sickert, had, as he put it, 'put her foot through it'. . . . My own feelings about the affair are not important. So much time has passed since I delivered the work that the whole undignified affair is for me past history.
>
> Nonetheless — some others may well feel differently [and he again expressed his view that the painting was supposed to revert to the House of Commons]. Your mother therefore had no right to destroy something which was not in fact her property: of course I am sure she did not know of the committee's plans.
>
> It can be argued, however, that for whatever reason the portrait was caused to be destroyed, it was an act of vandalism perhaps not without precedent, but rare in history, except in war time.

The whole thing had been a sorry story, Graham wrote: he had had to paint her father when he was being forced out by his own party *and* the Labour Party, and probably, from the outset, had been suspected of being an instrument of his enemies in the denigration of Churchill's image.

> I need hardly say that I had far too much respect and affection for him to lend myself in such a manner.
>
> To me your father was invariably kind and civilized — and with these qualities I should like to join yourself and your husband who, almost alone, were sympathetically understanding of the difficulties.

It was a dignified letter, though on one point Graham seems to have overstated his case: as we have seen, recollections differed about whether it was in any way firmly agreed that the portrait should revert to the Houses of Parliament on Sir Winston's death. There the matter rested until 11 January 1978, when the portrait's destruction was announced to a flabbergasted and fascinated world by Lady Spencer-Churchill's executors in a three-paragraph statement summarizing the facts of Mary Soames's letter to Graham.

Practically every newspaper, television and radio station in Britain must have telephoned Graham that day at the Lord Nelson. Its manager, Margaret White, recalled: 'You couldn't think Milford Haven could attract so much news. There were journalists waiting in the hall, and they even used to ask which was his room.'

Pier Paolo and Marzia Ruggerini were in Wales with Graham and Kathleen. 'I was amazed that his mood was just the same,' Ruggerini said.

He was only put out by the fact that he had to go and answer the telephone every five minutes. That evening, over dinner, I said to him: 'Now Graham, what did you *really* think when you heard?' He said: 'Pier Paolo, Lady Churchill burned the portrait. She didn't like it. *C'est un acte de vandalisme.* But it doesn't affect me.'

He felt no rancour and was not distressed, he told reporters. Asked how much it might now have been worth, he thought more than £100,000.[23]

In the intervening years there had not only been continued press speculation about the portrait's whereabouts and condition but also several requests to borrow it for exhibitions: from the Royal Academy, for example, in 1956, for its Winter Exhibition of British portraits; and in 1966 from Graham himself, for the German retrospectives of 1967. Now that its fate was known, there was no shortage of views about Lady Spencer-Churchill's action. *The Times* expressed a common opinion in a leading article of 13 January: 'A portrait of the greatest Englishman of his time by an artist who is arguably the best living English portraitist is an object of outstanding historical importance,' it said, lamenting the loss. But there were many who felt that personal freedom included the right to destroy portraits which pained loved ones, and the Churchill family received many letters of support.[24]

Mary Soames recalled that she and her husband had been 'aghast' when they were told of the portrait's destruction. 'It was very embarrassing. It had been the joint gift of the Houses of Parliament. People had subscribed to it. I don't think she thought of that aspect of it at all, which is quite curious, because she was a sensitive woman.' Mary Soames was annoyed when, almost a year later, Graham suggested on television that perhaps the portrait still existed: 'I don't even know that it's destroyed,' he said.[25] 'Nobody knows. I mean, it may well not be.' The comment implied that she and her fellow executors had told a lie and had been parties to defrauding the Inland Revenue of capital transfer tax, she felt, and she sent Graham a discreet warning not to repeat it. Such suspicions would have been banished by a clear statement of how the dark deed had been done. Mary Soames knew but felt that details were not relevant. Who did it was as uninteresting as who wielded the axe that executed Mary Queen of Scots, she believed.

Graham toyed briefly with the idea of painting the portrait again from the original studies, including those in the Beaverbrook collection. He was approached by 'a number of people', he said, to do so.[26] But he decided that it might look mean; there might be copyright problems; and it might not work. Certainly he could have asked £100,000 for such a recreation. Maybe, he mused, he should never have attempted the portrait: one could not compete with the media, which had made the faces of the famous so familiar and had given them an image to lose. He recalled nostalgically the frankness with which Velasquez and Goya had painted royalty, at a time when the Spanish court was more or less immured.

With Adenauer it had all been so different—and continued to be. On 4 September 1978 Graham flew to Bonn for the exhibition entitled 'Sutherland Paints Adenauer' mounted at the Adenauer Foundation at St Augustin, just outside the federal capital. It showed the main portrait and related works and was beautifully hung and catalogued. The genial West German President, Walter Scheel, was there and leading Christian Democrats. They were all charming to Graham; there were speeches and a teutonically thorough lecture on the history of political portraits. Press coverage was heavy, and Graham was hailed as the most significant living British painter.

There had been just a few newspaper and radio salutes at home to Graham's seventy-fifth birthday on 24 August 1978. (Henry Moore had celebrated his eightieth three weeks earlier with an exhibition of his drawings at the Tate and of his sculpture in Kensington Gardens, and the market for such tributes—which Graham felt his old friend richly deserved—had been saturated.) Although medical examinations revealed nothing wrong, he made arrangements with Kathleen and the Ruggerinis earlier that year to be buried in consecrated ground, in the cemetery of the twelfth-century church at St Ishmael's, in Pembrokeshire. A place of strange stillness, it lay a few hundred yards from the walled forest at Monk Haven which features in many of his last works.

These canvases, mainly very large and often done for Gianni Tinto in Turin, were invaded by a deep melancholy (as opposed to *Angst*). In one, *The Thicket*, he showed himself sketching: a small, hunched figure, grey of face, clothed in priestly black, against a background of writhing, menacing vegetation. Nature rarely wore a benign face in his work. Here it threatens to burst through the symmetry of the wall to claim its own. In *Path Through Wood*, his last major canvas, finished in April 1979, Graham reverted to an old theme, but it is the same exit-less thicket. This time the foreground is empty, and the threatening forms have moved dangerously close, rearing up as if to celebrate their victory, only just contained by a strange series of concentric circles.

And yet in 1978 and early 1979 Graham was also engaged on his relatively sunny and lyrical sequence of seventeen aquatints inspired by some charming, brief poems by Apollinaire, called (confusingly) *Le Bestiaire, ou Cortège d'Orphée*. Unlike the 1968 Bestiary, this was no gathering together of his more Gothic animal images but contained much that was new and fresh: an inverted tortoise strung like a lyre; a mouse chewing a plank, symbolizing time; three ibises—their legs, too, gave him difficulties—flying over the Nile. The pattern of co-operation with the Rossis was much the same as it had been for the 'Bees'. The sequence of private views in Rome, Milan and London in November 1979 put a terrible strain on his dwindling powers of endurance, but he hated to say no to friends. In each city there was a proportion of the total of 1568 original prints to sign. Once again, it was a considerable commercial success.

Even by his standards, it was a busy and peripatetic last year. Two months, between mid-April and mid-June, at the Villa Blanche represented the longest spell in one place. There were two other important openings: in March, that of the main works from the Picton Gallery at Marlborough Fine Art in London, and in Milan in June, under the auspices of the British Council, that of 127 of Graham's war drawings. This went on to Florence and was in Genoa when Graham died. By then arrangements had been made for Pier Paolo Ruggerini to buy those which Graham had retained—273 in all, some of them very small and many of them included in the exhibition.

In July, Graham had a final contact with the royal family when he received his third honorary degree: Oxford in 1962, Leicester in 1965, and now Cardiff, with Prince Charles, the University of Wales's Chancellor, presiding. The Prince of Wales had not, it seems, done his homework well enough, and asked Graham whether he did any work apart from portraits.

Although the October meeting of the trustees of the Graham Sutherland Gallery had brought a large measure of agreement on delicate issues, Graham continued to worry about its future. In the autumn he began to lose weight, eating less and less. He looked dreadfully tired at the 'Apollinaire' opening at Marlborough Fine Art on 20 November. Yet three days later he seemed much more his usual, often amusing self.

He returned to France with Kathleen on 24 November, in some pain after stubbing a toe badly on a door-stopper at the Connaught Hotel. The Ruggerinis arrived laden with gifts—caviar, a camera, a silver vase—at the

Villa Blanche on 22 December. He worked on the Airlie portrait. He and Kathleen lunched on Christmas Day at the Hotel de Paris with its manager, Fred Lauby, and others, including Alan Searle.

Three days later they went off to Kent. Graham sketched Hecht and still seemed fairly fit. In early January they made the pilgrimage to the Lord Nelson in Milford Haven. It was too cold to draw outside, and his arthritic knee prevented him from walking fast enough to keep warm. The Sulivans invited him and Kathleen to a reconciliation dinner with the Hanning Philipps. 'My heart leans out to you in gratitude for the marvellous way you arranged everything last night,' Graham wrote to them afterwards. 'We are humbly grateful and send deep love to you both and thanks.'

Saying goodbye that evening, Betty Sulivan realized that she and Jack would not see him again. Probably Graham sensed this too, at least with part of his mind. Yet on 24 January he had written to Harold Macmillan to discuss possible arrangements for sittings for a portrait for Oxford University to mark his twenty years as Chancellor. Macmillan himself had suggested Graham, believing him to be the most distinguished British painter then alive.[27] Graham favoured sittings in June, in Kent. He had also agreed in December to paint Sir Norman Reid, the outgoing Director of the Tate, for the Gallery's trustees. The commission was a symbolic healing of the old wound, though he had always had a high regard for Reid.

Graham was beginning to show all the symptoms of an enlarged liver. Bill George, a local doctor in Milford Haven who had become a friend, made arrangements for him to see the leading liver specialist, Professor Dame Sheila Sherlock, at the Royal Free Hospital in Hampstead. Graham was driven there in his Jaguar on 6 February. When a biopsy was performed on his liver, it was found to be enormously enlarged and tumorous. Organic growth, the relentless force of nature which had fascinated him all his life, finally killed him, after considerable pain, at 6.30 p.m. on 17 February 1980.

The critics, so often grudging to Graham in his lifetime, were more generous in death—though the obituaries were not, in general, written by those who had carped and patronized for so long. *The Times* spoke of his 'special eminence' among modern British artists, the *Guardian* of his 'special, if somewhat enigmatic position in British and European painting'. Anthony Curtis, in the *Financial Times*, said that his death robbed twentieth-century British painting of its 'greatest, most steadily productive genius'. The *Observer*'s Nigel Gosling saluted his translation of *Angst* into pigment 'in a language which will surely be understood for years to come'. Much of the popular and provincial press said he was 'regarded by many as the greatest British painter since Turner', an encomium probably attributable to the Press Association's obituary.

On 19 January Graham had asked to be buried in the beautiful churchyard at Trottiscliffe rather than at St Ishmael's in Wales, and the interment took place after a very private funeral service at a Roman Catholic seminary in West Malling.

When he died, plans were well in hand for a major restropective—the biggest ever held—of his work at the Tate Gallery in 1982. He had always hoped that it would be found to have 'unity in diversity' and was perhaps comforted to know that a proper assessment might at last be possible. Throughout his life he worried too much. In museums throughout the world, in thousands of homes and in untold minds his work lives on: at its best so intense, lyrical and passionate in its probing of the secrets of nature, and vibrant in its assertion of the energy of matter.

Listening to John Ormond's tribute, at a thanksgiving mass at Westminster Cathedral on 29 May 1980, how many landscapes flickered through the memory. As Kenneth Clark—who was there, representing the Queen—had seen so early on, Graham had changed the way we look at certain things. His life was not without its sorrows and disappointments, but he had the joy of both creating and revealing a new world of beauty.

Notes

All interviews are by the author unless otherwise indicated
GS = Graham Sutherland, KS = Kathleen Sutherland

Chapter 1 Surrey and Derby, 1903–21 (pages 19 to 42)

1 Interview with Michael Standing, Trottiscliffe, November 1980.
2 Information and evidence about GS's Derby antecedents from Mrs V. Langworthy, Derby Central Librarian; letters to the author dated 16 December 1980 and 8 January 1981.
3 Unless otherwise indicated, quotations from GS in this chapter are from two taped interviews, conducted on 17 July 1979 in Milford Haven and on 20 August 1979 at Trottiscliffe.
4 Letter to the author from the Countess of Sutherland, received January 1981.
5 Interviews with Dr Humphrey Sutherland, GS's brother, at Cumnor, near Oxford, 25 July 1979 and 13 August 1980.
6 Interview with GS's first cousin Aubrey Smith, Claygate, Surrey, December 1980.
7 Letter to the author from Rosemary Ainetti, personal secretary to Harold Macmillan, dated 14 November 1980.
8 Interview with GS's sister, Mrs Vivien Ingman, in Brede, Sussex, November 1980.
9 Interview with Lord Amulree, London, November 1980.

10 David Warren, *A History of Homefield* (Homefield Old Boys Association), unpaginated.
11 Anthony West, *John Piper* (London: Secker and Warburg, 1979), p. 15.
12 GS interviewed by Andrew Forge, *Listener*, 26 July 1962.
13 Information from an unpublished study by Alan Scadding, head of Epsom's History Department.
14 Letter to the author from John Piper, dated 3 January 1981.
15 Now in the collection of P. P. Ruggerini, near Milan.
16 Quotations from GS about Derby mainly from letter to the author received in November 1979 (undated). Others from earlier interviews.
17 Information about working life at Derby from Roland Bond, later Chief Mechanical Engineer of British Railways, in an interview in London in July 1980, five months before his death; and from Edgar Larkin, later Deputy General Manager, British Rail Workshop Division, in an interview in London in April 1980 and at the Derby Railway Works in September 1980.

Chapter 2 Student and Etcher, 1921–7 *(pages 43 to 59)*

1 Taped interview with GS in London, November 1979, from which all quotations in this chapter not otherwise attributed are drawn.
2 Interviews with Paul Drury in London, August 1979 and November 1980. Subsequent quotations are from the same interviews.
3 Information from early pages of a history of the Goldsmiths' College, *The Forge*, edited by Dorothy Dymond (London: Methuen, 1955).
4 Interview with Paul Drury.
5 Tribute by GS to Clive Gardiner in catalogue of a memorial exhibition of his work at the South London Art Gallery, Camberwell, London, 1967.
6 Interview with Paul Drury.
7 GS interviewed by Giorgio Soavi 1976; tape lent to the author.
8 Foreword by GS to *The English Vision*, catalogue of an exhibition at the William Weston Gallery, London, October 1973.
9 Letter to the author from GS, undated, received January 1980.
10 All are illustrated in Felix Man, *Graham Sutherland: Das Graphische Werk* (Munich: Galerie Wolfgang Ketterer, 1970), and in Edward Quinn (ed.), *Graham Sutherland: Complete Graphic Work*, with an introduction by Roberto Tassi (London: Thames & Hudson, 1978).
11 Reproduced in Douglas Cooper, *The Work of Graham Sutherland* (London: Lund, Humphries, 1961), plate 2b.
12 GS in *The English Vision*.
13 ibid.
14 Letter to the author from GS, received January 1980.
15 GS in *The English Vision*.
16 Letter to the author from GS, received January 1980.
17 Interviews with Milner Gray in London, December 1979 and January 1981.
18 GS in *The English Vision*.
19 Interview with GS in London, November 1979.
20 Oxford Movement: the name given to a small, Oxford-based group of Anglicans who in the mid-nineteenth century attempted to define the Church of England's position in world Christianity, and in so doing laid the basis of Anglo-Catholicism. Two of them, Henry Manning, an advocate of papal infallibility and of the 'ultra-montane' view, and John Henry Newman, a genuinely profound thinker, became cardinals, though in Newman's case only after considerable suffering and persecution.
21 Letters to the author from Father A. Whitehead, CRL, dated 19 August and 11 September 1980.
22 Letter to the author from GS, received January 1980.
23 Letter to the author from J. H. Hockey, May 1981. Hockey was a friend of GS at Goldsmiths', who also taught later at Kingston.
24 Letter to the author from GS, received January 1980.

Chapter 3 Teaching and Design, 1928–33 *(pages 60 to 73)*

1 GS interviewed by Melvyn Bragg and Bryan Robertson for the *South Bank Show*, London Weekend Television, shown 1 April 1979 (transcript of complete interview).
2 In the possession of Milner Gray.
3 Interview with Milner Gray in London, January 1980.
4 John Hayes, *Graham Sutherland* (London: Phaidon, 1980), p. 51.
5 This and several other letters from GS to Russell Alexander are in the Ashmolean Museum, Oxford.
6 Letter to the author from GS, January 1980.
7 Letter to the author from Diana Murray Hill, July 1980.
8 Letter to the author from Nina Sa-

govsky, November 1980.

9 Interview with GS in London, November 1979.

10 Letter to the author from Malcolm Fry, secretary of the Royal Society of Painter-Etchers, dated 26 November 1980.

11 Recalled by Richard Guyatt at an exhibition called '50 Years of Shell Advertising', London 1969.

12 Letter to the author from GS, January 1980.

13 In the quadrimestrial magazine *Signature*, no. 3, July 1936, published by Oliver Simon and the Curwen Press.

14 GS to Douglas Cooper, *The Work of Graham Sutherland*, p. 10.

15 ibid., p. 9 (illustrated).

16 In *Apollo* magazine, September 1962.

17 Interview with Henry Moore at Perry Green, Herts, July 1979.

18 The switch has hitherto been dated to 1932, but the school's annual report from 1933–4 states: 'During the year also Mr Sutherland took over book illustration classes, and excellent work has resulted.'

19 Interview with Robert Medley in London, June 1980.

20 Letter from Gerald Wilde to the author, January 1981.

21 Half a dozen designs have come to light at the old premises of E. Brain and Co. since the book's completion.

Chapter 4 Self-discovery in Wales, 1934–9 (*pages 74 to 93*)

1 Kenneth Clark, *Another Part of the Wood* (London: John Murray, 1974), p. 1.

2 ibid., p. 254. (Clark incorrectly dated it to 1935.)

3 ibid.

4 Interview with Sir Colin Anderson in London, October 1979, a year before his death.

5 Information from Frances Richards, his widow, February 1981.

6 Interview with Robert Wellington, in Hampshire, September 1981.

7 Printed as 'Welsh Sketchbook' in *Horizon*, no. 28, April 1942.

8 Introduction by GS to catalogue of the Graham Sutherland Gallery at Picton Castle, Wales, 1976.

9 Letter from GS to Giorgio Soavi, dated 11 March 1972, in the same catalogue.

10 GS to Douglas Cooper, *The Work of Graham Sutherland*, p. 11.

11 Oliver Simon, *Printer and Playground* (London: Faber & Faber, 1955), p. 121 (autobiography).

12 Pat Gilmour, *Artists at Curwen* (London: Tate Gallery, 1977) gives a good account of Simon's relationship with the Curwen Press.

13 Interview with John Piper in London, July 1979.

14 Letter to the Tate Gallery from GS, dated 11 November 1976.

15 The stamp designs can be seen at the National Postal Museum's headquarters, near St Paul's Cathedral.

16 Interview with GS at Trottiscliffe, August 1979.

17 Myfanwy Piper (ed.), *The Painter's Object* (London: Gerald Howe, 1937). Other contributors included Picasso, Kandinsky, Ernst, Léger, Nash, Moore and Piper.

18 Interview with Sir Roland Penrose, London, July 1980.

19 Reproduced as plate 1 in Robert Melville, *Graham Sutherland* (London: Ambassador Editions, 1950), unpaginated.

20 GS interviewed by Andrew Causey in *Illustrated London News*, 19 February 1966.

21 Interview with John Piper in London, July 1979.

22 Letter from Douglas Cooper to the author, dated 21 March 1981.

23 Letter from Alexandre Rosenberg to the author, dated January 1981.

24 Interview with Robert Wellington, September 1981.

25 Letter from GS to the author, received January 1980.

26 Letter from Paul Miller and interview in

Derby, July 1980.

27 Dirk Bogarde, *A Postilion Struck by Lightning* (London: Chatto and Windus, 1977), p. 224 (autobiography).

28 Letter to the author from Maida Lunn, October 1980.

29 Edward Sackville-West, *Graham Sutherland* (London: Penguin Books, 1943), p. 9.

30 Letter from GS to Clark, dated 7 September 1938.

31 Tate Gallery archives.

32 *The Times*, 21 September 1938.

33 *New Statesman*, 1 October 1938.

34 Letter from GS to Clark, dated 24 October 1938.

35 GS interviewed by Andrew Forge, *Listener*, 26 July 1962.

36 Melville, *Graham Sutherland*, unpaginated.

37 ibid.

38 GS interviewed by Forge, *Listener*, 26 July 1962.

39 GS interviewed for *South Bank Show*.

40 GS to Douglas Cooper, *The Work of Graham Sutherland*, p. 17.

41 For example the review by Roger Hinks in the *Spectator*, 30 June 1939.

42 Article by James W. Lane in *Apollo*, July 1939.

43 Article by Seymour Leslie in *Queen*, 9 August 1939.

Chapter 5 War Artist, 1940–5 (*pages 94 to 117*)

1 Letters from Clark to GS and KS, dated 5 and 13 September 1939.

2 Kenneth Clark, *The Other Half* (London: John Murray, 1977), pp. 22–4.

3 Letter from GS to the author, received January 1980.

4 Letter to the author, undated, received May 1981.

5 Information from Henry Moore, February 1981.

6 *Spectator*, 3 May 1940.

7 *New Statesman*, 10 May 1940.

8 *Sunday Times*, 12 May 1940.

9 The correspondence between leading war artists and the Committee is beautifully preserved at the Imperial War Museum in London.

10 Open letter from GS to Edwin Mullins, *Daily Telegraph Magazine*, 10 September 1971, from which all quotations not otherwise attributed are drawn.

11 Letter from GS to Dickey, August 1940.

12 To the author, January 1980.

13 Letter from Theyre Lee-Elliott to the author, February 1981.

14 David Vaughan, *Frederick Ashton and his Ballets* (London: A. & C. Black, 1977), pp. 188–94.

15 Letter from GS to Jane Clark, dated 31 January 1941.

16 Vaughan, *Frederick Ashton and his Ballets*, p. 193.

17 GS's open letter to Mullins, *Daily Telegraph Magazine*, 10 September 1971.

18 Interview with Henry Moore, Perry Green, Herts, July 1979.

19 Clark, *The Other Half*, p. 44.

20 Letter from KS to Eric Newton, dated 30 July 1941.

21 Interview with GS in Wales, July 1978.

22 Extracts in the *Listener*, 26 November 1941.

23 Letter, undated (probably June 1942).

24 Information from KS.

25 Interview with Kenneth Clark in London, October 1979.

26 Interview with Tambimuttu in London, January 1981.

27 Letter from GS to Vaughan, dated 7 February 1943.

28 Letters from GS to Colin Anderson, dated 5 May and 7 October 1943.

29 GS interviewed by Paul Nicholls, published in catalogue of an exhibition at the Galleria d'Arte Narciso, Turin, February 1976.

30 Letter from Clark to GS, dated 1 January 1944; GS's reply, 7 January.

31 Letter from GS to Clark, dated 8 February 1943.

32 Letter from Clark to GS, dated 15 February 1943.

33 Letter from GS to Anderson, dated 5

May 1943.

34 Letter from GS to Newton, October 1943.

35 Interview with John Craxton in London, January 1981.

36 Interview with Eunice Frost in Lewes, October 1980.

37 Interview with Jill Craigie in London, February 1981.

38 Malcolm MacDonald's father, Ramsay MacDonald, had split the Labour Party in 1931 by assuming the (largely titular) leadership of a coalition government which most of his party refused to support.

39 Interview with Walter Hussey in London, July 1979.

40 Keith Vaughan, *Journal and Drawings* (London: Alan Ross, 1966), p. 83).

41 Letter from GS to Clark, dated 14 September 1944.

42 GS's open letter to Mullins, *Daily Telegraph Magazine*, 10 September 1971.

43 ibid.

44 Historical note by Julian Andrews in *Sutherland: The Wartime Drawings*, with an introduction by Robert Tassi, translated, edited and with a foreword by Julian Andrews (Milan: Electa Editrice, 1979; London: Sotheby Parke Bernet Publications, 1980), p. 167.

45 Interview with Joseph Darracott in London, October 1979.

Chapter 6 Via a Crucifixion to Maugham, 1945–50 (*pages 118 to 144*)

1 GS, 'Thoughts on Painting', *Listener*, 6 September 1951 (from a radio broadcast on the Third Programme).

2 Letter from GS to Anderson, dated 9 April 1945.

3 Radio notes by Edward Sackville-West, *New Statesman*, 3 March 1945.

4 Information from Lady Dunsany, January 1981.

5 GS, 'Thoughts on Painting'.

6 ibid.

7 Letter from KS to Beaton, dated 31 August 1944.

8 Letter from GS to Hans Juda, dated 27 May 1945.

9 Interview with Elsbeth Juda in London, March 1980.

10 Recalled by John Craxton in interview, London, January 1981.

11 GS interviewed by Bryan Robertson, BBC Radio 4, 24 August 1978.

12 Interview with Robert Medley in London, June 1980.

13 Robert Rhodes James (ed.), *Chips: The Diaries of Sir Henry Channon* (London: Weidenfeld & Nicolson, 1967), p. 408.

14 Letter to GS from Curt Valentin, dated 9 March 1946.

15 Letter from Clark to GS, dated 26 November 1945.

16 GS's open letter to Mullins, *Daily Telegraph Magazine*, 10 September 1971.

17 Cooper, *The Work of Graham Sutherland*, p. 33.

18 GS interviewed by Andrew Causey in *Illustrated London News*, 19 February 1966.

19 GS to Douglas Cooper, *The Work of Graham Sutherland*, p. 33.

20 Letter from Clark to GS, undated.

21 Interview with Walter Hussey in London, July 1979.

22 Letter from GS to Clark, dated 8 August 1946.

23 Interview with Felix Man in London, December 1980.

24 Letter from Clark to GS, dated 2 September 1946.

25 Dated 15 November 1946.

26 In BBC film written and directed by John Read, first transmitted 7 December 1953.

27 Information from KS.

28 GS, quoted in *Daily Express*, 26 April 1958.

29 Letter from GS to Colin Anderson, dated 21 November 1946.

30 Information from a source close to Bacon.

31 In their respective interviews with the author.

32 Letter to the author from Rory Cameron, December 1980.

33 GS interviewed by Noel Barber in the latter's *Conversations with Painters* (London: Collins, 1964), p. 49.

34 Interview with Eardley Knollys in London, October 1980.

35 GS interviewed by Giorgio Soavi in 1977 (unpublished tape).

36 GS in BBC film directed by John Read.

37 Roderick Cameron, *The Golden Riviera* (London: Weidenfeld & Nicolson, 1975), p. 298.

38 GS interviewed for *South Bank Show*.

39 ibid.

40 Interview with Alan Searle in Monte Carlo, May 1980.

41 GS in *South Bank Show*. A similar account appears in Barber, *Conversations with Painters*, p. 51.

42 Cooper, *The Work of Graham Sutherland*, p. 40.

43 Chapman Pincher, *Their Trade is Treachery* (London: Sidgwick and Jackson, 1981).

44 Tom Driberg, *Ruling Passions* (London: Jonathan Cape, 1977), passim.

45 Interview with GS in Milford Haven, July 1979.

46 Information from Erica Brausen, May 1981.

47 GS interviewed by Giorgio Soavi in Menton, 1978 (taped).

48 Interviewed by Andrew Forge, *Listener*, 26 July 1962.

49 GS interviewed by Noel Barber, *Conversations with Painters*, p. 52.

50 GS, 'Thoughts on Painting'.

51 Cooper, *The Work of Graham Sutherland*, p. 58, and John Hayes's catalogue for exhibition of Graham's portraits at the National Portrait Gallery, June 1977.

52 Letter from GS to Fitzwilliam Museum, Cambridge, dated 5 December 1967.

53 Maugham, quoted in *Daily Express*, 16 November 1951.

54 Derek Hudson, *For Love of Painting* (London: Peter Davies, 1975), p. 103 (a biography of Sir Gerald Kelly).

55 Information from KS. Searle confirmed the figure of £300.

56 *Time* magazine, 13 June 1949.

57 GS interviewed by Andrew Forge, *Listener*, 26 July 1962.

58 GS interviewed by Hayes in National Portrait Gallery catalogue.

59 GS, 'Thoughts on Painting'.

60 ibid.

Chapter 7 Maximum Exposure, 1950–3 (*pages 145 to 165*)

1 GS interviewed by Barber, *Conversations with Painters*, p. 47.

2 Letter from GS, dated 15 November 1957, to compilers of Tate Gallery catalogue.

3 Cooper, *The Work of Graham Sutherland*, p. 34.

4 Letter from GS to Clark, dated 22 April 1951.

5 Letter from GS to Clark, dated 15 April 1951.

6 Pope Pius XII; the Rt. Rev. Hugh Watt.

7 Cooper, *The Work of Graham Sutherland*, p. 58.

8 GS interviewed by Cyril Ray, *Sunday Times*, 17 May 1953.

9 Quoted in *Daily Express*, 15 November 1951.

10 Cooper, *The Work of Graham Sutherland*, pp. 46–7.

11 GS interviewed by Bryan Robertson, BBC Radio 4, 24 August 1978.

12 Interview with Mrs Somerville in London, October 1980.

13 Michael Wishart, *High Diver* (London: Blond and Briggs, 1977), p. 94.

14 Reports from McEwen to British Council.

15 Cf. Cooper, *The Work of Graham Sutherland*, and Ronald Alley and John Rothenstein, *Francis Bacon* (London: Thames and Hudson, 1964).

16 GS to the author in Wales, July 1979.

17 Sackville-West first situated the painting on a veranda in his Penguin study of Graham's work (revised edition, 1955,

p. 11).

18 *The Times*, 19 May 1953.
19 See also his article, 'Trends in Contemporary Painting', *Listener*, 11 May 1950.
20 Interview with Harry Tatlock Miller in London, May 1980.
21 Letter from Jane Phillips to the author, dated 30 June 1981.
22 Letter from GS to Lord Beaverbrook, dated 9 September 1955.

Chapter 8 The Tate Affair, 1952–4 (*pages 166 to 182*)

1 Published in London, by Hamish Hamilton, in 1966.
2 Ronald Alley, *Catalogue of the Tate Gallery's Collection of Modern Art* (other than works by British artists) (London: Tate Gallery, 1981). The sculptures were destined for Peggy Guggenheim's gallery in London.
3 ibid.
4 Information from Ronald Alley and Sir William Coldstream, who became a trustee in 1949.
5 Information from a reliable source.
6 Generalizations of this kind are based on interviews with Tate trustees of the time, including Sir Dennis Proctor, Sir Colin Anderson, John Piper and Sir William Coldstream.
7 KS's diary suggests the former, Rothenstein's book the latter.
8 Letter to the author from Humphrey Brooke, February 1981.
9 Letter from GS to Clark, dated 8 February 1954.
10 Interview with Denis Mahon in London, November 1980.
11 Interview with Sir Colin Anderson, London, October 1979.
12 GS summarized the letter in his own to Clark of 9 February.
13 Douglas Cooper, *Nicolas de Stael* (London: Weidenfeld & Nicolson, 1961).

Chapter 9 the Churchill Portrait, 1954 (*pages 183 to 200*)

1 Jennie Lee, *My Life with Nye* (London: Jonathan Cape, 1981), p. 250.
2 Information from Dame Adelaide Doughty, May 1981.
3 Letter from GS to Mary Soames, dated 1 January 1978.
4 McLeavy was among those interviewed by Susan Barnes for an article on the missing portrait in the *Radio Times*, 28 November 1974.
5 Letter from GS to Lord Beaverbrook, dated 19 August 1954.
6 Rothenstein, *Brave Day, Hideous Night*, p. 334.
7 GS interviewed by Donald McLachlan, *Sunday Telegraph*, 20 January 1965.
8 GS interviewed for *South Bank Show*.
9 GS in *Sunday Telegraph* interview, 20 January 1965.
10 KS kept some notes on the sittings, over and above her brief diary entries.
11 GS in *South Bank Show* interview.
12 GS repeated this frequently; for example, in a letter to Beaverbrook, dated 21 March 1961.
13 GS interviewed by Honor Balfour, BBC Home Service, 3 December 1954.
14 GS in *South Bank Show* interview.
15 GS in interview with *Daily Mail*, 30 November 1954.
16 KS's notes.
17 Mary Soames, *Clementine Churchill* (London: Cassell, 1979), p. 632.
18 GS in *South Bank Show* interview.
19 GS to Susan Barnes, *Radio Times*, 28 November 1974.
20 Letter from GS to Beaverbrook, dated 9 September 1955, with notes of various sketches.
21 Lord Moran, *Churchill: The Struggle for Survival* (London: Constable, 1966), p. 620.
22 GS to *Daily Express*, dated 3 September 1954.
23 Letter from GS to Beaverbrook, dated 21 March 1961.
24 Interview with Felix Man in London, December 1980.

25 GS to Honor Balfour, BBC Home Service, 3 December 1954.
26 GS interviewed by *Daily Express*, 30 November 1954.
27 GS in *Sunday Telegraph* interview, 20 January 1965.
28 GS to *Sunday Express*, 31 October 1954.
29 KS's notes.
30 Nemon to *The Times*, 13 January 1978 (after news of the portrait's destruction).
31 GS in *Sunday Telegraph* interview, 20 January 1965.
32 Letter from GS to Newton, undated.
33 Partly from M. H. Middleton's brilliant description in the *Spectator*, 10 December 1954.
34 GS in interview with *Daily Telegraph*, 13 January 1978.
35 In *Looking Back*, serialized in the *Daily Express*, 1963.
36 GS in *Sunday Telegraph* interview, 20 January 1965.
37 Information from Dame Adelaide Doughty, May 1981.
38 Sir John Colville to *Sunday Telegraph*, 12 February 1978.
39 Interview with Mary Soames in London, November 1980.
40 Soames, *Clementine Churchill*, p. 716.
41 GS to Susan Barnes, *Radio Times*, 28 November 1974.
42 Letter from GS to Beaverbrook, dated 21 March 1961.
43 GS to *Daily Mail*, 30 November 1954.
44 Baxter's account appeared in the *Evening Despatch* of Edinburgh that day, 30 November 1954.
45 Noted in the *Evening Standard*'s Londoner's Diary.
46 *Daily Sketch*, 1 December 1954.
47 GS in *Sunday Telegraph* interview, 20 January 1965.
48 Maugham's letter undated; Anderson's dated 2 December.
49 *New Statesman*, 11 December 1954.
50 *Spectator*, 10 December 1954.
51 Letter to the author from Mary Soames, dated 25 June 1981.
52 GS to Honor Balfour, BBC Home Service, 3 December 1954.
53 GS interviewed by Hayes in National Portrait Gallery catalogue.

Chapter 10 The Coventry Tapestry, 1952–62 (*pages 201 to 222*)

1 Hayes, *Graham Sutherland*, p. 35.
2 Francesco Arcangeli, *Sutherland* (Milan: Fratelli Fabbri Editori, 1973; New York: Harry N. Abrams, 1975), p. 5.
3 Basil Spence, *Phoenix at Coventry* (London: Geoffrey Bles, 1962), p. 94.
4 *Observer*, 22 April 1962.
5 Spence, *Phoenix at Coventry*, p. 15.
6 ibid., p. 36.
7 Revelations 4: 2, 3, 6 and 7.
8 In a letter dated 16 January 1952.
9 Andrew Revai, *The Coventry Tapestry* (London: Pallas Press and A. Zwemmer, 1964), from which all other direct quotations are taken unless otherwise indicated.
10 Letter from GS to Eric Newton, undated (1962).
11 GS to Cooper, *The Work of Graham Sutherland*, p. 36.
12 Letter from GS to Spence, dated 26 June 1953.
13 Letter from GS to Spence, dated 24 January 1953.
14 Letter from GS to Spence, dated 26 June 1953.
15 Spence, *Phoenix at Coventry*, p. 58.
16 Letter from Provost Howard to GS, dated 1 September 1953.
17 Letter from Provost Howard to Spence, dated 31 December 1953.
18 Letter from GS to Spence, dated 21 January 1954.
19 Letter from GS to Thurston, dated 12 December 1954.
20 Letter from GS to Spence, dated 15 July 1957.
21 Revai, *The Coventry Tapestry*, p. 69.
22 Interview with Anthony Blee in London, January 1981.
23 Letter from GS to Spence, dated 15 November 1958.
24 *News Chronicle* report from Felletin, 20 January 1959.
25 Letter from GS to Pinton, dated 1

February 1959.

26 Letter from GS to Thurston, 27 May 1961.

27 GS's letter has not survived.

28 Letter from GS to Thurston dated 12 November 1961.

29 Letter from Spence to GS, dated 19 October 1961.

30 Letter from GS to Spence, dated 22 October 1961.

31 Letter from Spence to Pinton, dated 26 October 1961.

32 Letter from GS to Spence, undated.

33 Letter from Spence to GS, dated 21 December 1961.

34 Letter from GS to Sir Fordham Flower, dated 2 February 1962.

35 Letter from Pinton to GS, dated 6 February 1962.

36 Letter from Pinton to the author, dated 27 March 1981.

37 Thurston to *Coventry Evening Telegraph*, 24 February 1962.

38 *Daily Mail*, 27 March 1962.

39 *The Times*, 12 May 1962.

40 *Observer*, 20 May 1962.

41 GS to Revai, in *The Coventry Tapestry*, p. 50.

42 GS, reported in *Daily Sketch*, 21 August 1962.

43 Letter from Clark to GS, undated 1962.

44 Interview with Lord Iliffe in London, May 1981.

Chapter 11 Mainly Portraits, 1955–9 (*pages 223 to 238*)

1 Cooper, *The Work of Graham Sutherland*, p. 48.

2 *Burlington*, January 1957.

3 Letter from GS to Beaverbrook, dated 12 May 1955.

4 GS interviewed for *South Bank Show*.

5 Letter from GS to Maja Sacher, dated 14 September 1955.

6 Other artists shown included Philip Sutton, Donald Hamilton Fraser, Leonard Rosoman and Stefan Knapp.

7 GS interviewed by Hayes in National Portrait Gallery catalogue.

8 Interview with Elsbeth Juda in London, March 1980.

9 Letter from GS to Maja Sacher, dated 2 May 1953.

10 GS interviewed for *South Bank Show*.

11 Letter from Beaton to GS, undated.

12 Draft letter from GS to O'Higgins, dated 3 June (1957).

13 Helena Rubinstein, *Life for Beauty*

(London: Bodley Head, 1965).

14 *Evening Standard*, 4 October 1957.

15 *The Times*, 4 October 1957.

16 Letter from Mrs Eaton to the author, dated 31 March 1981.

17 Information from KS.

18 GS interviewed by Hayes in National Portrait Gallery catalogue.

19 GS interviewed in *South Bank Show*.

20 GS to *Daily Express*, 8 April 1959.

21 ibid.

22 Letter to the author from A. S. Frere, November 1980.

23 Clark to *Evening Standard*, 14 March 1960.

24 At Marlborough Fine Art in London.

25 Jennie Lee, *My Life with Nye*, p. 250.

26 Tribute by GS to Valentin in catalogue of opening exhibition of the Marlborough-Gerson Gallery in New York, November–December 1963.

Chapter 12 Acclaim and Hostility, 1960–5 (*pages 239 to 261*)

1 Report in *Daily Mail*, 6 April 1961.

2 Quoted by Wishart in *High Diver*, p. 174.

3 Facts drawn from various letters to GS and KS from Jeffress and others.

4 Palace sources.

5 Interview with Etti Plesch in London,

June 1981.

6 Letter to the author from Robert Simon, dated 9 June 1981.

7 Interview with Anthony Bell in London, November 1980.

8 *Daily Express*, 11 February 1964.

9 Interview with Father James Ethrington

in Acton, May 1980.

10 Letter from GS to Ethrington, dated 22 May 1962.

11 Interview with Felix Man in London, December 1980.

12 Note by Giso Deussen in the catalogue of an exhibition called 'Sutherland Paints Adenauer', at the Adenauer Foundation, St Augustin, near Bonn, September 1978.

13 GS in reminiscence at same exhibition.

14 Letter from GS to Adenauer (undated), received 21 October 1963.

15 Recalled by Felix Man in catalogue of the 1978 exhibition.

16 Letter from GS to Maja Sacher, dated

17 August 1964.

17 Clark to *Sunday Telegraph*, 13 January 1980.

18 Letters to the author from Lord Clark, dated 15 June 1981, and from Alan Clark, dated 9 July 1981.

19 Letter to the author from Cooper, dated May 1981.

20 Letter to the author from Louis Osman, dated 22 May 1981.

21 Interviews with Emery and Wendy Reves in Montreux, March 1981.

22 Letter to the author from Lord Butler, dated 2 December 1980.

23 GS interviewed by Hayes in National Portrait Gallery catalogue.

Chapter 13 The Italian Connection, 1965–70 (*pages 262 to 276*)

1 GS interviewed by John Ormond for a BBC Wales film, *Sutherland in Wales*, written and produced by Ormond and first transmitted 2 October 1977.

2 Interview with Pier Paolo and Marzia Ruggerini, Valle Lomellina, near Pavia, November 1980.

3 Interview with Giorgio Soavi in Milan, November 1980.

4 Giorgio Soavi, *I Luoghi di Sutherland*, introduction by 'Janus' (Turin: Albra Editrice, 1973); published in Britain as *The World of Graham Sutherland* (London: A. Zwemmer, 1973).

5 GS interviewed by Andrew Causey, *Illustrated London News*, 19 February 1966.

6 *The Times*, 18 November 1965.

7 Letter from GS to Maja Sacher, dated 8 January 1966.

8 Letter from Clark to GS, dated 23 May 1966.

9 Letter to the author from Lord Rayne,

dated 6 August 1981.

10 GS's introduction to the *Sutherland in Wales* catalogue of the Graham Sutherland Gallery at Picton Castle, near Haverfordwest.

11 Interview with Mrs Margaret White in Milford Haven, August 1980.

12 GS interviewed for *South Bank Show*.

13 *Sunday Times*, 19 May 1968.

14 *Listener*, 23 May 1968.

15 *Spectator*, 17 May 1968.

16 Letter to the author from Baron de Rothschild, dated 12 February 1981.

17 GS to the author, July 1978.

18 Hugh Cudlipp, *Walking on the Water* (London: Bodley Head, 1976), p. 310.

19 *The Cecil King Diary 1965–70* (London: Jonathan Cape, 1972), p. 176.

20 Letter to the author from Cecil King, dated 17 November 1980.

21 Letter to the author from William Paley, dated 28 October 1980.

Chapter 14 The Graham Sutherland Gallery (*pages 277 to 282*)

1 GS's introduction to the *Sutherland in Wales* catalogue, at the Graham Sutherland Gallery, Picton Castle.

2 Interview with Hanning Philipps at Picton Castle, August 1980.

3 Letter from Hanning Philipps to the author, dated 15 July 1981.

4 Information from Gordon Bennett, custodian of the Graham Sutherland Gallery, the Hanning Philipps and sundry files, on which much of this chapter is based.

5 Interview with Colonel and Mrs Sulivan at Benton Castle, August 1980.

Chapter 15 The Last Decade (*pages 283 to 305*)

1 Letter to the author from Lord Bath, dated 29 October 1981.
2 Interview with James Kirkman in London, January 1981.
3 Letter to the author from Sir Sacheverell Sitwell, dated 17 June 1981.
4 Letter from GS to the compiler of the Tate Gallery catalogue, 1974–6, p. 155.
5 Letter to the author from Lord Goodman, dated 11 December 1980.
6 Interview with Lord Iliffe in London, May 1981.
7 Interview with Lord Airlie in London, July 1980.
8 Interview with Emile Marzé in Menton, May 1980.
9 For example, *Conglomerate IV*, shown in Zurich, and *Poised Rock II*, shown in Milan.
10 *Observer*, 4 March 1973.
11 The encounter took place on 24 September 1972.
12 Recalled by Pier Paolo Ruggerini.
13 KS's letter to Cooper, dated 20 January 1975.
14 Cooper's letter to KS, dated 24 January 1975.
15 GS to the author at Milford Haven, July 1979.
16 Letter to the author from Gianni Tinto, dated 22 June 1981.
17 Roberto Sanesi, *Graham Sutherland* (Milan: Centro d'Arte/Zarathustra, 1979) with Italian and English texts.
18 *Financial Times*, 2 July 1974.
19 Interview with Mme Ferrari at the Villa Blanche, May 1980.
20 Letter to the author from Baer, dated 17 June 1981.
21 GS interviewed by Giorgio Soavi in about 1977 (taped).
22 Spurling in *New Statesman*, 15 July 1977; McEwen in *Spectator*, 23 July.
23 Independent Television News, *News at Ten*
24 Letter from Mary Soames to the author, dated 23 July 1981.
25 GS interviewed for *South Bank Show*.
26 GS to the author in Wales, July 1978.
27 Letter to the author from Macmillan's personal secretary, Rosemary Ainetti, dated 4 November 1980.

Appendix

Portraits in the order in which they were begun

Subject	Year of completion
1 Somerset Maugham	1949
2 Lord Beaverbrook	1951
3 Edward Sackville-West	1955
4 Sir Winston Churchill	1954
5 Arthur Jeffress	1955
6 Hans Juda	1955
7 Paul Sacher	1956
8 Helena Rubinstein	1957
9 Mrs Signy Eaton	1957
10 Mrs Maja Sacher	1958
11 Mrs Ramsay Hunt (*rejected*)	1957
12 Prince Max Egon von Fürstenberg	1959
13 Herschel Carey Walker	1960
14 Alexander Frere	1960
15 H.M. the Queen Mother (*sketch only*)	1967
16 Arpad Plesch	1961
17 Mrs Daisy Fellowes	1964
18 Sir Kenneth Clark	1964
19 Konrad Adenauer	1965
20 Douglas Cooper	1966
21 Cuthbert Simpson	1967
22 Charles Clore	1975
23 Emery Reves	1966
24 Giorgio Soavi	1968
25 Max Rayne	1969
26 Baron Elie de Rothschild	1968
27 Adolf Jann	1970
28 Cecil King	1970
29 Mark Longman	1970
30 William Paley	1971
31 Lord Bath	1971
32 Lord Plunket	1971
33 Sir Sacheverell Sitwell	1973
34 Lord Goodman	1973
35 Lady Marion Philipps	1974
36 Hanning Philipps	1975
37 Pierre Schlumberger	1976
38 Lord Iliffe	1976
39 Mrs Wendy Reves	1978
40 Milner Gray	1979
41 Lord Airlie	1980

Index

References to plates are in italics: for key to numbering, see list of illustrations

INDEX

INDEX

INDEX

328